RECALL TO INFERNO

The offer came secretly from Saigon. Three hundred of the Nazis' most superb S.S. troop would become an antiterrorist strike force. They would answer to no international convention. Operate under no restraints. Follow no law. They had their own supply dumps, transports, even copters. They wore any sort of uniform they wanted. They could do anything on or off the battlefield as long as they stopped the Vietcong. And as long as they didn't get caught.

Soon they were men with a price on their heads. Three hundred men against an entire army: striking fast, hitting hard, scorching the earth, and doing what no nation's soldiers before or after could do – winning.

**Also by the same author,
and available from NEL:**

Devil's Guard I:
The Battalion of the Damned
The Sonneberg Run

Recall to Inferno

Devil's Guard II

George Robert Elford

NEW ENGLISH LIBRARY
Hodder and Stoughton

Copyright © 1988 by George Robert Elford

First published in the United States of America in 1988 by Dell Publishing a division of The Bantam Doubleday Dell Publishing Group, Inc.

First published in Great Britain in 1989 by New English Library paperbacks

The Characters and situations in this book are entirely imaginary and bear no relation to any real person or actual happenings.

This book is sold subject to the condition that it shall not, by way of trade or otherwise, be lent, resold, hired out or otherwise circulated without the publishers prior consent in any form of binding or cover other than that in which it is published and without a similar condition including this condition being imposed on the subsequent purchaser.

No part of this publication may be reproduced or transmitted in any form or by any means, electronically or mechanically, including photocopying, recording or any information storage or retrieval system, without either the prior permission in writing from the publisher or a licence, permitting restricted copying. In the United Kingdom such licences are issued by the Copyright Licensing Agency, 33–34 Alfred Place, London WC1E 7DP.

British Library C.I.P.

Elford, George Robert
 Devil's guard II: recall to inferno
 I. Title
 813'.54[F]
 ISBN 0-450-49728-3

Printed and bound in Great Britain for Hodder and Stoughton paperbacks, a division of Hodder and Stoughton Ltd., Mill Road, Dunton Green, Sevenoaks, Kent TN13 2YA (Editorial Office: 47 Bedford Square, London WC18 3DP) by Richard Clay Ltd., Bungay, Suffolk.

Acknowledgments

The author wishes to express his sincere gratitude for all the moral, material, and professional assistance he received while preparing this book to: Nick Webb, Carolyn Caughey, Ian Chapman, Belinda Kirkin, Jane Holloway, Ian Lilley (England), Roy Cooke (Canada), Michael and Andrea Spata (U.S.A.), Roberto and Tamara Ollani, Mario de Luca, Giovanni and Mima Iacopi, the Fam. M. Falleri and G. Paolini (Italy).

GEORGE ROBERT ELFORD

Foreword

June 1952

The Battalion of the Damned of the French Foreign Legion had fought its way through the green hell of Cambodia and arrived at the Ho Chi Minh trail. We moved on, skirting the Red Highway, dealing death and destruction as we went.

Having realized that they couldn't beat us in the hills, the enemy embarked on a last desperate offensive. Not only the Vietminh but the entire Communist world joined forces to win that final and decisive battle. It was to be fought not with machine guns but with printing presses, radios, and loudspeakers —and not in the jungles of Indochina, now Vietnam, but in the capitalist world.

"S.S. marauders in the Legion massacre innocent civilians," screamed the Communist and leftist press.

"Hitler's scum at large in Indochina."

"How long will the French government tolerate . . . ?"

"Outrage! Outrage!"

And what the regiments of Ho Chi Minh could not achieve in five years, the international Communist fifth column accomplished in five weeks.

The international Communist parties' consternation could be well understood. "The S.S. marauders" were devastating the principal Vietminh supply route between China and Saigon. They had to stop us—at any price. The Battalion of the Damned had ceased to exist. It had lived 1,243 days, during which it destroyed 7,466 guerrillas by body count, 221 Vietminh bases, supply dumps, and camps; it liberated 311 military and civilian prisoners from terrorist captivity and covered roughly 6,000 miles on foot.

Once again the guns of Nguyen Giap, the guerrilla general, could roll freely. The jungle trails became highways and the forts of the Foreign Legion turned into graveyards. The French soldiers could fight bravely and go down gloriously. They were not permitted to win.

Like the American GIs a decade later.

Then came the disaster at Dien Bien Phu, but the Vietnam war did not end there. It did not end with the fall of Hanoi and the loss of the northern territories either.

It went on. . . . It is still going on. . . . It will go on for a long time to come because when the Communists have no external enemies left, they turn upon their friends and allies, on their own brothers.

In August 1954 the hard-core experts of the Foreign Legion's S.S. Battalion had been discreetly recalled. Now code-named Task Force-G, the commando group, three hundred strong, was officially in the service of the Saigon government—a group of mercenaries unshackled either by international conventions or by law. At long last the antiterrorist killer elite could fight their war the way they wanted, under the maxim: No mercy for the merciless.

Radio Hanoi called them the Commando of Death.

The Battalion of the Damned

South, dreary south,
Burning nights and days,
Green, rolling green,
Where Death rides on the trails.
You're weary? Carry on!
Until the bitter end,
You are Devil's Guard,
The Battalion of the Damned.

Go! Forward! March!
You are action bound,
Green, rolling green,
It's hell, man—all around.
Go! Forward! March!
The jungle looms ahead,
Brave! There's your grave,
The cowards are long dead.

You won't find no rest,
Till you fall on your chest,
And kick your soul away.
A stab in the back,
Or a shot in the head,
Your reward for the day.

Go! Forward! March!
Tread your dreary trail,
Kill, or get killed,
Fall but never fail.
Go! Forward! March!
Until the bitter end,
You are Devil's Guard,
The Battalion of the Damned.

—The marching song of the onetime German Battalion of the Foreign Legion in Indochina

Contents

PART ONE Recall to Inferno

1	Recall to Inferno	3
2	Operation THOR	21
3	Breakout from Camp Dizier	28
4	Rescue of the Third Regiment	40
5	Treason and Punishment	52
6	Raid on the Ho Chi Minh Trail	65
7	Havoc	86
8	The Coming of the Americans	96
9	Major General Clint McCory	117

PART TWO The Commando of Death

10	The Commando of Death	131
11	The Destruction of Bin Xuyen	152
12	Raid into North Vietnam	171
13	The Chinese Freighter	188
14	Deadly Dew	199
15	Silent Hawks	219
16	Holocaust in the Srépok Valley	244
17	Unconventional Warfare	269
18	War Without End	284

PART ONE
Recall to Inferno

1.

Recall to Inferno

It was perhaps my third encounter with Karl Stahnke, the one-time Gestapo agent, since our early days in Indochina, sometime in 1946, when French Military Intelligence had carried him off from our barracks in Viet Tri, near Hanoi. Then and there we were certain that Stahnke had had it but, contrary to our expectations, he hadn't been castigated for his wartime activities in occupied France. The counterintelligence group had simply decided to summon Stahnke's vast experience against the ever-increasing number of Communist infiltrators.

It is said that the ways of God are infinite, and Karl Stahnke must have taken the right one. He became one of the regional directors of the local SDECE, the *Service de documentation Exterieure et de Contre Espionnage*—an important official who lived in a flashy bungalow with his wife, Dagmar, a striking ash-blonde, tall and willowy and fifteen years younger than Karl. And to have a German wife was a genuine luxury in Indochina.

Stahnke had certainly come a long way from the World War II Gestapo cellars in Calais. When I later spoke to Erich Schulze about him, my friend's only comment came in the form of a nostalgic grunt. *"Na, ja,* Hans—the ranks fight and die. Officers come and go. Generals are substituted or retired. The ball-squeezers survive every calamity."

Erich was right. With the passing of years, Karl's messy past had been conveniently forgotten. Even his personal file had disappeared from the army archives. After all, he enjoyed unrestricted access to all confidential material.

At first I didn't even recognize him. He had put on some weight, divided his brilliantined hair, and wore a small, brushy moustache that lent his face a vague resemblance to Himmler. He probably liked that.

Only his ever-alert, unswerving, steely-blue eyes and intimidating personality remained. He was bland and patronizing. When I entered his plush office, he rose ponderously, circled his large desk, and advanced with a broad grin.

"Hans Josef Wagemueller." He beamed, squeezing my hand. The heavy rumble of his voice filled the room. "The holy terror of the Vietminh. . . . It's nice to see you again, and all in one piece."

With obvious delight in his square-jawed face and with his left arm thrown around my shoulders, he ushered me to a club chair then sat down himself, drawing a small glass-topped table between us. He called for drinks, threw open the lid of a silver-worked ebony box with a selection of expensive cigarettes, lighted a Royal for himself, and asked amiably, "How was life among the Gurkhas?"

His unexpected reference to my sojourn in Nepal startled me. "You still prefer to work with the tough ones," he continued, slapping me on the knee.

I chose a cigarette. He lighted it for me with a golden lighter. We observed each other for a while. I was curious.

"It's been a long time, Karl." I broke the silence after a while. "How could you ever find me there?"

Stahnke's mouth twitched into a half-smile and he opened his hands. "Keeping track of important people is part of my job, Hans," he answered candidly, then added, "Remember that your good friend Erich Schulze is still in active service."

"Of course!" Erich was working with the police of New Caledonia, and we corresponded every now and then. "Erich told you where I was and you hoodwinked old Krebitz into flying to Katmandu and talking me back here."

Stahnke threw open his hands. "I must confess it, Hans." Then he added emphatically, "We need you here—all of you."

I blew a small, ironical snort. "What for? To help the French carry the white flag?"

He shook his head and said placatingly, "It isn't as bad as that, Hans."

"Can it be worse than what it is?"

He observed me for a while somberly, then his voice changed pitch. "Perhaps you don't know yet, but there's a big change in the making," he continued suavely. "We won't be alone much longer, Hans. Our allies are stirring, with Uncle Sam in the first line. The Korean war ended but old Mao is shaking his saber toward the Nationalist islands of Quemoy and Matsu. He is also sending more military hardware to Ho Chi Minh. The Americans are becoming restless. The Sixth Fleet is on the alert. . . . *Jawohl, mein Junge.* Our friends are beginning to realize that if the French should lose Indochina, the whole of Southeast Asia might go red."

"Southeast Asia is pink enough already," I commented, then switched to a pleasanter tack. "Where is Erich?"

"He should be here by Monday," Stahnke answered reassuringly. "Also Helmut Riedl and a few others from your old outfit."

"Wo, for instance?"

"Rudolf Krebitz naturally . . ." He opened a folder, scanned some sheets of paper, murmured, "Medical officer Kurt Zeisl, Karl Stolz, Sepp Mueller, Horst Altreiter, Walter Winar, Otto Janaschek, Wilfred Resch, Gerhart Seyfert—"

"Seyfert?" I cut in. "Never heard of him."

He turned his attention to the papers. "You're right. Seyfert is a newcomer—from Brazzaville Congo." He glanced up. "There are plenty jungles too. . . . He is an expert. . . . Two years in Russia with an S.S. *Einsatzkommando.*"

I pursed my underlip.

"A Jew-flayer," I stated wryly. My overt indignation seemed to startle my host. Stahnke was probably ignorant of my acute aversion toward the onetime *Beamten* in S.S. uniform, who had been "fighting" for the *Vaterland* in the rear by doing dirty work for Heidrich and Kaltenbrunner, enriching themselves in the process. Stahnke knitted his brows. Perhaps he wanted to say something but checked himself. Anyway, his frown dissolved in a half-smile as he said, "That is the past, Hans—dead and buried. Seyfert was only doing his job, like thousands of others."

"A fine job he was doing too," I retorted.

Stahnke ignored my remark and plodded on listlessly. "I've managed to round up the best of your old outfit," he said. "Some were still in the Legion. Others had taken civilian jobs. A few tough fellows were coming from France and Algeria . . . even from Germany."

"You don't say. They must be crazy."

"Not crazy, but experts." he replied.

"How do the Amis fit in the picture, Karl?"

He shook his head slowly in a gesture of joking reproval. "You've been living on the top of the world too long and lost touch with reality down below."

"Not quite. I've been swearing a great deal about Dien Bien Phu, the armistice, and the loss of the northern provinces, for which we were fighting like mad for five damned years, Karl. The graves of my best companions are up there."

He nodded and replied somberly, "I know: Bernard Eisner, Pfirstenhammer, Schenk. . . . But it's going to be easier from now on. The land to protect is smaller. More compact. With every inch of Communist advance, the Amis are becoming more cooperative. Washington is already financing much of the war that would otherwise hammer France into bankruptcy. We are also getting excellent weapons. There's nothing to match them in the Communist arsenals."

"Which is, I presume, the only positive aspect of the French debacles," I commented with irony.

"In a sense—yes," Stahnke agreed. "The armistice means nothing to Hanoi. As far as the Reds are concerned, international agreements are signed only to secure political or economic advantage."

"And military ones." I straightened the record. "Legal or illegal."

"Yes, they aren't choosy," my host commented evenly. "The signatures on the Geneva agreement haven't dried yet but Ghiap is already testing our defenses in the north and along the borders with Laos and Cambodia."

"But for the world at large both countries are now free and independent."

Stahnke uttered a sound of bitter amusement. "Free and independent," he repeated disdainfully. "Prince Souvanna Phouma in Vientiane is perfectly free to obey Father Ho, like King Norodom Sihanouk of Cambodia."

"Or Hanoi will loosen the reins of its Khmer Rouge and Pathet Lao henchmen."

Stahnke laughed softly.

"I see I was wrong, Hans. You haven't lost touch with reality."

"There are newspapers and I've been listening to the radio, including Radio Moscow."

A brief pause ensued. We sipped beer.

Stahnke parked his mug, leaned closer, and said persuasively, "You are familiar with the land and its people, Hans. You know the Thais, the Meos, the Montagnards, and you also know the enemy better than anyone else. . . . Now they call themselves Vietcong."

"Vietminh, Vietcong. . . . It makes no difference. The first means Vietnamese people, the latter Vietnamese Communists. . . . It's one and the same outfit."

"But there is a difference," Stahnke contested. "Something you should keep in mind. The Vietcong are disciplined and devoted, ready to sacrifice themselves for Ho Chi Minh and his Communist party. Following the Chinese practice, the guerrillas are now divided into cells of three, to faciliate Marxist indoctrination and military training. For all practical purpose it's like living under the constant surveillance of four critical eyes. No one may slip in word or deed without the company's political officer being promptly informed, and he does his best to turn the individual into a perfect murder instrument of the party."

"Much like our S.S. used to be."

"Hey! Don't tell me that you've become an anti-Nazi?" Stahnke boomed but his voice carried a tinge of mild reproof.

"Why?" I chuckled. "Isn't it the truth? The Vietcong is ready to set fire to Southeast Asia for Ho Chi Minh and the Communist party. We burned half of the world for Adolf and the Nazi party. . . . Where's the difference?"

My comparison fell flat.

My host said soberly, "The difference is that for once in history we are on the right side, Hans."

"I wonder what the German Communists in the Soviet Zone are saying."

There was a pause, pregnant with thought. I drained my mug and leaned back expectantly.

Stahnke went on. "The coming months are going to be crucial for the Saigon government. As you probably know, the French are gradually evacuating the country, and Diem is not ready to face Hanoi alone. The transition period will probably foster increased terrorist activity. The Vietcong should be discouraged, and none could do it better than you, Hans. . . . How about having another short go at them?"

"How short?"

"Two years . . . two and a half at most," he replied, and his eyes kindled. "Starting with the rank of captain. There's a promotion for all of you and lots of fringe benefits."

"There should be plenty of fringe benefits to compensate for such mass idiocy, Karl."

He laughed contentedly. "Three thousand American dollars to begin with for you and Schulze—monthly, of course. Two thousand for the other veterans. Fifteen hundred for the *Mannschaft*."

"The enemy slugs aren't going to hit by the size of the paycheck, Karl. I want the same benefits for the whole team—let's say two thousand and five hundred."

"I believe it can be arranged."

"What else do we get?"

"A cash premium of five thousand and elevated pensions."

"For the survivors," I rounded it up.

He shrugged his shoulders. "There's no war without casualties, Hans," he said equably. "You'll also have plenty of booty."

"Who cares for the native rubbish?"

"Wrong! Today the Vietcong units are traveling with well-lined regimental coffers."

"If you say so. . . ."

"Whatever you might find after the battle will be yours."

After a while I asked, "Tell me, Karl—who is the brains behind our recall?"

"Your former boss, Simon Houssong."

"Colonel Houssong? I thought he was in retirement."

"They recalled him after Dien Bien Phu."

"A disaster he'd predicted six months in advance."

"That's probably why he was put back into uniform—a lieutenant general now."

"I'm glad to hear it. His promotion was long overdue. Perhaps because he understands the local problems.

"Houssong is a genuine admirer of yours, Hans."

"The feeling is mutual. What kind of a setup do they have in mind?"

"An independent force under your exclusive command, Hans. Coded Task Force-G."

"*G* for German, I presume."

"Likely."

I looked at him searchingly. "Am I to have a free hand?"

"Absolutely. I expected that question. . . . Well, this time no one is going to interfere. You'll have your own base, your own supply dumps, your own transports. . . . Perhaps even copters. Also your own funds."

"And I'll be dealing only with General Houssong," I added in a firm voice.

"Affirmative."

"And no meddling from Paris, for they have the gift of making the difficult impossible."

"As for Paris, you won't even exist, Hans," Stahnke answered levelly. "You may wear plainclothes, or uniform—any sort of uniform, but not a French one."

"That's okay with me. We might go Russian."

He laughed. "By all means. You may use any ruse you can invent, only don't let yourselves be caught."

"Saving the last bullet has always been one of our Ten Commandments."

"Well, just don't use it." He stuck out his hand. *"Abgemacht?"*

"Before I sign anything, I'd like to see Houssong."

"And I'd like to see old Giap's face when he learns that the damned Germans are back in business." Stahnke guffawed. "Well, three hundred men aren't a great force but they are veteran specialists. A hard-hitting lot."

"Fair enough. Just don't expect us to change the course of the war."

"All you'll have to do is to make the Communists pay a very high price for every yard of real estate they grab. Perhaps Moscow and Peking will find Father Ho a bad investment. The Ivan hasn't got the money to finance local wars all over the world."

I laughed in polite remonstrance. "You shouldn't pretend to be naive, Karl. You know as well as I that to Moscow, international troublemaking comes first. National welfare is only of secondary importance. They'll tighten the belts at home and keep manufacturing guns, cost what may. No Marxist regime can survive without weapons, and a tranquil world won't serve the revolutionary aims."

Nodding, Stahnke accepted my reasoning, then exuberantly described the benefits of the impending American aid: ultramodern weapons, warplanes, all-devastating bombs, deadly accurate rockets, the eventual support of the Sixth Fleet, and the possibility of Uncle Sam sending in troops.

Then and there I strongly doubted this latter proposal. "Uncle Sam is not likely take charge of a lost cause," I commented dryly. "He likes to win his wars."

"Merde alors, Hans, the Amis beat the daylights out of Japan. Don't tell me that they couldn't manage the Vietcong rabble?"

"They surely could and probably in a few weeks," I replied with conviction. "Provided that some of their experienced generals are permitted to run the war as they consider it necessary. Uncle Sam has his Rommels and Guderians but unfortunately also his Fuehrers and Keitels to shackle them. When the generals present a blueprint for victory, they are overruled by flaccid civilians, the majority of whom just couldn't care less about what's happening on the far side of earth. To them Vietnam is a forgotten place, a thousand miles behind God's back. Remember what happened in Korea? I'm still convinced that MacArthur could have stopped the Chinese intervention and preserved the Koreans' freedom."

"Sure, Hans—by using the atomic bomb."

"The mere threat of it would have sufficed," I stated. *"Merde aux yeaux,* Karl—if they aren't prepared even to threaten, then why spend money to manufacture it? But as far as I'm concerned, you make a weapon to use it." I waved a resigned hand. "You can't win wars by retreating. But that's all the great democracies of the West would ever do in the face of aggression. Retreat! Democracy might be a very pleasant system in a time of global peace, but what democracy has ever survived the challenge of powerful dictatorships? We can start the list with ancient Athens and finish it with France."

"America is strong enough to stop communism," my host replied.

I shook my head. "Not without the backing of her allies in

every important decision . . . something they would *never* do."

"Why not?"

"Because backing Washington would dent their national dignity, even when they are aware they're wrong. America is the most powerful nation in the world, and to snub openly at the strong is the privilege of the weak. It provides the weak with an illusion of strength. Uncle Sam's allies aren't necessarily friends too. Alliances are born of fear, not friendship."

Stahnke stared at me, perplexed. "Why, Hans—you no longer believe that communism can be stopped?"

"If you want to stop communism, the enemy within should be eliminated first. The open and disguised Marxist parties in the free world. Their organizations of subterfuge, their presses, paramilitary groups, propaganda centers, and financial resources. Because in a war their allegiance would belong to the enemy and in time of peace they could do more damage with street demonstrations and newspaper columns than the shell of a Red Army division might do in wartime."

He laid a restraining hand on mine and I broke off. *"O, du lieber Gott,"* he exclaimed jokingly. "You turned pessimist."

"I'm only trying to be consistent," I answered, rising from my chair. "But tell me one more thing before I leave, Karl. What is your role in all this?"

Stahnke threw out his hands. "Absolutely nothing. I'm only a third party, asked to contact you probably because I'm a German myself. Although should you happen to come across some useful information, or catch someone who might furnish it, I'd appreciate your collaboration, Hans."

"If and when we capture a top Commie, you'll be the first one to interrogate him," I replied.

"Vulcanize him," he corrected me with a grin, using the old Gestapo slang for the third degree.

Our reunion of old friends and companions of many past combats was joyful. Beer and wine flowed freely and untold stories were narrated, drawing cheers and laughter. Schulze, Riedl, Krebitz, and others of the *Alte Garde* were ready to book a place in hell, provided that I would do the same; not for rank, financial gain, or to fight communism—rather to revive the spirit of the old *Kameradenschaft,* or as Krebitz pointed out good-humoredly: "To get rid of our potbellies, fat, and muscle aches through regular physical exercise." It was surely mildly put but we truly enjoyed the encounter after such a long time.

The prospect of being an independent task force, *pro forma* in the service of the South Vietnamese government, had tipped the scale toward our acceptance. To our additional delight, manifested through wild cheers and a standing ovation, we also met two very dear companions: Erich and Riedl had brought along their wives, Suoi and Noi, who "didn't feel like staying behind to dust furniture and wash dishes."

"Here we are, Commander, sir!" Suoi greeted me with a radiant smile and kissed me on both cheeks. She was now prettier than ever.

"You aren't thinking of joining up again?" I asked teasingly.

"We most certainly do!" she stated resolutely.

Noi added, "We don't have children to worry about."

"Except your husbands," Riedl retorted.

"This is why we decided to come along," Suoi said, taking Erich by the hand.

"Where's your old battle dress?"

"We will have new ones made. More fashionable."

Krebitz chuckled. "Oh, I'm sure the Vietcong snipers will appreciate that."

Suoi stuck out her tongue at him. "Booo, old Himalaya bear. . . . We've seen snipers before." She patted Rudolf's slightly protruding belly. "Besides, you offer a much better target to snipe at."

Krebitz embraced them both in his strong bear hug. "It's nice to see you girls."

"You'll be seeing us a lot, Rudolf."

I interposed with pretended authority, "May I remind the merry community that I have not yet consented."

Suoi wheeled around, planted her clenched fists against her slender hips, furled her brows, and replied with immense firmness, "Just try not to consent!"

Erich burst into rippling laughter. "You'd better give up the idea of stopping Suoi, Hans," he boomed. "I've been trying to do that for three years. No going. Back in New Caledonia she'd insist on coming along when we went to shoot it out with robbers and killers."

"And Noi has a surgical nurse's diploma," Riedl cut in. "She's been assisting at serious operations and can be of real help to Kurt."

Needless to say, Zeisl, the medical officer, was in perfect accord. I accepted Suoi and Noi and also the revival of an old headache: their safety.

The following day we went to our appointment with Lieutenant General Houssong. He received us cordially and informally, questioned us briefly about the events of the past two years, then came to the point.

"Your coming job is going to be very different from the previous one," he began. "To start with, there'll be neither Legion nor air force to support and supply you, Wagemueller. Officially you'll be in the service of the Saigon regime—a rather shaky establishment with an army of inexperienced sucklings, incapable of providing you with any real support. While we are still here, things will go smoother, but the Legion is going to quit Indochina, except for a small expeditionary force to protect government installations and French property. Afterward you may count on what you can carry or take from the enemy but *never* on local promises. Especially not when it comes to cooperating with the South Vietnamese Army, which we equipped and trained for so many years with so little success."

"Are they really so bad, General?" Schulze asked.

"Worse!" General Houssong almost shouted. "In a tight situation they might refuse to fight, or simply abandon stations and decamp en masse. I'm telling you this so you have a clear picture. You'll probably hear more enthusiastic reports from the local authorities."

"Oh, we're quite prepared for it, General," I ventured, smiling. "We've seen local troops in action. Except for a few outstanding individuals, I was seldom impressed by what I saw."

"I believe you." Houssong nodded. "The local army was never reliable or solid, but since the division of the country it's been cracking up. The only young men who obey Diem's mobilization call are those who can't pay fifty thousand piasters to buy exemption from military service. Only students and sons of rich families join up willingly, because they'll soon become officers and obtain advantageous posts. Incredible as it might seem, of one hundred thousand call-up notices only about eight thousand have been obeyed. The army has thirty-four thousand deserters. The number of men missing in combat is six times higher than the number of dead and wounded. The missing ones simply went home."

It was a grim picture, but in a sense I could understand the local lack of enthusiasm. Why should the Vietnamese soldier sacrifice his life for Emperor Bao Dai? Or for the Ngo Dinh family? For the modern mandarins, the landlords who measured their properties not in acres but in dozens of square miles? Or die for the provincial governors and administrators, whose only concern was to enrich themselves while sitting near the cornucopia of fortune? What could be expected from lieutenants and captains who were given their rank because of good family ties and who would become majors and colonels in two years?

"Beware, Wagemueller," Houssong went on. "When we are no longer here you may depend on what you have in hand but never on what you are supposed to be getting."

"What about the Saigon generals?" I queried, half-suspecting Houssong's response.

"They excel in drawing little red and green arrows on operational maps—"

"—moving imaginary regiments—really only battalions or less—against fancy enemy targets that are no longer there." I couldn't refrain from continuing Houssong's track of thought.

"Precisely. The local staff officers live in luxury villas, drive around in Cadillacs and Lincolns, and their aversion toward communism is fueled only by the advantages of living in a capitalist system: decorations, money, and women. The colonels and majors falsify troop ration cards and pocket the wages and rations of entire phantom battalions. The few honest and devoted officers are sent to command some godforsaken outpost, to be killed by the Vietcong as soon as possible."

After a short pause, I asked, "General Houssong, may I ask why you accepted your recall from retirement?"

"Why do you ask?"

"Because you're a man who likes to win his battles."

"Every general likes to win his battles," he replied, then winked and added, "I accepted my new assignment only because I could work with you and your team, Wagemueller—which means winning my battles."

"I'm much honored, General. We'll try not to let you down."

"You should try not to let yourselves down.

"I presume you already know that you won't be operating in French uniform," Houssong continued, turning to the practical aspects of the future. "Rather jungle fatigues without insignias and badges. In fact, you should wear the black Vietcong garb when moving in the woods."

"I intend to do that, *mon général.*"

"Your war is going to be a war of wits," he went on. "Guerrillas against guerrillas. Fight the way you prefer. Set your own rules. The Diem regime is not bound by restrictions imposed upon the French forces. You may utilize every weapon and method. No one is going to question you, except your own conscience."

"Or a tribunal in Hanoi!" Schulze quipped.

Houssong shook his head. *"Ma fois,* Schulze, don't let that ever happen."

"Don't worry, sir. We have a long record of survival in Vietnam. It's going to be a good fight without the conventional shackles."

"Remember that the same may be said of the Vietcong."

Krebitz shrugged. "Who cares, General? Convention or not, Father Ho would hang us anyway."

"Once in every village," Erich cracked. "Slowly."

General Houssong smiled complacently. Then he brought up the subject of our operational areas that overlapped into Cambodia and Laos. "The Legion couldn't cross international borders. "Task Force-G may do it, hitting the Vietcong where Hanoi least expects it, perhaps right on the Ho Chi Minh trail. The local forces will probably get out of your way. They have to live with the guerrillas, but they aren't happy about Hanoi's truculence."

"What about some good raids into North Vietnam, General?" Erich proposed casually.

General Houssong's brows lifted. "Everything will be up to your own judgment, gentlemen. Should you find it feasible and think that you could manage it—come up with a good plan, like your raids into China back in the late forties."

We were content to work with General Houssong and wage the kind of war we appreciated in Vietnam. No rules. No regulations. No conventions. No reprovals. Return with results, no questions asked. In a war against terrorists this was the only acceptable rule.

Strike at their lair. Use every available ruse and weapon. Take no prisoners, whom some lily-livered or terrorized authority will free the day after, so that the killers might resume killing people. War against terrorists must be a total war. Hardcore terrorists are professional killers who had long since gotten rid of the last vestiges of humanity and who would unflinchingly slaughter twenty innocent bystanders only to murder a single individual in a queue. The prospect of imprisonment neither deters nor restrains them, for they are convinced that their companions at large will liberate them by force or through blackmail or more terror.

And here I might add that our cherished total war did not necessarily imply the sideline killing of civilians. When we executed guerrilla prisoners, we never rounded up their elders, wives, and children to share the same fate—unless they had been captured with a gun in the hand, or in the act of sabotage or murder. I still remembered Alexeiva Makarova, the frail, timid, soft-voiced Russian woman in Zhitomir, who worked in our field kitchen during the day; at night she was an ingenious partisan leader who had executed thirty German prisoners with her own hands.

Indoctrinated Communists are peculiar creatures who just don't fit into any logically established character pattern.

"You are not expected to win the war with three hundred men," General Houssong concluded. "*Alors,* Wagemueller, no unnecessary bravado, or risks. Damage the Vietcong as much as you may safely do but preserve your men and yourself."

I spent a week becoming acquainted with the newcomers to Task Force-G. Erich and Riedl organized an informal party in the army mess hall. I also invited Karl Stahnke, first because he was a walking encyclopedia of World War II names, places, and events, and second because of his uncanny ability to detect discrepancies in the sweeping stories some determined fellows might try to boost their "social standing."

Among the recruits was a onetime *Untersturmfuehrer* of the S.S., a certain Gerhart Seyfert, a stub-nosed, crafty individual with small, deep-set eyes and a garrulous nature. He was certainly not the typical Aryan and, probably resentful of not having been born tall, blond, and blue-eyed like good Teutons should be, he was still more anti-Semitic and racist than Dr. Goebbels had been. He would even call the North Africans "dirty Jews" or at best *"Verfluchte Zigeuner"*—"damned Gypsies"—and referred to the Senegalese as "niam-niam cannibals."

Our aversion toward Seyfert began with the visit of Lieutenant Bernard Berger, General Houssong's aide-de-camp. We were aware that Berger was Jewish. He even wore a small Star of David around his neck. It made no difference to us. We had long since realized that religious and racial discrimination was outright idiocy. The lieutenant was an extremely pleasant person, and whatever he promised us he fulfilled on the dot. I learned from Houssong that Berger's family had been killed in the KZ Bergen Belsen, yet not even his sad memories would induce him to show contempt toward us, former S.S. officers, whom he may well have considered indirectly responsible for the death of his parents and millions of other Jews. Only once did Berger mention that some die-hard Nazis were serving in the Syrian army—a fact we knew ourselves. Both Schulze and Krebitz had received tempting offers from Damascus and Cairo, which they declined. Krebitz just didn't feel like helping the Arabs kill more unfortunates, and from Schulze's point of view, working for the Arabs equaled serving Moscow and to him communism was worse than the Black Plague. I knew from many small remarks that inwardly Erich was genuinely impressed by the Israelis' resolute defense and subsequent victory in 1948.

After Lieutenant Berger left, I informed the men of the essence of our discussion regarding action plans. Gerhart Seyfer was present. Berger's name and face had caught his attention.

"Lieutenant Bernard Berger." He said out the name with slow deliberation and grimaced. "It sounds *Zhid* to me"—using the Ukrainian term for "Jewish."

Slapping him on the back, Riedl said patronizingly, "The Jewish problem was buried with your old buddy Kaltenbrunner, when they hanged him in forty-six, Gerhart."

Erich quickly added, "We know that you've had your fair share of the *Judenfrage*, especially its final solution."

Unwilling to let the situation deteriorate, I cut in. "I think you should drop the subject and leave the Jews alone."

Seyfert pursed his lips and heaved his shoulders. "Who cares? I guess they have paid enough for everything, past and future."

The way he said that made Erich jump. "The Jews?" he exclaimed. "They paid for what? For their wicked crimes against the Third Reich?"

"This is what we were taught to believe, isn't it?" Seyfert countered. "Some people can change their convictions. I can't. I'm only wondering because you attended the same school, together with Captain Wagemueller."

I shifted my face toward him and said rather icily, "You're wrong, *Kamerad*. We attended schools in Bad Toelz and not in Treblinka, or Baby Yar."

My comparison between the fighting S.S. training school and the infamous sites of mass extermination made Erich purse his lips and nod. "You should keep one thing in mind," I continued. "Contrary to your belief, we are not at all proud of the glorious manner your *Einsatzkommandos* contributed to the war in Russia."

Seyfert's chin lifted. He tried to counter rebuff with defiance. "You were with the S.S. in Poland and in Russia, Commander. Didn't you ever kill a *Zhid*?" he challenged me with a mediocre attempt at a leer.

"I sure as hell did, if the Jew was blazing away with a gun or was captured with the partisans. But when I captured partisans, I would rather question them about Soviet military dispositions than race and religion."

Schulze cut in. "And I used to be a *Panzer* commander, Herr Seyfert," he said disdainfully. "Stopped twenty-eight T-34s and knocked out over fifty artillery pieces. I lost six tanks and got wounded twice. Won the Iron Cross twice—something they didn't distribute to fellows around the KZ ovens."

His sardonic words and his emphatic "Herr" that referred to the civilian status of the *Einsatzkommando* personnel, despite their S.S. uniform, had had their effect. Schulze's bitter sarcasm shattered Seyfert's ego. "KZ ovens," he responded sullenly. "Do you really believe that propaganda crap? We shot a few thousand *Zhids*—all partisans and saboteurs—"

"Partisans and saboteurs?" Erich cut him short. "Seventy-year-old matrons and five-year-old kids. Come, Gerhart—you don't believe that shit yourself. In the summer of forty-two, when I was briefly hospitalized in Riga, I happened to be in the same room with one of the *Standartenfuehrers* of General Heinz Jost. He cheerfully boasted to me that by February his group had eliminated three hundred thousand Jews. There were four similar groups of butchers and if I remember correctly, you belonged to *Einsatzgruppe C.* Your score was slightly under the one hundred thousand—let's say—unarmed civilians. But now you're among real soldiers who didn't serve the *Vaterland* by filling mass graves. We probably lost the war on account of the Jews you slaughtered, so, in the future, just keep your beak shut."

Facing sullen hostility in every quarter, Seyfert shifted uncomfortably. "I was only obeying orders." He clung to the ultimate argument, which Erich dismissed with a negligent flick of his hand.

"Oh, we have all been doing that," he commented with a self-mocking snort. "Obeying orders . . . even the idiotic ones."

Later, when we were alone, he told me, "Something just doesn't tally in this Seyfert guy, Hans. Even here, in damned Vietnam, he's trying to be more Nazi than Hitler, and I'm wondering why."

There had been another Jew-eater in our ranks during our years in the Foreign Legion, narrated in *Devil's Guard:* former S.S. man Franz Stadler, whose meritorious service record was acquired around the pyres and furnaces of KZ Ravensbrueck for women. He was a former S.A. member and later ex-convict, who had been sentenced for raping a twelve-year-old girl. Later he was released upon Heydrich's order and given the KZ job as a reliable person. In any wartime S.S. *Kampfgruppe* on the front, Stadler would have been considered a cowardly bastard. In fact, he conducted a rather solitary life in our Battalion of the Damned.

During his early days, when he was still convinced that he'd many devoted listeners among us hard-core Nazis, Stadler used to brag about his various exploits in the concentration camp, not impressing but instead disgusting everyone. He described his infallible methods of eliminating Jewish "whores" by the hundreds and in the shortest possible time, while saving the useful parts, such as hair to fill matresses, fats for producing industrial grease, and gold teeth.

"We lined them up close behind one another, so that a single slug would drop three or four of the wenches—heh, heh." He chuckled. "One got commended for saving bullets for the front. . . . The young and comely ones were fucked first, so they wouldn't go to Moses without having had some fun."

But the men of my battalion were hardened soldiers who had gone through hell for *Fuehrer* and *Vaterland* and who loathed Himmler's KZ trash. After he had been dubbed *Krematorium Schwein* and *Kindschaendler*—child rapist—he clammed up. And when there was a particularly dangerous mission, Erich made it sure that Stadler wouldn't miss out. "He was with the S.S. for three years without smelling any gunpowder except his own," my friend used to say. "Let him feel what the enemy powder smells like."

Franz Stadler had been killed by the Vietminh at Dang-khe, near the Chinese border. We gave him a burial but no rifle salute. He didn't deserve any such honor.

Strange as it may sound, we were not blindly enthusiastic about everything the Germans had done before and during World War II.

2.

Operation THOR

The midday sun glowed overhead with stinging severity and not even the strong wind could lessen the oppressive heat, although it stirred enough dust to obscure the huts and the outlying paddies and compelled us to draw the linen dustguards over our mouths and wear goggles. The tense faces of my troops glistened with sweat. I was soaked to the skin myself and would have given anything for a dip in the nearby stream, which ran, we knew, in plain view of the Vietcong snipers.

The village seemed peaceful, ominously so. There were no adult men in sight, as no males of arms-bearing age would be left in any Vietcong village. The labor of tending the fields and paddies was left to small children, women, and elderly people.

The younger women were binding the stalks of dry rice; others were husking the harvest with pounders, while elderly men and young kids piled the sheaves in cone-shaped ricks. Elsewhere, small groups were thrashing grain on wide mats, while little girls were winnowing it with large round fans. In the murky ponds water buffalos idled, and in bamboo corrals small, bushy-maned Thai horses fed at mangers made of hollowed-out trunks. The idyllic scenery could have inspired any painter of rural life.

When I entered into the village with Schulze, Krebitz, Sepp Mueller, Jost Waldman, and ten troopers, the natives paid almost no attention to us. A few elderly women came to sit on the low balconies and nearby steps, conversing in low voices. A group of kids gathered and observed us with indifferent, curious, or hostile eyes. The handful of locals we tried to question wanted to know nothing of guerrillas, hidden arms caches, or food stores and scurried off as soon as they delivered their sullen replies.

Erich spoke to me in German.

"Mensch! This place smells like a king-size Vietcong warehouse. I can feel it all over my skin."

Sharing his sensation, I said, somewhat puzzled, "I'm wondering why shouldn't they defend it?"

Krebitz laughed softly. "But they are defending it, Hans." He astounded me. "In this very instant I can see a couple of apes with rifles."

"Where?" I asked tensely.

"Don't turn too quickly," he warned me. "They're behind the stack of sacks near the long house on piles. There's also a machine gun at the well between a pair of pithoi."

I shifted position and scanned the southern sector of the village without paying any attention to the places Krebitz indicated. Schulze joined my game of subterfuge. "I see the machine gun." He spoke between his teeth, waving a casual hand in another direction. "It's probably an old Russian *Goriunov* fit with a modern optical sight—which the monkeys left uncapped. It glints!"

Conversing casually, Krebitz pointed out more guerrillas lying behind various inconspicuous objects. Already a formidable observer when he came to Indochina, he had learned a great deal about guerrilla tricks from Ghia Xuey, our excellent Vietnamese guide in the late forties.

Sepp Mueller spoke in a low voice. "They're probably holding the entire southern sector and have us covered good and proper."

"There's no danger yet," Krebitz replied reassuringly.

Jost Waldman's chin snapped up. "What do you mean there is no danger? They might open fire at any instant."

Krebitz gave him a paternal smile. "Keep your shirt on, Jost. No one is going to shoot."

"You have a private agreement, or something?"

"The apes have several reasons for not being impatient," Rudolf continued, unperturbed. First, we are only fifteen men and the guerrilla band leader knows very well that a larger unit is hiding somewhere in the nearby woods. He'll measure it before deciding what action to take. Second, we don't yet constitute any danger to him. Third, he won't initiate a battle with all the women and kids in the open."

RECALL TO INFERNO

Waldman uttered a short nervous chuckle. "Since when do the guerrillas care for civilian casualties?"

Mueller tapped him on the shoulder. "They do care when those civilians happen to be their own kin," he said in a sure voice, baffling Jost even more.

"Where did you get that information from?" he blurted.

"Logical deductions," Erich cut in. "After you've ridden the *Karussell* with the Commies for five years as Rudolf has, you'll be drawing lots of deductions yourself."

Jost shook his head.

"The Vietcong boss here is a local ape, Jost," Rudolf explained, "and unless we push farther into the village, or start ransacking the huts, he won't show himself." He gave Jost a friendly wink, then added, "But when the locals begin to disappear, you'd better dive for cover."

"Then—what's going to happen now?" Waldman persisted, still looking lost. "They don't start it, we won't start it. Perhaps we should hoist the flag of truce and start negotiating."

Krebitz gestured toward me and Erich. "Our captains know what's going to happen," he replied. "We are probably going on a trip to get this damned wind into our asses instead of our eyes."

I knew what he had in mind. The strong wind was blowing from where the guerrillas had set up their positions. Krebitz wanted to leave the village undisturbed, retire into the woods, then attack it from the south, so that the Viets would receive the windblown dust in their faces.

A small but fine tactical point. The guerrillas had no goggles and might find it hard to shoot accurately with grit in their eyes.

Waving casual hands and trying to look as contented as possible, we withdrew along the coverless dirt road until it swung behind a hillock, then joined Task Force-G, camped down in the forest. Summoning Julius Steiner, Walter Winar, and Gerhart Seyfert, Krebitz left to reconnoiter the southern approaches.

After I briefed Riedl and Stolz on the situation, Riedl asked thoughtfully, "What if the apes are too strong for us, Hans?"

Schulze pulled a crafty smile and replied, "In that case, my friend, kindly remember that we're a crack unit that can do anything, even the impossible and worse. Just comport yourself accordingly."

"*Aber sicher, Herr Hauptman,*" Helmut answered flatly. "I should have remembered this crack-unit crap." And he began to sing one of his silly rhymes, to the tune of "The Three Little Pigs."

> Who's afraid of Father Ho,
> Father Ho, Father Ho,
> He is just an old scarecrow,
> Good old Father Ho.

He stopped and turned toward Erich. "What if the monkeys outnumber us five to one? I hope you'll come up with a good trick to fool them into losing."

"Negative, my friend. At such odds we shall eat them for breakfast. If the odds are worse, we might start thinking of tricks."

Sepp Mueller came scampering up on the footpath, his goggles pushed up in front of his forage cap. "We've just bumped off a pair of locals trying to sneak up on us," he reported, gasping.

"Guerrillas?"

"Wenches from the village."

Schulze waved a casual hand and said contemptuously, "Then you might as well call them Vietcong. . . . This whole damned village is Vietcong. I can smell them a mile upwind."

"Let's move!" I suggested.

Keeping under cover, we withdrew to where the rice paddies ended at the higher ground, which was covered with tall shrubs. Sheltered from hostile observation, the commando made a ninety-degree turn and continued along the imaginary arch of a semicircle that took us where we wanted to be—a good mile south of the village, where we met Krebitz. He told me that the ground south of the village offered good cover and that the guerrillas were still facing north. He estimated that there were about two hundred Vietcong, but we couldn't guess how many civilians might join the fray once it got started. The odds were only two to one against, a "fair going," according to Schulze.

Krebitz decided to advance and occupy a hillock behind the

village, from where his sharpshooters could easily hit the mortar and MG crews, and also a number of guerrillas sheltering themselves the wrong way.

To our luck the wind was still blowing toward the enemy, carrying dust and the kind of microscopic matter that can cause great discomfort in the eyes and nostrils. Unwilling to risk a change of wind, Task Force-G prepared for assault by forming three groups under the command of Schulze, Riedl, and me, each equipped with a pair of flamethrowers, the most effective antiguerrilla weapon. The Vietcong could stand up against a lot of fire from guns but not against the liquid fire of the "roasters." Most times the mere wind of the searing-hot tongues of flame would be enough to send them scattering head over heels. To be frank, we would do the same.

I signaled advance.

The going was easy. The tall grass and undergrowth gave us cover and the dust helped. At a distance of about four hundred yards from the first huts we split. Erich's group moved toward the west, we toward the east, while Krebitz occupied the hillock in the center.

The last stage we completed in short dashes from bush to bush and from mound to mound, then crawled still closer, until the distance between us and the first guerrillas narrowed to a grenade's throw. I knew we had the enemy in the bag.

The red flare arched above the huts. Krebitz opened up with three machine guns and twenty automatic rifles. The effect of the sudden rain of steel was devastating. The guerrillas spun around, at first dumbfounded, then terrified, and made a desperate attempt to counter the unexpected aggression from the hill. Gruppe Drei gave them no chance to realign mortars and machine guns. The sharpshooters began to kill the crews. An instant later Schulze's commando tore into the village with guns blazing and flamethrowers setting fire to everything incinerable. Gruppe Drei shifted aim and was now decimating a Vietcong platoon. The enemy effort was of little use, for the MG targeted Schulze while, coming from the east, my own troops caught them in the open right flank. Only one of the machine guns had managed to fire briefly before Karl Stolz's flamethrower blew the crew from its sandbagged platform. Five blazing human torches dashed screaming toward the paddies, tottered and crashed to the ground. In a matter of minutes the Vietcong positions had been overrun. Scattered groups stood up and fought with bayonets, machetes, and rifle butts but when we came to grips, the game would invariably go our way. We had a clear superiority of brawn and the enemy was still handicapped by the dust blowing into their faces. Most were struggling half blind and completely uncoordinated.

Descending from the hillock, Gruppe Drei burst into the village center, triggering the mad stampede of a mob of hollering civilians, streaming toward the woods. Women, children, elderly people fled for their lives, carrying only small infants and shabby bundles; knocking down one another, ducking before the whining richochets, screaming and lamenting. We did not deliberately shoot at them, but with slugs flying in every direction some casualties were inevitable, especially when a group of escaping Vietcong dived into the running mass.

Gruppe Drei's men moved from hut to hut, kicking open doors, ripping down walls, spraying the interior with submachine-gun salvos. One hut with five guerrillas inside was virtually cut in half by the slugs. Ignorant of what might be stored in the huts, the men refrained from using grenades.

After fifteen minutes, organized resistance ceased but the killing continued in the open, in the huts, on the pile-supported porches and under them, inside cow and pig pens and barns, as the troops gunned down Vietcong survivors wherever they were found. Perhaps a handful had gotten away with the civilians but even so, Gruppe Drei counted 280 corpses, 60 of them noncombatants.

C'est la guerre. When the guerrillas fired from the milling crowd of civilians, my troops fired back.

The price of victory was four dead and sixteen wounded.

Task Force-G occupied the deserted village and the men ransacked the huts and outhouses. From beneath floors, from henhouses and pig pens and from carefully camouflaged pits, Krebitz extracted at least ten tons of arms and ammunition and, to our astonishment, six crates of heavy artillery shells. Perhaps the guns were already on their way south, somewhere along the Ho Chi Minh trail in Laos or Cambodia.

We replenished our supplies of hand grenades and such mortar shells as we could use. Krebitz rounded up a hundred hens and ducks—for dinner. With the arms cache mined and the huts burning, Task Force-G marched away in plain sight of anyone who cared to look, but after a mile or two we changed direction and vanished in the hills.

3.

Breakout from Camp Dizier

While we were marching north in the shady valley of the Song Ba River, beneath the 7,000-foot-high "Mother and Child" peaks, I received a call from General Houssong, advising me to proceed to Camp Dizier, some sixty miles to the north. I was to confer with the local French commander regarding a possible raid against a Vietcong camp in the neighborhood. General Houssong didn't think it necessary to take the whole commando to Camp Dizier. To discuss the raid Schulze and I would be sufficient, but I decided to take Riedl along too.

After leaving Task Force-G on a convenient and easily defendable hillock with ample water, we hitched a ride with a South Vietnamese convoy headed to Plei-ku and arrived in the camp by noon. Camp Dizier was a fortified base roughly 180 miles north of Saigon and only 30 miles from the Cambodian border, situated along the *Route Colonial* 19. The French forces were about to evacuate the fort and hand the installation over to the Saigon government.

As chance would have it, we ran into a full-scale guerrilla offensive with strong North Vietnamese support, launched probably to intimidate the newly arrived Saigon recruits and perhaps to scare them into quitting the camp.

Colonel Desmond D'Arcy, the commander of the garrison, treated us to a fine lunch and later dinner, after which we retired.

At 8 A.M. the next morning the colonel was already sitting behind his desk, drawing up a list of officers and ranks for promotion or citation. A soldier of long experience, D'Arcy knew that timely rewards would uplift the men's spirit and he had the notion that the last three weeks before the fort was to change hands would be difficult ones. The colonel had gone to bed around 2 A.M. after giving another look at the fortification works in the northeastern sector. During the past ten days there was a sharp increase of guerrilla activity and the engineers could work only at night, lest they become victim to Vietcong snipers, recently furnished by Moscow with some telescopic rifles.

At 8:25 the roof of the trenched headquarters began to tremble. "Intense enemy artillery fire!" Colonel D'Arcy jotted down in his diary, then hurried to the observation post to see what was happening.

The long-expected Vietcong offensive had begun.

Its first salvo had bashed in the wooden barracks wall and blew us from our bunks, causing a great commotion. We hurried to the headquarters complex, buffeted by the nearby detonations, stumbling over heaps of rubble. *"Voilà*—a Vietcong offensive," Colonel D'Arcy greeted us, then, noticing our disheveled state, asked, "What happened to you?"

"Rien de tôut, mon colonel," Schulze answered huskily. "We were blown from our bunks."

"They hit the officers' quarters?"

"Only one wall."

He gestured toward the distant hills. "Giap wants to pull another Dien Bien Phu," he said gravely. "He isn't going to succeed."

There was nothing yet to see. One could only hear the terrific and continuous thunder of the artillery barrage of guns and mortars; it lasted for thirty minutes. For the moment the commander could do little but contact the various units around the defensive perimeter and ask for situation reports. The enemy barrage forced everyone into shelters, which had been its exact purpose—to enable the assault troops to advance unhindered almost to the foremost wire entanglements, while the reserves positioned themselves in the thick underbrush and behind huge termite hills. The shells had blasted some barbed-wire coils and a section of the minefield in the northern sector, where the enemy commander intended to strike first. Apart from three companies of North Africans and one of paratroops, the rest of the garrison consisted of inexperienced Vietnamese soldiers who seemed lost in the pandemonium. Naturally the Vietcong counted on the strong demoralizing effect of the prolonged barrage. While squatting in foxholes and trenches and sheltering in underground casemates, inexperienced troops would be frequently overcome by the sensation of impending disaster.

Then, all of a sudden, the guns fell silent and through the smoke and dust the first assault troops appeared. The outermost fortifications opened up and the mobile artillery joined in. Wanting to give a hand to the defenders, we gathered our weapons and rushed to a nearby shell hole.

At first glance I saw that the Vietcong onslaught would be a massive one, employing several battalions. All the same, the first enemy attempt to break through the battered obstacles foundered in the determined defensive fire of the paras and North Africans. But it was not long before we began to suspect that on this particular occasion the principal adversary was not the Vietcong but the North Vietnamese Army, equipped with field artillery, tracked assault guns, T-34 tanks, and multiple rocket launchers. The guerrillas were playing only an auxiliary role, mostly that of the expendable *Kanonenfutter.*

After the aborted opening assault, Hanoi's artillery opened up again, this time for fifteen minutes, in the best tradition of conventional warfare. The gunners ought to have had excellent advance observers, for after a few *Abtastschuesse,* ranging shots, their shells landed right on the French positions. First they blasted away more of the obstacles, then they shifted toward the center and Fort Ypres with the command post. The bombardment still continued when the enemy infantry embarked on its second attack.

The Moroccans and Algerians fought tenaciously. The paras were formidable but the Vietcong now seemed resolved not to cede an inch of the gained ground. Regardless of losses the enemy lines surged forward; their sappers were prying loose the sagging perimeter in the northern sector, where the new fortifications had not yet been completed; less ferocious attacks were taking place against the other sectors as well.

"Forward to kill!" the guerrillas yelled their battle cry. *"Xung-Phong!"* The platoon leaders urged their men, *"Di! Di!"* as they sprang or crawled over the torn bits of coils and the shredded corpses of their fallen comrades, in repeated human-wave assaults, which reminded us of our old battles on the plains of the Ukraine with the resounding "hoorays" and the charging masses of outspread infantry.

RECALL TO INFERNO

The guerrillas were advancing like army ants on the move, despite the murderous opposing fire. Hundreds were mowed down by the machine guns or blown to smithereens by antipersonnel mines, mortar, and artillery shells. One must pay Caesar his due; the Vietcong we saw here were superbly trained soldiers, utterly fearless in the face of death.

Even our habitually contemptuous Schulze conceded that the attackers of Camp Dizier were neither "jungle dwarfs" nor "stupid monkeys of Father Ho" but top-quality soldiers.

But who could really tell? Perhaps most were not guerrillas at all but North Vietnamese regulars, only clad like the Vietcong.

Squatting in the shell hole not far from the headquarters entrance, Erich turned toward me and said casually, *"Herr Kommandant, es ist ein vollbescheissene Angelegenheit hier."* Which roughly translated into "Commander, sir—the situation here is full of shit."

It was indeed.

Scarcely fifteen hundred defenders, of whom only six hundred were seasoned troops, had to stem the assault of at least two enemy regiments.

And to add to our concern, the pilot of Camp Dizier's solitary copter reported the presence of a North Vietnamese battalion in the nearby hills with twelve Soviet T-34 and Josef Stalin tanks and six tracked assault guns.

The exercise field and the passageways between the semi-ruined barracks turned into an inferno of bursting shells, grenades, and Molotov cocktails. Automatic weapons clattered incessantly. The paras' flamethrowers belched fifty-foot gouts of fire. Men yelled, cursed, howled in pain, screamed in anger, fear, or death throes. A few paces from where we clung to the slippery declivity of our shell hole, a French lieutenant raised his Mitra to fire at a group of charging Vietcong. Before he could pull the trigger he was hit in the head and tumbled lifeless to the ground.

My own gun had jammed but Erich and Helmut's two brief salvos stopped the enemy. Vaulting over the ledge, I dived for the dead lieutenant's Mitra, then crawled behind a stationary troop carrier where Schulze and Riedl joined me a few minutes later. But it was no shelter at all, for the bullets seemed to be flying in every direction and the hail of slugs was so intense I wondered if the different groups of Vietcong were not hitting each other as well as the defenders.

Artillery shells and mortar bombs whizzed overhead, while Russian-made *Katyusha* rocket launchers played their deadly music.

Firing his submachine gun, Schulze yelled over the din, "Hans! This looks like real war!"

"Who cares?" Riedl shouted back. "We're devil's own guard. Not even Lucifer would take us. . . . Besides, there's a truce between Saigon and Hanoi." And he ducked as a slug whizzed past his head.

"Why won't you sing one of your stupid rhymes now?" Erich taunted him. "Who's afraid of Father Ho?"

Whereupon Helmut promptly began to holler,

> We are sitting in a mess,
> In a mess, in a mess.
> Old Giap may kiss my ass,
> Tra la-la-la-la . . .

Then he started to blaze away at the enemy infantry, shooting up a group of Moroccans barricaded in the semidestroyed mess hall.

The North Vietnamese assault guns lumbered into view and converged on the exercise field, firing point-blank into whatever still stood. Only the concrete pillboxes checked their farther advance until, crawling over the mounds of torn flesh of their dead comrades, the enemy sappers smothered them one after another. The Vietcong had suffered at least a thousand casualties before Bunker Lafayette, on the western perimeter, fell silent.

But life comes cheap in the Orient. As I later learned, it was the North Vietnamese General Tan Quang Bun, Giap's right hand, who directed the assault, and Giap never cared a fig for losses—so long as there were results.

I was immensely relieved that I'd left Task Force-G in a safe place. Had it come along, it would have been compelled to fight and probably suffer prohibitive losses. Deep within I was still preoccupied, not so much on account of our own fate, but wondering what Task Force-G would do without us. The situation looked grave.

The mere fact that the North Vietnamese had been able to concentrate some ten thousand infantry, armor, and artillery barely two miles from the fortifications, without being spotted either by aerial or land reconnaissance, would be the best way to describe the terrain the French were obliged to fight on.

The situation was deteriorating. After their initial brave stand the North Africans lost their élan and had only one goal —to survive. Now they scarcely poked their heads out of the trenches and foxholes. The paras bore the brunt of the fighting, and they fought manfully; not only did they stop the guerrilla advance and knock out a pair of assault guns, but they stormed and recaptured a machine-gun emplacement. The North Africans, who should have given them covering fire, ducked into shelters and lay low.

One of the French *chars* clattered around the gutted officers' mess, lurched to halt, and lobbed a shell into the side of a North Vietnamese troop carrier at barely thirty yards. The vehicle exploded, jettisoning jagged pieces of armor, instruments, wires, bits of uniform, and chunks of flesh. Fire, smoke, and dust engulfed the screaming survivors.

Firing, crawling, and firing again, we made our way behind the tank, but by the time we arrived some wounded paras and Moroccans had already taken the safest places and I didn't feel like pulling rank to dislodge them. Here rank meant nothing. We were only desperate men trying to survive.

I spotted a hand lying in a muddy groove and recognized it by the silver signet ring on its battered index finger. I scanned the ground for the corpse of Lieutenant André Duprés and found it ten yards away, partly buried in a pile of debris. I grabbed a bit of cloth, picked up the hand, crawled over a tangle of corpses, and placed it next to the unfortunate officer's mangled wrist. He was killed by a fist-size shrapnel in the chest. I don't know where I got the inspiration to leave my safe shelter and enter a shower of bullets only to pay a last honor to a corpse. "Are you out of your mind?" Erich browbeat me later. "There's a war going on here, if you failed to notice."

Somehow my impulsive gesture made me feel content; perhaps it was rooted in the unsaid wish of all of us to be buried in one piece.

Suddenly one of the paras yelled a shrill warning. The tank began to move—backward. We had just enough time to dive and roll out of harm's way. A few wounded and a pair of Moroccans were too late. I saw the tracks roll over them, mashing arms and legs into the churned-up ground, drawing brief shrieks of agony and instant death. The battle turned into a savage free-for-all, where no one cared for anyone else. The enemy shells continued hammering us, blasting even the ruins. Rafters, shards of brick, and rugged pieces of corrugated tin roofs careened through the air and knifed into the ground or the bodies of those who happened to be lying there.

We darted back into our old shell hole, the only safe place around. At least the front-line troops stubbornly believed so. "Lightning would never strike the same place twice," the proverb ran, and for some silly reason we believed that it should be the same with artillery shells.

Colonel D'Arcy stood in the sandbagged entrance of his bunker. His face was drawn and pale, as if all the vitality had been leeched out of his body. He was shouting orders that no one seemed to hear, let alone obey, gesticulating with his gun. For some strange reason he darted from the entrance and stopped on the ledge of our hole. Remaining upright, perhaps dazed, or just beset with impotent rage, he began to blaze away with his automatic pistol.

"Er ist voll Verrueckt geworden!" Erich swore. "Where does he think he is? In the Luna Park, shooting at rubber ducks?" He reached up and, grabbing the colonel by the ankles, jerked him into the hole.

I spotted a handful of Vietcong racing toward the headquarters' entrance. One was about to lob a grenade when Erich hit him in the head. The guerrilla crashed to the ground, together with his primed grenade. Six of his companions followed him into the Communist paradise—hell.

Wiping the sweat and dirt from his face, Erich said casually, "I think we should get out of this mess."

I asked flatly, "All right—how?"

"Break out toward the south."

"All three of us?" Riedl queried with an ironic chuckle.

RECALL TO INFERNO

"Immer nach dem Lage handeln," Schulze answered. "One should act as the situation warrants."

"Warum eigentlich nicht?" Riedl agreed. "Why shouldn't we try? There aren't more than five hundred Vietcong to eliminate. Child's play . . . *Kinderspiel."*

"What's your idea?" I asked Schulze.

He showed me a flare gun. "This thing here . . . If we could pump a flare into one of the assault guns, it would raise a hell of a fire and smoke inside and probably drive the crew into the open. We seize the vehicle and make a break for it."

"Until the artillery sends us the good night, Charlie," Riedl cracked.

"Kuhscheiss," Erich commented. "Cowshit. The French won't fire at us while we're racing away from the fort, and the North Vietnamese will take us for one of their own. . . . What do you think of it, Hans?"

"I don't feel like stopping a slug here or hanging in Hanoi. Start looking for the vehicle."

Riedl shrugged. "It sounds crazy but it might work. Most of his crazy ideas work."

"Like the dam we built in the hills to flood the Vietminh rats in the Ca-bang Valley in 1950," Erich remarked, firing his submachine gun. "That's four Congs less," he commented contentedly.

"It was in fifty-one," Helmut retorted.

"Anyway, it worked," Schulze said.

We suggested that Colonel D'Arcy come along, but now that he was somewhat composed, the camp commander wouldn't even discuss the idea of abandoning his post. "I must return to the bunker," he repeated over and over. "To the phone and the wireless. Relief might be coming, or at least the air force."

Firing like mad and tossing grenades and crawling across heaps of rubble and corpses, we escorted him safely into his bunker.

At 1:15 P.M., after three hours of incessant fighting, Captain Delmont, the commander of the western sector, reported that further resistance would be useless and senseless because all his artillery and machine-gun positions had been put out of action and his company now comprised a mere forty-four men. With his face drawn, Colonel D'Arcy authorized him to surrender; a proposal Delmont flatly refused. Instead of raising the white flag, he ordered *à la bayonette* and stormed straight into the enemy ranks. A few minutes later the gallant officer died in action. Forming a hedgehog stand around his body, his Algerians fought until they fell dead or wounded, and in the end extracted a terrible toll from the enemy. Shamming death, one of the mortally wounded Arabs waited until the Vietcong swarmed over the place and began to frisk the corpses for valuables, then set off a crateful of hand grenades, blowing up himself and everyone else in a two-hundred-foot circle.

Lieutenant Clairmons, who was in charge of six howitzers on the eastern sector, sounded almost as if he were crying when he reported that his Moroccans had decamped and he was unable to defend his guns.

Once again the Communist propaganda had scored a bull's-eye. For some months the Vietcong propagandists had been urging the colonials to turn their weapons against their imperialist overlords, join with the Vietnamese Forces of National Liberation, and fight for the freedom of their homelands. "If you cannot, or will not, fight against the French, then surrender," the leaflets and broadcasts urged. "You will be treated generously, rewarded, and sent home or to any other country you choose."

Many colonial troops had heeded the call. The Communists have weapons other than guns but just as effective.

By 2:30 P.M. the situation became critical. The defenders were restricted to a six-hundred-yard circle around the HQ bunker. The enemy tanks never moved. Perhaps General Bun did not wish to risk his cherished armor during the initial attack and later they were no longer needed. Overall superiority in manpower and artillery were sufficient to win the battle, although not completely.

Such was the situation when Erich's chance unexpectedly presented itself. A North Vietnamese assault gun halted scarcely fifteen yards from our shelter and began to shell a gun emplacement still held by the paras.

"Here we go!" Schulze yelled, and before we realized what was happening, he darted forward, vaulted onto the rear armor, lifted the lid of the observation port, fired a flare through the gap, and slammed down the cover. The fiery projectile must have terrified the crew, for the rear door flung open and five North Vietnamese regulars dropped from the billowing smoke. Erich's submachine gun toppled them in a wink.

"Move!" He beckoned us, clambering into the vehicle where we joined him, dodging bullets. "Keep the door open for a while," Erich shouted as he dropped into the driver's seat. Riedl settled behind the machine gun and began to hammer a cluster of guerrillas darting toward us. I occupied myself with the turret gun, checked the shells, and swore aloud. They were low-velocity shrapnel against soft targets and would be quite useless if some of the North Vietnamese tanks decided to give us the pursuit.

I tapped Erich on the shoulder.

"Keep away from those tanks," I shouted. "I won't even tickle them with the shells we have."

As he revved up the engine, he shouted over the din, "Try to blast their crews, Hans. They're all in the open, watching the show."

He spun the half-track and started to race along the rubble-covered parade way toward the wrecked eastern sector; we rolled over debris, discarded weapons, craters, corpses, and played havoc among the bewildered guerrillas who occupied the captured Moroccan trenches, knocking over field artillery, crushing mortars and machine guns to sheet metal and their crews to minced meat. Seeing the red North Vietnamese ensign with the yellow star, the enemy troops in our way suspected nothing until we crushed them to death.

Whistling, Erich smashed through a pile of broken logs and wires that had once been the camp gate and watch tower, while Helmut was sending long strings of slugs into a scattering group of Hanoi officers around a Russian UAZ truck with wireless. He was singing merrily, "Who's afraid of Father Ho . . . Father Ho . . . Father Ho . . ."

But there's no sharper spur to victory than good spirits in defiance of peril.

Erich yelled, "Get ready, Hans!"

I ran the turret sixty degrees and targeted the foremost Josef Stalin tank stationary on the forest line with its crew lounging around the squat turret.

They received my four-inch greeting dead center and pitched

off the armor, flying like rag dolls, while others nearby dived for cover. I loaded and fired and fired again five or six times in rapid succession to pin the tank crews to the ground.

Riedl was hollering above the din of the engine and tracks,

> Vater Ho ist ein Vogelschreck,
> Bald sitzt Er bis zum Hals im Dreck.

Another of Schulze's "crazy" ideas had worked. The North Vietnamese artillery didn't fire at us and the French guns, too, let us go. We were "running away."

Finally one of the T-34s began to roll, firing as it clattered over bumpy ground, bouncing up and down, lobbing shells all over hell's half acre, while Erich drove our much-faster half-track in a crazy zigzag line. For a while the tank ran parallel with us with its gun slung sideways, firing at random. But, as "even the blind hen might find a worm," I wanted to get it off our tail. There was only one way to do it, and I gestured to Schulze. He understood and halted for an instant, just long enough for me to aim, keeping ahead by three feet, at the foremost transport wheel of the T-34. My shrapnel hit the two center ones. The track snapped and fed itself flat on the ground. The tank spun around and stopped dead.

"It seems it's our lucky day," Riedl commented.

Speeding through sparse woods, we ran into a Vietcong logistics camp of tents, with stores and a first aid station, all of which Erich crushed, while Helmut and I blasted scattering groups of terrified guerrillas and four trucks into oblivion.

"How much gas we have?" I shouted to Schulze.

"There should be enough for another fifty miles—if the damned Russian indicator works."

But as it turned out, it was not to be our luckiest day, thanks to the unexpected appearance of six fighter bombers, probably on their way to Camp Dizier—late as usual.

Two of the warplanes peeled off the formation and dived for us. I tried in vain to contact them over the Chinese wireless set of the half-track.

"Those shitheads are loaded with rockets!" Riedl yelled. Erich swerved sharply and drove into the brush just as the road behind us erupted with fire and smoke. The assault gun rocked.

I banged my head against the gunlock and swore. Erich stepped on the brake. Riedl threw open the rear door and we bolted for the woods.

The rockets of the second plane turned our comfortable transport into scrap metal.

"Verfluchte Scheisskerl!" Erich swore, shaking his fist after the climbing plane. "Instead of blasting the tanks of Father Ho, he's making us walk thirty miles in this damned heat. Asshole!"

Camp Dizier, or what was left of it, was relieved by an armored brigade two days later.

Colonel D'Arcy was still defending the HQ complex against tanks and infantry with his surviving 275 men, most of them wounded. We were pleased to hear that every one of them was later decorated and promoted, for they truly deserved it.

Erich told me later, "You know what? If we had taken Colonel D'Arcy along we would have wrecked his career."

"Probably," I agreed.

But we were resolved to return with Task Force-G to search for the Vietcong camp in the jungle from where the offensive against Camp Dizier had begun.

"I bet the base is crammed with tanks and artillery," Riedl said.

Krebitz added thoughtfully, "I'd like to find the road those tanks and howitzers took to get here in the first place."

4.

Rescue of the Third Regiment

Counterguerrilla operations in Vietnam were never a picnic—not even with tank, artillery, and aerial support, but going into action during the semiannual monsoon period signified a prolonged sojourn in a steamy, misty, soggy green hell. The persistent rain swelled the rivers, flooded the lowlands and valleys, grounded aircraft, and severely restricted overland transport.

Naturally the rainy seasons were periods of increased Vietcong activity. The enemy relocated troops, hauled supplies into the South Vietnamese heartland and the delta, and attacked outlying bases and fortifications with redoubled effort. Monsoon rains could be so intense that visibility would be reduced to zero and every other sound would be obliterated by the downpour, especially in the forests. Weary sentries of military installations could be surprised and killed, camps stormed and overrun, and supply convoys seized.

The weeks of the southern monsoon in July and the northwest monsoon in January were periods of Vietcong gains in every province. In the absence of warplanes and copters the Mekong between the Cambodian frontier and the delta would be abuzz with clandestine shipping. After having been supplied with Chinese 12.7-mm machine guns and 4-cm antitank guns, the Vietcong no longer feared French and South Vietnamese gunboats. Instead of escaping, they would engage and often sink them.

To the French Expeditionary Force the monsoons were periods of lethargic inactivity. The North African soldiers suffered a great deal and usually sank into sullen, apathetic moods.

The rainy seasons never grounded Task Force-G. Dry or wet, we would be in the hills, trekking along remote trails, in jungles and swamps, striking the guerrillas when and where they least expected it, causing Hanoi tremendous losses in men and material. We also endured hardships; even the Russian winter seemed a mild inconvenience in comparison.

Task Force-G was in the mountains of Chu Pong, skirting the river Drang with the small village of Plei-kia, where some Montagnard tribesmen, resolute enemies of the Vietcong, were defending themselves with bows and arrows and a few obsolete rifles.

It was on the plateau of Chu Pong that the unbridled fury of a storm caught and bogged us down for thirty-six hours. We were unable to advance one thousand yards to take shelter in the forest.

Our advance came to standstill under a small cluster of trees that offered no protection at all. The wind howled and blustered through the branches, tearing leaves and boughs. The deluge was of almost solid intensity; it came down like shotgun pellets, and the violent wind right in our faces made progress impossible. The men could barely carry the weight of their equipment and when they tried to struggle on, the wind spun them around and flung them off their feet. It was blowing so furiously that even breathing became difficult. All we could do was to turn our backs to it, squatting on the ground, wrapped in our burlaps.

The sky seemed to split apart, and between the thunderclaps lightning flashed. Some struck the nearby cliffs with the sickening roar of a heavy shell. Shouting over the pandemonium and gesticulating wildly, I urged the troops to lay down guns and other metallic objects that might attract lightning.

When the rain abated after about six hours, the wind began to blow harder than before. Erecting shelters was out of the question. We were unable to unfold burlaps, or get poles set, for everything was promptly blown away and went downhill in shreds. One may dress against cold or warm but little can be done against rain, whipped by a gale. The water found inlets through our watertights, by way of collars and sleeves, and soaked everything underneath. Neither cigarettes nor food—not even biscuits—could be handled.

After a miserable night the wind lost some of its ferocity, and we managed to drag ourselves into the forest to rig our burlaps between the branches. Then we had at least makeshift shelters. Out came the bags with spare fatigues and dry underwear, while the soaked clothes were fastened upon the branches where the wind more or less dried them. Still, another day would pass before we could resume our march.

After covering about four miles, our advance guard came to a dirt road with a wooden bridge across the Drang, fortunately intact and devoid of traps. Either the Vietcong had not been there recently, or the guerrillas needed the bridge themselves—as it was the only one to Plei-kia. Beyond the Drang the dirt road ran north over undulating, forested ground between a pair of tributaries, flowing two miles apart.

Dusk was falling when we stopped briefly to eat and don our straw hats, bamboo helmets, and other Vietcong garb. Our precaution was superfluous. The bad weather had sent the guerrillas into shelter. Krebitz and Gruppe Drei crawled to within fifty yards of the foremost huts, occupied by the Vietcong. The dwellings toward the center were burnt or semidestructed with corpses lying between them. The village had been taken by the guerrillas, although the small number of dead in sight led us to believe that most inhabitants had managed to flee into the woods and were perhaps safe. Plei-kia itself was unimportant to us, but the village could serve the Vietcong as a convenient base for future attacks on Dang-duc, farther north on *Route Colonial 19*.

I divided our commando of 130 men into six assault groups, each equipped with a pair of machine guns and one flamethrower.

Making a short detour, Schulze advanced to cut the road toward Duc-ko, while Altreiter and Stolz occupied the steep banks of the two lateral streams to prevent the enemy from escaping in either direction. With sixty troops, Krebitz, Riedl, and I moved into the village from three directions. Thanks to the wind and to Krebitz's accurate survey, our trailblazers eliminated a pair of sentries in the open and three more perched on a pile-supported landing with a thatched-roof overhang. Using silencers, our sharpshooters shot them in the head without drawing as much as a feeble sigh. The same fate befell two guerrillas who exited from a hut to relieve themselves.

Gruppe Drei advanced right to the huts, where the guerrillas seemed to be in a cheerful mood—their carefree chattering and guffaws could be heard clearly. Inside the huts fires burned, illuminating the doors and windows, casting long dancing shadows on the walls. In the largest hut someone played the harmonica and a dozen throats sang a brisk revolutionary song, which a trumpeteer tried to back somewhat dissonantly.

Two undamaged huts looked vacant. Rudolf recognized them for what they were: the "gardrobe" where the Vietcong had left their equipment and supplies, mostly mortar shells, hand grenades, and ammunition.

Our assault initiated (and perhaps also concluded) with a salvo of fifty grenades flung into and around the huts, the combined power of which equaled that of a large aerial bomb. The bamboo-straw huts virtually deflagrated, and even the debris shriveled in the subsequent gouts of the flamethrowers. In barely ten seconds the guerrillas lost 70 percent of their complement, and the survivors were unable to rally. Some were blinded, others suffered severe burns or lacerations, and all succumbed to Gruppe Drei's bullets. None of our machine guns or submachine guns fired. There was no need. The dazed, bewildered enemy were dispatched by single rifle and pistol shots, and the handful of Vietcong who managed to escape ran into Schulze's blocking party, and fled into a cave where a flamethrower made short work of them.

News can travel fast even in the wilderness. Scarcely an hour after we recaptured Plei-kia a group of rugged Montagnards strolled into the village with their women and children in tow. The inhabitants had heard the explosions and saw the conflagration and rightly asserted that the guerrillas had been evicted by the "French."

With their dwellings and provisions lost, the tribesmen were in a pitiful situation. The captured Vietcong stores could provide for only a few days. We gave them as much canned food and cereal as we could spare, banking on enemy stocks we might seize later on. Kurt Zeisl treated the wounded locals, then Erich led the headman and his two sons to the Vietcong dump, waved a casual hand about, and told them flatly, "Everything's yours. When the Communists show up here the next time, put up a good fight."

The Montagnards' delight was boundless, especially when Krebitz and Stolz demonstrated how everything, including a pair of mortars, worked.

They treated us to a good dinner of rice and fried fish. We overnighted in the village and the next morning the troops helped the people with the reconstruction. By the time we departed in the afternoon, 60 percent of the dwellings had been rebuilt.

Our northward march continued in the comforting certainty that we left behind a reliable "garrison" of brave warriors. Personally I could never understand why the French brought Africans to Indochina in the first place instead of recruiting the Montagnards, who were known for their stamina, bravery, and trustworthiness, not to mention their familiarity with the country, its climate and people.

We advanced toward Colonial Road 19 in our traditional *Frachtzug*—"freight train"—manner, a slow but safe process, with Krebitz and his trailblazers half a mile ahead and Riedl's platoon forming the rear guard. After a couple of miles I caught up with Rudolf, sitting on a log and studying the map, jotting down compass readings.

"We should leave the road here and continue in the forest toward Dang-duc," he suggested, showing us the proposed route and the point where he wanted to reach Road 19.

"Do you want to bypass Duc-ko and the French garrison?" I asked, scanning the map.

He nodded. "Also Dang-duc—and come to number nineteen hereabout. . . . Both villages must be crawling with Vietcong spies."

"In Dang-duc there are only some Saigon gendarmes. Perhaps fifteen men."

"Who, strangely enough, had not been killed by the guerrillas," Schulze added emphatically. "There should be a good reason behind this most unusual Communist clemency."

Riedl spoke. "You mean a sort of, er—gentlemen's agreement? . . . You don't see us and we won't be shooting?"

"Something along that line," Krebitz confirmed.

I said, "Rudolf is right. We should avoid the villages."

"There's a good trail across the hills." Rudolf astounded us. The men murmured with delight, for the prospect of cutting a ten-mile path through the virgin wilderness did not appeal to them.

"Come along," Krebitz beckoned us.

Picking our way through the thorny shrubs, we followed him into the roadside thicket and after some fifty yards came a clear path. "An old Vietminh trail," Rudolf explained, making a sweeping gesture toward the untrodden grassy path with mushrooms growing here and there. "It's not been used for months or was forgotten completely."

"How on earth did you find it?" I exclaimed.

"By chatting with some Montagnard friends," Rudolf replied with a grin. "I'm always wide open to useful information."

I appreciated Krebitz's aptitude. While on a mission in enemy-dominated territory, we preferred to keep our contact with the local people to minimum or to avoid them altogether. Statistically defined, of a hundred natives only about twenty would be genuinely friendly. The rest might be divided into forty neutrals, thirty Communist sympathizers for ideological, financial, or safety reasons, while the remaining ten were bona fide Hanoi spies. Our First Commandment demanded secrecy and that we trust no one outside our innermost "society." The second maxim reminded us that we should always move quickly and silently and kill swiftly. The third one inspired us to show no mercy to the merciless and spare none of the enemy.

Following Rudolf's trail, soon we came to one of the many nameless tributaries of the Drang, all which we had long since dubbed with female names, such as Karin, Susy, Mitzie, Helga, and the like. The stream was swollen with rainwater but the partly rotten and ominously sagging plank bridge across it was covered with reassuring spiderwebs. A few timbers were felled and the trailblazers reinforced the wobbly structure, then Task Force-G crossed over. Two hours later we came to a large cave in the rocky hillside. The reconnaissance party found it vacant and dry, and I decided to halt there for the whole day. We were not bound by timetables. Our objectives were Vietcong dumps, camps, supply convoys, relief and first-aid stations, and whether we hit those on Wednesday, Friday, or the next Monday made no difference. We never lacked targets.

In the cavern, with fires burning inside, soup, tea, and coffee boiling, and clothes drying, it felt like heaven, like being in a first-class hotel on the French Riviera. Men habituated to hardship can content themselves with little.

The following evening we arrived at Colonial Road 19, three

miles past Dang-duc and only thirty miles from the Cambodian border, without encountering any locals, friendly or hostile. The Mekong flew a hundred miles farther west. The region was known for clandestine Vietcong traffic.

We advanced in a far-strung column, marching during the hours of darkness, resting in the roadside undergrowth during the day, clad like guerrillas. We spotted several enemy groups trodding eastward: armed Vietcong and load-carrying Dang Cong coolies, pushing heavily laden bicycles, carts, and wheelbarrows. Not wishing to give away our presence, we let pass unmolested convoys of company strength or larger. Those of only a platoon or two were overwhelmed and eliminated, especially during the misty morning hours. Gruppe Drei left behind neither corpses nor any suspicious clue, and the men cleaned up every site of action. Not a single cartridge would be left lying around, unless captured Chinese or Russian weapons had been used. Enemy convoys disappeared along *Route Colonial* 19, but the subsequent arrivals had not been alarmed by the sites of former disasters.

More dreary miles. More rains and thunderstorms. More hardship. Damp, misty mornings and long, tense periods of waiting: like a spider in its web, looking for a victim.

We killed more guerrillas. Seventy-two by body count. One third of them were mere boys, barely fifteen but already trained assassins and saboteurs, ready to perpetrate the most hideous atrocity at the Party's bidding. Sixteen of our victims were women, armed and wild and quite willing to surpass their men in brutality. One girl, however, Schulze had spared. She was only twelve, braided and frightened, with some garbled native name. Erich dubbed her "Hanoi Rose" and made her march along, fastened to Walter Winar's belt with a thin chain, for she would probably have bitten through any cord. "She'll eventually become domesticated," Erich told me, and I wished him good luck. The alternative would have been to shoot the girl too.

Our fast-growing ledger recorded nearly three hundred victims since we left Saigon. We were still undetected and could move freely because we never permitted anyone to escape and ring the alarm bell in Hanoi. The enemy knew nothing about our activities, our whereabouts.

RECALL TO INFERNO

Task Force-G reached the Cambodian frontier in the early-morning mist. The road branched off northward and from the milky whiteness emerged the smoldering ruins of a small fortified camp: a ghastly site with North African and South Vietnamese corpses scattered far and wide.

"What a fine welcoming spectacle," Krebitz commented as he threw an invisible cordon of security around the fort. The trailblazers and sharpshooters took position in the vacant, blackened rooms. Others began to search for survivors but found none. The guerrillas had done a thorough job.

Sepp Mueller came across the badge of a dead Moroccan—the flaming grenade with its regimental insignia REI 3. The unfortunate Arab legionary belonged to the *Troisième Regiment Etranger d'Infanterie*. Fingering the badge, Schulze commented nostalgically, "The Third Regiment. . . . They were holding a bridge at Fu-li on the river Dai last July. Only a few weeks before the armistice. The regiment must have been evacuated from the north quite recently."

"From one hell into another one," Jost Waldman retorted with an ironical snort. He covered the dead Arab's face with a bit of cloth and weighed it down with stones.

Suddenly we became aware of distant gunfire and muffled explosions. Krebitz, Mueller, and Waldman grabbed their gear and darted off to see what was going on. We concealed ourselves in the fort and, while waiting for Rudolf, Riedl added four more Vietcong to our list of victims. Unaware of our presence, the guerrillas strolled into the compound to search the corpses for valuables that had been overlooked by their predecessors. Helmut shot them as they squatted next to some dead Moroccans.

Rudolf returned with bad news. Near the river Sé Son, two miles from the camp, the guerrillas were decimating a colonial unit bogged down in the marshes.

"Probably the survivors of the Third Regiment," Erich said.

"Moroccans, Algerians, and Senegalese," Krebitz elucidated. "The apes are all around them—holding the dry ground and a hillock. The wretches can neither escape nor defend themselves, and unless we relieve the pressure they'll be gunned down to the last man."

"What's the enemy strength?" I asked.

Krebitz considered for a moment. "At least two companies
. . . perhaps more."

"That's long odds," Riedl commented wryly. I was considering our chances. We were only 130 strong, but I knew by experience that the element of surprise would promptly cancel 30 percent of the enemy superiority.

"Ah, was," Erich exclaimed. "We've been fighting under worse conditions and won. Remember Operation Triangle. We were only six hundred but wiped out over a thousand Vietminh."

"I also remember that we packed over a hundred machine guns and twenty flamethrowers," I commented levelly. "And we had Eisner and Pfirstenhammer." I turned toward Krebitz. "Do you think we should intervene, Rudy?"

"We could certainly get the apes with their pants down, Hans," he answered. "The terrain is good. Ample grass and shrubs, but we should move quickly."

Tired as they were after a long march, the troops accepted the additional hardship. We hurried to the scene of action.

The moment I caught a glimpse of the spreading marshland of the Sé Son valley, I knew that the Third Regiment was in an awful mess. The Vietcong had pushed the colonials into the coverless bog that the river had recently flooded, and the unfortunate fellows were having a rough time wading through pits and holes filled with swirling eddies; sinking up to their chins and sometimes deeper, nearly drowning in the slimy mud, trying to put distance between themselves and their tormentors. The guerrillas occupied the high ground and were shooting at the easy targets at leisure. The North Africans were men of deserts and barren hills, cast into an utterly alien and hostile environment. Now they could not stand erect or extricate themselves, once the mud had engulfed their feet. They struggled on, daring a rain of slugs that raked the surface around them, tossing up funnels of water. Their only relief was the foggy cover of mist, which heaved and rolled, exposing some men, concealing others. But whenever the mist momentarily lifted the snipers would strike home, a few Legionnaires would freeze, double up, crumple, and go down like stone under the weight of their equipment. And whenever the stragglers came to a small dry mound with sparse shrubs, more fugitives would perish in the struggle to secure a foothold in the bushes.

Hollering abuse and guffawing, the guerrillas were target-practicing at the bobbing heads, using only rifles and pistols braced against tree stumps or logs. Through the field glasses we saw bills changing hands. "I bet they're making wagers." Erich swore quietly. *"Verdammte Gelbschnautze."*

The Vietcong were gunning down the men in the water, and all the while a loudspeaker blared from the hillock, calling the colonials to surrender—in Arabic!

I also spotted a few French officers and NCOs. A tall, bearded captain was trying to exhort his troops to turn deaf ears to the enemy propaganda and keep going, but the officers were primary targets and the snipers hit them one after another.

There was no time to make preparations. We just split into three *Kampfgruppen*, set up our mortars and machine guns on the best available sites, and opened up with everything we had, hoping that in their confusion the enemy would mistake us for a battalion. With guns blazing and bayonets fixed, the three assault groups charged forward and swept the Vietcong from the hillock. The beleaguered colonials were instantly relieved. The guerrillas had more urgent doings at hand than target-shooting.

Victory followed with amazing speed.

The Vietcong machine guns and mortars had been left unattended while their owners had gathered near the water to disport themselves with handguns. Gruppe Drei captured them and turned them against their former owners. On the narrow stretch of flat ground between the hill and the swamp the troops of Stolz, Sepp Mueller, and Altreiter were beating the daylights out of the smaller and lighter Viets in a hand-to-hand brawl. When it came to grips the enemy could not win. Some of our brawniest companions would simply wrench the rifle from the adversary's hand and smash the butt over his head.

The colonials in the marsh were not idle for long. They'd pulled themselves together and began to do some target-shooting of their own. Unhindered now, the Moroccans and Algerians waded ashore and set up their MGs to rake the far side of the hill, which momentarily puzzled us, until Julius Steiner came skidding down the slippery declivity, shouting "There's another bunch of shitguys in the forest!"

There was indeed—two more companies. A perfect surprise, due to lack of reconnaissance. Some three hundred guerrillas who had been resting in the woods now rushed to the scene of action. The Third Regiment's machine guns forced them to discard the idea and take shelter. The colonial guns had clear command of the flat and pinned down the enemy reinforcements.

Soon the rest of the colonials were on dry ground. They fixed bayonets and charged the enemy under the command of a French sergeant, whose presence of mind had turned a near rout into blazing victory. The sudden turn of tide kindled the North Africans' fury into roaring rage. Shouting garbled battle cries, wielding their rifles like they were clubs, and with drawn machetes, the colonials threw themselves upon the Vietcong, standing or lying—fit or wounded. Ignoring blows and slashes, they bore their foes to the ground and hacked them to pieces. A few paces from where I squatted, a Moroccan corporal knocked a guerrilla to the ground, held his victim down by the shoulders, and, howling madly, tore out his jugular—with his teeth! A group of Senegalese ripped the clothes off four screaming Vietcong, spread-eagled them, and sliced off their private parts.

Seeing this brutal ferocity, other guerrillas turned and fled into the forest, pursued by the raving colonials. All organized resistance broke. Our troops were already strolling around the hill, bayoneting wounded Vietcong and prisoners. The battle of the Third Colonial Regiment ended in the jungle where some 160 prisoners were slaughtered with machetes amid wicked laughs and dirty oaths.

In the encounter the enemy lost 376 men. Our own losses were three dead and eight wounded. The colonials fared worse. They had lost 760 ranks, 8 officers, and 11 NCOs. The only survivor of rank was Staff Sergeant Jean Pelletier from Narbonne, a professional soldier for sixteen years.

Battered, worn, and bleeding from several slashes, he reported to me after the engagement. While Zeisl treated his injuries, the sergeant called my attention to the lack of guerrilla baggage. The customary jute and canvas bags with personal possessions were missing from the field. Pelletier was sure that the luggage had been deposited somewhere in the forest.

The colonials loved booty, and Krebitz offered a hand at

finding it. The Vietcong sacks and bags were soon discovered concealed in a crevass and in a dry brook, covered with branches. Ammunition, foodstuff, watches, money bags stuffed with French and local bills, bottles of rice liqueur, tobacco, and eight thousand cigarettes was a fair haul. Save for two thousand cigarettes, we ceded everything to the colonials as their legitimate booty of war.

The survivors of the Third Regiment retired to the provincial capital, Hue—spreading wild stories about the fearless German attack against "thousands" of Vietcong and their subsequent salvation through the heroism of Task Force-G.

5.

Treason and Punishment

Task Force-G did not always win. On two subsequent expeditions we failed to reach our objectives and suffered losses in men and matériel, although the reverses were not due to any bad planning or carelessness on our part. Nor should they be credited to Vietcong ingenuity.

We were in the hills of Chu-don, a few miles west of *Route Colonial* 14, which connected Plei-kiu with Saigon and Nhantrang on the South China Sea. A dirt road connected the highway and the village of Plei-me. We bypassed it in favor of a tedious trip across the wilderness, skirting the foothills of the Chu-don range. "Safety before speed" was our Fourth Commandment. We never observed timetables, not even if delay meant we'd miss an important Vietcong convoy. There would always be others.

Our raids were invariably prolonged affairs, seldom lasting less than two weeks. In practice, we remained in the hills as long as we had ammunition. Frequently we could replenish our dwindling supplies from captured enemy stores. Then we'd keep going beyond the expedition's scheduled distance and duration.

The raid had been planned by General Houssong and was based on recent intelligence, telling of the existence of a large guerrilla dump in a cluster of caves in a ravine near Plei-me. The dump was supposed to consist of four hundred machine guns, thirty mortars, a pair of Russian-made multiple rocket launchers, and ammunition, all which the Vietcong planned to distribute to the various guerrilla cells active around Plei-kiu.

We advanced with extreme caution because, apart from ourselves, we also had Suoi and Noi to take care of. In many past engagements the girls had displayed fearlessness and stamina, and I had no valid reason to turn down their request to come

RECALL TO INFERNO

along, although their presence had surely given me a constant headache.

Camouflaged with green twigs, which rendered the troops almost invisible against the jungle background, Gruppe Drei approached the ravine, with the rest of Task Force-G tailing five hundred yards behind. At a suitable place we halted to prepare our weapons and were ready to move, when Krebitz called me over the walkie-talkie and requested that Erich and I come over. Curious, we advanced to where Gruppe Drei had taken position in the brush-covered declivity, overlooking the caves. Without preliminaries, Rudolf suggested that we should have a look through the binoculars.

The caves were indeed conspicuous. The ground in front of the entrances showed traces of recent activity—footprints and grooves of heavy objects dragged along the path and broken bits of wooden crates. In fact, the outlines of some crates in the gloomy interior could also be discerned. Without removing his field glasses from his eyes, Krebitz asked, "Tell me, what strikes you odd?"

I looked again, then scanned the neighborhood, observed the trees, the underbrush, but saw nothing extraordinary. With his binoculars roving between the caves, Schulze mumbled, "Strange . . . Why should they leave some crates near the entrance of each cave?"

Now that he said it, I realized the oddity myself. I shifted my eyes toward Krebitz and saw him grinning contentedly. "Because the assholes wanted us to see those crates and dash into the ravine, jumping up and down like kids under the Christmas tree."

"It's a trap!" Schulze swore spitefully. "A damned trap!"

"So it is," Rudolf agreed, "and the leader of the apes must be a newcomer hereabouts if he believes we'd swallow such clumsy bait." He dropped his field glasses to his chest and added, to me, "You should return to Riedl and throw up a good defensive perimeter, Hans. I think it's going to be hot here and very soon."

"What about you?"

"I'll watch the place for a while."

"You have only sixteen men," I reminded him warily.

"You might need covering fire."

"I don't feel like risking you for any Vietcong treasure, Rudy."

He shook his head. "There's no Vietcong treasure here, Hans," he said with conviction. "The crates are empty. So are the caves. But the ravine might be full of trip mines and the hills full of guerrillas."

"Then you'd better return with us," I replied. To speed up Rudolf's decision, I added, "You may consider it an order."

He shook his head and smiled. "All right, then—let's move—but carefully—without showing much of yourselves."

We began to crawl, first sideways like fiddler crabs, then backward, from bush to bush. "Do you think we're being observed?" Erich asked in a low voice.

"I know we are," Krebitz replied.

We continued our wary withdrawal but barely covered twenty yards when a solitary shot rang from an overhang and a slug buried itself in a stump ten inches from my shoulder.

"You see what I meant?" Rudolf commented. "Now we should get the hell out of here."

The same instant the underbrush on the far side of the ravine erupted with automatic fire and a couple of heavy mortars opened up, blasting six-foot craters in the acclivity. No longer crawling but darting from tree to tree and from boulder to boulder, we fled toward the clearing where the task force had bivouacked, tailed by machine-gun salvos.

The enemy mortars registered with precision, as if they had been positioned in advance, anticipating our approach. Only God knew what kind of devilish surprise awaited us had we descended into the narrow ravine.

Riedl and Sepp Mueller had already set up our mortars and were busy shelling the forest behind us. The troops were positioned along a low ridge, ready to repel the enemy infantry, should they pursue us. And pursued we were. We barely reached our line when a disorderly mob of Vietcong emerged from the thicket and came charging across the clearing, firing from the hip, hollering *"Xung-phong!"* At first glance it was evident that we didn't face seasoned veterans or North Vietnamese regulars, only a bunch of Communist fanatics, perhaps with a string of easy victories against the South Vietnamese

RECALL TO INFERNO

recruits to their credit. Theirs wasn't the proper way to attack Task Force-G.

"Dil Dil" the foremost runners cried. The clearing was about one hundred yards wide. The charging Vietcong received the full firepower of my troops at a distance of about sixty yards and couldn't last long.

"Keep firing!" I urged the men. "The bastards have no idea how to shoot but don't let them come close enough to hurl grenades."

Krebitz pushed Suoi and Noi into a depression, and Gruppe Drei's men piled a wall of knapsacks around them. Noi protested. She wanted to look after the wounded. Rudolf rebuked her with a crisp "We haven't got any wounded. When Zeisl needs you, he'll call."

The foremost guerrilla lines staggered, pitched left and right, crashed to the ground, as if some giant hand had pulled the very soil from under their feet. Over two hundred perished in the withering fire of machine and submachine guns. When Stolz and Jost Waldman began to sweep the ground with their flamethrowers, those who sheltered in the tall grass broke cover and bolted for the woods. Only a few made it.

I rose to one elbow and glanced around. "Any casualties?"

The men passed the question along the perimeter.

"No casualties" came the happy confirmation.

"Where's Krebitz?"

Altreiter waved a casual hand toward the forest behind us. "He's gone to secure our rear."

"Do you think they'll come again?" Waldman asked, wiping dust and dirt from his face.

Schulze shook his head. "Not after the reception we gave them."

"Now they'll try their luck with the mortars," Sepp Mueller commented. "I think we should change position."

I was of the same opinion.

Riedl helped Suoi and Noi to their feet.

"Keep low," he cautioned them. "There might be snipers in the bushes."

Thinking that the 102-mm Vietcong mortars could cause a great deal of damage, I was about to displace our line toward the south, when a trooper arrived from Krebitz and reported, between gasps, "The way to Road fourteen is free. Come quickly."

We scrambled and bolted into the forest. By the time the first enemy mortar shells exploded in front of and behind the ridge we had occupied before, Task Force-G was safely out of range.

Our second futile effort had occurred in the marshes of the delta where we intended to destroy a number of sampans loaded with guerrilla supplies.

Here, too, the Vietcong had known our target and route in advance. We were attacked during a crucial river crossing and suffered thirty casualties before we could extricate ourselves from a very tight situation.

Three of our flamethrowers and four machine guns were defective—something that never happened before. The abortive missions and malfunctioning weapons carried a sinister ring of treason, and we were obliged to accept the painful reality of a saboteur in our ranks. Twice the Vietcong had been ready to receive us at the right time and in the right place. The enemy must have gotten advance warning and the weapons had been sabotaged.

But by whom?

How?

When?

We could only spin vague theories. A spy in Task Force-G? It was hardly conceivable. Nevertheless, the hard facts pointed irrefutably in that direction. Minor details had been leaked that could not have come from any source other than our own camp. The flamethrowers and machine guns were not accessible to outsiders.

Gathering in Stahnke's office, we discussed the grave matter. A prolonged debate ensued over a dozen personal files. In the end our search narrowed down to six names, men who had known the key details, apart from Schulze, Riedl, Stolz, Altreiter, and myself. They were Julius Steiner, Gerhart Seyfert, Otto Janaschek, Jost Waldman, Wilfred Resch, and Walter Winar.

In order not to arouse suspicion or unjustly offend anyone, we pretended to interview the men "proposed for promotion."

Our first subject of inquiry was twenty-seven-year-old Jost

Waldman, who had just celebrated his tenth anniversary in uniform, first a German, then a French one. He was a tall, supine, blue-eyed fellow with curly blond hair and a carefree teenage look—that was, however, misleading. Jost was a tough, resolute fighter with a vast fighting experience, accumulated during the last ten months of World War II.

He had joined the twelfth S.S. *Panzergrenadier Hitlerjugend* Division in April 1944, at the age of sixteen, awash with fanatical patriotism like all his Hitler Youth companions. He had been assigned to the 1st Battalion of the 25th Regiment, transported to Normandy a few days after the allied landing. They were to delay the British-Canadian advance on Calais.

Serving a PAK 75 antitank gun, Waldman and his companions had knocked out seventeen enemy tanks and assault guns in the Calais–Falais–Lissieux triangle. He had participated in the battle for Carpiquet village and the nearby airstrip, defended by 360 Hitler Youth against two Canadian battalions with artillery and armored support. None older than eighteen, the men of the *Hitlerjugend* division were fired with Nazi ideals, quite ready to die—so ready that by the end of August their division had been reduced to three hundred soldiers, ten tanks, and zero artillery. In a single late June afternoon, Jost had lost a cousin, five former classmates, and nearly all his superior officers and NCOs, many of them burned alive by Canadian flamethrower tanks. Himself wounded by shards and wood splinters, Jost destroyed two tanks with his *Panzerschreck* bazooka. Six Canadians had been captured and were about to be escorted into the rear when Jost, nearly hysterical and perhaps in shock, grabbed his *Schmeisser* and gunned down the prisoners, qualifying himself for the allied list of war criminals.

After the bloody combat for Hill 112, which the Canadians had dubbed Calvary Hill, Jost and some others fell prisoner to the British. Knowing what fate awaited him once the enemy discovered his identity, Jost made use of the momentary confusion caused by a short-lived German counterattack and escaped, made his way back to the German lines, and earned himself the Iron Cross.

I knew that Waldman had suffered a great deal for what he had done in Normandy. "Those poor Canadians were only doing what they had been ordered to do," I heard him lamenting once. "To them it could have been the end of the war. . . . A year later they would have gone home to their families. I killed them in cold blood—also their parents, wives, and children. . . . They shouldn't have given me the Iron Cross but the firing squad."

He would never go near or even look when we gunned down Vietcong prisoners.

When he entered into Stahnke's office, Stahnke greeted him with a broad smile and a boisterous announcement.

"This should be a happy day for you, Jost. I've just heard the news that your onetime commander in Normandy had been released from jail."

Jost's face lit up.

"The *Sturmbannfuehrer* Krause?" he exclaimed.

Stahnke shook his head. "No—not the commander of your *Kampfgruppe* but someone higher up."

"*Standartenfuehrer* Wuenschel"

"Still higher."

Staring at Schulze, then shifting his eyes toward me and Schulze, Jost considered for a moment, then his chin came up.

"There was only one man higher up, old *Panzermeier*," he exclaimed, calling General Kurt Meier by his nickname.

"Right, Jost," Stahnke confirmed. "He is free."

"But he was condemned to death by the British."

"The sentence had been commuted to life in jail but Meier was released a few days ago."

"I'm glad to hear it." Jost beamed. "He shouldn't have been jailed at all for he hadn't done anything. . . . He wasn't even near Lissieux when we—I—killed those prisoners." His voice caught.

I said quietly, "All the commanding officers were held responsible for the actions of their troops. There had been other killings too."

"I know . . . I'm sorry . . ."

The poor fellow looked miserable, bitten again by remorse. Jost had gunned down six prisoners and couldn't live with their ghosts; we had gunned down hundreds of guerrillas without thinking of them twice.

Julius Steiner of Gruppe Drei, an ex-paratrooper, had been eliminated from the list of suspects in fifteen minutes. His prompt, unswerving answers regarding his service in Belgium, Greece, and Italy tallied in every aspect with what we had on file. His escape and travel into the Foreign Legion matched our own experience down to the smallest detail. He had even known our onetime French drillmaster, Sergeant Maurier.

Walter Winar had enlisted in the *Wehrmacht* in November 1939 and had been trained to drive tanks. His combat service began with the 10th *Panzer* Division of General Heinz Guderian. Winar drove his tank (or rather tanks, for he lost four of them) from the Ardennes, through Sedan and Noyens, to Dunkirk. When Erich asked him casually which were his neighboring units, Winar replied without hesitation, "The *Grossdeutschland* and the *Leibstandarte* Adolf Hitler."

He had spent three years in France, been wounded by the *Maquis*, participated in the occupation of Vichy France, then fought rearguard actions against the Americans in the Rhone Valley. He fell prisoner but escaped and hid in the Alps to live like a hermit in caves and vacant sheds. When the weather began to grow chilly he made his way to the sea with the idea of going into Spain. The gendarmes arrested him in Beziers, but he was generously permitted to choose between a prison camp or the Foreign Legion. Winar opted for the latter.

Otto Janaschek had been in Russia from the first day of Operation Barbarossa until the eventual retreat. During the last weeks of the Third Reich he ended up with General Schoerner's phantom army—Hitler's last hope of salvation.

"I was there till the very end," Janaschek narrated. "When the Fuehrer promoted Schoerner to *Feldmarschall* and ordered him to move his divisions to relieve Berlin . . . But what divisions?" He chuckled bitterly. "They existed only on the Fuehrer's operational map. All Schoerner had were a few ill-equipped regiments. I was carrying a light MG-42 with exactly twelve cartridges in the belt. Our division possessed two Panzer Vier-H, with the wrong ammo for the gun, four *Jagdpanzer*, a couple of Goehring assault guns, and two Tigers with about five rounds for each and fuel for twenty miles."

Janaschek's record and interview showed no discrepancies.

As for Wilfred Resch—we could have eliminated him from the list without posing any questions. Although I did not know him personally before he came to Vietnam, he was an *Alte Ka-*

merad of Schulze and me from the last days of the war, east of Liberec in Czechoslovakia. Resch, too, had been up in the mountain pass but belonged to the unfortunate battalion that surrendered to the Red Army under the command of Colonel Steinmetz, and that had been slaughtered on the narrow road as they marched downhill singing, under the flag of truce. Resch had managed to roll into the rushing waters of the ravine and hid in a crevass until—having stripped the German corpses of valuables—the Russians left. Hiding during the day, moving at night, he made his way to Koblenz in the French zone. He was arrested and transported to a POW camp in Bordeaux. One day a major happened by, asking for volunteers to serve in the Legion. Resch had signed up.

Which left us with Gerhart Seyfert, whose S.S. *Einsatzkommando* credentials made him an unlikely subject for collaborating with the Communists. His 120-man commando alone had gunned down fifteen thousand Jews in the Ukraine. After the war the members of *Einsatzgruppen* were tried and executed in the East and the West alike.

We scrutinized his file minutely. Seyfert had enlisted in the Legion quite some time after the war—in 1949—ostensibly after he had been identified as a former member of Himmler's death squad, guilty of war crimes and crimes against humanity. He had been living in Berlin under the alias Gerhart Stahler, and he enlisted in the Legion under that name, giving bogus data with regard to his wartime service as a master sergeant of the 136th Wehrmacht supply battalion of *Heeresgruppe* B. After a period of training in Sidi-Bel-Abbes in Africa, he volunteered for service in Indochina and eventually ended up with us.

On his very first day with Task Force-G, Seyfert confessed his true name and that he had not been in the Wehrmacht but belonged to the S.S. *Einsatzgruppe* C of *Brigadefuehrer* Dr. Thomas, Kommando 4-A, headquartered in Poltava. Since it is established practice in the Foreign Legion to ask no questions about one's past, Schulze had asked, "How come you decided to give us your genuine credentials?"

"Because I didn't want to fool you; nor am I foolish enough to believe that I could have fooled you for any length of time," Seyfert replied in a very straightforward manner.

"You acted wisely," Schulze had told him then and there. "It would have been awkward if some of our veterans of the Kiev district caught you in telling wild stories."

Seyfert's explanation sounded reasonable and also plausible. Many of us had enlisted in the Legion with bogus papers and might have done the same thing in his place. We never bothered with looking deeper into his past.

But now a number of discrepancies began to show up. Karl Stahnke had soon discovered that the *Einsatzkommando* 4-A had not been based in Poltava but in Charkov and that by the winter of 1942–43 its commanding officer, Dr. Thomas, had been replaced by *Brigadefuehrer* Rasch.

Krebitz then reminded us that Seyfert had been absent from our second aborted trip because of a foot sore.

He was a frequent guest in the cabaret Grand Monde, one of many run by the Bin Xuyen organization, the Saigon version of the Italian Mafia. The Bin Xuyen controlled scores of bars and restaurants, among other nonrelated enterprises, and much of the city's vice through a well-equipped private army of two thousand local gorillas. Stahnke was certain that the Bin Xuyen cultivated tender ties with Hanoi. It was quite possible, because Hanoi would never hesitate to engage even capitalist and reactionary allies when it came to destabilizing the Saigon regime. The Communists are not selective about fellow travelers who might help them win their cause and who might be hanged later on at leisure.

The Grand Monde and the bars of Cartinet Street were major places of entertainment, and naturally a large number of soldiers spent free evenings there. We were no exception. But nightclubs in Saigon don't come cheap. Yet Seyfert never ran short of cash.

The curious facts kept emerging. After some additional checking and counterchecking, we decided that neither his army pay nor the occasional booty taken from dead guerrillas would have sufficed to maintain Seyfert "on the go" at the rate he was going.

A polite check of Seyfert's personal belongings yielded nothing suspicious, save for a savings account number with Credit Lyonnaise and some letters from a certain Advocat Dr. Fritz Sigel of Munich, verifying the transfer of some money, the interest on invested inheritance.

"What I don't like is the irregularity of the payments," Stahnke commented thoughtfully as he was making notes. "You see, dividends and interest on capital investment are being paid regularly."

Having talked to Seyfert's closest buddies, it came to our knowledge that his outings in Saigon would usually end in a bar called Chez Muong, where Gerhart was apparently having an affair with one of the waitresses, Yvonne—a native girl with a French name. Since Chez Muong was frequented by French and South Vietnamese officers, Stahnke considered it likely that the Vietcong had some "eyes and ears" there. He placed the bar under surveillance, and the rest of the story ran like a good detective thriller.

Mademoiselle Yvonne turned out to be the sister of a resident Vietcong activist, a Hanoi agent whose job was not to fight or sabotage but to organize and report.

In the end, Stahnke procured a "tongue." In his terminology, this signified that a couple of Karl's hit men would quietly nab someone employed in the bar and persuade him or her to talk about "interesting subjects."

Sometimes the randomly lifted client could not tell anything about Vietcong or Hanoi connection but in most instances would come up with the names of others, capable of enlightening Uncle Stahnke. In the end, after a couple of middlemen had been "vulcanized," Stahnke would arrive at the agent he sought.

In the current affair the spy was a certain Monsieur Trengh Can Thy, a commonplace fellow in his early thirties who owned a radio-TV repair shop behind the Petrusky Lyceum. Stahnke's midnight raid on the shop netted him a powerful transmitter that packed enough kilowatts to convey fraternal greetings to Moscow—let alone Hanoi.

The Vietcong agent was quietly carted off to Stahnke's "laboratory of truth"—an annex of the Des Mares camp. By three o'clock in the morning, "Comrade Trengh has had his flutters and had lost," in Karl's words. Can Thy's confession amounted to a list of enemy agents active in Saigon, Da-nang, and Hue and (no longer surprisingly) one right in our ranks: Sergeant Gerhart Seyfert, a lieutenant of the Soviet NKVD, delegated to the recently established STASI, the State Security of the German Democratic Republic, which closely followed the protocols of onetime Gestapo boss Kaltenbrunner's RSHA.

Riedl promptly dubbed it "Gestaposi," to everyone's delight.

We wanted neither an official inquiry into the inglorious affair nor a mass exodus of Hanoi spies. After having discussed the matter with Stahnke, he resolved the problem in the best Gestapo tradition.

By seven in the morning Trengh's corpse was back in the shop with a neat Chinese bullet hole in the head. Karl arranged for some convincing disorder, lifted the cash from the safe, carried off some radios, and left the place for the Saigon police to ponder over.

ROBBERY AND MURDER, the newspapers reported. Hanoi had no reason to be alarmed. Such and similar crimes were daily events in Saigon, and even the signs of brutal physical torture fit neatly into the overall picture. As one of the enthusiastic reporters suggested: "The victim was brutally tortured probably to reveal the combination of his safe."

We didn't feel like publicizing the affair. It was decided that Seyfert should not be arrested or even interrogated.

He should die in action.

As Stahnke explained, "You'll be happy, Moscow will be happy, the STASI in Berlin will be happy, and Hanoi will replace Monsieur Trengh with another resident agent—and I'll be happy, too, because we might round up the whole Hanoi network piecemeal. . . . No arrests and trials, mind you—only convenient incidents. A car crash here, a short circuit there; a gas explosion somewhere else. No arrests, no alarm. Hanoi will keep replacing the perished agents and we collect intelligence in the meantime."

We sent Seyfert on a bogus mission with Krebitz and Gruppe Drei. When the group returned without the traitor, the troops were told that our unfortunate companion had been killed by a Vietcong sniper.

I sent a brief note to his parents in Berlin stating that their son had died a soldier's death, knowing that the NKVD would have a copy of it the day it arrived. Neither the East Germans nor the Soviets would suspect anything. Seyfert had been sent to Vietnam to destroy the hated German commando from within, and soldiers do die in action.

From Trengh Can Thy's confession we learned that Seyfert had been important enough to have his reports forwarded directly to the North Vietnamese general Tan Quong Bun, a close collaborator of the Supreme Commander, Vo Nguyen Giap.

"We gave the *Scheisskerl* a burial," Krebitz told us on his return. "There was no salute, though."

6.

Raid on the Ho Chi Minh Trail

The battlegrounds of South Vietnam were much different from those in the north. The jungles were denser, more humid, and steaming hot. In the Mekong delta hundreds of brooks, river branches, shallow canals, and treacherous morasses hindered wheeled transport and sometimes even infantry operations— although the Hanoi convoys kept rolling southward as if moving on a highway. And in a sense the enemy did have a highway, which ran from the northern province of Bui Ciu, through Laos and Cambodia, into the South Vietnamese heartland. A branch even extended all the way to the delta, so cleverly camouflaged that not even air reconnaissance could spot and map it.

And with Laos and Cambodia now "fully independent," the main segment of the Red Highway was immune from hostile land operations.

But not from those of the "outlaws" of Task Force-G.

Commando strikes into Vietcong-controlled territory called for meticulous planning in the utmost secrecy. None of our supply and transport requirements would ever follow the regular service protocol. My requests were handed over to General Houssong in person, who would arrange for equipment and vehicles and have everything delivered to our base two miles outside the city in a maximum security zone.

No go-betweens were ever permitted to learn a single particular regarding our strength, weapons, or destination. Nor could the omnipresent Vietcong spies procure any useful information.

Task Force-G would depart during the night in a convoy of trucks closed with burlap, usually with a number of vehicles running empty. At some preselected point the convoy would split, the empty trucks continuing one way, the laden ones taking another road. During the hours of darkness no Hanoi observers could tail us in cars or scooters for any distance without arousing suspicion, being stopped and advised to lay by for half an hour or take another road. Those who persisted despite our warning would be fired upon.

We were planning a long haul—a raid across the Mekong into Cambodia, carrying enough supplies to last for several weeks. The expedition called for fifty-pound backpacks for each man plus personal weapons. Needless to say, after two years of "vacation" we were still somewhat out of shape. We were also older.

I had just celebrated my forty-third birthday. Schulze was turning thirty-seven. At forty-five, Rudolf Krebitz was the eldest, with Kurt Zeisl, forty-four, running a close second. We were certainly no longer young titans with plenty of muscle in reserve.

Task Force-G would search for the southernmost offshoot of the Ho Chi Minh trail. I decided to begin this mission with a diversion in the delta, forgo wheeled transport, and insist upon copters. After a moderately heated exchange with the local air force commander, General Houssong, our "patron saint," had managed to procure a squadron of copters.

Saigon virtually buzzed with Vietcong "eyes and ears." No troops could ever leave the city without the enemy being informed of its strength and direction within half an hour. Stahnke estimated that there were at least fifty clandestine transmitters operating in and around the capital. The number of WTs with ranges up to eight miles were inestimable.

Stahnke was convinced that a permanent guerrilla signal link connected the resident spies with Vietcong command posts in the jungles and swamps. Short-range messages sent by the principal agent would be picked up by the first link, who would relay it to the second link, and so on, until the report reached its destination. All the drivable roads were covered with signal links, masquerading as roadside vendors, beggars, or common peasants tending their fields.

Air travel was the only way to frustrate enemy surveillance, but even so, one had to leave the airfield in the wrong direction.

Only one hundred strong, we departed under the cover of twilight and flew a crazy zigzag pattern to keep the enemy spies confused.

With the landing pads barely touching the ground, the troops disembarked in the delta in two minutes. The copters then rose and departed, continuing the zigzag antics.

We landed in a small clearing under a few inches of water, covered with weeds and low bracken, and waded toward the south. The muggy, sodden air of the marshes lay heavily on us but it was the exact place where no French or South Vietnamese troops would ever venture.

Krebitz spotted a small group of guerrillas tredding toward Tra-vinh, a tiny hamlet in the morass. It looked like a good start for a diversion, and we began to tail them over the worst possible ground—if one may call that endless bog ground.

The guerrillas, about twenty strong, were certainly local fellows, for they knew the swamps well enough to get ahead of us. From a wireless communication we learned that the evening before they had blown up a couple of army trucks in My-tho, a township south of Saigon, fortunately without killing anyone.

For a while we lost sight of them, but Krebitz's self-assuredness did not diminish.

"Sooner or later they'll retire into one of the two villages in the neighborhood, where we can capture them at leisure," he reassured me.

The only negotiable trail consisted of tufts of grass above the murky surface, upon which the guerrillas left ample imprints to follow.

We were in no hurry. The way the Vietcong had taken led straight to a dead end on the seashore.

A couple of miles before Tra-vinh, we came to a patch of dry ground with some thickly wooded hillocks. All of a sudden the succulent odor of grilled meat wafted on the air. Being the youngest among us, Jost Waldman climbed a tree and sat for a while scanning the land around.

"Was gibt's?" Riedl called him. "What's up?"

"I see some huts," Jost yelled, waving a hand in the direction. "Perhaps a village."

Krebitz checked his map and hollered back, "There should be no damned village here."

"It's not really a village, only a couple of dwellings. . . . Built of wood, it seems."

"Any movement?" I asked.

"I can't see anyone around."

Schulze wrinkled his nose and sniffed into the air. "If there's smoke and a fine smell, then somebody must be cooking something."

"Which reminds me that it's past lunchtime, fellows," Helmut reminded us, tapping his belly. He rolled his eyes and blew a wishful sigh. "What a heavenly scent."

Waldman clambered down. "There's also a trail about a hundred yards to the right," he reported.

"Well, let's take it," Erich said, shouldering his submachine gun.

"Where does it lead?" Riedl asked.

"To roast chops!" Erich replied promptly.

"Let's move on!" I waved a hand.

We marched into an "adventure" that befitted a comic strip. It was a welcome diversion from our dreary routine.

All of a sudden a sinewy, bowlegged, and white-bearded little old man materialized in front of us, like an apostle from the New Testament. Wielding a cane longer than himself levelly in his extended hands, he barred my way and screeched all fire and truculence.

"You may not go any farther, soldiers of ill-fortune. This is a sacred place!"

I raised my hand good-naturedly and Task Force-G halted. Pulling his most amiable smile, Erich asked, "Are you a priest, Grandpa?"

The old man's chin came up. "I am the guardian of the sacred shrines."

Schulze promptly reassured the apostle that we were extremely pious people who deeply respected the local deities.

"You see, Grandpa—whenever we come across a local temple we pay homage to the native saints."

"There's no temple here. No saints!"

"Then who is living in the huts?" Erich persisted with charming simplicity.

"Shrines. . . . No huts. . . . Nobody is living there. . . . Only the spirits of our forefathers."

"Cooking lunch?" Riedl cracked, and the troops around us burst into wild guffaws. "What about the smoke?"

"What smoke?" the patriarch queried shrilly, then rolling his eyes heavenward, he intoned, "Woe upon the men who profane the sacred shrines. . . . What you saw were only wisps of morning mist."

"It's past noon, Grandpa," Erich reminded the apostle placidly. The old man stood his ground. "When the spirits gather they look like smoke."

"And smell like roast beef!" Helmut continued with his verbal antics, drawing more laughter.

I said quietly, "I'm sorry, Father, but we must inspect your shrines."

"Which we'll do with great reverence," Erich added.

The long cane came up again, pressing against my chest. "Then—let me go ahead," the apostle insisted, straining himself against Schulze's gentle tug. "I must appease the spirits and prepare them for your intrusion."

He seemed irrepressible.

Krebitz said, "You must stay right here, Grandpa. We can negotiate with your ghosts ourselves," he added, tapping the stock of his submachine gun.

Gruppe Drei quietly circled the sacred place and captured eighteen Vietcong candidates, for they were mere boys, playing war, and who would not even try to fight it out despite their Chinese rifles and hand grenades. Indeed they looked more like scared youngsters caught with their hands in the bag and their pants full. They were busy with grilling meat and fish. Finding themselves in a ring of bayonets, some began to snivel and cry.

Their fifteen-year-old "general" was the grandson of our bowlegged "guardian of the sacred shrines"; the five fisherman's huts served as "headquarters" and "base" for the local "people's army of liberation."

Seeing his kin threatened, Grandpa gamboled down the trail to embrace and protect him. The troops broke into renewed laughter. I turned to Krebitz.

"*Also, Herr Krebitz—alles durchsuchen.* . . . Collect the hardware and have a look what else they have in the huts."

Grandpa dragged his fretting grandson in front of me. "Don't shoot him, Officer," he pleaded, in tears, wringing his hands. "He is only a silly boy. . . . All of them are silly boys."

"They were silly enough to blow up those trucks in My-tho."

"But nobody was hurt!"

"Fortunately."

"Not fortunately," he protested. "Ky wanted to do it when the streets were empty."

"But why would he do such a thing?"

"The boys thought if they blew up the army trucks the Vietcong commander would accept them in his group."

"And if the Vietcong had accepted them, they would be dead now," Schulze cut in sternly. Then he cocked his head and asked, "By the way, Grandpa—where is this Vietcong commander?"

The apostle hemmed and hawed, shifted uncomfortably. Erich chambered a cartridge. Krebitz did likewise.

"In—in Cân-tho" came the hesitant response.

"His name?"

We got the name too. The guerrilla regional commander was a local farmer.

Krebitz and his men returned, hauling bags and boxes.

"Grenades and cartridges," Rudolf stated curtly. "Five more rifles. We smashed them already."

"Smash the others too. The grenades we can use."

"What shall we do with the kids?"

"Give them the absolution for those trucks in My-tho."

He grinned and called for two of his brawniest troopers, Metzler and Schindler, who came, rolling up their shirt sleeves.

"Convince the kids that it's not nice to blow up trucks," I advised them. "For the good of their souls."

One by one the guerrilla candidates were taken before the "executioners" and forced to lay prone on a stool. Each boy received a dose of reeducation with the flat of a trenching spade: a dozen fair strikes to each bottom, after which we released the hollering group of would-be soldiers of Father Ho.

"If you try it again, we'll return to burn down your village and shoot every one of you!" I warned them in farewell.

They vanished in a jiffy and we turned our attention to the pile of grilled goodies that Steiner's attentive care had saved from burning to ashes.

After lunch we marched toward the Cambodian border but stopped briefly in Cân-tho to pay a visit of courtesy to the Vietcong commander. We found him sleeping happily on top of three tons of weapons and explosives, while his two sons were busy with greasing submachine guns and placing them into oilcloth bags. Wasting no time, Krebitz and Stolz strung them up on a rafter, then blasted the guerrilla warehouse.

Task Force-G left the Mekong after Lang-xuyen and turned northward across the marshy plain in the general direction of Kampong in Cambodia. Somewhere in the distant hills the Ho Chi Minh trail was supposed to branch off, crossing several tributaries of the Mekong. Our "road" ended in an extensive green swamp of algae, waterweed, and mosses; knee-deep and pestilential, swarming with water snakes and leeches. Krebitz, who had gone ahead to reconnoiter, reported the presence of another river. Unmarked on our map, it flowed into the Mekong some miles to the west. Such mystery rivers and streams were common in Vietnam.

We joined Gruppe Drei on a patch of high ground near the river. Beyond the far bank loomed miles of billowing foliage, dark and motionless, wild and untamed.

"I think, once we're across, we'll find the delta branch of the Ho Chi Minh trail quite close," Krebitz told us, but he didn't like the peaceful appearance of the distant woods.

The sun dipped beyond the hills of Cambodia. The morass became alive with the steady chorus of frogs and the shrill calls of lizards. The incessant buzzing of mosquitoes drew incessant curses. Covered with their waist-long mosquito nets, the men looked like an army of white ghosts.

I wanted no fires kindled. We ate a cold meal of corned beef and sardines with canned beans and the customary vitamin pills.

As he burned leeches off his legs with a cigarette and swore nonstop, Riedl blew a frustrated sigh. "By the time we get across this damned river we'll be needing a blood transfusion."

Likewise preoccupied, Karl Stolz commented with a chuckle, "We might be up to more bloodletting when we hit the Ho Chi Minh trail."

We still had a couple of hours before darkness. Krebitz, who seemed somewhat restless, wanted to make another short reconnaissance trip. After summoning a few of his men, he disappeared in the riverside bog, returning twenty minutes later—alone—with a mysterious expression on his face.

"I left the men to keep an eye on the site," he told us. "Let's move!"

"What site?" I asked, clambering to my feet.

"A cluster of huts. Apparently abandoned."

He led us to a narrow causeway built of trunk halves and boughs upon short piles driven into the swamp but barely two inches above the surface. Gruppe Drei's men were scanning the place through binoculars. The causeway was a long one. As we advanced warily, a handful of bamboo huts with thatched roofs came into view, still a good two hundred yards deeper in the morass.

A nameless hamlet in the middle of nowhere?

Harmless fishers' huts?

Vietcong cache of arms and ammunition?

I turned to Krebitz, whose attention seemed riveted on the plankway, as he cautiously advanced until he abruptly stopped and raised a hand.

"Halt!"

He beckoned Steiner to join him. Both men squatted down, drew their bayonets, and warily pried loose one of the planks, exposing a primed grenade that a careless step would have set off.

"The huts are not empty," he commented as he defused the grenade and tossed it into the water. "I think we bumped into a real Vietcong warehouse—everything neatly booby-trapped."

"It's a good site," Erich commented appreciatively. "Well hidden. No wonder the copters never spotted it."

"Kindly remember that we are in Cambodia," Riedl remarked.

Schulze waved a dismissing hand.

Sepp Mueller laughed softly. "The copters don't care, we don't care, the Vietcong don't care. . . . What the hell for an independent Cambodia?"

"Because after the British quit India it became fashionable to play the independence game," Erich responded. "It's the domino effect, Sepp. You tip over the first stone and the whole row of dominos topple. Soon every cannibal chieftain with a thousand *niam-niams* in his tribe will want to be king, president, prime minister, or at least ambassador to the United Nations. It's the trend of the times." Then he reverted his attention to the huts.

Krebitz moved on and discovered an impressive array of devilish devices, among them Russian-made "jump mines" that, when touched off, would spring four feet high and explode in the intruder's face. A simple lost foot or shattered leg wouldn't satisfy the Communist bloodlust.

Rudolf and Steiner found more loose planks that activated shooting devices and signal projectiles. By the time we came to the hundred-by-sixty-foot platform with the huts, in pitch dark, Gruppe Drei had deactivated sixteen traps.

Their positions could be recognized by a pattern of casual axe incisions.

As I didn't want to reveal our presence by using battery torches, I postponed the survey of the huts until daybreak. We spent the night on the relatively dry platform in comfort under the mosquito nets.

The huts had no windows and their entrances were covered with bamboo mats, unprotected and inviting. Krebitz, however, disliked such invitations. Instead of trying the doorways, he cut holes in the walls. With good reason. All the entrances were booby-trapped in the best Russian partisan fashion, with charges powerful enough to maim a person without damaging the stores.

The moment I entered the first hut I knew that our expedition was already successful. The platform in the swamp was a major Vietcong dump. The huts were crammed with wooden crates and metal containers bearing Russian, Chinese, Czechoslovak, French, and to our delight, East German inscriptions.

Machine guns, submachine guns, rifles, pistols, bazookas, mortars, grenades, field phones, wireless sets, and hundreds of ammunition boxes constituted a prize haul, the total weight of which Krebitz estimated at about thirty tons.

Sepp Mueller found twelve flat-bottomed barges suitable for shallow-water traffic, which also told us how the crates had gotten to the platform. They had been shipped down the Mekong, then rowed upstream along the tributary and into the swamp.

All this despite our fighters and copters, which regularly patrolled the border areas. Even as we ate breakfast, we saw three fighters streaking northward, barely one hundred feet above a forest, flying in a perfect V formation.

"The pilots don't seem to care a fig for the landscape down below," Riedl remarked as the planes streaked past the huts.

Schulze waved a hand. *"Ah, was*—they're probably enjoying the excursion to use up their daily quota of fuel."

Krebitz asked thoughtfully, "What shall we do with the guerrilla hardware, Hans? We can't blow it up. The detonation would be heard twenty miles away."

"Sure." Erich nodded. "The apes are still in the dark about us. Otherwise they'd have defended this place tooth and nail."

Stolz said gravely, "We'll have to wreck everything piece by piece."

"Why not dump everything into the swamp?" Jost cut in.

"That wouldn't render the machine guns and mortars useless," Krebitz replied. "And shells are watertight."

I said, "Select what we can still transport, especially bazookas and hand grenades, Rudy. The rest we'll have to break up."

Rudolf did so, then we got down to the dreary job of damaging everything else. We broke firing pins, springs, trigger mechanisms, hammered chunks of wood into mortar barrels, scattered cartridges and grenades in the swamp. One hut containing grenades and other weapons the men of Gruppe Drei rigged with a charge and timer set for sixteen hours, although Krebitz also booby-trapped a couple of crates, just in case the owners should come to fetch something sooner.

We left the platform by boat, traveling first-class, courtesy of Father Ho. Near the river the men camouflaged our transports with leafy branches, then advanced to the fringes of the riverside thicket. One barge with Krebitz, Steiner, Stolz, and eight troopers, continued to the far bank.

Fifteen minutes later I got the all-clear signal and we crossed over to land on firm ground. The men unloaded and holed the boats. Krebitz distributed the baggage. The officers were no exception. Erich's fair share was one of the dismantled mortars. I got a pair of bazookas and a knapsack of shells. Riedl carried a 12.7-mm machine gun.

With Krebitz and his trailblazers up in front we set out by the compass, cutting our trail while trying to make as little noise as possible. Every now and then Jost Waldman would climb a tall tree to look for signs of human presence in our proximity: smoke and circling crows and vultures. After four hours of hard going, during which we covered perhaps three miles, the jungle began to thin out. Yet this decreased rather than increased our speed. Sparser woods permitted, not only our advance guard but also the enemy, to see farther. We suspected that the southernmost section of the Red Highway was not very far.

According to aerial photos, there ought to have been a small river ahead, only about twelve yards wide but with slushy ground on both banks and quite deep. Like many similar natural phenomena, the river did not exist for the cartographers in France.

Wherever it was possible, the Ho Chi Minh trail followed rivers and streams. Thousands of Vietcong and coolies constantly on the move with hundreds of pack animals, permanent camps, first aid and rest stations, and guardhouses demanded a steady supply of water.

We camped down for the rest of the day, cleaned and checked our weapons, then changed into Vietcong garb, donned straw hats and bamboo helmets, and waited for Krebitz to survey the neighborhood.

Around 7 P.M. Rudolf and his party returned, after hacking a path to the nameless river. He left four troopers with a walkie-talkie on the bank.

"There's a footpath before we come to the river," Krebitz stated, "just outside the marshes. . . . We followed it for a few hundred yards. It leads to a plank bridge with a guardhouse. . . . A pair of lookouts. After the bridge the path turns westward and probably runs straight into the Ho Chi Minh trail."

"How far can the trail be?"

"Not more than two miles from the river, Hans."

Erich cut in, "Do you think we can take the bridge?"

Krebitz shook his head. "The last stretch of ground before the bridge is quite coverless," he said. "There's also a phone line running from the guardhouse, and if we attacked the bridge, the Viets farther inland would be alerted."

"What do you suggest?" I asked.

"We should ford the river and approach the guardhouse in the woods on the far bank."

"Yes," said Schulze. "They wouldn't suspect an attack from the west."

"That's what I think," Krebitz agreed. "The lookouts might even take us for comrades coming from the Ho Chi Minh trail on the way to the delta."

It was already too dark to attempt the swamp and the river. We bivouacked in the forest for the night, which we spent in darkness. Those who wished to smoke punched a hole in an empty tin can and kept the glowing end of the cigarette inside.

Shortly before sunrise the commando traversed the morass. To our cursing bemusement, we served as breakfast for the local leeches. Stolz volunteered to cross the river and survey the far bank. As he waded into the murky shallow, we followed his progress with anxious eyes. He maneuvered himself forward in the expanse of water lilies and floating weeds, pushing a makeshift float with his knapsack and submachine gun; he waded, then swam with slow breaststrokes, barely stirring the surface.

The far bank was silent, blanketed with the sort of threatening tranquillity that gives one the creeps. We had the strong sensation that the enemy was there, but why, we couldn't say. It was only an uncanny feeling. Perhaps our sixth sense manifested itself from the depths of long years of experience.

Instinct prevailed over logic more than once.

In the jungle not even silence can be interpreted positively. The adversary might be astute enough to permit the advance of a single man, who would then signal "all clear" and an entire platoon might be wiped out while in the water, encumbered with equipment and unable to fight back.

We had played that game a hundred times—letting a handful live in order to kill a hundred.

Camouflaged with leafy twigs, our sharpshooters were invisible under the brush, with their eyes narrow on the telescopic sights, mouths set in thin lines, and trigger fingers rigid. Their spotters conned their target sectors, only twenty yards wide for each man. The silence increased their tension.

Strange as it may sound, we always preferred the report of guns to sinister tranquillity, particularly in the jungle where there was no visibility beyond a few yards. When we heard bullets whizzing overhead and the dull thuds as they hit the trees, we knew where our adversaries lurked and could oppose them. Krebitz and his sharpshooters were experts in knocking out even unseen snipers and enemy machine-gun crews

Were the Viets luring Stolz into a snare?

But to our luck, such was not the case. Suddenly the undergrowth on the far bank erupted with machine-gun and rifle fire. Bullets plunged into the river around Stolz, ripping across the surface, throwing up small fountains. He sank deeper into the water but moved steadily forward, now keeping somewhat to the left and downstream. Gruppe Drei's spotters began to scan the thicket, while the sharpshooters readied their guns. The site of the machine gun was soon determined. The sharpshooters fired a salvo of four explosive slugs—one aimed directly at the muzzle emission, the others ten inches above and twenty-five inches to the right and left destined for the gunner and his observer, and belt feeder or magazine changer. The MG fell silent but the rifles kept firing at Stolz. Hindered by our sharpshooters, the Vietcong snipers found it advisable to change position.

Stolz arrived in the reed-strewn shallow and began to lob grenades, then we heard the sharp reports of his Mitra, followed by profound silence. Karl called over the WT and announced flatly, "You may cross over, Hans."

Fifteen minutes later Task Force-G stood on the west bank and, as we soon discovered, within two miles of the Red Highway from Hanoi to the delta.

Fortunately there were no large Vietcong encampments nearby. The six lookouts belonged to the platoon that manned the guardhouse at the bridge—some fifteen guerrillas, three of whom had rowed upstream in a small boat to investigate the cause of the previous turmoil. Gruppe Drei captured them, and Krebitz wasted no time in persuading them to talk. The prisoners were young men, strong in Marxism but weak in brawn. Once they were separated and taken out of sight of one another, they quickly lost much of their Communist steadfastness. When one saw Steiner emerging from the woods, wiping his crimson-stained bayonet, he instantly felt like talking. He gave a good description of the guardhouse and his companions there, who carried only World War II Russian rifles. He also described another guardhouse right on the Ho Chi Minh trail. Krebitz wanted confirmation, which the second prisoner eagerly furnished after a couple of kicks and punches. Only our third captive wished to remain a tough fighter of Father Ho. When Rudolf queried him, he threw up his chin and sneered with contempt. "Quang Ku is not going to tell you anything!"

Pursing his lips, Krebitz told his men to strip the prisoner. When the resolute fighter of Father Ho was lying in the grass naked like Adam in Paradise, Steiner, our chief trailblazer said nonchalantly to Steiner, "Fetch a stick of dynamite with a three-minute fuse, Julius."

Steiner returned with the dynamite. "What shall I do with it?" he asked.

"Grease it a little and shove it up in Quang Ku's ass!" Krebitz answered.

The prisoner sat bolt upright and announced, "Quang Ku will tell you all you want to know."

We also learned of the existence of a permanent Vietcong camp twenty miles to the south; about relay stations at thirty-mile intervals, the regular patrols along the trail, lookout platforms on trees, and all sorts of useful information.

We turned the three, stripped to loincloth, loose. One cannot walk fast barefoot in the jungle. Krebitz advised them to return home into their villages. "The Vietcong will soon know that you informed on them and if they catch you, you'll surely hang. . . . Here, take these."

He tossed them a bagful of canned food and a machete.

There was no trail on the west bank. The guerrilla lookouts had come by boat. After a brief conference, we decided to change our plan. Using the boat, Riedl, Stolz, Steiner, and Jost Waldman were to float downstream and, if possible, knock out the guardhouse and capture the bridge. The rest of us would recross the river and take the footpath Krebitz had mentioned before.

Clad like the guerrillas and sheltered by the floating mist, Riedl and his companions had no difficulty in tying up right at the bridge. The foremost sentry waved a hand and asked what the earlier shooting was about. Riedl answered with a 9-mm slug through a silencer, while Stolz treated the second sentinel similarly. The foursome stormed the guardhouse and encountered no resistance. Six Vietcong were in their bunks; two were having breakfast while a third was reading a book by Lenin. All died in a matter of seconds.

Stolz picked up the book and spat. "Lenin." He sneered.

"The devil who stirred up all this Communist shit." Then, as if speaking to the corpse, he added, "Well, now you may join Lenin in hell and learn all about the revolution right from the professor—the much good it'll be to you."

Jost cut the phone wire, then the four men sat down to wait for us. We arrived an hour later muddy and spent but content with what we saw.

Krebitz wanted to booby-trap the bridge and the guardhouse, but Sepp Mueller came up with a better idea. "Instead of attacking the apes in the guardhouse on the Ho trail, why shouldn't we lure some of them here?"

"How?"

"By setting fire to this joint. They'll see the conflagration and send a party to investigate."

"It's a good idea, Sepp," Schulze agreed. I was of the same opinion.

We positioned ourselves along the footpath, with Gruppe Drei lying in ambush farther west to tie the bag once we got the guerrillas inside. Stolz and Mueller set fire to the guardhouse, and it wasn't long before Krebitz reported over the WT, "They're coming, Hans!"

"How many?"

"Twelve apes with rifles."

"Kinderspiel," Erich commented. "Child's play."

"I guess the submachine guns are reserved for the bastards fighting in Vietnam," Riedl cut in.

I spoke to Krebitz. "After they pass your position, Rudy, advance to the junction and knock out the guardhouse."

"All right."

A small group of Vietcong came trodding down the path. I waited until they were fifty yards away, then ordered fire.

When we arrived at the junction of the Ho Chi Minh trail, Gruppe Drei had already eliminated twenty-six guerrillas and captured the guardhouse.

The long search was over. An important segment of the Red Highway was in our hands—the main Vietcong artery that we were resolved to bleed for a while.

What our astonished eyes beheld was not really a trail but a four-yard-wide road that had been cut across virgin jungles, ravines, and mountains—the result of the incessant labor of thousands of people over many years. Its surface was hard earth with sections of gravel and timber, laid in the depressions where water was likely to collect during the rainy seasons. At every opening in the woods, overhead netting with green bits of canvas concealed it from aerial observation.

"Men! This is great!" Erich exclaimed. "Grand enough to run second to the Chinese Wall."

It was indeed a genuine marvel of Vietcong ingenuity.

I sent a brief coded message to Lieutenant General Houssong to let him know that Task Force-G had reached its objective.

Schulze deployed sentries around the junction, then we discussed what should be done next. We had several alternatives. The commando could march either toward the north or south to destroy whatever enemy objectives might lie in its way. We could also stay where we were and ensnare oncoming Vietcong convoys, although it was against our principles to remain in one place for long, and sooner or later Hanoi would start wondering about the missing convoys. In the end we opted for holding the junction for a few days, then following the trail toward the Mekong delta, for the guerrillas would probably accumulate most of their supplies in the southern section for an eventual assault on the South Vietnamese capital.

As the first step we had to eliminate some enemy outposts, depending on the station we occupied. The guardhouse was equipped with a primitive telephone switchboard featuring three sets of wires. Apart from the wires running to the riverside guardhouse we destroyed, there were two others strung up on the branches, stretching north and south. In order to avoid inconvenient calls, Krebitz cut them both. As soon as dusk fell he sent a platoon south under the command of Horst Altreiter, while he marched off toward the north with Walter Winar and fifteen troops, tracing the overhead wires. Eventually he came to a wooden bridge across a ravine, with a makeshift platform rigged up between the branches of a tree. The platform was vacant but the men spotted the muzzle of a machine gun. The four guards were squatting on the bridge around a kerosene lamp, playing a game of Mikado. Confident in their Vietcong garb and conical straw hats, the platoon closed in boldly. The guerrillas clambered to their feet and looked on unsuspectingly with shouldered guns. *"Chieu hoi!"* one of them called, raising a hand in greeting. In a wink they were overwhelmed, bayoneted, and pitched into the rushing stream. A pair of troopers occupied the machine-gun platform. The rest of the platoon plodded on. The telephone wires guided Krebitz to a watchtower. The three lookouts there also were surprised and eliminated. Leaving Walter Winar and five men in the tower, Rudolf returned to the junction.

Shortly afterward Altreiter arrived, after having eliminated three guerrillas in a hut two miles to the south and replacing them with four troopers. Now secure against surprise from either direction, we bunked down to sleep in turns.

In the early morning we heard a distant dull detonation, followed by a louder second explosion.

Grinning and gesturing toward the border, Krebitz commented, "The huts in the swamp, boys—blowing up." Then, glancing at his wristwatch, he added, "It didn't go by the timers we set. . . . I guess the brave soldiers of Father Ho had gone to fetch some ammo for an action in hell."

Schulze, Riedl, Krebitz, and Gruppe Drei converted the junction into a deadly trap. The troops drove a thirty-foot trench across the road and covered it with branches and gravel. Along either side pits were dug with sharpened stakes placed in them, everything carefully camouflaged. Machine guns and flamethrowers were positioned at convenient spots to cover a three-hundred-yard section of the road and all possible ways of escape. Still not satisfied, Krebitz had a dozen tall trees hacked halfway through and mined, then stretched trip wires between the shrubs to activate them.

In a shed, Jost Waldman found bales of jute sacks, which the men carried off to sit or lie on. Krebitz commandeered the sacks and had them filled with earth, to reinforce the guardhouse and turn it into a bunker with gun slits facing the trail.

Our net was cast. We were looking forward to catching the fish. The next morning we caught the fish, and it was a whale.

The first rays of the rising sun barely tinted the eastern sky when Winar called over the WT to report the coming of a convoy. "It's still too dark to see details but we can hear the squeaking of cart wheels and the approaching *pat-pat* of many feet" he reported tensely.

"How far are they?"

"A few hundred yards.... Shall we stay up here or get lost in the woods until they pass the tower?"

"You'd better get lost," I advised him. "Just in case someone should talk to you or ask questions."

"They might become suspicious if they find the tower vacant."

"That'll be the lesser one of two evils," I replied. "Quit the tower but stay close and keep your eyes peeled. We must know exactly what the convoy consists of."

"Okay."

"And don't let yourself be caught, eh?"

"Don't worry, Chief," Winar answered with a chuckle. "I'll keep my last bullet."

"Arschloch!" I commented flatly, and hung up.

Ten minutes later he called again and spoke in a subdued voice. "The convoy is passing us now.... Two companies of Vietcong up in front.... Some thirty bullock carts driven by men and women, also armed.... A large group of coolies with backpacks.... Over a hundred.... Wait.... One hundred and fifty would be a closer guess. Hey! There's also a platoon of North Vietnamese regulars led by an officer."

"All right, be careful, Walter."

Schulze spat. "Hanoi regulars in neutral Cambodia, marching toward South Vietnam, with which they are at truce." He said contemptuously, "Father Ho is surely not bothered by international agreements or national frontiers."

I turned my attention back to Winar. "How many are they?" I asked over the walkie-talkie.

"The regulars? Perhaps sixty—but wait.... There are more bullocks coming with artillery pieces.... *Donnerwetter!* Six howitzers and a pair of *Katyushas.*"

"Is that all?"

Winar uttered a soft laughter. "Why, Commander? Do you want to bag the whole North Vietnamese Army?"

"I wish I could.... Did anyone stop at the tower?"

"Negative. We might as well have remained on the platform."

"Return there after the convoy left. There might be others on the way here."

I hung up and went outside to where Erich, Helmut, and

Rudolf were giving last-minute instructions. The troops scrambled and rushed to their respective positions. I remained in our guardhouse bunker with Gruppe Drei's sharpshooters Paul Kretz, Rolf Schneider, and Alois Fuchs. Jost Waldman sidled down behind our heavy MG. With its explosive bullets it was, for all practical purpose, a small cannon.

The men we left at the bridge called. "The convoy is marching into the first bend, Commander."

There were four bends between the bridge and the junction.

The minutes dragged on. There was no sound except for the quiet whisper of the overhead foliage and the distant creaking of wheels.

Tense faces. Tight trigger fingers. Beads of perspiration.

At long last the foremost Vietcong company marched into view. Concealed along the road, our troops tracked their steady advance yard by yard. When the enemy came within seventy yards, I fired the red flare.

For an instant the convoy froze, then exploded with screaming men and women and bellowing bullocks scattering in every direction—spinning, crumpling up, and crashing to the ground. Some bullocks bolted and overturned their carts. Others crashed into Krebitz's trench. From either side of the road the automatic weapons sputtered and the flamethrowers set fire to carts, men, and beasts. Scampering groups of guerrillas with their clothes on fire ran amuck in a rain of tracers and detonating grenades.

Imagine what happens to closely packed people and beasts when they unexpectedly find themselves in the murderous crossfire of twenty machine guns and eighty automatic rifles and submachine guns and a hail of grenades—at a distance of twenty to seventy yards. No orders could be given, let alone executed; no platoons rallied and positioned for defense; no attack organized. The general panic and the instinct of survival through blind escape overrules every other consideration.

A platoon of Vietcong darted toward the guardhouse and collided with a string of heavy MG slugs that literally blew their legs from under them. Shrieking with terror and pain, guerrillas and Dang Cong coolies darted for the woods, tumbled into the pits, and became impaled. The North Vietnamese platoon made a desperate attempt to break away toward the north and ran into Stolz and Steiner's party with flamethrowers belching fire from only fifteen yards.

Positioned to have perfect command of the road, our sharpshooters were picking up individual targets at the rate of three to five in a minute. The road and its immediate flanks were coverless, while our troops occupied the undergrowth on either side and staked pits and mines blocked access to the forest.

One group of bewildered Vietcong were darting first this way, then that way—looking desperately for a gap in the trap, dying all the time. In the end the survivors dropped their guns and raised their hands. Their futile hope to survive through surrender was mercilessly swept away by Waldner's MG salvos.

All of a sudden a gigantic explosion rocked the ground and a pair of carts disintegrated in a funnel of fire and smoke, leaving a thirty-foot crater and blowing everything and everyone from the road in a fifty-foot circle. Around the guardhouse it rained splinters of wood and metal, torn branches, and chunks of flesh. When the smoke lifted we saw a mangled bullock caught in a tree thirty feet from the ground, a human head embedded in our earthwork like a cannonball. The trees that Krebitz had mined were blown and crashed onto the road. Wherever I turned I saw mangled bodies, torn legs and arms, shoulders with only the shapeless pulp that had once been a head still attached.

The detonation was so violent that one of our MG emplacement sixty yards away was buried under a shower of debris.

Our machine guns stopped firing. The flamethrowers were turned off. The men of Task Force-G surged forward to finish off the enemy wounded.

Schulze came, holding a handkerchief against his bleeding nose. In reply to my worried query, he said, gasping, "I'm all right, Hans—just got the decompression when the carts blew up."

"Any casualties?" I asked anxiously.

He shook his head. "I don't think so. . . . Perhaps a couple of gunners got hit by the cascading debris."

Krebitz glanced at his watch.

"Twelve minutes!" he emphasized.

Twelve minutes. In that time we'd created 422 enemy corpses, 60 of them women, 100 mere kids hoodwinked into the glorious war of liberation by Father Ho. . . . Plus the mangled corpses of 58 North Vietnamese regulars, most of them burned beyond human semblance.

Task Force-G suffered no loss, save for bleeding noses and ears, bruises and sprained muscles caused by falling debris.

Contrary to our original plan, we decided to move on. It would have been impossible to create order out of the chaos we'd created, and the huge explosion might have alerted the Vietcong camps farther inland. I ordered Winar to blow up the bridge and watchtower, then report back with the lookouts.

From the few intact carts, Krebitz selected what we could use, mostly hand grenades, and used the rest of the explosives to booby-trap a section of the road and the woods around it, including the guardhouse and the path to the river. Never lacking ideas, he had the howitzers and the multiple rocket launchers towed into the thicket, loaded and targeted on the guardhouse and the road toward the north; he rigged everything with trip wires and primed grenades, some linked to the carts and corpses along the trail. Before we departed he gave a last inspection to his trap and commented contentedly, "Well, when the apes come to put the place in order they'll set up a fine artillery barrage right in their own faces."

"Wouldn't it be better to destroy the artillery, Rudy?" I asked, ever cautious.

He assured me, "Don't worry about the artillery, Hans."

He had rigged everything in such a way that once they were fired, the howitzers and rocket launchers would set off their own primed mines and destroy themselves.

Krebitz seldom left anything to chance.

7.

Havoc

The wholesale destruction of an important Hanoi convoy without any loss to us fired our troops with enthusiasm and self-confidence. They were now quite ready to attack Vietcong targets anywhere, anytime, even inside North Vietnam. With their fighting spirit soaring, no one would even think of returning to Saigon. Our provisions were ample, as we'd been able to replenish them from captured enemy stores. During three weeks in the wilderness we had barely touched our canned food but consumed those taken from the guerrillas: Chinese canned meat, fish, and vegetables. "Delicious and easy to come by," according to Karl Stolz. "The next time we go on an expedition we shouldn't haul fifty-pound backpacks," he joked. "Only guns and some spare mags. Everything else would be provided by Father Ho anyway."

Boldly, but not carelessly, we marched along the Red Highway, destroying bridges, lookout platforms, guardhouses, rest camps, and supply dumps, mining and booby-trapping the trail behind us, causing immense death and devastation to Hanoi. Soon our ledger of Vietcong dead surpassed the one-thousand mark, still without any fatal casualty to us. Our "luck" was due to both our tactics and Krebitz's alertness plus the element of surprise. We refrained from engaging the enemy in open combat but rather surprised them when they were exposed, while we remained in carefully prepared positions, offering no target to fire at. The machine guns and flamethrowers were always positioned in such way as to prevent our adversaries from coming close enough to hurl grenades. When we spotted Vietcong with bazookas, Gruppe Drei would eliminate them first. The mortars seldom gave us trouble. They were transported dismantled. Once we opened fire, usually from a distance of 80 to 120 yards, the guerrillas could neither assemble nor position them. Our machine gunners pinned them to the ground and the sharpshooters killed those who dared to stir from the grass.

Abandoning the Ho Chi Minh trail for a while, we skirted the Mekong. Using bazookas, mostly those taken from the Vietcong, Schulze and Riedl destroyed a fuel dump and a pier with ten sampans tied up alongside, laden with boxes of ammunition, ready to leave for the delta. We added one hundred more victims to our steadily growing list.

Krebitz captured a Cambodian patrol of eight regulars and their sergeant. We disarmed the terrified lot and let them go, prompting bowing thanks, happy half-grins, and enthusiastic handshakes. We couldn't even question them or understand a syllable of their garbled words of gratitude, for they spoke neither French nor Vietnamese, only Khmer.

"I guess the poor devils live in a sort of limbo between freedom and Communist slavery," Riedl commented afterward, "not even knowing which side to take."

Schulze snorted sarcastically. "One shouldn't expect King Shihanouk to oppose the Vietcong. Giap could seize Phnom Penh in a day."

After almost completely annihilating a guerrilla camp twenty miles southeast of Kompang, which also resulted in the destruction of a Vietcong first-aid station and field hospital complex of forty large tents and barracks with everyone inside, we heard the Hanoi broadcast calling us "The Fascist Commando of Death" for the first time. The name stuck. In a matter of days Hanoi's alternative to Task Force-G had become our nom de guerre.

After we returned to Saigon, from God knows where, the men procured a few hundred canvas badges: white skulls with crossed bones in a black quadrangle, which they stitched onto their battle fatigues, berets, and forage caps.

"Here comes the new *Totenkopf Kommando*," Schulze exclaimed with good humor.

"Fascist death-head commando, according to Hanoi," Riedl cut in. "We might as well add the S.S. stripes."

"Not for you, Helmut," Erich replied tauntingly. "The Brandenburgers were *Wehrmacht*."

"Admiral Canaris's outfit," Krebitz quipped. "Tough guys."

"Tougher than many S.S.," Riedl agreed.

Lieutenant General Houssong accepted our new regimental insignia with a smile.

"I think that after your fray along the Ho Chi Minh trail you deserve your skulls and bones," he commented. "That's all you left for Hanoi to collect. Skulls and bones."

"We are the first new S.S. *Totenkopf Kampfgruppe,*" Schulze stated. Then, extending his right arm in the Nazi salute, he yelled, "*Heil* Diem!"

Houssong laughed softly. "Just don't start calling each other *Sturmfuehrer* and *Obersturmfuehrer.* . . . Although I don't think that Diem would mind it."

The destruction of the Vietcong hospital complex had had difficult: the reluctant decision to execute fifteen physicians and male nurses who refused our generous and unusual offer to accompany us to Saigon. We spared four surgeons and eight female nurses who had consented, and permitted them to come along under the stern warning that the slightest hostile action, or attempt to escape, would result in their execution. So, our young "Hanoi Rose," whom Schulze treated well and who was no longer fettered, would have company.

We entrusted our prisoners to the care of our medical officer, Kurt Zeisl, and Gruppe Drei.

The execution of the hospital personnel was not a senseless act of brutality, only a sad necessity. The guerrillas were always hard up for medicines and medical care. Hanoi could replace lost fighters and weapons, but not doctors and trained nurses. Without their help thousands of wounded or sick guerrillas could not be nursed back to more action, and even minor injuries might bring death through infection and gangrene.

The executed doctors were all North Vietnamese officers. By offering them a choice I discharged my obligations as a civilized being—something I rarely remembered in the jungles of Vietnam and Cambodia.

We continued our work of devastation for sixty miles along the Red Highway. Task Force-G overran another camp of tents and bamboo huts defended by a Vietcong company of about two hundred men. The enemy had a couple of well-positioned machine guns that were difficult to knock out. Unwilling to risk the life of a single trooper, I satisfied myself with occupying a dominant hill from which our mortars and bazookas demolished the enemy positions one after another, causing multiple explosions and a conflagration. Finally the Vietcong abandoned the site and withdrew into the woods.

Since the enemy still controlled the approaches, we didn't enter the camp or try to engage them but made a two-mile detour to bypass the camp altogether and moved on. Our work had been accomplished. There was hardly anything left for the enemy to salvage, and the prospect of killing a few more Vietcong was not worth the risks involved in jungle combat against an alert and well-armed foe.

After this interlude we began to notice the first signs of enemy alertness. Our going became more difficult. Krebitz and his trailblazers encountered heavily defended obstacles. Our days of merry freewheeling along the Ho Chi Minh trail were over. The news of the previous disasters had reached Hanoi, and their countermeasures began to have an effect.

Task Force-G left the trail and marched eastward in the direction of Tan-vinh, a village on the border. Our diversion, however, did not confuse the enemy and in the foothills of the 3,000-foot Mount Ba Dinn we encountered the first Vietcong blocking party, deployed to bar our way back to Vietnam.

The enemy commander had anticipated our route.

Playing his game astutely, he refrained from firing at Krebitz and his advance party of ten troops, although they were within three hundred yards of the low, wooded hill with shrubbery on its crest where a guerrilla company lay in ambush with a four-inch howitzer and a pair of MGs. The rest of the Vietcong reception committee, two more companies with a pair of howitzers, waited on the eastern slope and on the nearby hillocks, ready to envelop our column. By then, perfectly aware of our strength, the enemy commander permitted Krebitz to move unhindered in the hope of luring our entire complement into the trap.

It was only a few Chinese cigarette stubs and discarded matches that placed our keen-eyed Rudolf on the alert. The stubs were dry and must have been discarded only a few hours earlier. Had they been even a day old the tobacco would have been sodden after the morning dew. Immediately on his guard, Krebitz could even see what was invisible.

Drawing northward in a lazy arch, the reconnaissance party came across more conspicuous marks: squashed tufts of grass and deep grooves imprinted by wheels carrying a heavy load.

Krebitz returned into the woods where we waited. "The hill ahead is occupied by the Vietcong with a field gun and probably machine guns," he stated. "There should be more of them in the nearby hills, perhaps also with artillery." He paused, observed me and Erich, then asked, "What do you intend to do?"

"What do you suggest?"

He considered his answer. "We can't proceed in the open. There might be a whole battalion deployed in the hills."

Schulze said thoughtfully, "If they've taken the trouble of hauling howitzers into this wilderness, they want to finish us good and proper."

"We should turn south," Riedl suggested.

Krebitz shook his head. "There are swamps in the south."

"Then what?"

"I think we may still bank on the element of surprise."

"What surprise?" Riedl exclaimed. "They know we're here."

"But they don't know that we know that they're there," Krebitz responded with a laugh.

I said, "Tell me your plan."

"Well, for one thing the enemy knows that we're only one hundred strong," Rudolf began. "We should split and form three groups. One group of twenty men should seize the first hill with the howitzer. The second group of forty troops should secure the crest against counterattacks. The rest of Task Force-G should advance in the open toward the swamps in the south but out of machine-gun range. Fearing that we might escape the trap, the enemy commander would probably leave concealment and redeploy."

"Wait a moment!" Schulze cut in. "If they see forty men moving away they would realize—"

"No, they wouldn't," Krebitz broke in. "You mean the missing sixty." And with a triumphant expression on his face he delivered his clincher. "The Vietcong in the hills will see one hundred men moving away from the ambush site. Our whole force! Because the prisoners are going to join the forty troops and the men will carry scarecrows clad in our spare fatigues and berets."

We accepted Krebitz's ruse on the spot.

The troops got down to work, each pair preparing a dummy rigged up of suitable boughs and properly dressed, which they were to carry on shoulder-to-shoulder poles. In less than an hour our third group of forty troops turned into a unit of one hundred and ten, with our prisoners obliged to carry their own dummies. Since the men themselves were camouflaged with green twigs, from the distance of a mile our scarecrows should have appeared quite realistic to enemy observers on the hillock.

The makeshift hundred embarked toward the southern marshland under the command of Horst Altreiter, keeping out of machine-gun range but in plain sight of the Vietcong.

It was not long before Jost Waldman, who was observing the enemy-occupied hill from a tree, reported movement.

"I think they're turning the gun around," he called tersely. "A company is leaving the slope toward the south."

"To block Altreiter," Schulze said.

"The Fascist Commando of Death," I corrected him jokingly.

Krebitz called Altreiter over the WT. "Watch them, Horst! They're going after you."

"I've seen them," Altreiter reassured us. "I sent a couple of men ahead with flamethrowers."

"How many tanks you have left?"

"Four."

"You should use them sparingly. . . . What about the prisoners?"

"Still docile like good sheep."

"Just don't let them take off in the confusion."

"Where should they go? Into the swamps?"

Confident that the enemy was no longer paying attention to our part of the forest, keeping under cover, we drew a semicircle and arrived at the shrubby hillock without difficulty. Sepp Mueller, Walter Winar, and four troopers embarked on the tedious uphill crawl, while we positioned ourselves in the tangled undergrowth and set up our eight mortars and eleven machine guns, facing the opposite hill but also to give support to Altreiter if necessary. The flamethrowers were deployed in the first line.

Protected only by twelve guerrillas, the howitzer on the crest opened up on Altreiter's group, now a way to the south. Making good use of the Vietcong preoccupation elsewhere, Mueller, Winar, and the four troopers dashed onto the crest with submachine guns blazing and lobbed grenades into the two machine-gun nests. They mowed down the gun crew and their protectors. Only four guerrillas survived the unexpected assault and tried to escape downhill, but the sharpshooters killed them before they covered fifty yards.

Four slugs. Four dead. Head and face shots.

Mueller and his men took possession of the howitzer and the machine guns and opened up on the enemy guns on the other crests, while Schulze and I spread out our meager force to secure Sepp against counterattacks.

Sepp Mueller and Walter Winar were expert gunners. They blasted the enemy howitzer from the nearest crest with their third shell and sent its crew topsy-turvy down the declivity. Within a few minutes the second howitzer also fell silent. Our men on the crest turned their attention to a line of enemy mortars on the hillside. The magnificent foursome at the captured gun worked like a team of robots, loading, targeting, and firing in rapid succession, with Winar shifting aim on the go, the troopers shifting the carriage. The howitzers kept roaring, blasting the enemy-occupied hills, wrecking mortars and machine guns, killing their crews; then Sepp Mueller turned his attention to the guerrillas in the open.

The companies that had gone after Altreiter now turned back and dashed toward the hills, but the shrapnel bursting among them forced the runners to take shelter. I've seen many great artillery duels in Russia but never gunnery like that of Sepp and Walter.

Relieved from pressure, Altreiter lunged after the retreating companies now pinned to the ground by Mueller. We saw Horst's flamethrowers belching fire, burning down grass and bushes. He must have been quite close to the enemy.

"What the hell is he doing?" Erich exclaimed anxiously. "Does he think he has a hundred men?"

Dusk was falling, as was Sepp Mueller's impunity. A Vietcong company deployed in the brush now charged forward in a desperate attempt to silence the howitzer and the murderous machine guns. Some heavy mortars on the far side of the adjacent hill, out of Mueller's sight, began to hit the acclivity where we sheltered, but as the gunners corrected elevation the detonations crept toward the crest.

From the smoke, dust, and cascading earth, Krebitz and Steiner emerged black with dirt and sweat. They rolled into the depression where I lay.

"Call Sepp and tell him to quit!" Rudolf gasped. "There's a whole damned company coming with bazookas. He'll be knocked out."

Overhead the howitzer roared again. I called Mueller over the WT. "Sepp! Blow your gun and come down here, while you can still do it," I rasped.

"All right, Hans—just a few more rounds. . . ."

"Immediately!" I shouted. "The Viets are crawling up on you with bazookas."

"I'm already giving them hell."

The gun thundered twice more. The shrapnel landed in the center of the advancing enemy. A dozen guerrillas cartwheeled in the air; others pitched into the grass.

"Did you see that?" Sepp exulted over the walkie-talkie. "A company, you say? By the time they arrive they'll be only a platoon."

"What about the MGs up there?"

"Ran out of ammo."

"Come down, you idiot!"

"I'm coming in a moment," Sepp temporized.

I turned to Schulze. "Let's give Mueller all the support we can." I gestured toward the Vietcong, crawling uphill like ants. "He's in shit."

Another report of the howitzer was followed almost instantly by a sharp double explosion. Overhead the Vietcong broke into wild cheers.

"Sepp!" I called repeatedly. There was no answer.

Altreiter, who had a better view of the crest, called, "Hans! I think Sepp has had it. There are guerrillas all over the crest."

Riedl covered his face with his hands. Erich blew a gasp like an enraged bull before charging and I felt miserably downhearted.

"Keep firing, you idiot!" Krebitz yelled at Riedl. "This isn't time to mourn. The crest is taken but we should stop the reinforcements."

"I think we should get the hell out of here," I croaked, "before they start hurling grenades on us."

"Schulze! Where do you think you're going?" Rudolf cried, but Erich was already out of the hollow, summoning his men.

"I'm going up to the crest!" he called.

"Not on your life!" I shouted, but he was gone, crawling away and uphill.

Some thirty Vietcong had managed to break through our ring and reach the crest. The rest of them were beaten back by Steiner and Stolz's flamethrowers. For a while the enemy took shelter in the brush but when it began to burn, they broke cover and fled precipitously, dashing right into Altreiter's field of fire and going down by the score.

Unaware of the impending disaster down below that threatened their comrades, the Vietcong platoon on the crest was celebrating their victory over Sepp with wild hollers and yells. Schulze wouldn't permit them to celebrate for long. With only twenty troops he stormed the crest to meet the enemy head-on in a vicious brawl. Enraged as they were, his men crushed the guerrillas, killing twenty and capturing fifteen. Stolz and Steiner turned the howitzer against the still-resisting platoons on the plain. No longer exposed to fire from above, I ordered my own men to advance against the remnants of the Vietcong companies, some two hundred demoralized guerrillas, deprived of their cannons, mortars, and machine guns. Teaming up with Altreiter, we delivered a two-pronged assault. For some minutes the enemy resisted tenaciously but when the flamethrowers began to singe them, they withdrew under the cover of dusk. Leaving behind all their equipment and supplies, they fled toward the northeast. We found the corpse of their commanding officer. Although clad like the Vietcong, according to his papers he was a major of the 266th Infantry Regiment of Hanoi's army.

Schulze and Krebitz recovered the seminude corpses of Sepp Mueller, Walter Winar, and their companions. Using bayonets or knives, the guerrillas had carved five-pointed stars into their chests and cut off their noses and ears.

Even in the heat of combat they found time to commit an act

of bestiality. The expression of screaming agony on Winar's face told us that the savagery had been perpetrated while our unfortunate companion was still breathing.

We had more casualties. Sixteen altogether, whom we buried in a crater with military honors and marked the site with boulders laid out in the form of a cross.

Our wounded were treated by Zeisl and the prisoner surgeons and nurses. The surgeons had even operated—extracted slugs and sewed up deep wounds under the beams of battery torches.

Schulze had his fifteen prisoners bayoneted. Our list of victims passed the two thousand mark.

Task Force-G had also consumed 80 percent of its ammunition in that single engagement, all the flamethrower tanks and hand grenades. Gruppe Drei spent several hours canvassing the ground to collect serviceable enemy weapons and ammunition for the trip home, for we were practically disarmed.

8.

The Coming of the Americans

As far as our Commando of Death was concerned, American involvement in Vietnam began with the arrival of Captain Mike Spata and Staff Sergeant Joe Starr, both World War II veterans and counterguerrilla experts, two men with similar professional qualifications but vastly different temperaments.

Spata and Starr had been introduced to us by General Houssong, as kind of semiofficial observers, delegated by the U.S. Armed Forces to procure on-the-spot impressions regarding the state of affairs in Vietnam.

A former university chemistry lecturer, Spata was a typical intellectual. He had a medium build with back-swept light-brown hair, blue eyes, and a pair of gold-rimmed spectacles. Soft-spoken, always composed, and highly cultured, judged by his appearance alone no one would ever consider Captain Spata a soldier. On the contrary, he looked like the antithesis of anything martial.

Yet he was a much-decorated officer with many years of combat experience, first with the Nationalists in China, then in Burma, and later on the Pacific theater of war against the Japanese.

Joe Starr was lanky but muscular; dark-haired, crew-cut, and square-jawed. A man of a cheerful, "devil-may-care" character. He came from Colorado, if I remember correctly. Slow-moving at the first impression but, when necessary, he could be swift like the strike of an adder. Jungle fatigues, a Colt .45 revolver tucked into his Western-style belt and holster studded with cartridges, high Texan boots; a knapsack loaded with vitamin pills, antimalaria pills, water disinfectants, and foot sprays constituted his equipment. The troops promptly nicknamed him Sheriff as they had dubbed Spata Professor.

During the war, Starr had been serving in a commando of the U.S. Marines. He had gone through every imaginable hell from

Guadalcanal to Okinawa. From the first day we considered him an expert *Kamerad* and our equal in every sense of the word. And after we saw him hit five tin cans in rapid succession with his revolver, Starr also gained the respect of Gruppe Drei's sharpshooters.

The Americans were only observers, officially prohibited from participating in armed actions, but Captain Spata loathed office walls and preferred to be on the field. Joe Starr was apparently quite ready to forget certain regulations he disagreed with —particularly when it came to the "exchanging of forty-five-caliber greetings with the fuckin' Commies."

He fumed a great deal about how the United States had been helping the Russians to survive the war—only to be stabbed in the back by Stalin shortly afterward—and that was all old Roosevelt's fault, who would readily believe what Uncle Joe bullshitted.

Laughingly, Erich reminded Joe that this was no news. Even Churchill had stated after the 1948 Berlin blockade that the allies had slaughtered the wrong pig.

Starr loved action. The more dangerous it was, the more he liked it. When, on the first day, I asked him why he ever volunteered to come into our green hell, Starr replied with a shrug, "To look for trouble, I guess." The troops burst into laughter, and he was liked from that very instant.

"Well, Joe—you'll have all the trouble there is!" Schulze reassured him with a friendly slap on the back.

Our two observers should have spent much of their time with the South Vietnamese Army but, as Starr had put it, "There's not a shit to watch." Both preferred to march along with Task Force-G instead, sharing our hardships and perils. Captain Spata was snapping pictures with his tiny Minox camera and took notes and Starr got wounded on his second trip, which he considered a kind of baptism by fire—by the Communists. He had already been "baptized" twice by the Japs.

We were in the foothills of the Khon Tran mountains, about 150 miles northeast of Saigon, assaulting a Vietcong camp in a clearing in the woods. The opposing fire was determined, and we could gain ground only by crawling from tree to tree. There was a machine gun positioned in a hollow tree that blocked our advance for over an hour. Starr was lying next to me in a sodden gully and Riedl asked him teasingly, "Hey, Joe—what do you think of the Vietcong now?"

Starr turned halfway and answered in the same spirit, "In combat I don't think—I fight!"

He asked for a couple of grenades. Julius Steiner accommodated him.

"What do you want to do?" I asked somewhat nervously, for I didn't want to return to Saigon and report to General Houssong the death of one of his observers.

"We can't sit here until Christmas," Joe answered crisply. "I'm going to blast that hillbilly from his hole."

"You're not supposed to fight, Joe," I reminded him, but he was already crawling away like a lizard, approaching the enemy MG at an angle, while the slugs raked the green tangle around him.

"He is surely no chicken," Steiner commented, and began to blaze away with his Mitra to provide Starr with covering fire. Then he slung the gun onto his back and crawled after Joe. I opened up myself to distract the Vietcong gunners, thinking that Captain Spata was going to be mad about Starr's martial venture. Riedl joined my effort to pin down the snipers firing in the direction of the dauntless sergeant who, despite the odds, had managed to come within twenty yards of the hostile machine gun.

We heard the double blast and saw the fire and smoke. The hollow tree tilted, then crashed down, burying a handful of guerrillas and wrecking the MG. Schulze and Riedl summoned their troops, lunged forward, and dislodged the enemy from the woods.

I found Starr sitting on a stump, pressing a handkerchief against his upper left arm, which was bleeding profusely from a three-inch slash. Krebitz bandaged it up temporarily and had Starr escorted to our improvised first-aid station where Zeisl, Suoi, and Noi were treating our wounded.

Blowing a deep sigh, Starr dropped on a log.

"Bullet?" Noi asked as she unwound the blood-soaked bandage.

"Splinter," Joe replied flatly, and winced as a segment of lacerated skin ripped away with the gauze.

Noi disinfected the wound and called Zeisl, who examined

Joe's arm, requested him to move his elbow and fingers, then said jokingly, "All right, Sergeant—there's no need to amputate."

"How kind of you, Doc."

"Neither ligaments nor nerves are damaged. You were lucky, though."

"This is what you call luck around here?" Starr cracked. "I'd be a lot luckier not to have been hit in the first place."

He fumbled in his pocket for a cigarette. Zeisl lighted it for him.

"I'm afraid you arm will need some stitching," Zeisl said. "I have no novocaine left, so you'd better brace yourself."

He offered Starr a canteen with cognac. The American took a mouthful and nodded. "Go 'head, Doc." "I'm so booked up on aches that I can't possibly feel any worse before a day or two."

Noi gave him an antitetanus shot.

Erich, Helmut, and Krebitz chased the Vietcong onto a precipitous crest that overhung their burning camp. After a bitter fight at close quarters, using mostly bayonets, machetes, and rifle butts, the first signs of victory appeared on the eastern extremity of the plateau, where Riedl had pushed the guerrillas to the edge of a three-hundred-foot drop. In the northern sector, Krebitz had more difficult going, but once the sharpshooters eliminated the enemy machine gunners, his attack, too, gained impetus. The battle ended when Erich forced the largest resisting group against a rock face and Stolz advanced against them with the flamethrowers. The Hanoi-delegated political officer opted for surrender instead of being roasted. He was spared together with the Vietcong commander and a couple of Communist Party activists whom I wanted to send to Karl Stahnke. About 140 Vietcong were then hurled into the rocky abyss together with their weapons.

We were about to leave the plateau when Starr arrived on the double with the Colt in his good hand.

"You're too late, Sheriff," Erich greeted him. "The fray's over."

"You don't say!" the American cried. He shifted his eyes around and observed the enemy dead with an expression of disappointment, then reverted his attention to Schulze. "No prisoners?" he asked, somewhat mystified.

Beckoning Starr to follow, Erich strolled to the precipice and made a sweeping gesture. "Down there!"

Joe stared at the broken weapons and bodies. "How come?"

"Mass suicide," Schulze lied with the most innocent expression he could muster. "When the apes found themselves trapped they just jumped off the overhang. . . . Such things happen quite often. These soldiers of Father Ho are quite fanatical. You see, they wouldn't even leave their weapons to the damned imperialists."

"And what about those guys?" The sergeant gestured toward the group of Communist prominents being led downhill by Krebitz.

"They're Hanoi Party men," Erich replied casually, "caught at the last moment. One of them is a *Zampolit* of the North Vietnamese Army."

"*Zampolit?* What the heck is that?"

"I'm sorry. . . . That's the Russian term for political officer."

"A North Vietnamese officer here?" Our sheriff stared. "So close to Saigon?"

"Oh, such tourists from the north are quite frequent, Joe. Why shouldn't they visit us? There's an armistice."

We always tried to spare our American friends from "indecent spectacles" for mutual benefit. Before we gunned down our prisoners or wounded Vietcong, Spata and Starr would be railroaded somewhere else on some pretext. Our observers were newcomers to Vietnam, still imbued with humane sentiments, chivalry, and the Geneva Convention. Since we were getting along very well, I didn't feel like providing any ground for friction. Captain Spata would surely protest vehemently against some of our established practices.

When Captain Mike Spata visited Erich and me in our office for the first time, we had a brief discussion about aspects of the irregular war we were waging. During our discourse, Spata remarked, "You know that many people in the States believe that the Vietcong are brave patriots who fight for their freedom, like our forefathers had been fighting under Washington."

Schulze pursed his lips and said levelly, "You Americans are idealists, trusting and benevolent. The Vietcong are subhumans. You shouldn't waste your confidence on them."

Spata uttered a soft chuckle. "I thought this superman-subhuman idea died with Hitler," he retorted.

"Not here," my friend stated positively. "Perhaps it won't be long before you come face-to-face with some genuine subhumans, Mike. They even look like apes."

Riedl entered. Hearing Schulze's last sentence, he rolled his eyes and intoned with mocking solemnity, "All men are equal before God, O people—including the Papuan cannibals and the Vietcong apes. . . . The only trouble is that hereabouts God is called Lenin and Ho Chi Minh is his prophet. A thousand miles to the north the prophet is Mao."

From my drawer I extracted a small red-bound book and slipped it to Spata. "Mike, you'd better read this before you do any observing in Vietnam."

Spata picked it up gingerly and read the title. *"The Revolution Will Win. . . ."* He glanced up. "What's it all about?"

"The Vietcong. . . . The author, Truong Chinh, is the Hanoi chief of propaganda but the name is only a nom de guerre meaning Long March. Truong's real name is Dang Xuan Khu. We almost captured him in 1950. He beat Krebitz by five lousy minutes."

Captain Spata flipped open the book, thumbed through a couple of pages, read the chapter headings, and wrinkled his nose. "It must be a pile of red nonsense."

"The Vietcong fights and often wins according to the maxims of this red nonsense."

Erich cut in. "Truong's book is plain Mao plagiarism, worded to suit local conditions. All the same, it's the Vietcong version of God's truth."

"Once you read it, you'll know better what kind of an enemy we are fighting against," I added soberly.

"Did you fellows read it?" Spata asked somewhat skeptically.

I nodded. "Certainly, Mike—and also Mao, Chou En Lai, and scores of other works written on the subject of guerrilla warfare by Russian and Western experts."

"Only the French high brass would never even touch such layman's literature," Riedl added.

Spata asked, "Are the French really so incompetent?"

I shook my head. "I wouldn't use the word *incompetent*. The majority of the general staff officers are excellent theorists, only they stubbornly refuse to believe that primitive rebels can effectively oppose a modern mobile army. This view of theirs remained unaffected by the disaster at Dien Bien Phu and the loss of thirteen northern provinces. The western military leaders tend to ignore the fact that those primitive rebels have been fighting against modern armies for fifteen years, counting the Japanese occupation."

There was a pause. Spata said meditatively, "Perhaps you're right. . . . It's the age-old mistake of underestimating the enemy. Even our generals would often refer to the Vietcong as 'those raggedy little bastards in black pajamas.'"

Aimed mostly at Erich, I replied with a mild smile, "We, too, call the guerrillas jungle dwarfs, apes of Father Ho, *Schweinhunde,* or *Scheisskerle,* but there's no longer conviction behind such derogatory remarks, rather only frustration. With their well-earned victory in the north the guerrillas have also earned our respect and in a sense even our admiration."

"Sure," Erich blurted. "We gun them down with great admiration, Mike." But he also conceded that the Vietcong had accomplished what the French General Staff considered a "dream of fantasy"—the concentration of four infantry divisions three hundred miles from their operational bases in the Tonkin district, equipped with heavy artillery and perfectly supplied, despite their complete lack of motorized transports and constant aerial strikes. They had turned the "dream of fantasy" into genuine nightmare when they swamped and captured Dien Bien Phu, together with General de Castris and his staff officers.

I made the saga of Dien Bien Phu an obligatory study for the troops of Task Force-G, so that they could better understand the nature of the Vietcong enemy: no longer a ragtag group of local desperados but a disciplined and well-organized army of devoted Communists, who counted their ranks in divisions, brigades, battalions, and companies.

Spata sipped some whiskey, then said quietly, "We learned a trick or two about jungle warfare against the Japs, Hans."

"I'm sure you did," I conceded. "But tough as they were, the Japanese were regulars and the Vietcong are not. They fight like wild beasts."

RECALL TO INFERNO

Schulze interposed, "If they'd only fight, but they don't fight, only slaughter, maim, and destroy in cold blood. They kill sucklings in the crib and maim even the dead. Believe me, Mike—if you treat them humanely they'd take it for a sign of weakness and fear. You cannot expect a spark of goodwill from the Vietcong, let alone reciprocity."

"Therefore you exterminate them."

His response momentarily threw us off balance.

"Well, we sure try to kill as many Vietcong as possible," I said.

He observed me steadily. "Those hospital personnel in Cambodia weren't exactly Vietcong, Hans," he said pointedly.

"You know about them?"

"I know that Task Force-G accepts no surrender and takes no prisoners."

"I gave those fellows a choice."

Captain Spata blew a sigh of mild exasperation. "That may be—but we're still supposed to be civilized men. . . . I grant that sometimes it might be very difficult to remain civilized."

"Wait until you see some of the outrages perpetrated by the bastards," Riedl said. "Afterward you'll be hollering for the H-bomb or at least some poison gas."

After a few weeks of relative tranquillity, when we engaged only in minor forays around Saigon, our American friends were to participate in a real action and witness the naked severity of death in Vietnam.

Only six miles from where the borders of South Vietnam, Laos, and Cambodia converged, the French forces, the Saigon troops, and Task Force-G were engaged in a large-scale offensive against a Vietcong village with a fortified guerrilla camp on a nearby hill, protected by the river Sé Kong, a cluster of cliffs, and precipitous ravines.

In the tangled woods were two Vietcong regiments equipped with artillery.

It was a genuine symphony of death: the sharp, incessant staccato of small-arms fire, the whizzing of artillery shells, the brief hiss of descending mortar bombs, and the screaming fighter bombers in dives, followed by the earsplitting detonations of their bombs and rockets. A rapidly expanding funnel of smoke towered above the guerrilla base on the forested hill, which gradually transformed into a hundred-foot wall. More and more explosives plunged onto the crest, tearing foliage, uprooting trees, toppling tall boulders. The wall of smoke expanded like some uncanny monster. It rolled and heaved, a shapeless living entity, growing bulkier, as if it were drawing life and power from destruction. But it was a familiar monster. We knew it from our battles in Poland and Russia.

Another squadron of warplanes erupted from the clouds and dived into the wall of smoke, dropped their cargo, and streaked skyward.

Observing the spectacle through his field glasses, Captain Spata commented, "I wonder if there's anything left to bomb."

Speaking from experience, Schulze reassured him that our elusive adversaries were quite clever at surviving such hammerings. "The artillery and the air force are probably blasting lots of empty huts, fuel drums, and crates, Mike," he said airily. "Also mock-up artillery positions with wooden guns and mortars made of stovepipes, while the guerrillas are sitting it out at a safe distance, together with their real equipment."

Sergeant Starr's chin came up. "Don't they know it?"

"Who?"

"The air force, for instance."

Erich shrugged. "They probably do," he replied matter-of-factly.

The Americans stared. Starr shook his head. "This is all Chinese to me. . . . Then why the hell the bombing?"

Riedl laughed softly. "Just look at the spectacle, Joe. . . . The planes are also shooting films and photos. How fine everything will look in the newsreels and plastered over the newspaper pages. The generals and the country fathers at home will congratulate each other and say how well everything is going here."

"That's pure bullshit," Joe commented.

"This whole damned war is bullshit," Erich replied. "This is likely the last large-scale French participation in the Vietnam war. The Foreign Legion is going to quit soon but it wants to quit with *gloire.*"

"You mean—it's only a farewell show?" Spata asked wonderingly.

RECALL TO INFERNO

"Something like that, Professor." Schulze nodded. "Otherwise why this huge concentration of men and firepower? Just look around. North Africans, French paratroops, South Vietnamese, artillery, fighter bombers, assault guns, and tanks. . . . The Vietcong camp on the hill isn't important enough for all this show of force."

"What about the two Vietcong regiments in the woods?" Spata queried.

"The Laotian and Cambodian borders are only a few miles away, Mike. If anything should go wrong those regiments would simply cross the border and camp down where neither the French nor the Vietnamese can follow them."

"You can," Starr stated.

"Sure," Schulze commented. "Task Force-G with two hundred and seventy-five men against two Vietcong regiments. . . . No longer the Commando of Death but a dead commando."

Starr said with a grin, "Yeah, a slip of memory. You aren't a division."

At 11:30 A.M. the bombardment stopped. The colonial battalions and the South Vietnamese troops charged forward to assault the fortified village, which had, so far, been spared. As a matter of fact, it had not been defended by the Vietcong at all. Senegalese and Moroccan companies were leading the charge, the former screaming like madmen, shaking their weapons as if they were spears or clubs, and dashing into a murderous guerrilla crossfire of machine guns, mortars, and field artillery, coming not from the village but from the green tangle that flanked it.

The assault faltered almost instantly. The colonials turned tail and fled back toward the Sé Kong, which the French engineers had spanned with a pontoon bridge.

"*Voilà,*" Krebitz commented sarcastically. "There goes the offensive of fifty yards."

Since it was not our task to participate in open combat, I led Task Force-G away from the scene in a wide semicircle. Taking advantage of the tall shrubs along the riverbank and the enemy's distraction, I wanted to seize a dominant elevation from where the Vietcong, or rather perhaps the North Vietnamese, were shelling the North African positions.

As I expected, we encountered no opposition. The guerrillas' attention was riveted on the colonials and South Vietnamese, now hemmed in around the bridge. Once again masquerading as guerrillas, we made our way behind the hill where a dirt road led to the crest picketed loosely by an enemy platoon, dispersed in a wide arch. The six sentinels directly in our way were quickly killed by the sharpshooters, while those farther away mistook us for companions and waved friendly hands. We waved back, hollered greetings, then disappeared in the greenery, climbing toward the crest, from where a pair of howitzers were shelling the colonials. Just before coming to the crest we stopped and Krebitz went to reconnoiter. From where we sheltered, the rolling battle down below was in plain view with hundreds of Vietcong crawling slowly but inexorably toward the river and the bridge.

Krebitz returned. "It's okay, Hans. . . . There's only the gun crews and some fifteen apes with rifles."

I rose. "Let's move!"

Our commando swarmed onto the crest, mowed down the bewildered gunners and riflemen, and took possession of the four-inch guns. The troops shifted the carriages, Schulze and Krebitz realigned the howitzers, then opened up. One fired at the enemy guns positioned on the adjacent hills, the other hammered the guerrillas advancing on the bridge. Our unexpected interference caused a great confusion on the plain that soon turned into disorderly retreat.

Schulze began to knock out the enemy guns.

With Riedl, Stolz, Altreiter, and the Americans, I returned to the river.

The guerrilla assault units had fled into the village. The French and South Vietnamese troop carriers and half-track assault guns left their concealment on the far bank and crossed the bridge. The colonials cheered. A red flare knifed into the dull sky, drew a lazy arch, then started to fall. The assault guns, mortars, and field artillery opened up. The South Vietnamese machine guns joined in.

Long lines of tracers tore into the village. Shells burst between the dwellings blasting balks, bricks, bamboo walls, and planks, turning everything into cinder and ash. From the billowing smoke rose desperate shrieks. Within a few minutes the village turned into a raging inferno that, swept by the wind, swiftly consumed everything that could burn and spread to the nearby paddies where the water halted the flames.

I spotted a lean shape darting from the village, screaming in terror, jumping over shell holes, smoldering wood, corpses, ducking between strings of tracers. A grinning Senegalese corporal braced his rifle against a tree stump and took aim.

"Let him go, man!" Captain Spata yelled in French. "He's only a kid." Unperturbed, the corporal pulled the trigger. The boy staggered, spun around, and crashed to the ground.

The Senegalese spat. "Boys like him do much shooting in this country," he stated coolly. Then he yelled something to a native companion and their group began to advance toward the huts.

An assault gun came clattering by, stirring a cloud of dust and throwing mud left and right. Riedl yelled, "Can't you move slower, *Scheisskerl*?"

The din of the engine obliterated his call, but we saw the gunner's head pop up behind the armor plating. His helmet, earphones, and face were covered with a gray crust of dust, creased with canals of sweat. He made an indecent gesture with his right forearm as he jolted up and down with the movement of his vehicle that translated into a sort of quiet "fuck you."

"Gibt es dein Muttil" Helmut returned the courtesy. "Give it to your mother."

I shifted my field glasses toward the crest with Schulze, Krebitz, and Gruppe Drei and saw with relief that all was well. They were still shelling the Vietcong positions.

The North Africans and the Saigon troops dashed into the village, which was defended only halfheartedly. The bulk of the Vietcong had withdrawn farther west, into their camp, leaving the village at the mercy of the colonials. The Senegalese were first to enter, hollering as they advanced—not to scare the enemy but to boost their own courage. The Africans were a superstitious lot. Darkness and silence scared them. Hence their habit of shrieking and burning everything in sight. They butchered everyone they came across.

Our Americans were aghast at the spectacle of unbridled savagery.

"This isn't war but genocide," Spata commented disdainfully. "Something the Japs did in China and Bataan."

Riedl waved a hand. "Wait until you've seen the rest of the carnage. . . . And kindly remember that the Nazis did not contribute to the spectacle."

The colonials virtually wiped out the Vietcong village. We entered twenty minutes after its conquest. The ruins were still burning and some Vietnamese auxiliaries were dumping corpses into a gully.

Most victims were women, children, and old people. Only a few dozen corpses were clad in Vietcong garb. Faithful to their traditions, the colonials had been saving on ammunition. (Cartridges and grenades could be turned into cash on the Saigon black market.) The victims had been bayoneted, hacked to pieces with machetes, or had had their brains spilled with rifle butts. Mangled kids and squashed babies lay trampled into the dust. Seeing them, our Americans' fuses blew. When we came across some Africans camped down next to a heap of maimed corpses—munching, playing dice, guffawing, and displaying what they had looted—Spata and Starr were hell-bent on decimating them with a couple of submachine-gun salvos.

"Don't jump to conclusions," Erich counseled Spata. "Just take a good look at the fellows and imagine them wearing only loincloths, shaking shields and spears in a wild war dance to the tune of tom-toms. They're subhumans like the Vietcong, stripped of their spears and bows and put into uniforms to receive the blessed benefits of civilization—machine guns, automatic weapons, and flamethrowers. They can barely count past twenty and their deadly toys delight them. . . . It's fun to set houses on fire with flamethrowers instead of torches."

"Why are you mad, *mon général?*" a Moroccan sergeant chided Spata sarcastically after a vehement verbal reprove. "Bac Ko was a Vietcong village, and our order says that Vietcong villages must be wiped out."

"Including babies and children of four?" Spata retorted scornfully.

The sinewy Moroccan waved a hand about as if trying to dismiss a boring subject. "This is a bandit village, General—"

"I'm a captain!" the American cut him off.

The Moroccan shrugged. "Captain, colonel, general—to me the same—sir," he added after an instant. "The people of a bandit village must die. You pick a boy of ten and he can shoot like a commando marksman."

"We were talking about children of four!" Starr interposed.

The sergeant spat again. "Children grow up and become guerrillas. I let a boy get away today and he cuts my throat tomorrow."

The same evening the Americans did not feel like eating and complained a great deal about the African butchers.

"How can they possibly sleep at night?" Captain Spata exclaimed in exasperation.

Schulze explained to him that the African butchers can sleep very well. "They've grown to manhood slaughtering each other in tribal wars, and killing is about the only creative activity they're capable of doing," he said.

The South Vietnamese went hunting for dogs, shooting them on sight—something they had learned from our onetime Battalion of the Damned. Once the army departed, the village would be built up again, the Vietcong would reoccupy it, and consequently the soldiers would return one day to destroy it once more. The enemy won't be alerted by the barking of dogs.

The battle for the Vietcong camp about a mile west of Bac Ko continued all day long. The colonials and the South Vietnamese attacked it from the village and Task Force-G forced open the rear entrances. The paratroops did not participate in the action, only secured the communications and the bridge. The fighting ended around 7:15 P.M. when Riedl and Krebitz mopped up the last resisting groups around the burning communications hut. Gruppe Drei, Schulze, and Riedl had captured some 150 Vietcong, who surrendered rather than face our roasters, and secured themselves a new lease of life. With an eye on our Americans, we handed them over to the Saigon troops who beat them badly but did not shoot them.

Suddenly we became aware of the clatter of rotor blades and for an instant the men froze, staring flabbergasted at the green copter that emerged from the forest barely a hundred yards from where we stood.

"Schau 'mal das an!" Erich exclaimed, pointing. *"Ein verdammte Hubschrauber."*

"It's Russian!" Altreiter yelled. Krebitz threw an inquisitive glance at me.

I gave him my nodding consent. "Go ahead, Rudy!"

"They aren't corporals and sergeants traveling in that copter, that's for sure," Stolz added as Gruppe Drei's men began to blaze away at the engine and rotor transmission.

A dark jet of oil spurted from the ripped cowling. The engine began to sputter.

A trail of smoke. The copter dropped back onto the trees. The crackling of branches. The clatter stopped. With a dozen troops in tow, Riedl and Krebitz bolted for the woods. A few minutes later Spata and Starr joined us. Schulze called their attention to the column of prisoners now being escorted toward the river and said emphatically, "There they go—the prisoners.

"You seem to have done a great job here," Starr complimented, surveying the devastation.

"We can't complain," Erich answered amiably, and called for Altreiter. "Say, Horst—why won't you show our friends the captured guns and ammo?" And when the Americans were facing Altreiter, he gestured toward the far side of the camp.

"*Jawohl*, Chief!" Horst nodded understandingly, and the three trodded off to where I wanted them to be.

Soon Riedl came running, shouting and gesticulating. "Guess what we've got!"

"A couple of Hanoi top brass."

He grabbed me by the arm. "Russkies!" he replied exultedly. "Three of them. . . . And a North Vietnamese colonel in the bargain. . . . Come!"

We needed no further prodding. Led by Helmut, we rushed into the clearing where Krebitz guarded the prisoners.

"One major, one captain, and a lieutenant," Rudolf announced.

"*Himmel, Gesaess, and Naehgarn!*" Erich exclaimed, staring at the sullen group. "*Es kann nicht wahr sein.* This cannot be true."

"And a Hanoi colonel," Riedl reminded us.

I gave the red quartet a salute, which they returned sullenly. We observed each other, measuring, contemplating.

The overall situation had not changed since the late 1940s, when we had captured and executed four Soviet advisors, who were then buried under tons of rocks in the hills of North Vietnam to forgo any diplomatic hassle between Paris and Moscow.

Naturally we knew that Russian and Chinese military advisors were on active duty with the North Vietnamese Army and consequently in the Vietcong ranks, which, by 1954, could not be distinguished from the Hanoi regulars.

Both Moscow and Peking had accepted the calculated risk that some of their delegates might die in action or, even worse, become prisoners. By Soviet moral standards it was better to lose an officer in action than have him captured by the enemy. Prisoners would be interrogated, subjected to intensive capitalist propaganda, and perhaps later sent back as agents. This principle had weighed heavily on the Soviet decision not to adhere to the Geneva Convention. As Stalin reasoned, if the front-line troops knew that the enemy would treat them well, they might prefer desertion or surrender to dying in the trenches.

Dead soldiers neither talk nor come back as enemy spies.

Naturally we could not place our Soviet prisoners on public display without involving Paris in a political muddle and triggering Moscow to violent accusations, blatant lies, and perhaps retribution.

The French would not accept them. The Diem government would not know what to do with them either, and I surely couldn't keep them for any length of time without crossing swords with Starr and Spata, who would probably want to send them to America. And if I consented, a week later Moscow would be sending protest notes to Washington, and *Pravda* would be raving about "the U.S. agents who had kidnapped three Soviet citizens from North Vietnamese territory, where they were inspecting the distribution of hospital equipment, donated by the Russian Red Cross." The lords of the Kremlin were superb liars.

Spata and Starr would certainly raise hell against any proposal to shoot the prisoners. I was already scraping my mind for an alternative solution. When my companions asked me what I intended to do, I told them flatly that I would probably release the Russians, as the best way out of a tricky problem. Schulze and Krebitz were in accord.

I shifted my attention to the sullen group.

The Soviet major was the amiable sort: round-faced, stocky, and fair, with healthy red cheeks. Seeing me and Erich, he rightly assumed that we were in command. The major drew himself up and gave us another peremptory salute, which the dyspeptic-looking captain with brooding eyes and the flat-faced, beetle-browed North Vietnamese colonel promptly imitated. I introduced myself and Schulze and noticed that our very names had drawn instant frowns and expressions of concern. I was certain that our names were known to our unwelcome guests.

The major spoke stiffly. "I am Major Vladimir Lazarev. My companions are Captain Yuri Larkin and pilot Lieutenant Alexei Kolosov." He gestured toward the Hanoi officer. "Colonel Quang Ho Tanh is our host in Hanoi."

"Hanoi is a long way from here, Major Lazarev," I responded with a thin smile. "But welcome in the Republic of Vietnam all the same." I tried to look cheerful to alleviate the Russians' consternation, but the major's face remained stony.

He continued, "I demand to be treated as officers of the Red Army and prisoners of war, who may not be compelled to give any sensitive information to the enemy."

"Enemy, major?" I asked sharply. "To the best of my knowledge we aren't at war with the Soviet Union."

Since the major seemed to know well how to pitch his voice precisely between politeness and truculence, I found it expedient to rebuke him with a quiet addition. "You may ask but not demand anything, *tovarich* Major. And because we are not at war, we may treat Colonel Quang as our prisoner of war but not you."

The North Vietnamese colonel's face showed instant relief. His fingers were unsteady as he picked a cigarette from his golden case. Erich offered him his lighter. He acknowledged the courtesy with a smile like a rent in canvas. The major went on, no longer aggressively but in a friendly tone. "Then, if you prefer, you may simply consider us three ordinary Soviet citizens in distress, Captain Wagemueller."

"Yes, it sounds better," Riedl quipped. "A group of tourists lost in a zone of war. . . . It happens."

"There's an armistice between the two Vietnams," the major said in a tight voice, miraculously enough without choking on the joke he was telling. He seemed somewhat embarrassed, though.

Erich's ironic response was instantaneous. "Is there an armistice?" he asked innocently, glancing around for confirmation. "I presume the battle that ended half an hour ago was only a game of cowboys and Indians with a few hundred corpses for the sake of excitement."

The major cleared his throat. Captain Larkin spoke for the first time. "The Vietcong is not the North Vietnamese Army," he said somberly.

"Who are they?" Schulze asked amiably.

"The South Vietnamese workers and peasants who fight for their freedom against an oppressive regime."

"Amen," my friend added, waving a hand. "Come, *tovarich* Captain, you don't believe that *Dreck* yourself. . . . Even in the Red Army one should possess a certain level of intelligence to become a captain."

The captain swallowed the polite affront and Riedl cut in. "And if we're talking about workers fighting against an oppressive regime—what about the East Berlin riots last July?"

"We are in Vietnam and not in Berlin." Major Lazarev brushed aside the inconvenient theme, and I didn't feel like getting into a hopeless political exchange.

"Stop pestering our guests," I told Riedl with joking severity. "You know damned well that anything they can possibly tell you has already been printed in countless ideological volumes."

I shifted my eyes toward the major. "*Alors,* Major Lazarev— what shall I do with you?" I asked, mildly amused. "You surely understand that your presence here must be kept *sovershenno sekretno,* because you shouldn't be here at all."

My expression "top secret" in Russian astounded the officers.

"You have been in Russia," Captain Larkin said, stating a fact rather than asking a question.

"Almost three years."

"With the German *Wehrmacht,* I presume—"

"With the German S.S.," Erich corrected him. "S.S. Panzer. . . . Twice decorated with the Iron Cross—naturally for outrages against humanity, Captain Larkin. I guess if I had gunned down a few hundred Jewish kids or Russian POWs, I would have earned the Knight's Cross too. . . . They were distributing them for such things."

Unperturbed by Erich's acidy outburst, Major Lazarev spoke in a controlled though mildly reproving tone. "First, serving

Hitler, then the French—now you are mercenaries of the Diem regime. . . . Of course we have heard of you, Captain."

"I'm sure you have, Major. Our public relations with the Communist press have always been first-class."

The major turned his eyes to me. "You are known to gun down your prisoners. If this is what you intend to do, then permit us to write a note to our families, which I hope you shall forward, and be done with it, without denigratory preliminaries. We are both officers and we both know the rules of the game. You have your ideals, we have ours, and it would be pointless to argue about who is right and who is wrong."

I said levelly, "I have no intention of shooting you, Major Lazarev. On the contrary. We decided to let you go."

"Go where?" he blurted, utterly baffled.

"Back to Hanoi. . . . Home. . . ."

I always appreciated character and bravery, and Lazarev had certainly displayed the best qualities of an officer. My unexpected statement, however, made the Russians stare dumbfounded. The cigarette dropped from the captain's fingers. Lazarev mumbled something unintelligible and began to wipe his glistening face.

"You decided to do—what?" He wanted to make sure.

"To let you go," I repeated, amused by the look on his face. "For old enmity's sake," I added jokingly. "We've been fighting each other since July 1941. You may return to Hanoi. Not Colonel Quang, though, for he will have to go to Saigon and do a great deal of explaining."

The Hanoi colonel shifted uncomfortably but said nothing. He had probably expected to be shot out of hand and was only happy to accept the suggested alternative.

The Russians were still fretting over what they probably considered a sort of dirty Fascist trick—like the slogan *"Arbeit Macht Frei"* above the concentration camp entrances or the signs SHOWERS on gas-chamber doors.

Captain Larkin said sullenly, "Do you plan to shoot us in the back?"

"Slushaite, tovarich Kapitan," I rebuked him sharply. "I have never broken my promises yet, so there's no need to be insulting. *Idite!"*

Speaking to the major, I added, "I'm afraid that you'll have a long walk, Major. The closest Vietcong camp is about fifteen miles distant—in Laos. Perhaps you'll run into some guerrillas with a wireless set and request another copter."

I turned to Krebitz. "Rudolf, give our Russian colleagues a couple of canteens with water, some provisions, a compass, and a chart of the region."

Erich gathered the three Red Army holsters with automatic pistols and nonchalantly handed them back to the baffled threesome, who were still staring at us with incredulous eyes.

"Keep these, *tovarich* Major. Trekking in the jungle can be dangerous. Apart from the Vietcong there are other ferocious beasts at large. Wolves, leopards, bears—even tigers."

We conducted our perplexed captives to the trail that issued from the guerrilla camp and ran into the green tangle.

"That's your direction," I said, pointing. "Keep going until you run into the first Vietcong lookouts but be careful because sometimes they shoot first and ask questions later. . . . Anyway, your Soviet uniforms should help."

"It's still bright enough to march a couple of miles," Erich interposed. "Perhaps you should camp down somewhere for the night and continue in the morning. . . . *Dosvidaniye.*"

The Russian still fidgeted. The major wiped his face, while Captain Larkin's eyes were roving between the trail and our silent group. At Schulze's gesture our men shouldered their weapons, and at long last Major Lazarev became convinced that there wasn't any devilish ruse behind our magnanimity and he muttered a halfhearted *"Spassiba gospodin, Kapitan. . . .* Thank you, Captain. I don't really know what to say."

"You shouldn't say anything but move! It's getting dark."

He turned toward his companions. *"Paidom, tovarichi.* Let's go, comrades."

They had the decency to salute us, then took the trail, walking warily first; the pilot lieutenant and Larkin kept turning back until our still-shouldered weapons dispersed the last vestiges of lingering suspicion and their steps became more brisk. In a few minutes the three Red Army officers disappeared in the jungle.

Krebitz handed me a map case that he had taken from the

wrecked copter. "There are some Russian documents here, Hans. Do you want to have a look?"

I waved a dismissing hand. "Send everything to Stahnke, Rudy. My Russian isn't good enough to understand what is it all about."

9.

Major General Clint McCory

Major General Clint McCory was a handsome, silver-haired stocky man in his early fifties, quiet-spoken and exuding and almost palpable steadiness. His hair was cut short. He had a tanned face with fine features, a thin moustache, and mild blue eyes. His spotless uniform fit his muscular frame perfectly and featured the ribbons of twelve decorations. In all, he was the sort of man who would have looked smartly clad in a jute sack.

He received us cordially and seated us around the oval conference table already set with glasses and various drinks packed in ice. There were crackers, boxes of cigarettes, and cigars. He took his seat, flanked by Major Roy Cooke, Captain Mike Spata, and Captain Ryan Dart of the Special Services. Present were General Houssong and his aide, Lieutenant Bernard Berger, Captain Pierre Dessault of the French Military Intelligence, and a South Vietnamese general. There was also a tall, exquisitely dressed, silver-haired, and very regal-looking civilian, a certain Jeff Robertson, a wartime OSS major, now working for the Central Intelligence Agency, whom we instantly nicknamed CIA count.

"Gentlemen, it's a pleasure to meet you," General McCory began with a complacent smile. "As you probably know, I was sent here by my government to have a closer look at the state of affairs in Vietnam."

He shifted his eyes toward me. "I believe that Captain Wagemueller is in charge of Task Force-G. . . . The letter *G* of which might be interpreted either as German, or G-men—both sufficiently tough."

His words drew soft laughs around the table and brought a content smile to Erich's face. Turning toward him, the general continued levelly, "Captain Schulze, the second in command, has a daredevilish disposition and hair-trigger temperament. . . . Lieutenant Krebitz, your chief trailblazer and inventor of clever ruses. . . . Lieutenants Riedl, Altreiter, and Stolz. . . . Don't be surprised but I have known about you for quite some time and appreciate your accomplishments before 1952."

The general leaned back in his armchair, observed us for a short while, then added, "First of all, I'd like you to brief me on the present situation—in a few words, I mean."

Since he posed his question while looking at Schulze, my friend thought it expedient to answer rather unceremoniously.

"I can brief you, sir, in four short words—if you'll excuse me for my terminology—the situation is pure shit."

I chuckled. Major Cooke repressed a smile. Jeff Robertson grinned. General McCory seemed mildly amused.

"Well, to tell you the truth I've suspected it," he commented with good humor. "It stinks all the way to Washington, and that's one of the reasons why I'm here. What's the core of the problem?"

I said, "Wrong people in the wrong places, sir. Incompetents in responsible positions playing pinball games with the lives of thousands of troops."

General McCory threw back his head and laughed. "This isn't a NATO meeting, is it?" he asked, drawing polite chuckles. He wiped his forehead and face, then asked, "Do you agree, Captain Schulze?"

"One hundred percent, General," Erich replied.

McCory's attention reverted to me. "Do you believe that another sort of leadership could bring the war to a successful conclusion?"

I opened my hands. "It'd be very difficult to win this war, sir," I temporized. "There are Vietcong cells everywhere, well integrated in the urban and rural communities. The remaining French and South Vietnamese fortifications are constantly under attack. Hanoi doesn't care a fig for the armistice agreement—"

"That we know," the general cut in. "To Hanoi the war in the south has nothing to do with the north. The Vietcong are dissatisfied local workers and peasants fighting oppression." He glanced at me. "Please continue."

I went on. "There might be a way to render the south impregnable and to cut off Hanoi's interference, but I doubt if anyone would care to consider it."

"Tell me. I'm interested."

"Well, sir—in my opinion, instead of trying to fight the enemy cells separately and repel aggression all over the country, striking in every direction of the compass, it might be better to erect a long fortified defensive line along the frontiers with Laos and Cambodia."

"You mean, a sort of Maginot Line?"

"Something of the sort, sir," I answered levelly. "A patch of barren ground, one hundred feet wide with barbed-wire entanglements, minefields, and concrete pillboxes at regular intervals with permanent garrisons. Such a line would render the Ho Chi Minh trail useless. It would prevent infiltration and supplies from the north, and without supplies the local guerrilla cells would simply run out of steam."

Captain Dart interrupted. "To build such a fortified line would be very costly, Captain Wagemueller. The frontier is over fifteen hundred miles long."

I said mildly, "Useless air attacks, artillery strikes, and daily battles can be costly, too, sir. Not to speak of the cost in lives," I argued. "I believe that in the long run—because we should be thinking in terms of years—the defensive line would come cheaper."

Schulze cut in. "Please remember that the Soviet-inspired Iron Curtain is ten times longer, and we know that it is very difficult to cross the Russian border illegally."

"Hmm . . ." General McCory cleared his throat. "In any case, your suggestion isn't something to be discarded out of hand. I'll certainly take note of it, Captain."

He thumbed through a file, scanned some pages, then glanced up. "For the moment let's revert our attention to the actual situation, which should be bettered. My government is ready to increase assistance substantially."

"In which case we might still win," Riedl quipped.

The general continued. "But I must tell you beforehand that Washington likes clean jobs."

"That's all right with us, sir," Erich cracked. "We never leave survivors to give press interviews or testify before the United Nations."

Schulze's blatant farce prompted another wave of soft guffaws.

The general chuckled. "I see I should have said clean *wars* instead," he corrected himself, stressing the word.

I raised a hand. "Unfortunately, we cannot play it fair with the Vietcong, sir," I said levelly. "They utterly disregard conventions, the basic code of moral conduct, and snub at civilized manners. Gentleness only makes them suspicious. It would certainly never evoke their gratitude. If you spare the life of a Communist guerrilla, he wouldn't be thankful to you but consider you a weakling, someone easy to scare and destroy."

General McCory nodded understandingly. "We're aware of this paradox."

CIA Count Robertson interposed quietly, "Have you noticed any substantial changes in guerrilla tactics and armaments lately, Captain?"

"Certainly. The Vietcong now has semi-track assault cars, night scopes, four-inch howitzers, multiple rocket launchers, and Josef Stalin tanks."

"Inside South Vietnam?" Major Cooke asked in wonder.

"Not permanently, sir. But assault tanks, artillery, and rocket launchers did participate in the near-successful assault on Camp Dizier last year. Otherwise the heavy armaments are stationed in Laos and Cambodia, not far from the border."

"The tanks and assault vehicles carry North Vietnamese insignias?"

"Correct, sir. As I said before, Hanoi doesn't care a fig for international agreements or borders."

General McCory's eyes rested in my face. "Could Task Force-G attack the bases of those mechanized units, Captain?" he asked gravely.

"We've conducted such expeditions in the past, General."

"Inside Laos and Cambodia?"

"It makes no difference to us. We aren't bound by legalities either."

"To our luck!" Erich added. "Otherwise we might be smelling flowers from three feet below by now."

"If and when you plan to do any such raid, let me know."

"Me too," our CIA count cut in. "There might be certain instruments and documents I'd like to have a look at."

"When we're ready, I'll let you know, Major Robertson—"

"Call me Jeff," he said. "We might be doing a lot of business together."

"All right, Jeff. You may discuss the details with Rudolf Krebitz. He's a good delivery man of Communist goodies."

I turned my attention to General McCory. "As a matter of fact, sir, we're thinking of a raid into North Vietnam proper."

My announcement drew some skeptical and baffled expressions mixed with admiration.

"Why not?" I continued. "If Hanoi can operate in South Vietnam, I can't see why we shouldn't return the courtesy."

"Such a venture might be extremely dangerous, don't you think?" Captain Dart commented, toying with his pencil on the map spread before him.

I shook my head. "Not more dangerous than operating in Laos or Cambodia against the Vietcong," I replied in a firm voice.

"The Vietcong are not the North Vietnamese Army."

"Lately there isn't much difference between the two. The Vietcong High Command is sitting in Hanoi."

"That we know," Major Cooke remarked.

"Besides, our onetime Battalion of the Damned operated exclusively in what is now North Vietnam," I continued. "We know the terrain well. We're familiar with every road and every trail and with every village where the Communists have garrisons."

McCory rubbed his hands and said, "Well, I can neither approve nor disapprove any such venture but if you think you can do it, go ahead. I wish you good luck."

The South Vietnamese general spoke for the first time. "Perhaps a couple of costly incursions into North Vietnam would induce Hanoi to scale down its troublemaking in our part of the country," he said in halting English. "Ho Chi Minh spares no effort to wreck our democratic system."

This latter statement drew polite smiles of amusement around the table.

"Perhaps we should say semidemocratic system," General Simon Houssong commented, inducing quiet chuckles in the American ranks.

From my briefcase I extracted a sheet of paper bearing official North Vietnamese heading and seal. "This is Communist Party

Directive number 2342, which we took from a captured Vietcong functionary," I explained, offering the paper to General McCory, who read it aloud for the benefit of his fellow Americans.

"—Lao Dong. Central Committee. Political Department Section five, et cetera. . . . The Geneva Armistice agreement calls for a truce between the National Movement of Liberation and the French forces and between the two Vietnams. This, however, should not mean the end of our struggle against the capitalist and reactionary forces in Saigon. The division of our country is only a temporary arrangement. It permits us to prepare ourselves for the final struggle. The Diem government must be done away with. The southern provinces must be liberated. Therefore we should reinforce our ranks and redouble our efforts to win new cadres in the south through education, convincing, and Marxist steadfastness and incite them to revolt. Pursuing this noble aim, our resident activists in the southern provinces should not hesitate to enter into alliance with dissatisfied groups or individuals; not even if those should be openly reactionary and anti-Marxist. The responsible comrades should remember that after the Japanese invasion of China, comrade Mao Tse Tung would not only make peace with the Nationalists of Chiang Kai Shek, but he would ally himself with the internal enemy against the more dangerous external one. But after the victory over the invaders, comrade Mao also eliminated the internal enemy. We should not hesitate to follow the proven Chinese example. After our victory and the unification of our country, our reactionary allies might be reeducated or, if necessary, eliminated. . . . Signed Truongh Chin."

The general glanced up. "Who is he?"

"The North Vietnamese analogue of our Dr. Goebbels, General," I enlightened him.

During a brief pause for drinks, the CIA count turned to me and said, "These are the kind of papers I'd like to collect and study, Captain."

"Just call me Hans, if you don't mind. . . . These kind of papers we used to discard because of weight, Jeff."

"That's a mistake."

"We'll let you have them in the future. I believe that our intelligence chief, Karl Stahnke, still has a file."

"I've already studied those," Robertson replied flatly, somewhat surprising me.

"You did?"

"There were even some Soviet documents."

"I know. Were they interesting?"

"To me every enemy document is interesting. Where did you get those?"

"From some captured Russians after the battle at Bac Ko. . . . Why? Didn't Stahnke tell you?"

"He's a rather clammed-up sort, Hans."

"It goes with his job."

"What did you do with the Russians?"

"We let them go."

Jeff stared. "Let them go where?"

"Back to Hanoi," I replied. "What else could I do with them?"

Robertson shook his head and said reprovingly, "The next time kindly let me have a chat with them first."

I opened my hands. "Now that we know each other—why not? But Russian prisoners are rare like the white raven."

General McCory asked for attention. The discussion continued, now concentrating on the military hardware we needed.

I asked politely, "Do you mean us in particular or the French forces in general, sir?"

"Let's talk about Task Force-G, Captain Wagemueller. The French requirements I've already discussed with General Ely."

"I've prepared a list, sir."

"All right. Let me have a look."

Schulze handed the relevant papers to Captain Dart, who passed them on to the general, then distributed copies to everyone else. The general began to scan it, nodding every now and then, making pencil marks. After a while he lifted his face and said with charming simplicity, "Your requirements aren't exactly modest. . . . Four assault guns, five amphibious tanks, ten troop carriers, twenty precision rifles with night sights, fifty flamethrowers, two thousand trip mines, twenty transreceivers, ten heavy machine guns, fifty light machine guns." He halted and glanced up. "You call the 12.7-caliber MGs light machine guns hereabouts? . . . Wait! Twenty-five thousand rounds of explosive slugs for rifles and light MGs? I'm afraid that explosive bullets are prohibited under the Geneva Convention."

"So are poisoned arrows, darts, and punji stakes, General McCory," I replied mildly. "Also bamboo bombs and cholera-infected excrement dumped into wells and rubbed onto grenades and shells—a most popular Vietcong practice."

"That may be, but the Pentagon will strike it anyway."

"Understandably," the CIA count cut in with slight irony. "Nobody is shooting poisoned darts in Washington."

Schulze turned to General McCory. "May I ask you, General, to strike the word *explosive* and substitute it with *hollow*."

The general seemed puzzled. "Just what do you mean by hollow?"

"Only the empty casing without the lead fill," Erich explained. "We can do the filling ourselves."

"With explosives?"

"Yes, sir—and forgo any possible objection in Washington." Erich resolved the problem with an innocent grin, drawing polite chuckles and repressed smiles.

Captain Dart spoke. "I'm sure that such bullets could be manufactured, but that might take time."

"Oh, we can wait." Erich persisted. "They'll come in handy later on."

General McCory shook his head. "Folks, you're irrepressible," he commented, his voice warm with pretended indignance. "General Houssong was right when he described Task Force-G as an indispensable wild bunch."

Schulze nodded. "We are, sir. But I doubt if you'd prefer to work with a bunch of rabbits."

Now even the general laughed as he waved a resigned hand. "I'll see what can be done about your slugs." He chuckled, shook his head, and reverted his attention to our list, only to look up again almost instantly.

"Two gliders with auxiliary engines and infrared photo equipment. . . . What the hell for?"

"You see, General, aerial observation is a vital element of the job we're doing," I explained. "The guerrillas are constantly on the move along the Ho Chi Minh trail, in the hills of South

Vietnam, on the rivers and canals of the delta. Only planes and copters can detect them, but unfortunately they make a lot of noise. The Viets hear them coming from afar and, by the time the pilots arrive, everything's safely hidden beneath the foliage. The gliders could sneak up on them and catch the monkeys with their hand in the sack."

"I understand."

"Personally, I consider it a sound idea," Major Cooke said. "But what's the engine for?"

Robertson said, "To gain altitude in the absence of upcurrents and for returning to base in windstill."

General McCory asked, "Do we have that sort of glider, Jeff?"

"Affirmative, General. Two-seaters, fitted with a forty-five-horsepower engine. That's about the power packed into a VW Beetle."

"And the infrared gadgets?"

"Available, sir."

I was elated. "In a month those gliders will cause the Vietcong more damage than a squadron of B-26s might do in half a year, General," I said enthusiastically.

"Okay. Let's see the rest." He turned back to our list. "Twelve scuba tanks, masks et cetera—one compressor," he read aloud. "The Vietcong has no navy."

"It does, sir," Schulze countered. "Four and a half gunboats armed with machine guns and two-inch cannons."

None of the Americans caught Erich's joke. Captain Dart asked, puzzled, "What do you mean by four and a half gunboats?"

"I mean that the fifth one was blown up by Lieutenant Krebitz," my friend replied with a grin. "Half of it sank, the bow with the pom-pom remained above the water. The guerrillas are using it as a fixed gun platform."

I took over. "The Vietcong have a large number of river transports, General, barges, sampans, rafts—some of them motorized. Normally they travel at night and lay by the bank camouflaged during the day because of the fighter and copter patrols. They would be extremely vulnerable to underwater attacks."

"Sounds sensible to me," Robertson commented.

"It is." Erich rammed the nail home. "The gliders would guide Task Force-G to the right place at the right time."

For some weeks both Erich and Krebitz had been nagging about the scuba gear, and I had the odd sensation that they were concocting something special and secret, a scheme in which the scuba equipment would play a great role. But whenever I made a pointed remark my query was brushed aside with evasive generalities. Erich's scheme must have had something to do with Captain Spata, whom he began to cultivate intensively, and the fact that the American used to be a chemistry lecturer had given me some ideas, none very sound or confirmable.

We left the meeting in excellent spirits. Lieutenant General Clint McCory and his fellow officers, especially Major Cooke, with his never-spent cigar, had made a good impression and substantially increased our optimism.

American assistance would certainly weigh heavily in the balance and could frustrate enemy designs. Naturally we did not expect immediate and significant changes for the better, with instant victories all over the map, but American help could certainly set back Hanoi's schedules and perhaps provide enough time for the Saigon government to form a cohesive army.

When we shook hands, CIA Count Robertson spoke in German for the first time. *"Also glueck auf!"*

We were astonished because during our previous encounters he spoke only English or French.

"Don't tell me that you're an Austrian!" Erich exclaimed, referring to Robertson's accent.

The CIA count answered with a smile, "My mother was—from Eisenstadt in the Burgenland."

"Why didn't you say so in the first place, instead of letting us sweat it out in English?" Riedl asked.

Robertson grinned. "First I wanted to eavesdrop a little on your private blabberings," he replied with good humor, and winked. "It goes with my job."

He shifted his eyes toward me and asked, "I hope you don't

mind my little, er—subterfuge, Hans? Anyway, you weren't double-dealing."

Pleasantly amused, I told him nonchalantly, *"Ganz Amerikanisch gesagt,* Jeff—chuck you, farlie."

PART TWO
The Commando of Death

10.

The Commando of Death

It was time to pay a visit to the Vietcong base of the combined guerrilla and North Vietnamese forces that had attacked Camp Dizier with armored and artillery support.

Task Force-G, 280 strong, left Saigon in a convoy of trucks, headed for Camp Dizier, which was to be our operational base. Colonel D'Arcy and his North Africans were no longer there but the new commanding officer, Colonel Ca Phan Cop of the South Vietnamese Army, received us cordially.

The fortified camp had been rebuilt and turned over to the Saigon government. It was now manned by two thousand local troops and a platoon of French paras.

We were accommodated in two comfortable wooden-stone barracks with separate two-berth officers' quarters with bathroom and shower, all very clean and modern.

Even a casual survey of the camp revealed ample evidence of U.S. help. The soldiers were carrying brand-new American automatic rifles, helmets, belts, canteens. We saw American machine guns, troop carriers, rapid-fire guns, howitzers, bazookas, tanks, and heavy mortars. The old guns of Fort Lafayette had been replaced with heavy six-inch ones, and the pillboxes were also fitted with multiple rocket launchers.

The South Vietnamese troops were young, cheerful, healthy fellows who seemed confident of the future. They must have heard of our Commando of Death before because they tried to make our sojourn there as comfortable as possible and did everything to please us.

Colonel Ca Phan Cop, a small, stubby man with a perpetual smile, proudly showed us around to demonstrate the important changes and improvements in Camp Dizier, now called Camp Liberty. He called our attention to six new pillboxes with one principal and three auxiliary gunports that enabled the crew to defend them against attack from any direction.

Fuel and ammunition had been placed in concrete-covered underground shelters. The fuel cisterns, too, were twenty feet below the surface and under concrete slabs.

The colonel showed us his pair of copters, parked inside deep earthenworks with sturdy overhead netting, removable with the help of winches.

There were three layers of steel-mesh nets with a twenty-inch gap between them. "Against mortar shells," the colonel said. The steel links should arrest the falling projectiles without exploding—his own idea, which we'd have liked to see in action. It was like World War I antitorpedo nets lowered into the sea along battleship hulls.

"No more Vietcong surprise attacks against Camp Liberty," the colonel stated firmly. "We have sentinels two miles from the camp in every direction. If the guerrillas want to try it again, they'll get a bloody nose. We are ready for them."

Extensive minefields with automatic signal devices, ten-foot-high barbed-wire coils, and antitank obstacles reinforced the defenses. Squat, concrete bunkers with no windows, only gun slits, replaced the earlier wooden watchtowers.

The camp seemed strong and threatening.

During lunch in the officers' mess we encountered several of the colonel's subalterns and also the commander of the French paratroop detachment, Major Charles Lapautre, with whom we had a pleasant chat. He invited us for a drink in the adjacent bar and introduced us his second, who, to our immense delight, was former lieutenant, now captain, Jean Marceau—one of the prisoners we'd liberated from a pestilential Vietminh pit in the jungle four years earlier. Needless to say, the happy event was celebrated with endless handshakes and toasts. Marceau recounted his miraculous escape from certain death, after months of miserable captivity, to his superior.

"When I asked for more food for the men, the Vietminh commander forced us to eat shit," he recalled. "He said it was a great distinction for the colonial pigs to eat shit of the Vietminh heroes. . . . But afterward they had their dinners too." He chuckled. "Remember, Hans? You made them chew up their leaflets, then gave them printing paint for pudding." He burst into guffaws. "If Wagemueller hadn't found us we would be all dead."

"Not quite, Marceau. It was Bernard Eisner who made the Commies reveal your dungeon."

"Oh, yes—Eisner . . . the fellow who blasted off the balls of a terrorist to make the others talk. What happened to him?"

"He died in action a few months later, Jean," Schulze said grimly.

Marceau's smile faded. "I am sorry to hear it," he said somberly. "He was a tough soldier."

"Yes, he was hard-hitting," I said.

"There was also a friendly Vietnamese with you—"

"Ghia Xuey, our guide. It was he who discovered your footprints in the first place."

"Is he with you?"

"No. Unfortunately we don't know where Xuey is. I wish we did."

Major Lapautre turned toward me. "What are you up to now, Captain Wagemueller?" he asked cheerfully. "Are you going to raise hell in Hanoi?"

I laughed softly. "Perhaps one day it will be Hanoi's turn to receive a visit from Task Force-G," I replied jokingly. "Father Ho is high up on our list. It's very tranquil up north."

"No wonder," Marceau commented. "Father Ho keeps all his troubles south of the seventeenth parallel."

"Where are you going from here?" Lapautre asked.

There were several Vietnamese officers at the table, so I preferred to ignore his query. "We'll talk about it later, Major," I said casually.

He nodded. "You're right. . . . Why don't you join in the evening for coffee or a drink?"

"Not here—"

"In my lodgings."

Bien sûr. Why not?"

Marceau asked, "What do you think of Camp Liberty?"

"To be frank, I'm not impressed," Krebitz said.

"Why not?"

"Bunkers, trenches, barbed-wire entanglements, artillery and minefields, while the neighboring heights are left for the enemy to climb. . . . Just like at Dien Bien Phu."

Marceau laughed. "Yes, come to think of it. . . . Where the Saigon troops cannot drive, they won't go. . . . The Amis made their life too comfortable with all those Jeeps, trucks, and troop carriers."

"Place a couple of guns and mortars up on those crests and you can shell the camp to smithereens," Krebitz added, shaking his head slowly. "Will these people ever learn anything from past debacles?"

"No, they won't," Major Lapautre said. "Not without a commanding general who is ready to learn himself, and no general would ever admit that his martial knowledge is wanting."

"True." Schulze nodded in assent. "What did Hitler learn from Stalingrad? From Voroniez or the *Kesselschlacht* at Kursk?"

In the evening, when we were alone with Lapautre and Marceau in the major's room, I informed him that we were after the Vietcong base that had attacked Camp Dizier. Major Lapautre, who had lost some eighty paras during that assault, became all fire and enthusiasm.

"You are about to realize our dream, Wagemueller." He beamed. "To carry the war to the jackal's own lair, which we were never permitted to do. There should be a haul across the border."

"So we hope. Artillery, rocket launchers, assault guns, tanks . . . lots of fuel and ammo."

"There must be a huge base somewhere in the western hills with a good road to the north," Erich added.

"In Cambodia," Major Lapautre stated with a nod. "In the hills of Ratanakiri."

"Are you sure?"

"If the North Vietnamese artillery and tanks are still there."

Krebitz said, "They never withdraw anything, only bring more. If the North Vietnamese outfit is still there, we'll find it."

Marceau said, "And when you set out for Cambodia, count us in."

Rather surprised, I asked Lapautre, "Do you intend to join the fray, Major?"

"Bien sûr, pourquoi pas?" he replied evenly. "Sure, why not?"

"Can you do that? I mean, your—"

"—superiors in Saigon?" He finished the sentence with a laugh. "They are too busy packing suitcases. I was sent here to protect the fort while it was being rebuilt. Now the job has been completed and, lacking other specific orders, I should say that we are free."

"Aren't you supposed to return to Saigon?"

Major Lapautre winked. "But we will be returning to Saigon. Who'd say anything against a small detour?"

"Through Cambodia?" Erich quipped.

"Sure." Krebitz grunted. "The Ho Chi Minh trail is supposed to be better and safer than many of our highways."

The prospect of having sixty veteran paras along pleased us.

After discussing the matter with Schulze, Riedl, and Krebitz, I decided to leave the Americans in the fort. I couldn't risk their falling prisoner to the Vietcong in Cambodia, which the Communists would surely exploit to the utmost, playing it right up to the United Nations and naturally the world press, with the properly prepared and signed "confessions." But when I suggested this to our friends, both men jumped at my throat and argued vehemently against it.

"Well, Hans, damn it—we'll leave our papers, ID badges, photos, and even personal letters in the custody of the colonel. We'll dress like any of you and even keep our last bullet. Dead men sign no confessions," Captain Spata proposed angrily.

I remained adamant. "I can't report to Houssong that you shot yourselves in order to avoid capture," I replied sternly. "My answer is still no."

At length, sulkily, the Americans resigned to my decision. Erich told them consolingly, "No one here doubts your courage, Mike, and we'd like to take you along. . . . Honestly we would. But think it over. Your government is trying to keep Cambodia and Laos independent and neutral as long as possible, and an incident would gravely jeopardize this aim. We're moving not against guerrillas but the Hanoi regulars. In the future, when we march into Cambodia or Laos to hit the Vietcong, with less risks involved, you'll come along. It isn't a question of not trusting your ability or resolution to face perils, only a matter of higher considerations."

Major Lapautre agreed with my decision. "If anything happened to *les Americains,* you'd be held responsible, *mon ami.* The President would be mad and Task Force-G might lose support."

He also agreed that it was prudent for me not to say anything about our destination in the officers' mess during the lunch. "Not that I distrust Colonel Ca Phan and his officers, whom I consider excellent companions, but—"

"Yes—*but*," I cut in quietly. "This *but* is omnipresent in Vietnam, Major. We learned the hard way that it's better to avoid it altogether. That's why we survived until now."

He nodded understandingly. "When do you intend to leave?"

"The day after tomorrow."

"In the morning?"

"Yes, at dawn—along Road nineteen."

"Toward Plei-kiu?"

"Only for some miles—until we're out of sight for curious eyes. Then we'll leave the highway and cut through the woods in the direction of Moc-den."

"A shortcut through the jungle?" he asked, his brows arching.

Erich unfolded his map. "We know an abandoned Vietminh trail here." He traced our planned route.

"It should be a hundred miles long," Captain Marceau commented thoughtfully.

"Eighty," Krebitz said. "As the crow flies. . . . I know that the paras think in miles flown, but across the hills and ravines it'll be closer to a hundred and fifty."

I asked Lapautre, "Are your paras up to such a long trek?"

"We marched three hundred miles through Laos to relieve the pressure on Dien Bien Phu," he replied. "My men are ready to jump into the fires of hell and they never complain."

"I wish there were ten divisions like you," Schulze remarked.

Major Lapautre smiled. "The same may be said of your commando. There would be no communism in North Vietnam now."

"In North Vietnam?" Riedl retorted exuberantly. "There'd be no Reds anywhere in Asia!"

"Don't exaggerate," Erich cracked. "We'd need a few more platoons to liberate China."

The following morning, Krebitz and twelve men of Gruppe Drei embarked on a long reconnaissance trip. Rudolf wanted to survey the place where the enemy tanks and assault guns had been stationed before the assault on Camp Dizier. Naturally the South Vietnamese had already examined the site on more than one occasion but I refrained from questioning either Colonel Ca Phan or his subordinates. It would have given them an idea about our destination.

Doing it the hard way, Krebitz and his men marched off. Riedl, who had been present during the assault and knew the place well, went along.

It was late in the afternoon when the reconnaissance party returned, soaked and muddy but quite content.

"We had a good look at the site," Krebitz said. "There's no road in the proper sense of the word. The assault guns and tanks came through the forest."

"We saw the traces of their slalom between the trees," Riedl cut in exuberantly, "uprooting those that couldn't be circumvented."

Months had passed since the attack but despite the monsoon rains and the fast-growing vegetation, Gruppe Drei was able to follow the grooves imprinted in the soggy soil by the heavy vehicles.

"We didn't go all the way to the Sé San," Krebitz told us, "but the tracks continue toward the river."

"They must have built a bridge," Schulze said thoughtfully.

"I can't recall seeing any bridge on the reconnaissance pictures," Jean Marceau said.

"It could have been removed after the withdrawal," Riedl suggested. "Or else it was built a foot under the surface."

"Aber sicher!" Erich exclaimed. "Like over the Sa Lo in the north. We caught the Vietminh marching across such a bridge," I explained.

All of us remembered the battle at the Sa Lo, in which Bernard Eisner died.

Krebitz continued, "It won't be difficult to find the site where the vehicles had crossed the river. The tracks are still visible."

Major Lapautre and Captain Marceau were in accord.

Lapautre said, "I think the expedition is less dangerous now than it would have been right after the Vietcong assault. Right then the enemy surely kept its way of retreat under surveillance, but five months is a long time."

"The camp might even be abandoned or relocated," Horst

Altreiter said. "Or else, if it's still there, it might be even larger now."

Krebitz said, "I'm sure that it's still there, crowded with armor and artillery, everything perfectly concealed in the jungle." He studied the map and traced an imaginary line with the tip of his forefinger. "The Laotian section of the Ho Chi Minh trail follows the course of the Sé Kong. It traverses the river below the confluence of the Sé Kong and the Sé Kamane, then continues southward into Cambodian territory—to Siem Pang —from where a dirt road runs across the Sé San to Ratanakiri."

He drew a circle with his pencil. "The base should be somewhere inside this circle!"

"I think so myself," Lapautre said.

Erich squared his shoulders. "If it is, then we're going to find it," he stated resolutely.

The next morning we left in the direction of Plei-kiu in the north, but once we were out of sight, Task Force-G and its paratroop reinforcement drew a semicircle toward Moc-den, then continued in the direction of the river Srépok, which flowed south of Ratanakiri. We moved by the compass, cutting our trail most of the time. Gruppe Drei was marching ahead, followed by Lapautre and Marceau with the paras. Schulze and I advanced four hundred yards behind them with Riedl and fifty troops making up the rear guard.

On this exceptional occasion our total strength came to 350 men; 16 heavy and 90 light machine guns, 120 submachine guns, 20 flamethrowers, and 30 light mortars, plus bazookas and hand grenades.

Task Force-G had never been so strong, and we looked forward to action with confidence.

Before Moc-den we hit rough terrain and our advance slowed down. There were canals and streams to traverse, thorny thickets to hack a path across, and steep acclivities to negotiate, but we remained out of sight to hostile eyes and did not encounter locals.

It took us three days to reach an offshoot of the Srépok River and cross into Cambodia southeast of Ratanakiri, where we bivouacked on a wooded crest.

Krebitz had lost his footing and tumbled into a fissure, spraining his left ankle. Zeisl advised him to rest for at least ten hours. To give Rudolf a break, Riedl and Karl Stolz marched off to reconnoiter the country, still following the old tank imprints. A couple of miles inside Cambodia the trial widened and revealed evidence of improvements. The tree stumps had been removed and depressions and muddy sections were paved with boulders and trunks.

According to the compass the road led toward the Stung Treng–Moc-den Road, which, if our calculations were correct, was six miles to the south.

There was a shallow stream, perhaps twelve feet wide, which the enemy armor had crossed and which Riedl's platoon negotiated without difficulty. This tributary of the Srépok merged with the Sé San farther west, to flow into the Mekong eighty miles away.

To Riedl's astonishment, a trail emerged from the tangle, six feet wide and running north. Here the enemy convoy had split. The tanks and assault guns continued along a southwesterly course, while the UAZ Jeeps and trucks had turned northward.

In order to save time, Helmut sent Stolz with five men to follow the tank tracks, while he surveyed the trail the trucks had taken. The two agreed to meet at the junction in about four hours, at 5:30 P.M.

Some instinct told Helmut that he had come close to an important discovery, so he scouted the guerrilla trail with redoubled attention. After some miles his platoon came to a small clearing, where the trail continued in a ravine, which disclosed the customary evidence of frequent human presence—discarded rubbish. He decided to leave the path and cut across the nearby hill.

Helmut's caution was richly rewarded. To his astonishment, from the crest he could see a large, quadrangular army camp.

Guardhouses, barracks of wood and stone, a cluster of tents, a few trucks, and the turret of a tank—everything was hidden beneath the rich foliage.

He found the camp of the enemy armor and artillery.

To avoid the risk of alerting the enemy, Riedl overcame a strong desire to creep closer and gather details. Rudolf Krebitz would know better how to do it. Instead, he retraced his steps and marched back to the junction, where he found Stolz and his men already having dinner. Stolz had pushed all the way where the road to Siem Pang linked up with the Stung–Moc-den motorway.

"The tanks went in the direction of Siem Pang," Stolz reported. "There's a guardhouse with barrier at the junction, manned by Cambodian regulars."

The two men exchanged experiences and compared distances on the map. Riedl concluded that somewhere six to eight miles distant from the bridge across the Sé San, there must be a deviation into the North Vietnamese base he had spotted earlier. He computed the approximate site of the camp, then the reconnaissance party embarked on its long trip back to Task Force-G. Darkness caught them in the woods and going became difficult. Because the men needed a good rest after having covered some twenty-four miles during the day, Riedl decided to bivouac for the night.

Wireless silence was the order of the day, but short, prearranged signals were permitted at intervals. Stolz sent us the "everything's okay," which relieved us of our day-long state of anxiety.

Daybreak found us on the trail. We met Riedl's party on a wooded hillock overlooking the stream.

Helmut excitedly briefed us on the situation, and the discovery of the enemy base fired us with enthusiasm. Krebitz, who insisted that he was all right now, wanted to have a closer look at the jungle installations and prepare a rudimentary scheme of them. He chose Jost Waldman, Julius Steiner, Paul Kretz, and ten men from Gruppe Drei, apart from Riedl, who knew the way and who volunteered to make the trip again. Captain Marceau and six paras wanted to go along and, since it was a joint venture, I willingly consented.

"Don't make any move before I return," Krebitz advised me before leaving. "And don't worry about us either. It might be a long trip and perhaps we'll stay overnight. If this is the camp we want, the enemy will be strong in armor and artillery and our plan must be perfect. The element of surprise must be absolute."

We shared his view, and Marceau said jokingly, "Rudolf is like a good paratrooper who would never jump into the great unknown."

"There's no place to jump there anywhere," Riedl commented. "You'd all land on the treetops."

Krebitz and his party left and we decided to set up our base right where we were, and prepare the equipment for the coming assault. The troops rigged up their burlaps between the lower branches and began to sort out their gear, setting aside what was to be left behind, mostly provisions and spare clothes. The paratroops had done likewise and deposited their personal belongings, documents, and army tags. Major Lapautre was familiar with our "game rules," one of which prescribed that no corpses should be left behind.

The North Vietnamese, Chinese, and Russians could trespass in the Republic of Vietnam, but should there be a single French corpse or prisoner for international display, the Communists would start yelling their heads off, about "the latest French violation of the armistice and aggression against neutral Cambodia."

Communist arrogance and double-dealing knew no limits. They would lie the sun out of the sky and try to convince anyone who cared to listen that black was white and mortar shells were only white doves of peace. And unfortunately, to the world at large, Father Ho was the brave leader of a small, underdeveloped nation that had been oppressed by the Japanese and French colonialists, abused and exploited for decades. Naturally there would be no mention of the small, insignificant details such as roads, bridges, hospitals, and schools built by the French, without whose presence most of the natives would still be dull-witted illiterates.

The hordes of Father Ho had never built anything. They had only destroyed.

The full moon shone high in the night sky when Krebitz beeped his recognition signal to our perimeter sentries and reentered into the camp: a line of soft-moving shadows with faces and hands blackened and boots wrapped in rags to deaden sound.

Krebitz, Riedl, and Marceau wanted to discuss the result of their trip immediately, but I stopped Riedl's exuberant opening with a raised hand.

"Have your dinner first," I suggested. "The enemy camp's

been there for quite some time and the Viets won't be leaving now."

"The camp is crawling with Hanoi regulars," Marceau exulted. "Fourteen tanks, twenty semi-track assault guns, forty UAZ trucks, some with howitzers hitched behind—"

"Everything neatly lined up, Hans," Helmut cut in. "Ready to be blown to hell."

"Let's hear, Rudolf."

Krebitz took over. "Well, we made it all around the perimeter," he said between bites and gulps from his canteen. "It's a North Vietnamese outfit all right, well housed in wooden barracks and thirty-eight tents."

He spread a diagram on the slab of stone we used for a table. Schulze and Stolz illuminated it with their hooded battery torches.

"Here!" Krebitz continued, pointing. "Headquarters, telecommunications barracks, officers quarters. . . . Over here, semiburied fuel and ammunition dumps. . . . At first we followed the Jeep trail, which leads to the southern entrance. On the right side are water cisterns with a pipe running to the stream. There's a small pump house here."

"What are the dots?"

"Latrines," Krebitz replied. "Outside the enclosure. The main entrance is here, facing west, with a dirt road to the Siem Pang highway and the village of Vo-sai on the river Sé San."

"How far is the village?" Erich asked.

"Six miles, I'd say. We couldn't go that far, but there's a phone line connecting the guardhouse with the camp and probably with some other installations near the village."

"Probably," Shulze said. "They wouldn't leave the bridge without protection. Perhaps there's a guardhouse."

"Or another camp," I interposed.

Studying the map, Major Lapautre traced a way toward Laos. "This is probably the road the vehicles took from North Vietnam to Cambodia," he said. "Siem Pang, Ban Phone, Chephone, and Quang Binh above the demarcation line. The base is certainly a permanent one, and Hanoi considers it immune against attack."

"They sure do," Krebitz agreed. "The camp has hooded electric lights and the watchtowers are fitted with searchlights."

"How many watchtowers?" I asked.

"Six. They're all below the treetop level."

"Against aerial reconnaissance," Schulze commented.

"The whole camp is concealed under the trees," Krebitz said. "You can't see a damned thing from above. Not even from the nearby hills."

I asked, "What about the approaches?"

"Excellent," Riedl replied. "Forested hills on every side with tall grass and shrubs right up to the perimeter wires."

"Barbed coils?"

He shook his head. "Simple wire mesh."

I turned toward Krebitz. "Minefields?"

"No mines, no traps."

Major Lapautre cut in. "The bastards must feel themselves at home in Cambodia."

"They *are* at home," Erich replied. "It's Ho Chi Minh who runs the country, and the fact that Hanoi prefers to maintain Cambodia independent and neutral for the time being is only a part of his grand strategy. For one thing, it keeps the French air force away from the Vietcong communications and permits a lace of bases near the border for the eventual invasion of South Vietnam."

"Sicher," Riedl said. "Should Father Ho ever capture Saigon, independent Cambodia wouldn't last for a year."

"Six months," Erich corrected him. "Nor would Laos survive. Hanoi's dreaming of a Southeast Asian empire."

Lapautre turned toward Krebitz. "Any suggestion how to attack?"

Rudolf nodded. "By dusk, along the entire perimeter," he said, leaning over the map. "With mortars on the eastern hills we may wreck the installation, then move in from every direction at the same time. Here." He drew our attention to some marks. "Tanks and trucks lined up in rows."

"A swift assault with bazookas and flamethrowers could wipe out the lot," Stolz said.

"If the tanks are ready to roll, I would spare a couple of them," Erich stated, drawing curious glances.

"What for?" Stolz queried.

Schulze replied, "You ask? You were a tank driver yourself.

Won't it be fun to go on the rampage with some T-34s and Stalins?"

Stolz laughed. "I'm game, Erich."

"May I continue, gentlemen?" Krebitz cut in.

Erich threw out his hands. "But of course, Rudy. Go ahead."

Krebitz turned his attention to the scheme. "There shouldn't be much infantry in the camp," he went on. "Thirty-eight tents, each capable of accommodating about six men, should make around one hundred and eighty, probably tank and assault gun crews and artillery men. There might be two platoons of infantry to man the guardhouses, watchtowers, and gun emplacements."

"Where are they?" Lapautre asked.

"Along the dirt road," Marceau replied.

To Krebitz, Schulze said, "I'll take care of the northern sector. Gruppe Drei should pin down the crews and prevent them from reaching the tanks."

"That's exactly what I intend to do." Krebitz nodded.

Erich scanned the scheme. "Not much infantry, eh?"

Riedl chuckled. "Even the size of their latrines confirms that," he said with a grin. *"Sitzbank mit vierzehn Loecher.* Accommodation for fourteen assholes. Of course, the top cadre asses have private outhouses inside the compound."

With the help of Krebitz's design we drew up an assault plan.

Krebitz with Gruppe Drei, Schulze with seventy-five men, and Riedl with sixty troops were to move along the stream, knock out the pump house, and set up the mortars on the eastern and northern elevations. Erich should move into attack position against the parked tanks and semi-tracks, while Riedl would attack the fuel dump and the main entrance. Major Lapautre's paratroops were to strike the guardhouses and MG emplacements along the dirt road, cut the phone line, and destroy the ammunition depo. With the rest of the men, I would strike the camp from the south.

The general assault would begin at a red flare.

We marched off at 4:15 A.M., and by 7:00 our thirty mortars were in position and the five assault groups had occupied their respective stations.

We broke radio silence for the first time to confirm mutual readiness. At 7:12 A.M. I told Jost Waldman to fire the flare.

Like our previous surprise attacks, this, too, triggered instant confusion. By some freak chance the first ranging shots landed on top of the communications barracks and blew it apart, and afterward it began to rain fire and steel, as all thirty mortars opened up, hitting the barracks, headquarters, parked howitzers, and tents. At the same time Sculze blasted the two northern guardhouses and a section of the wire-mesh fence, and his troops began to demolish the armored vehicles with bazookas and flamethrowers, while a thunderous detonation, swiftly rising flames, and smoke announced that Riedl had reached his primary objective, the fuel dump.

My hundred troops poured slugs into the collapsing tents, now abuzz with scantily clad Vietcong and Hanoi regulars. Tracers, incendiaries, and explosive bullets raked the entire camp. Half-crazed soldiers poured into the open from the collapsed tents and barracks and ran blindly in every direction. The guardhouses and machine-gun nests were knocked out. Perforated by hundreds of slugs, the water cisterns spilled their contents onto the sloping ground where, mixed with burning gasoline and diesel fuel from the wrecked trucks, it flowed toward the center of the camp, engulfing more vehicles and the field artillery.

In the meantime Major Lapautre and Captain Marceau's paras occupied the guardhouses and MG positions along the dirt road, cut the phone wires, and blasted a trench across the road to prevent the escape of tanks or trucks. This precaution proved unnecessary, for Erich was already in possession of the parked armor and was busy disabling them, save for a pair of Josef Stalins.

From the underbrush Krebitz's sharpshooters knocked down the bewildered runners and the few who tried to resist.

I called a halt to the mortar bombardment over the walkie-talkie, for we were already inside the camp and ready to demolish what was still standing. My men stormed across the tent complex, already flattened by the shells and burning, corpses littering the passageways. Krebitz had captured the camp commander, a Hanoi major, and his aide-de-camp, a captain. The rest of the officers were already dead, together with most of their troops.

We converged in the center of the camp where Major Lapautre and a few of his paras joined us. Happily enough, none of the five assault teams had suffered losses, as the enemy had no time to organize any coherent defense. Nor could the enemy escape—the entire perimeter was covered by the paras and Gruppe Drei. Half an hour later fighting inside the camp gradually stopped but the fray continued around the Siem Pang road.

Unexpectedly it gained intensity.

Unknown to us, a Vietcong infantry camp lay next to the village, on the far side of the river. It had been alerted, perhaps by wireless. It must have been a large camp, for the paras, left to guard the bunkers and MG emplacements, reported the arrival of twenty truckloads of guerrillas who spread out along the road and tried to advance. Lapautre and Marceau were about to board a UAZ truck to drive back to the junction when Schulze stopped them.

"Try to block the junction, Major, and tell your men to hold their fire when they see a couple of Josef Stalins coming up. They'll be ours!"

"Magnifique," the major responded. Marceau slipped behind the steering wheel, their escort of paras jumped aboard, and they drove off.

"Go and fetch those tanks," I said to Erich. "On the double."

Summoning Karl Stolz and Jost Waldman, Schulze hurried toward the burning motor pool.

I called Riedl. "How many trucks are serviceable, Helmut?"

"Four."

"Get your men together and hurry to the junction. The paras will need a hand."

"What's the big shooting out there?"

"Enemy reinforcements from a camp in the village."

"Scheisse!" He spat. "How many?"

"Twenty truckloads."

"That might be anything up to four hundred Viets."

Distant unmistakable detonations interrupted our discourse. Krebitz came running with Steiner and Paul Kretz in tow.

"Those are artillery shells!" he shouted.

An instant later Captain Marceau called over the walkie-talkie. "We have some assault guns to tackle, Hans. Do you have any bazookas left?"

"I'm sending you something more substantial than bazookas," I told him. "Schulze is taking off with a pair of Stalins."

"Bless him!" Marceau exclaimed. "He should hurry up."

"Can you hold on?"

"For a while—sure, but it's getting hot here. We haven't got any grenades left, but fortunately the Viets don't know that."

With some troops from Gruppe Drei squatting or sitting on the rear and front armor, the two heavy Josef Stalin tanks rumbled through the camp gate. Behind them rolled three trucks with Riedl's men, carrying bazookas. Schulze and Stolz, standing in the turrets, waved.

"See you later!" Erich shouted over the din of engines and tracks.

The convoy disappeared in the direction of the junction. I turned to Krebitz. "I must know the number of guerrillas in that riverside camp and their equipment. Where are the camp commander and his adjutant?"

"I locked them up in one of the officers' latrines," Rudolf replied. "That's the only barracks still standing."

"Bring them here."

The Hanoi major and captain were brought forward.

"How many Vietcong are in the camp near the village?" I asked without preliminaries.

"Enough to wipe you out, fascist brigands," the major retorted, sneering. Otto Janaschek's heavy backhand blow sent him reeling. He staggered against Rudolf, who grabbed him by his lapels and drew his bayonet.

"Listen, you red bastard, we have no time for mutual courtesies. How many guerrillas are in the village and what equipment do they have?"

Sullen, contemptuous silence. Krebitz repeated his question, waited, then his right fist jerked forward, plunging the bayonet into the camp commander's groin. With a bewildered look in his eyes the major gasped, paled, clutched at himself, and sank to the ground. Coolly, Krebitz wiped the blade in the adjutant's jacket and said, "Perhaps you want to be more reasonable, *tovarich.*"

"E-eight hundred," the captain stuttered. "Six assault vehicles. . . . Trucks and Jeeps with machine guns."

"What else?"

The captain shook his head. "Nothing else."

The camp commander was still groaning in agony. Krebitz drew his pistol and shot him through the head.

"Your Radio Hanoi is calling us the Commando of Death," he said to the captain in a voice of ice. "That's all you'll ever get from us—death! But you were reasonable and we'll let you go. Return to Hanoi and tell what you have seen here. There'll be more such spectacles. Many more."

He turned to the guards. "Take him back to the latrine until we're about to leave, then let him go."

The adjutant was led away. I spoke to Rudolf. "Demolish everything, then return into our camp, Rudy."

He stared. "What about you, Hans?"

"I'm going to give Lapautre a hand."

"But the real fray has just begun," he protested.

"And you're out of it, together with Gruppe Drei. You've already done more than your share and your ankle needs a rest." I noticed that he was limping.

"But—"

"No but." I spun him around. *"En avant marchez!"*

"Jawohl."

He limped away, hollering at his troops. I assembled my group and marched off toward the junction. By the time we arrived the sounds of the battle had moved northward. I saw the burnt-out shells of two assault guns and a string of wrecked trucks. Major Lapautre and Captain Marceau were waiting for me in front of the battered guardhouse.

"The Viets are escaping toward the river," Lapautre informed me. "Schulze and Riedl are pursuing them, but it was tight here before the tanks came."

"Casualties?"

The major's face clouded. "Five dead and sixteen wounded . . . some seriously."

"Did you call Zeisl?"

"He's already attending them."

"If I can be of any more help, don't hesitate to ask."

"We could use the trucks to transport our wounded."

"To Camp Dizier?"

"Why not?" Captain Marceau asked. "There's a road."

RECALL TO INFERNO

I shrugged. "You're right. If the North Vietnamese could use it, why shouldn't we?"

A UAZ Jeep with a sergeant and a pair of paras tore down the road, raising a cloud of dust. They came to a skidding stop. The sergeant sprang from the driver's seat and saluted.

"The Viets are fleeing toward the Laotian border," he reported, addressing Lapautre; then, turning toward me, he added with a conspiratorial grin, "Your men are raising hell in Vo Sai with those tanks, Captain."

"I can well imagine it," I replied flatly. "May I borrow your Jeep?"

"Certainly, sir."

I slipped behind the steering wheel, beckoned Altreiter and Steiner to join me, then burned rubber toward the river. The six-mile stretch of dirt road disclosed ample evidence of Erich's handiwork: three more demolished assault guns, five wrecked trucks and overturned trailers, scores of corpses on and around the road.

As we approached the river, we heard the heavy rumble of tank engines but no shooting or detonations. I stopped on the bridge, where the high arch provided a good view of the north bank. A few hundred yards to the right the Vietcong camp was in shambles. Piles of smoldering rubble. The guardhouse at the bridge had been blown into the river and a platoon of Cambodian regulars were sitting under guard.

Riding in the Stalin tanks, Erich and Karl Stolz were having a merry romp in the village, driving through the houses and gardens, leveling everything in sight but ignoring the scattering population. I actually saw them halt and wait until some locals moved their laden carts out of harm's way or salvaged their bundles, razing the dwellings only afterward.

Noticing me, Erich drove up to the bridge and shouted from the turret. "It seems that we settled the account for Camp Dizier, Hans."

"With interest," I hollered back. "But what the hell are you razing the village for?"

He shrugged. "I thought we should teach the natives that if they accommodate the Vietcong they might be looking for trouble."

"Bullshit! They can't do a damn about the Vietcong."

Schulze threw out his hands. *"Alles in Ordnung,* Hans. The tanks are Hanoi's property. Phnom Penh may send a protest note to Father Ho."

"All right, now finish your game and return to the junction. Do you have enough fuel?"

"I got an extra five hundred gallons from the guerrilla camp."

"Sehr gut. We'll be driving back to Camp Dizier."

"Das ist aber nett, Hans," he replied. "That's kind of you."

"We have some wounded who must be transported."

"How many trucks?"

"Four."

"I think we have two more. Also some Jeeps."

"Bring everything to the junction, Erich."

"What about the tanks?" he asked.

"Blow them up," I replied without thinking.

"Kuhscheiss, Hans. Why not keep them?"

I waved a hand. "Keep them for all I care, but move!"

I drove back to the junction. Twenty minutes later Erich and Stolz arrived with the tanks, leading three trucks and a few UAZ Jeeps. Lapautre asked with a laugh, "What do you plan to do with those *chars*? You can't sell them on the black market."

"Perhaps I'll present them to Colonel Ca Phan, or else we drive them back to Saigon."

"The tracks will be worn flat by the time you get there," Marceau cracked.

"Where's Rudolf?" Schulze asked.

"I sent him back to our camp." Then, speaking to Riedl and Altreiter, I added, "You should drive down there with the Jeeps and take Krebitz and our luggage to the Moc-den road."

"We blew up the Sé San bridge," Stolz announced casually.

"Good! It should keep them busy for a week."

"Our personal present to Giap," Schulze added.

By 6 P.M. we were across the border and past Moc-den, driving merrily along the colonial road toward Camp Liberty, with Gruppe Drei's men sitting astride on the tank turrets and the armor. The colonel almost keeled over when he saw the two heavy tanks with North Vietnamese insignias roll into the fort with a string of vehicles in tow.

Schulze and Stolz sprang from the turrets. Making a sweeping gesture toward the tanks, Erich said to the flabbergasted commander, "A present for you, sir. . . . With the compliments of Task Force-G. The next time the Vietcong shows up you may give them the shake of their lives."

The stolen trucks and Jeeps we used for transport back to Saigon. "You may keep them," General Houssong told me over drinks. "The vehicles are your legitimate booty of war."

Krebitz, Stolz, and Riedl sold the lot to some local landlords for a fair amount of cash. It would have been difficult to get spares for them.

A couple of weeks later we learned from intelligence reports that our raid had cost Hanoi around $4 million in destroyed war matériel and 1,200 casualties.

11.

The Destruction of Bin Xuyen

The year of 1955 began with trouble in France, in Vietnam, and along the seas of China. After a long-drawn-out political skirmish in Paris, French President Coty had finally named a prime minister, Monsieur Mendès-France. The new government didn't last long. It collapsed after a month. For ten days France remained without a government. The prolonged political crisis fostered Socialist ideals, represented by the new government of Christian Pineau, whose nomination stirred little enthusiasm in Saigon's military circles.

By then it was well established that the Socialists should begin their social reforms by scaling down the supplies to the armed forces, quite regardless of international political circumstances or military situations. Random nationalization of important industries would be the order of the day, upsetting production and delivery. Lieutenant General Houssong and his aides seemed vastly relieved when, only one day after its nomination, the National Assembly voted no confidence in Pineau's cabinet of four Socialist ministers.

"It's good news, Wagemueller," Houssong told me exuberantly after the evening radio newscast. "I prefer not having a government at all to having a Socialist one. Socialism is the first step toward communism. Pineau might have a great deal of goodwill, but his ministries would have been penetrated by Communist plants in a few weeks."

When the radical government of Edgar Fauré gained parliamentary confidence, the sighs of relief in Saigon must have been audible all the way to Paris.

Good-for-nothing Emperor Bao Dai was spending most of his time on the French Riviera, leaving the affairs of the state in the hands of interim prime minister Ngo Dinh Diem. The people of both Vietnams were still looking forward to the general elections to determine the nation's future.

But neither Ho Chi Minh nor Diem wanted free elections, which were specified by the terms of armistice. Being in firm control of their part of Indochina, the Communists did not need them, and the Saigon regime could not afford them. It hadn't done a thing to improve the lot of the population. Diem's position was certainly not enviable. Apart from being obliged to resist unceasing aggression from the north, Saigon itself was on the verge of turmoil. The prime minister, a plump little man who waddled like Donald Duck and whose principal preoccupation was to establish a sort of Ngo Dinh dynasty with family hegemony over the Republic of Vietnam, would never even dream of fostering even rudimentary social reforms, especially for the benefit of the impoverished peasantry. In reality, Diem was governed by his brother, Nhu—a lithe man of fragile stature, perhaps the Martin Borman of Saigon. For some reason, Nhu found it very entertaining to persecute the Buddhist priesthood, which turned them into devoted enemies. In fact, he excelled in turning not only the priests and the illiterate masses but also the educated intelligentsia into Communist sympathizers.

And both top men in Saigon were dominated by Nhu's introverted, boundlessly ambitious, and cynical wife, who already fancied herself empress of Vietnam.

The dissatisfaction was skillfully exploited by the local version of the Sicilian Mafia, the so-called Society of Bin Xuyen, which controlled hundreds of local enterprises and much of the city vice through a two-thousand-member army of local thugs.

For all practical purpose the Bin Xuyen was already a state within the state. The organization paid no taxes, ignored the law, collected monthly ransom from thousands of small businesses that wished to survive; it made and unmade district officials, judges, prosecutors, police officers, and had even managed to infiltrate into the armed forces through General Van Vien, the Minister of Public Security. Through the good offices of Vien a large number of local police stations had fallen under Bin Xuyen control. The suburb of Cholon was completely subject to the local warlords, so much so that Bin Xuyen gangsters were maintaining checkpoints side by side with the local police.

There were also two militant and fanatical religious sects, the Cao Dai and the Hao Hoa, both deeply rooted in ancient feudalistic traditions and both ardent opponents of social reforms, which they considered a threat to their existence. For the moment the two sects were quiet, much like steam under the lid, waiting for the inevitable showdown between the government and the Bin Xuyen. They were waiting to see who won before deciding which side to take.

Karl Stahnke had long suspected the existence of some tender link between the Saigon underworld and the Vietcong, thus Hanoi. "Economical and political gangsters can work well together," I remember him saying once. "The Bin Xuyen works toward internal upheaval, which suits Hanoi's long-range plans."

While scouting in the marshlands of Cao Lanh, near the Mekong, we captured a sampan with seven crates containing submachine guns, rifles, mortars with shells, and ammunition. The four locals on board could not have loaded the heavy crates. Krebitz was sure that they were only carriers, simple boatmen, who hauled freight against payment. This fact was verified through their subsequent and none-too-gentle interrogation. After a couple of punches and some tickling with the bayonet, the owner of the sampan confessed that they had received the shipment at Tan Chan, a village close to the Cambodian frontier, in exchange for a small parcel wrapped in oilcloth, obviously money. Schulze wanted to know who had delivered the crates on board. The owner had no idea. "Some local people, I think," he replied evasively but Krebitz quickly refreshed his memory, and when Erich asked, "What do you think now?" the owner thought they were some Vietcong.

The crates were to be shipped down the Mekong, then through a tributary and some canals to My-tho, where a couple of men from Saigon would be waiting with a refrigerator truck marked Ca Ban Meat Company.

At first none of us doubted that the weapons were destined for the local Vietcong. I sent a coded message to Karl Stahnke and asked him to meet us in My-tho. We decided that Krebitz, Stolz, Altreiter, and Jost Waldman should change into local garb and accompany the barge to its destination.

By the time we arrived, Stahnke had already seized the truck. The driver and his six companions were driven into his headquarters in the Des Mares camp, together with the crates and the meat-company vehicle. The sampan's owner and his companions were permitted to leave.

Schulze and myself were present at the "interrogations." First the prisoners were stripped naked by a pair of burly *Mitarbeitern*—Stahnke's assistants—Herr Wachtel and Herr Rosner, who wore only training slacks, gym shoes, and T-shirts. A third hulk of muscles, Herr Stoppel, sat on a low stool, toying with a rubber truncheon. His expression was one of sheer boredom.

Herr Wachtel placed papers and pencils on a long table with bench and said stiffly, "Name, address, place of work, name of your *Schweinhund* commander, and his address. Who gave you the money for the shipment and where?" He pursed his fleshy lips and added with chilly emphasis, "Every single lie—ten minutes of physical exercise in the care of Herr Stoppel."

The prisoners stared, dumbfounded and terrified. Three of them began to write but stopped after a few lines. Others could not write at all. Suddenly Herr Rosner and Wachtel were on top of them, jerking them to their feet, shouting, *"Marsch raus!* Outside!"

The protesting group of bewildered locals was herded into an adjacent chamber with iron hooks and chains hanging along the filthy, blood-splattered walls and sinister-looking instruments lying on wooden racks. Herr Stoppel began swearing. "You goddamned red bastards of Father Ho," he shouted as he tossed the prisoners to Rosner, who in turn forwarded them to Herr Wachtel, each delivering a few hard punches and kicks, hollering all the while.

"Verdammte Terroristen!"

"Communist bastards!"

"Fuckin' red whoresons!"

Amid vicious punches, blows, and kicks.

Herr Wachtel shouted, "Some of you Ho Chi Minh scum can't even write, but you understand the language of the machine gun, don't you? . . . Now you should sing about weapons and ammunition, about the local Hanoi cadres, about your training. . . . You'll either sing *Scheisskerle* or have your balls poached like eggs before getting a slug between your eyes."

The prisoners began to sob and protest even more vehemently against being called Communists and Vietcong. Their protests were quickly silenced by more blows, as the brawny threesome got down to real business. The catch-as-catch-can between the walls began with the incessantly cursing hulks chasing their screaming adversaries.

Shrieks, yells, and desperate pleas were to no avail. The "vulcanizing" continued.

Smoking a cigarette, Stahnke said casually, "I know that our prisoners are not Vietcong but belong to the Bin Xuyen gang, which is planning to raise hell in Saigon and very soon."

At the end of the softening-up process, the prisoners were barely able to move. Lying in their own muck—a mixture of blood, excreta, and urine—every one of them confessed that a large-scale uprising in Saigon would take place in two days' time, led by the Bin Xuyen, backed by rebellious government troops and also by the Vietcong.

Stahnke studied them closely, then—with instinct born of experience—he selected a shallow-cheeked, sinewy individual, a certain Na Bhan Nhom, and told us in German, "He's the weakling of the lot."

He summoned Herr Stoppel. "Take the fellow into my office."

Herr Stoppel stared. "He's all blood and shit."

"You have a water hose, haven't you?"

"Ja—natuerlich, boss."

Stahnke beckoned me to follow him upstairs where he offered us some drinks.

"I've been expecting this," he said equably. "Any day now. . . . There are one hundred and sixty-three police stations in and around Saigon. Ninety of them are controlled by the Bin Xuyen." He waved a hand. "No wonder with General Van Vien in charge of public security. It's like giving the beef to the wolf to guard."

"Van Vien should have ceded his office to Colonel Ngoc Lee this morning," I said.

"Alas, he did not. Instead he posted armed sentries around his ministry."

There was a knock on the door. Herr Stoppel brought the prisoner in, now washed, dressed, and patched up but shaking like a leaf.

"Let him have a chair," Stahnke said curtly.

Stoppel pulled over a chair and pushed the man onto it, grunting. "If you shit on the carpet I'll plug your ass with the cork of a twenty-gallon keg. . . . Don't twist your damned neck around—I'm here. Sit still!"

Stahnke rose, circled his desk, swung another chair in front of his desk, and sat down. "Cigarette?"

"If—if I may . . ." the prisoner muttered, astonished.

Karl gave him a cigarette and lighted it, then leaned back, crossed his legs, and spoke in a quiet, balanced voice. *"Also mein Junge,* I am Uncle Stahnke, the chief confessor around here. By nature I am curious but also impatient. . . . Watch whatever you're going to tell me because one single lie will take you back into the cellar and this time through a one-way door. . . . When will the rebellion begin?"

"The day after tomorrow" came the thin-voiced response.

"Sir," Karl reminded him, stressing the word. "We are very courteous people here."

"Yes—sir."

"So is better. At what time?"

"Around noon, sir."

"Where?"

"They plan to open fire against the Palace of Independence, sir."

"That's Diem's office," Karl commented, then turned back to the prisoner. "With what?"

"With some mortars."

"How many mortars?" Stahnke raised his voice. "Look, son, don't make me use a winch to drag out your words."

"There should have been fifteen mortars, sir."

"But now there'll be only nine because we captured six."

"Yes, sir. . . ."

"What else will be attacked?"

"I—I don't know, sir."

"Do you want to return downstairs?"

"No, sir. . . . Please no." The fellow pleaded, wringing his hands. "Honest to God, I don't know. We were assigned to fetch the crates and deliver them to Monsieur Thy at the meat company. . . . The lords would never tell us anything important."

"The lords, eh?" Stahnke said with a nod. "Who is Thy?"

"The warehouse manager. Hon Thuy Thy."

Karl rose, signaling the end of the questioning. "Herr Stoppel. Take the fellow back in his cell."

"His cell? *In Ordnung.*" With a heavy hand he pulled the prisoner to his feet. *"Komm, Ferkel."* He ushered Bhan toward the door, calling him piglet.

The man fidgeted and shifted. "Please, sir," he said to Stahnke. "I don't know anything else. . . . Don't beat me again."

"You're going into your cell. If you told me the truth, you'll be free in a few days."

He sat down behind his desk and called General Houssong's aide. "Lieutenant Berger, do you know anything about a certain Hon Thuy Thy, working with the Ca Ban Meat Company?"

"No, the name's unknown to me but I can ask Captain Dessault."

"Please do."

After some minutes Berger was back on the line. "Hon Thuy Thy is a former police commissar on pension."

"Did he work with the Cholon precinct?"

"Correct. How did you know?"

"I guessed."

Berger said, "The Ca Bán company is run by the Bin Xuyen people but the former Minister of Public Security owns thirty-five percent of the shares."

"General Van Vien?"

"Oui."

"Why did you say former?"

"Van Vien was cashiered two hours ago," Berger said. "By the order of Diem."

"Do you happen to know where he is now?"

"At home, I presume. Why?"

"It's too long a story to tell it over the phone. Is General Houssong in his office?"

"Until four in the afternoon."

"Please advise him that I'm coming over with Wagemueller and Schulze to discuss a very urgent matter."

"Straight away. Is it about the rebellion?"

"That's right. It'll begin at noon the day after tomorrow."

"Come on over."

"One more thing, Berger. Who's the head of the Ca Ban company?"

"Wait a moment." There was another short pause, then Berger said, "Chairman Thiu My Lanh."

"Thanks a lot."

Stahnke replaced the phone, rubbed his hands together, and announced exuberantly, "My friends, the big machine of Uncle Stahnke begins to roll." He called his three gorillas.

"Herr Rosner, go and find out where the chairman of the Ca Ban company, Thiu My Lanh, lives."

"Jawohl—and then?"

"Then get down to work."

"Ausradieren?" Rosner asked. "Erasing?"

"I want Thiu here in one piece—tonight! But do it with the utmost discretion."

"Sehr gut. Es wird gemacht," Rosner replied. "It'll be done."

After the burly trio left, Karl said, "You know, they aren't only brawn and no brains, Hans. The fellows are quite clever and absolutely reliable. You give them the most impossible order and they'll figure a way to carry it out."

"Where did you get them, Karl?" I asked with a chuckle. "Are they old Gestapo buddies?"

"Ex-policemen—worked with the criminal police of Munich during the war. I recruited them straight from Germany."

"How the hell?" Schulze blurted, puzzled.

Stahnke smiled. "Through the friendly intervention of some old Gestapo buddies," he answered with good humor.

Herr Stoppel and company were indeed efficient. The same evening they had sequestered the chairman together with his Citroen limousine, driver, and four armed bodyguards, right in front of Thiu's mansion in Cholon.

Handcuffed and blindfolded, the chairman and his entourage were driven to Stahnke's "laboratory of truth" and locked in separate cells.

Stoppel reported, "Monsieur Thiu is in the cooler, together with his driver and four other shitheads."

"That's good," Karl said, rubbing his hands. "The machine is rolling. . . . Anyone see you?"

"The gatekeeper and a guard inside the park."

"That's bad!"

Stoppel shook his head. "Not bad, dead!" he retorted, a grin spreading over his heavy-boned cheeks. "Both of them."

"That's good again. Now go and have dinner."

Karl suggested that we should dine, too, then have a chat with Thiu.

The chairman of the meat company was close to sixty, and it wasn't necessary to persuade him to sing. He sang voluntarily. As a member of high standing in the Bin Xuyen organization, he could sing the kind of tunes Stahnke liked to hear. Thiu's revelations were of utmost importance and urgency. By morning Karl was able to forward a thirty-page report to Captain Dessault with a copy for the commander of the expeditionary forces. Within a few hours the report lay before Ngo Dinh Nhu, the brother and first counsellor of Prime Minister Diem.

Besides Van Vien, two more generals, Nguyen Van Ty and Van Sang, had been named as rebels in the pay of the Bin Xuyen. Consequently the local intelligence was able to compile a list of 160 officers who were secretly conspiring with the Bin Xuyen. But that was not all. High court judges, prosecutors, and thirty district chiefs of police had all been receiving double wages for years: one from the state and a larger one from the gangster empire, in which they held various nominal positions, like chairman, director, manager, and supervisor. It was no wonder that very few of the Bin Xuyen bandits ever saw the inside of a jail.

The beginning of the uprising had been fixed for 1:00 P.M. on April 28, signaled by simultaneous attacks on Diem's office, the army general headquarters, and the Ministry of Public Security. The rebel forces were concentrated along the Rue Gallieni with assault forces assembled in the Petrusky Lyceum, which also housed the Bin Xuyen arsenal.

By 10 A.M. the loyal government troops were ready to deliver a preemptive strike, but for some inexplicable reason, Diem hemmed and hawed and withheld the order to attack. He acknowledged the early warning and moved into a less exposed wing of his palace. He also accepted the French tanks, dispatched by General Ely, to protect his person but he wouldn't take the initiative.

"Diem is an idiot." Erich fumed. "We offer him the Bin Xuyen on a silver plate yet he wants to take them the hard

RECALL TO INFERNO

way." Both General Houssong and Captain Dessault were of the same opinion, and the prime minister's behavior remained one of the unsolved mysteries of the South Vietnamese puzzle.

As Monsieur Thy had informed us, the rebels began to shell the Palace of Independence at 1 P.M. with simultaneous assault on various other government buildings. At long last, around half-past two, the government forces began to respond, then went on the offensive. Task Force-G, too, received the order to move, from no less an authority than the new Minister of Public Security, Colonel Ngoc Lee. He requested that I attack the rebel forces that occupied a dozen buildings along the Rue Paulus. Without hesitation and somewhat coolly, I informed the minister that I would not sacrifice a single man in house-to-house combat, as that wasn't their task at all. The colonel was astounded. At first he tried to order me, then he pleaded, threatened, and pleaded again. In the end he phoned Houssong, who called me and fully approved my decision.

We were veterans of countless urban battles, from Stalingrad to Berlin, and knew only too well what it was like to hold a four-story building, while the enemy occupied a similar one across the street. We knew the implications of fighting in cellars, in attics and roofs, from room to room, up and down on staircases, suffering heavy casualties from grenades exploding in narrow places; or being shot in the back by snipers who, before being eliminated, would invariably claim a few victims.

A commander who takes his troops into urban combat must be prepared to accept 50 percent casualties. I was not prepared to accept even as few as 5 percent just because a vacillating prime minister would not permit a timely and well-prepared preemptive strike that would have caught the rebels unprepared.

In the end General Houssong resolved the tricky problem. Knowing well that Diem would never consent, he told Colonel Lee that Task Force-G would move against the rebel strongholds with fifty flamethrowers, the only effective weapon against enemy troops fighting from cellars and attics. Fifty roasters could have burned down half of Saigon. Needless to say, the colonel promptly agreed that Task Force-G should be preserved intact for the war against the Vietcong. Whereupon I generously offered to give a hand at the Petrusky Lyceum, where the government troops were being blocked by a minefield the insurgents had laid.

Krebitz thought that with the help of a few heavy machine guns firing explosive bullets, he could open a way for the troops. He found a suitable apartment house with windows facing the lyceum park. Moving through back rooms and holes opened in the walls, the security forces delivered six MGs. Using tables and chests to improvise gun platforms, Gruppe Drei set them up, while our sharpshooters occupied themselves with rebel heads and chests that popped into view every now and then. When everything was ready, the MGs opened up on the mined yard, combing through the grass and flowerbeds with methodical precision: three guns horizontally, the other three vertically, with the slugs hitting at twenty-inch intervals. The continuous sharp crackle of the bullets was frequently interrupted by the resounding detonations of the exploding mines. Fire, smoke, and cascading gravel covered the park and from the lyceum windows came shouts. The muzzle of a submachine gun poked into the street from one of the upper windows, but the hands that held it never got the chance to pull the trigger. Kretz and Schindler hit the sniper between the eyes, just as they knocked out everyone else who tried to aim a gun from any other window.

Our heavy MGs blasted three wide lanes across the rebel minefield, then, as the government troops surged forward, they shifted fire toward the windows. The heavy slugs wrecked the makeshift barricades and killed the rebels behind them; tore through walls and doors, playing havoc in the interior, pinning down the defenders, barring them from positions that might enable them to attack the soldiers. We began to lob rifle grenades into the building, causing even more confusion, while the troops burst through the blasted gate and occupied the ground floor.

Comfortable and safe in their sheltered gun slits, Gruppe Drei's men began to pick up the fugitives as they darted from the lyceum.

In the other districts of the capital the fighting continued thoroughout the day, causing many fires and much destruction. Another strong rebel group had besieged the the army housing center and the offices of the army paper, *Caravelle,* where the editors and newsmen, including General Gambier's son, resisted until the paratroops broke the blockade. The Des Mares camp, too, had received its share of mortar shells, which wounded five soldiers.

Around midnight the fighting shifted toward the suburbs. Task Force-G moved to dislodge the insurgents from the Cholon district, cleaning up police stations and isolated points of resistance, gunning down armed civilians and uniformed rebels; captured soldiers and policemen would live or die according to the situation of the moment. If and when they had been captured in the presence of Saigon officers, they would be escorted to a camp and handed over to the security forces of Colonel Lee. When there were no inconvenient eyes around we shot them regardless of white flags or raised hands.

"They refused to surrender or disregarded our challenge to halt." Krebitz formulated our official justification for the executions. Dead troublemakers wouldn't be amnestied to pick up the gun again and kill more people.

We heard the midnight newscast of Radio Saigon. Prime Minister Diem announced that the larger part of the rebel forces had been killed or captured and that Emperor Bao Dai had called him from Cannes and graciously inquired about the state of affairs in his capital! I think if Bao Dai had been in Saigon we would have gunned him down too.

In the early-morning hours we caught some sleep in the empty bunks of a deserted rebel barracks.

By 11 A.M. the next day the insurgency was virtually crushed with the capture of the cabaret Grand Monde—the last rebel stronghold, or what was left of it. Sporadic fighting continued in the suburbs and in the countryside for a few more days. Task Force-G participated in it with enthusiasm. Fighting in the open country was more to our liking. Particularly so after Diem announced that the battle would continue until the Bin Xuyen organization was totally exterminated. We took the prime minister's statement literally.

Protected by the paratroops and an armored brigade, the French quarter suffered no damage, but in the city some twenty thousand people remained without homes. Needless to say, during those crucial days in Saigon the Vietcong did not remain inactive. In thirty-six hours Hanoi's guerrillas had attacked twenty-three military and civilian installations in the various provinces, from My-tho in the delta to Da Nang in the north: isolated forts, police stations, bridges, telephone exchanges, motor pools, landing strips, electric transformers, and others. The Vietcong assaults were perfectly coordinated with the events in the capital.

With the exception of the fellow who had informed Stahnke of Bin Xuyen's designs, the prisoners in Karl's "laboratory of truth" had been shot, too, including the chairman of the Ca Ban company. The corpses were loaded into the limousine and the refrigerator truck and driven to Cholon by Herrs Wachtel and Rosner. After parking both vehicles, they blew them up with grenades.

"An unfortunate mortar hit," Stahnke commented wryly. "Such things happen during insurgency and street fighting. They were all mafiosi anyway."

When I asked him casually what happens to some truly innocent people he had hauled in, Stahnke replied with professional conviction, "My dear, Hans—when I decide to haul in someone, I'm already ninety percent certain of his guilt. The remaining ten percent would usually show up after I scrutinize my client for a few minutes. Most of my clients are professional bandits and terrorists who will never change for the better, only for the worse. The best solution is to eliminate them for the benefit of mankind."

Karl Stahnke had a very low opinion of legal processes, which he contemptuously called "merry domino games between judges and lawyers." He said, "When you catch someone with his hand in the bag, he is guilty. If you put him into jail, you'll only turn him into an even harder crook. It's in prison where the small-time chicken thief learns the methods of the heavy trade. A professional crook remains a professional crook, and the only way to stop him is to put a slug between his eyes. Instead of police the honest community needs eradicators. That's right. Death squads, my friend. If you want to put an end to crime, violence, drug abuse, murder, go about it radically. It's the only way. No lawyer, no judge, not jail, but a bullet in the head. And believe me, after you gunned down the first two hundred crooks, the rest would change profession."

I couldn't criticize him for we had a very similar view regarding the Communists.

With Krebitz and Gruppe Drei, Schulze was turning the district of Cholon upside down, looking for Bin Xuyen bosses.

Acting on a tip he got from Karl Stahnke, he managed to corner one of the top *padrinos,* a certain Ngo Binh Try, the number-three man in the underworld society, together with his colleagues and gorillas. Throwing a cordon around the huge park where the boss's palatial mansion stood, the troops joked a great deal about the Commando of Death going to dislodge a mafioso from his pleasure nest. As a matter of fact, the pleasure nest turned out to be protected with electrified fences, armored gates, land mines, and steel cupolas in the park equipped with heavy machine guns and 4-cm PAKs—antitank guns, quite capable of beating off even armored attacks. Binh Try's gorillas were a small army of experienced gunmen, the cream of the Bin Xuyen hit team.

It wasn't long before Erich requested my assistance, for all he could do was to prevent escape from the fenced park.

With 150 troops I drove to Cholon, arriving just in time to repel a breakout attempt of five luxury limousines headed by armor-plated trucks with gun slits from which a dozen machine guns sputtered. The convoy stopped and beat a hasty retreat when Waldner and Janaschek turned on a pair of flamethrowers to deliver a fiery salute across the road. The fugitives retired into the mansion. Krebitz got down to work. Julius Steiner blasted the gate with a bazooka, and we spread out in the park under the cover of the smoke canisters that blinded the MG cupolas, which were then knocked out one after another.

There was a sculpted fountain in the garden, perhaps a hundred yards from the mansion. It depicted an angel blowing a trumpet. Riedl insisted that it was the Angel of Death, trumpeting on the Day of Judgment, which we found a befitting allegory. Never running short of humor, Helmut tied our fancy Jolly Roger to a bayonet, crawled up to the angel, and stuck it between its left fingers. The skull and crossbones had an unexpected effect on the thugs in the mansion.

To our astonishment, a large white sheet appeared in the center window and a voice called through a loudspeaker asking for a truce and our acceptance of a negotiator. I consented and three well-dressed men, who looked more like top business executives than terrorists, exited through the massive wooden door. With Schulze, Krebitz, and Riedl flanking me, I received the Bin Xuyen envoys in front of the fountain. Speaking in the name of Monsieur Binh Try, the spokesman of the delegation, a flat-faced, stiff character of about fifty, boldly proposed that we should concede free passage to My-tho in exchange for $500,000!

This casually presented business proposal prompted wild guffaws in our ranks but the envoys' faces remained stony, unmoved.

"Where is this five hundred thousand dollars?" Erich wanted to know.

Erich's skeptical sarcasm didn't even stir the flat-faced gangster spokesman. He gestured toward the mansion. The gate opened again and a large suitcase was placed on the landing.

"There it is!"

"Faut-il prendre cet argent?" Krebitz asked, but Schulze raised a restraining hand.

"We're going to fetch it ourselves," he said. "Come along."

Shouldering his gun, he walked up to the marble-stepped, colonnaded portico and picked up the suitcase, opened it briefly, then shut the lid. "It like seems half a million, all right."

"Unless it was printed in Hong Kong, or right in Saigon," Krebitz said.

"The bills aren't new," Schulze said.

They returned to the fountain with the suitcase. I threw an inquisitive glance at Schulze. He nodded. Krebitz broke into laughter and Riedl followed him. The threesome from the mansion looked on, baffled.

Fingering the lapels of the spokesman's expensive suit, Rudolf chuckled. "Now, tell me, boss—what should stop us from taking the mansion, frying everyone inside, and keeping the money all the same?"

"Because in that case you would not gain a cent" came the flat response. "The mansion is mined and so is the fountain we're standing next to. One only has to press the plunger."

"You're bluffing," Erich said.

The flat-faced envoy shrugged, raised his hand, and an instant later, halfway to the mansion, the gravel lane erupted with a resounding detonation.

"That was a mine, all right," Rudolf commented appreciatively.

"I am not bluffing," the Bin Xuyen spokesman said with a ghost of a smile. He drew apart the flowery bushes right next where I stood to disclose a land mine with wires.

"There are three more mines, Commander."

"You'd blow up with us."

"Yes, we would go to hell together. . . . What do you say?"

I said casually, just for the fun of it, "Make it one million and you can leave in peace."

He accepted the double figure without batting an eye. "All right, Commander. Hold your fire."

"Do you mind if we—er, change location?"

"Not at all. Just leave the money where it is—for the time being. If you try to cheat on us, you'll get only cinders."

"Don't worry. We always keep our part of a bargain." I glanced at my watch. "You have time until half-past six."

"Sufficient."

The three men withdrew. The white sheet stayed in the window. Ten minutes later the door opened again and a second suitcase was placed into the portico.

"Voici comment conclure la guerre," Riedl cracked. "This is how to finish the war."

"I wonder how many more suitcases they have ready?" Erich commented. "What do you intend to do, Hans? Let them go?"

I shrugged. "Why not? They're paying well for the passage, and the Bin Xuyen is not the Vietcong. Diem will seize all the organization's assets anyway, the money too."

"That's right," Riedl agreed. "Why shouldn't we reimburse ourselves for all the trouble of the past three days?"

"I'm curious about where they want to go," Erich said.

"Not to Hanoi for sure," I replied. "My-tho means Cambodia. A pleasant boat trip along the Mekong to Phnom Penh and from there to Bangkok. In a few weeks time the Bin Xuyen chairmans, directors, and managers will be sitting in plush hotels in Paris, Rome, London, and New York, and in a month or two they'll be running new companies. Money opens every door."

Our flat-faced spokesman returned with the second suitcase. "One million dollars," he said wryly. "Do you wish to count the money?"

"There's no need. It'd be very stupid of you to trick us. Your boss may leave for My-tho with his entourage. We'll let him pass."

I wanted to lift the suitcases onto the Jeep but Krebitz stopped me. "Let me have a look first," he said emphatically. "We're dealing with gangsters."

"You mean booby traps?"

He emptied the suitcases into a pair of jute sacks and tied them up. "They're playing it fair, Hans," he remarked.

Twenty minutes later the convoy of limousines left the park. The leading vehicle halted at the demolished gate. The rear window rolled down and inside we saw Monsieur Ngo Binh Try with his wife and three children. He was a pleasant-looking man of about forty-five. He beckoned me to lean closer.

"All that you find in the mansion is yours," he said quietly. "Persian carpets, Chinese vases, antique furniture . . ."

"And get blown up in the process of collecting?" Krebitz asked.

Try looked at his golden watch. "You have ninety minutes. At seven thirty-five the mansion will blow up. Diem and his clan may collect the shards."

I said, "Who cares? We have no place for carpets and Chinese vases."

"As you wish."

I waved a hand. "You may proceed. *Bon voyage.*"

The convoy rolled into the street and disappeared toward Tan-an, on the road to My-tho.

Erich patted the sacks with the money. "This is one of the reasons why I like to work with you, Hans."

I slapped him on the back. "All right, let's go home."

"Why shouldn't we look for another big fish?" Riedl asked. "After all, we're mercenaries now."

Krebitz wrinkled his nose. "I don't like that term, Helmut."

"All right, soldiers of fortune."

"A fortune of some three thousand dollars for each man," I added.

We gave twenty thousand to Karl Stahnke and his burly assistants. After all, it was Karl's tip that led to our bonanza.

Captain Spata and Sergeant Starr were waiting for us in the map room, both in a tense mood.

"What's the situation?" Spata asked tersely.

"Haven't you heard the radio newscast?" I asked tauntingly.

"Who the hell understands the local blah-blah." Mike grunted. "We're sitting here on nails since last night, locked up in this damned concentration camp of yours, Hans."

"How come?" Krebitz cut in.

"You know well how come. The guards wouldn't let us leave."

"By my explicit order," I enlightened the Americans. "The rebels were shooting all over Saigon—mostly from behind, and we couldn't risk losing you, Mike."

"I like your good heart, Commander, sir," Spata responded grudgingly but with a smile hovering on the corners of his mouth. "I sure did lots of observing from here."

"How are things now?" Starr asked.

"It's all over. The rebels are either dead or locked up. Only very few managed to get away."

I slipped a bundle of bills on the table. "This is yours."

They stared. "What the heck—"

"Six thousand hecks. Your share."

"Our share of what?"

"Task Force-G received a cash premium for cleaning up the city."

"From whom?" Starr wanted to know.

"From the government," I lied amiably.

"Don't pull my leg." Spata waved a hand. "No government pays that fast. . . . Besides, we didn't participate."

"We have five men in the hospital and they, too, received their shares. . . . Damn it, Mike, one day you insist on working with Task Force-G, the other day you refuse your share. Well, we're a closely knit society, if you haven't noticed it."

In the end they acquiesced.

A few days later U.S. General Lawton Collins, the personal envoy of President Eisenhower, landed in Saigon to discuss the technicalities regarding the U.S. government's pledge to train the South Vietnamese army.

Three days after Collins's arrival the Saigon parliament deposed Emperor Bao Dai. Diem assumed full charge of the country.

The Hao Hoa and Cao Dai sects, which remained neutral during the insurrection, now hurriedly expressed their loyalty to the Diem government. Had the rebels won, they would have expressed the same loyal sentiments to the Bin Xuyen or to General Van Vien.

12.

Raid into North Vietnam

General Houssong summoned Schulze, Krebitz, Riedl, and I for a meeting in the map room of his headquarters, where we also encountered Captain Dessault of the Military Intelligence, Lieutenant Berger, Captain Spata, and the American major Roy Cooke.

The major shook hands with us, lighted a cigar, observed us with interest, then said in a pleasant, balanced voice, "Gentlemen, I'm very pleased to meet you again and I hope we'll all get along well. I've been assigned to this camp in the capacity of advisor and, unofficially though, Task Force-G also belongs here. Naturally I've heard of you before and read some reports on your accomplishments, which General Houssong has kindly placed at my disposal. I also had a long discussion with Captain Spata, who has participated in some of your recent actions. Consequently I realized that I should concern myself with the Saigon army. You don't really need anyone to advise you, because you know damned well how to cope with any situation."

This opening statement went down very well with us and prompted polite smiles and quiet grunts of assent. It also inspired our instant sympathy, because we disliked nothing more than ranking newcomers trying to talk down to us.

"Don't continue, Major Cooke." Schulze beamed. "We'll get along very well together."

"But I must continue," the major insisted good-humoredly, puffing at his cigar. "First because that's what I'm being paid for, and second because, believe me, gentlemen, sometimes even you need counsel—if not what to do, then what not to do."

"There are two things we never do, Major." Irrepressible Erich took the floor. "We never run."

"But if we do it's forward!" Riedl interposed, drawing soft chuckles.

Schulze continued. "Second, we never give a moment of tranquillity to Hanoi's terrorists, regardless of whether they're common bandits or if they camouflage themselves as freedom fighters or patriots."

General Houssong smiled complacently. Major Cooke raised his hand, asking for silence. The room stilled.

"Well, there's also a third," he resumed emphatically. "Frankly, you should give more thought to bettering your image before the world and should never let the beast in you get the upper hand."

A brief pause ensued. I said quietly, "Major Cooke, we are aware of American sensitivity to public opinion, but it is not so with us. We've long since stopped caring what people might think or say about us. You see, sir—the more distorted the image the Communists paint of us, the wider berth they will give to Task Force-G."

Erich cut in. "It's already the very last thing on earth the Commies want, to run into the damned Germans."

"German fascists!" Riedl corrected him.

Cooke shook his head and looked amused. "You have many enemies, and not only on the Communist side," he remarked, but it was a fact we knew well.

Krebitz said, "For over six years in Vietnam we've been doing our best to gather as many enemies as possible."

General Housson's eyes sparkled with delight. Major Cooke said, "We also have the Western world to consider." His tone was mild. Neither approving nor disapproving, but his polite reminder prompted Erich to respond.

"You mean the press, sir?"

"First of all."

"Well, we've already been shoeshined by our free, democratic, but rather pinkish press men to such extent that we've become more black than a Senegalese in a coal pit, Major. There's no redemption for the onetime S.S., so there's no need for us to become lily-livered or, as you would call it, humane. In the eyes of the world we're wild beasts, and this attitude will never change. We got used to living with our stigma."

"And that's where you're wrong, Captain Schulze," Cooke said, stabbing with his forefinger. "There are thousands of rehabilitated S.S. guys in Germany. They're working, pursuing businesses, leading normal civilian lives. You can't go on fighting forever either."

"We're far too militant to settle in the civilian life and become fine, law-abiding citizens, Major. We're habituated to give orders and not to receiving them. Our trade is war and the weapons are the only tools we are familiar with. I don't think that we could ever cope with the small, irritating hassles of everyday civilian life: the petty bureaucrats, the red tape, garrulous traffic cops—restrictions. Why?" he added with a chuckle. "If a cop gave me a speeding ticket, I'd probably make him swallow it at gunpoint."

Major Cooke opened his hands. "In that case," he replied patiently, "I believe that many of you would be welcome in the new German *Wehrmacht*—er, what do you call it?"

"*Bundeswehr*," I told him.

Erich waved a dismissing hand. "No, thank you," he said. "I would be bored to death."

"I'm certain that the new German army will be superbly equipped and quite active."

"Active where?" my friend wanted to know.

"In the field of practical exercise, where officers of your experience could be most needed."

Erich shook his head and answered soberly, "Major Cooke, we don't like the idea of playing soldiers. We *are* soldiers. The *Bundeswehr* is only a midget reincarnation of its former *Wehrmacht* self, and it'll never be permitted to grow into a giant."

"Why should it?"

"For the simple reason that the Red Army is a giant. Only Germany can prevent the Bolshevization of Europe."

"But today Germany is no longer alone," Major Cooke reminded Erich in a soft voice. "You have friends, with my country in the first line."

"Well, sir—America hasn't done much to help another friend and ally, France, at Dien Bien Phu, when a single bomber raid on the scale of Hamburg or Dresden would have wiped out Giap and his Vietminh divisions in half an hour. . . . In any case, I would prefer a Germany that needed no protectors."

I noticed that Erich's Dien Bien Phu bit had hit the major below the belt and I thought it wise to intervene before my somewhat sardonical friend should ruin the meeting's amiable atmosphere.

"Major Cooke," I said, "General Houssong has informed me that you were bringing some good news for us."

The major seemed much relieved by the chance to change the subject. "What I brought isn't news, but hardware." He beamed. "Some of the stuff you requested from General McCory. A pair of powered gliders, scuba equipment, heavy and light machine guns, some with infrared scopes, and precision rifles, likewise equipped for shooting at night—and twenty thousand hollow cartridges."

The earlier good humor of the meeting instantly returned.

Major Cooke turned toward me. "Well, what'll you do with your new toys, Captain?"

"We might start raising hell in North Vietnam," I answered casually.

The major's brows arched. "Are you serious?"

"We never joke about Hanoi and the Vietcong."

"How do you propose to get there?"

I shrugged. "The Ho Chi Minh trail in Laos is perfectly suitable for two-way traffic, Major. If the Vietcong can march south, Task Force-G is quite capable of moving in the opposite direction."

General Houssong leaned closer to me and said in a conspiratorial voice, "We might have such an expedition for you all lined up, Wagemueller."

"A good haul, *mon général*?"

"Come to my office the day after tomorrow around four in the afternoon. Bring along Krebitz, Riedl, and naturally your hair-triggerish friend, Schulze."

Speaking to Houssong's aide-de-camp, I asked, "When can we have the American stuff?"

Fumbling with his papers, Lieutenant Berger said, "By tomorrow noon—except for the gliders, which'll stay on the airfield."

"Of course."

Captain Spata shifted his chair and tapped me on the forearm. "I told you, when Uncle Sam decides to move, he moves quickly."

"What about the amphibians and the troop carriers?"

"Coming by freighter."

We could hardly wait to take possession of the American "goodies." Krebitz was the most excited among us, particularly because of the infrared scopes. "Mensch!" he exulted. "Imagine us sitting on an overhang in pitch dark, knocking off Father Ho's soldiers as they walk along the trail."

Few of us could sleep that night.

The following morning six army trucks rolled into our compound, headed by Lieutenant Berger in a Jeep. We received him like kids rejoice over the coming of Father Christmas.

After a hurried lunch we drove to the airfield with Spata and Starr and our three pilot candidates whom Krebitz and Schulze had "excavated" from the ranks: Stefan Escher, Hubert Mohr, and Hansjuerg Woss, who had flown gliders before the war.

The resources of Task Force-G were ample. In our ranks served blacksmiths, electricians, bomb and demolition experts, engine mechanics, tank drivers, artillerymen, field engineers, weapons smiths, and even one expert of submarine mines and torpedos.

Naturally none of our airmen had ever seen a glider with an engine, and they marveled over the special equipment and instruments for night flying, observing, and photography. Their tanks could hold enough fuel for three hours of powered flight, which, according to Escher and Woss, had little to do with range, as most of the time the gliders would be driven by the wind and the upcurrents. The engines served only to gain altitude when necessary, or for flying back to base in windstill.

The next afternoon we reported to General Houssong's office where we found the same officers present, including Major Cooke. He queried us about the equipment and received our most sincere thanks.

Then General Houssong began. "Wagemueller, you'll have the chance to repeat your splendid Man Hao raid in China, back in the early fifties."

"Ma fois, mon général, you don't want to send us into China, I hope," I replied with mock concern.

"No, nothing that far." Houssing chuckled, while Major Cooke rekindled his perpetual cigar. "We're thinking of a fine little raid into Ho's empire."

"Naturally you're free to accept or refuse the job," Dessault added.

Schulze asked, "What's our objective?"

"Not far north of the seventeenth parallel. Near the provincial capital of Hue Tien."

"Dong Hoi?" I asked.

"*Oui.* What do you think of it?"

"The raid is possible through Laos, but what is there worth to destroy?"

"Captain Dessault will tell you," Houssong replied.

Dessault glanced up and cleared his throat. "There's a large fuel and ammunition depot two miles south of Bo Trech," the intelligence officer explained. "Two hundred thousand gallons of gas and diesel fuel in drums. Six semiburied depots for artillery shells, small-arms ammo, and dynamite." He checked his papers, then went on. "Also two hundred tons of land mines and hand grenades."

Krebitz whistled softly. "When that stuff blows up they'll hear the detonation all the way to Peking."

"We hope they'll hear it all the way to Moscow," Major Cooke replied. "Much of the hardware is coming from the USSR. T-34 and Stalin tanks, Molotova trucks, artillery, and troop carriers."

Captain Dessault slipped a handful of aerial pictures across the table. Some had diagrams attached, elaborated with circles, arrows, and legends.

"Where did you get this picture from?" I asked. Neither French nor Vietnamese aircraft would ever venture north of the demarcation line.

"From the Pentagon," Cooke said.

"Your pilots have done a great job, Major," Schulze complimented. "The photos must have been taken from very low altitudes."

"They were taken from an altitude of fifty-five thousand feet, using special cameras carried by a special airplane."

"Well, they must be very special to show the watchtowers and the tanks with such clarity. . . . There's even a bridge or something from the shore to the middle of nowhere."

"The North Vietnamese are constructing a pier of pontoons," Dessault explained. "To faciliate the unloading of a Chinese

RECALL TO INFERNO

freighter, the *Huang-Po*. Fifteen thousand tons laden with military supplies. The freighter is due in a week but she can't approach the shore closer than two hundred and fifty yards."

"One of the reasons for our reunion," General Houssong remarked. "You might kill a pair of flies with a single blow, Wagemueller. The supply dump and the freighter."

Speaking to me, Cooke asked, "What do you think of it?"

"We'll be ready to leave by the morning, Major Cooke."

Housson leaned toward the major. "I told you that Wagemueller's team would never shrink away from anything."

Captain Dessault spoke. "You must go with a very small force. Maximum twenty-five men—flown to Hue, then trucked to the Laotian border . . . Somewhere near Khe Kanh. From there you'll be on your own."

I excused myself and walked to the large wall map. Schulze, Krebitz, and Dessault joined me. With the pointer, I began to trace the imaginary course of our trip.

"From Khe Kanh to Lang Mo, about fifty miles. . . . From there, along the river Hoi across hilly ground to Bo Trenh, another twenty-five miles."

Krebitz cut in. "Over mountains, cutting our trail. Perhaps we can reach the target in one week."

"You must!" Dessault emphasized. "That's when the *Huang-Po* would be casting anchor. You should hit before they unload her."

"We must hit freighter and dump at the same time, then run for dear life," Riedl said with a grin.

"You can't return the same way," Dessault reminded me.

"I know." I nodded. "The garrisons will be alerted."

Studying the map, Krebitz spoke. "We might continue toward Bai Dinh in the northwest, then enter into Laos along the road to Phao."

"There's a strong garrison at Bai Dinh," Dessault warned us. "You should bypass it."

Schulze pursed his lips. "Roughly one hundred miles of rough going back to Khe Kanh."

Riedl said, "The Vietminh walked four hundred miles from Tonkin to Dien Bien Phu."

"Over roads," General Houssong said. "You'll be going over hills and across uncut forests."

"Ten miles a day," Krebitz remarked. "Even if we travel light."

"That's another point," Major Cooke cut in. "You should travel light and avoid trouble with the Laotians."

"We'll be clad like any Vietcong, Major Cooke," I told the American. "Black pajamas, helmets of latania or bamboo with greenery tucked into the string mesh. But should it come to a fight, I'd be compelled to prevent any witness from reaching Vientiane to cry of French intrusion into Laotian territory."

Then, noticing Cooke's worried expression, I said, "You shouldn't worry on that score, Major. We've covered hundreds of miles without ever been spotted by either Laotians or Cambodians. We're good at avoiding unwanted contacts."

"But what if someone should see you from a distance, without your being aware of it?"

"From a distance we'll be the Vietcong to any casual observer. Vientiane could protest in Hanoi."

"That's something they'll never do," Houssong remarked.

Major Cooke said gravely, "You should bear in mind that Washington is trying to maintain friendly relations with Vientiane and Phnom Penh."

I decided to leave Erich with Task Force-G for other assignments in my absence and selected only twenty men for the expedition, including Riedl, Krebitz, Jost Waldner, Julius Steiner, and six Gruppe Drei sharpshooters. I expected Schulze to open up with a barrage of arguments against his exclusion but to my pleasant surprise he seemed to understand the necessity of not leaving Task Force-G without a competent commander. Goodnaturedly he even offered to make some resounding diversive strikes in another direction to occupy Hanoi's attention elsewhere.

The men Krebitz selected were the most experienced veterans who accepted the coming trial of force with enthusiasm. They had long since wanted to poke their fists under Giap's nose and welcomed the chance to play Vietcong in Ho Chi Minh's own country.

Krebitz and Riedl selected our equipment with extra care. Hollow charges with timers, plastic explosives, and incendiary bombs were high on our list. We were to carry submachine guns and precision rifles with silencers, firing our self-manufactured explosive slugs. We would have liked to take along the American infrared guns but the battery, scope, and torch would have been a great burden. We limited the total weight of equipment per man to thirty pounds, including weapon, ammunition, and six grenades, which did not leave much room for food. We took biscuits, sardines, soup cubes, tea and coffee, which had to last until after the raid. On the return leg of the trip we could procure food at gunpoint, if necessary. And we could always count on coming across mungo, orange, and breadfruit trees, which grew everywhere.

Much of the flight and the trip by trucks we spent poring over the maps and aerial photos of the zone we intended to penetrate. There were abundant photos in the intelligence archives, and Krebitz outlined the best route across the Giai Truong range. He also marked enemy objectives that we were to avoid: hamlets, rural garrisons, bases, roadblocks, and guardhouses.

Julius Steiner volunteered to lead a commando against the Chinese freighter, and the men he suggested for the job were excellent swimmers and demolition experts. The hollow charges and incendiaries were to be transported by small inflatables, sprayed black. We hoped that by midnight, the time of action, the ship's crew would be sound asleep.

Following my explicit order, the truck drivers halted two miles outside Khe Kanh, which village I wanted to bypass. Dawn was lighting up the skyline when we marched off and the first rays of the sun found us already past the village and high in the mountains, following the course of a small tributary of the Sé Kong. From the rugged heights we had a good view of the road and the Laotian border post with a handful of soldiers lingering around the guardhouse and the barrier. There was virtually no civilian traffic along the road, and when a Vietcong convoy came by, the Laotians would discreetly turn the other way to observe the flora and fauna of the nearby hills, proving that peaceful coexistence with the Communists was possible under the maxim: "You don't annoy us and we will let you live."

Krebitz advanced by the compass in the direction of a hypothetical point on Hill 1883, five miles north of the Laotian village of Tse Pong. Hacking our way through the green tangle of creepers and thorny brushes, keeping under cover, we followed the trailblazers and reached the site in five hours. After resting, the commando continued in a northeasterly direction, toward the North Vietnamese village of Lang Mo, about fourteen miles distant as the crow flies. The way we crawled in tortuous semicircles, it was closer to twenty-five miles. Sometime we came across footpaths, trodden by hunters, woodcutters, or mountain tribesmen. When Krebitz declared them safe to take, our rate of advance increased considerably. Even though Krebitz had indeed selected the easiest route to follow, some hard climbing and slippery descents couldn't be avoided.

We entered into North Vietnam. The frontier was a jungle of age-old latania trees invaded by creepers, through which we had to cut a long tunnel. On a muddy declivity Riedl slipped and dropped on his bottom on top of a protruding root. He sat there gasping for air, while Krebitz and Steiner rushed to his side. "Did you hurt yourself?" Rudolf asked anxiously, helping Helmut to his feet. "Are you all right?"

"Of course I'm all right." Riedl gasped, imitating Erich's voice. "I feel fine. I'm a superman of Task Force-G who can march on, fight, and win—even with his balls squashed. . . . You know, Rudy, it's quite a bit of luck that you found the easiest way, which is only excruciating. A more difficult one would be murderous."

The ground rose and dropped, with precipitous rock faces and steep-walled gorges alternating at rare intervals. Sometimes we had to use hooked ropes to descend along a particularly rough declivity. And all the while we cut our trail, we were following a comfortable one down in the valley that traced the course of a stream with countless rapids, through tiny hamlets. Our commando advanced over unbroken ground, through gorges with menacing overhangs, over and beneath wobbly boulders, exposed to constant threat of landslides. Riedl's previous estimate of doing ten miles a day was a gross overestimation, and I already began to worry about our timetable. The ammunition dump could wait but the freighter, *Huang-Po,* might be unloaded by the time Steiner arrived.

During the war on the Russian front I sometimes read Livy's account of Hannibal's crossing of the Alps. Now it occurred to me that our trip was very similar to the struggle of the Carthagians in the roadless mountain wilderness. Except that Hannibal had commanded tens of thousands of men who cleared obstacles and built roads in a jiffy.

Here and there, where the ravines widened enough to permit a modest cultivation of rice or tobacco, a few dozen flimsy huts crowded together, made of bamboo with roofs of grass laid in several layers of cross-shaped patches. Sometimes our advance guard would come across dwellings just below the hill crest, where a handful of families sustained themselves by raising pigs and growing corn and poppies on the declivities, the wild vegetation of which had been burnt off. The barren black patches would always warn us of human presence, and sometimes we were compelled to make mile-long detours in order not to be discovered.

Toward the despised *Thays*—the Westerners—every eye in the country would be hostile.

Whenever the towering cliffs and steep drops gave way to small flatlands, seldom more than a mile or two across, there would be more huts and also peasants, plowing narrow patches of arable land, plodding behind their buffalo-drawn hoes.

After fourteen hours of hard trekking we had covered about twelve miles. When we reached a small clearing with water bubbling from the rocks, I ordered halt. Using spirit cubes that burned smokeless, the men prepared their only warm meal of the day, then we bunked down for the night.

We rose at daybreak, and I delivered a last reminder to the men. "Take care not to drop anything, especially not tissues, matches, cigarette boxes, and stubs. Whatever you wish to discard should be buried. Whenever we come to sandy or muddy patches of ground, the last men should erase our imprints, using twigs."

We plodded on a few hundred yards behind Krebitz.

Despite our precautions, we ran into a peasant on a hunting trip with his ten-year-old son, whom the trailblazers captured. This most unwelcome incident delayed us for two hours. The safety of our group demanded that the prisoners be eliminated, but here even Krebitz was against killing them. The man was an invalid who had lost his left arm fighting against the Japanese.

His son was a skinny, frightened boy with big bug eyes, who wouldn't stop sniveling.

But we couldn't just release them. They lived in a twelve-hut hamlet in the valley, only half a mile distant. Rudolf went to look for the place and saw a good trail running toward Lang Mo and also some penned Thai horses. When he returned he told me rather glumly that it would take a rider an hour to reach the nearest militia camp and trigger red alert in the entire district.

Jost Waldman resolved the dilemma quite ingeniously. He had spotted a cave farther uphill and suggested that we should convey our prisoners there, tie them, and block the entrance in such a way that it would take them several hours to free themselves. Jost also concocted a way to do it. He explained his idea to Rudolf, who agreed that it sounded plausible.

Bound by the wrists and ankles, the frightened twosome were propped up against a boulder. Krebitz suspended a sheathed bush knife above the peasant's thighs; the other end of the string he fastened to a twig, which he tucked into a fissure in the rock with a dynamite primer and timer, everything out of reach. He explained to the terrified locals that after two hours the primer would blow the twig and the knife would drop into his lap. "With some effort you will be able to draw it and cut yourself loose."

The peasant kept nodding. He understood that they weren't to be killed, and everything else suited him. Just for the sake of a wobbly pretense, Rudolf questioned him about the way to Ne Nhom, in Laos, and if there were soldiers on the border.

He also warned the man sternly, "When you return to your family, stay at home and keep your mouth shut. If we find out that you talked, we'll return and erase your hamlet from the face of earth with everyone in it." Happy to be alive, the peasant shook his head in denial. He wouldn't talk.

We left them with a canteen of water and the food they had been carrying, then blocked the entrance of the cave with loose boulders, figuring that it could be five or six hours before they would be back in their hamlet.

The commando moved on with redoubled effort to put distance between the cave and ourselves. All the men were relieved at how the tricky problem had been resolved.

The second night we spent on a crest overlooking the Hoi valley with another settlement of twenty huts and a militia guardhouse. Krebitz counted twelve soldiers with rifles and an individual with a submachine gun, likely their commander. From the guardhouse a phone line stretched northward, fastened to roughly cut saplings. The behavior of the North Vietnamese troops did not suggest any state of alarm. Krebitz was probably right when he asserted that the peasant wouldn't talk.

In eleven hours we covered another seven miles, and according to my estimation, Lang Mo was still a good eight miles distant. But even seven miles was ample under the circumstances. We negotiated climbs and declivities where it took seventy minutes to advance five hundred yards. Even though we might not be able to reach the Chinese freighter in time, I considered the safety of my men more important than the destruction of a shipload of arms. Should we miss the *Huang-Po*, we would content ourselves with wrecking the supply dump.

The next day we moved on. The advance guard was well ahead and out of sight, and we followed short signals sent by Krebitz over the WT. Wireless communications were avoided but we had some twenty-five signals of long and short beeps that signified danger, all clear, civilians, hamlet, guardhouse, camp, halt and wait, open fire, cease fire, encircle, reinforce, and the like.

We came to a place where phone wires crossed the stream to continue on our side of the ravine. There was a bridge of boughs and rough planks and a cluster of huts on the edge of some open ground, covered with tobacco plants. A mile past the hamlet we hit a declining path that led to the trail along the stream. Krebitz, Stolz, and Jost descended to cut the phone link, making it appear a natural accident. They toppled the pole into the river and rolled a large boulder to where it had been.

Our expedition continued without incident and on the ninth day the dreary trekking ended on a wooded hill—eight hundred yards from the huge North Vietnamese Army dump and about one mile from the shore where the freighter *Huang-Po* was resting at anchor at the end of the pier of pontoons.

To our relief, it was evident that the work of unloading was only about to begin. There were trucks parked on the shore, two of them fitted with cranes.

I decided to attack both targets at midnight. Julius Steiner, Jost Waldman, and four demolition experts were to leave for the shore at 10 P.M., swim out to the freighter, board it, and mine the cargo holds with the timers set for 12:30 A.M. At the same time we would accomplish our job in the dump, setting the timers for 12:45 A.M. We calculated that by the time the freighter blew up, we'd be back on the hill where Steiner and his party were to join, us and we would leave immediately in the direction of Bai Dinh and the Laotian border.

Resting in the underbrush, Krebitz plotted the route Steiner should take across the railway line and road, where the elephant grass and shrubbery spread almost to the shore. He made a last inspection of the demolition charges, floats, and timers, then turned his attention to the supply dump.

"It's the largest *verdammte Lager* I've ever seen in Vietnam," Riedl said as he shifted his binoculars along the fenced perimeter. "Two guardhouses, eleven watchtowers, six ammo depots, at least five thousand drums of fuel.... They've even got a railway sliding."

"And trucks, tanks, Jeeps, troop carriers, and artillery," Karl Stolz added.

"Thirty-two T-34s and eight Josef Stalins," Krebitz completed the list. "Fifteen pieces of artillery.... They look like 105-mm howitzers.... Twenty Molotova trucks with 12.7-caliber MGs.... Sixteen Jeeps with 37-mm guns."

"Heilige Strohsack!" Jost Waldman exulted. "There's enough stuff here to keep an armored division on the move all the way to Saigon."

"That's where they want to go eventually," Stolz said.

The dump lay close to the Hanoi railway and road, and about a mile south we saw an army camp of tents with more trucks, tanks, and artillery.

"Moscow and Peking are surely not wasting time equipping Giap." Krebitz grunted, his eyes glued to the field glasses. "One thing is sure, Hans, that army—"

"—camp rules out a direct attack on the dump," I cut in.

"Richtig," he said with a nod. "Whatever we might do must be done in absolute silence."

"That damned camp wasn't on the aerial photos," Riedl said.

"Not the fault of the American reconnaissance," I replied. "It must be a very recent addition."

"It's only tents," Krebitz said. "You could set them up in a few hours."

We turned our attention back to the dump.

Krebitz called out, "Watchtowers at three hundred yards. Simple barbed-wire fence but illuminated at night by light bulbs at twenty-yard intervals." He scratched his head and looked at me grimly. "It's going to be very difficult to get inside without shooting, Hans."

"So it seems."

Jost cut in. "We should have arranged for a timely overflight to provide for a blackout."

Krebitz's chin snapped up and he turned briskly. *"Fliegeralarm hast g'sagt?"* he exulted. *"Jawohl!* An air-raid alarm! You've hit it, Jost. Only we don't need airplanes to cause a blackout."

Rising to one elbow, he slapped Waldner on the back. "You sure hit it!"

Waldner stared, baffled. "Hit—what?"

But Krebitz's attention was already back on the enclosure. "Have a look, Hans," he said after a while. "What do you see on the double pylon between the three wooden barracks and the fence?"

I shifted my field glasses to the spot he indicated and understood what he had in mind. "The transformer box of the power line, coming from the highway."

Rudolf nodded. "Using silencers, a pair of explosive slugs should knock it out."

"They'll hear the detonation in the watchtower."

"Short-circuiting condensers do pop," said Riedl. "And we'll have a fine blackout."

"There's a catch, though," Stolz said meditatively. "Army camps usually have a generator for emergency."

"They do here too," Krebitz agreed. "It's probably in the wooden shack next to the pylon. . . . You see the insulators and the cables? But by the time the Viets start it up, we'll be inside, planting mines."

"What about coming out?" Riedl asked.

Krebitz grinned. "When we're ready to leave the camp, Kretz will stop the generator, too, with a bazooka."

"It sounds practical," I commented. "But everything should be timed to the second."

"Leave all the timings to me," Rudolf said reassuringly. "We'll be through with the dump in ten minutes."

"Ten minutes might not be enough. The ammo cellars are surely locked, and we can't just shoot away the locks."

"Who wants to get inside?"

"What do you mean?"

"Now you sound like a newcomer." Rudolf shook his head. "With all those fuel drums bursting so close to the ammo cellars? Remember what happened at Man Hao? The burning fuel is going to flow right into the cellars."

Of course, Rudolf was right. The exploding drums would create a sea of gas and diesel oil, swamping the ground, flowing like lava, whipped by subsequent detonations.

I said, "You're right, Rudy. Post a pair of sharpshooters three hundred yards from the transformer house and another pair close to the generator shack."

"I hope your idea will work," Stolz said.

"Well, just make sure that you carry something to write with," Riedl quipped.

"What for?"

"To sign the register of Old Peter—should Rudy's plan misfire."

Jost Waldman, who hadn't heard the expression before, stared. "What Old Peter are you talking about?" he asked, puzzled.

"The holy one."

At dusk we synchronized our watches. When it was dark enough, Jost Waldman, Steiner, and four troopers left for the coast.

With action plotted in every detail, lying in the three-foot grass, we waited. Shortly before midnight our groups crawled closer to the camp perimeter, now lighted with powerful electric bulbs. Riedl and I with six men were to penetrate the western section of the wired enclosure and mine the fuel drums and some of the parked trucks. Krebitz, Stolz, and five men would enter from the north.

The minutes passed tensely. The air was hot and damp, and I could feel rivulets of perspiration trickling down my back and chest, drenching my undershirt. The men were taut-nerved with unease written on their faces. Every instant someone would glance at his watch.

The seconds crept past the minute mark and the minutes seemed like centuries.

13.

The Chinese Freighter

Julius Steiner, Jost Waldman, and their party encountered no one on the way to the beach. The highway was empty of traffic, except for occasional military vehicles whose headlights could be seen from miles away. The *Huang-Po* was lighted sparsely, as was the pontoon pier, where sentries paced their dreary hundred-yard beat back and forth. Farther in the south the lights of Dong Hoi glinted between the trees, but Bo Trach, to the north, lie wrapped in darkness.

The six men undressed quickly, piled their clothes into a crevass between the boulders, inflated their small floats, and waded into the water.

"I hope there aren't any sharks around," Jost whispered to Steiner, who joked.

"You have a sharp combat knife, Jost."

"Combat knife." Waldman snorted in disgust.

"Ah," demolition expert Kurt Seidlinger said. "Any shark that has a go at you will bite into a nice pot of TNT and turn itself into Chinese shark-fin soup, already cooked."

"Thanks for the consolation," Jost replied dryly. "I guess we'll be the noodles."

"Hsss!" Steiner hissed under his breath. "The water carries your fancy talk all the way to Japan."

They swam on with slow breast strokes, heading for the anchor chain in the prow, the links of which should be large enough to provide footholds.

The hull loomed closer and closer. The commando rested. Hanging on to the floats, they surveyed the vessel carefully. Steiner counted eight lighted windows and portholes, but no guards were visible anywhere and everything seemed quiet. There were four sentries on the pier.

Faithful to the teachings of their great Mao, who wrote in his little red book that "men who sleep well at night will march better in the morning," the crew had probably bunked down. The officers were either in their cabins or had gone to visit Dong Hoi, perhaps invited by their local hosts.

The anchor port was close enough to the deck for a man to haul himself aboard.

Taking his binoculars from the float's watertight pocket, Steiner gave the superstructure another look from prow to bow. He scrutinized the masts, the bridge, and also the pier where he spotted a pair of soldiers, holding fishing rods, but they would be out of sight of the seaward anchor.

Careful not to make noise, the commando swam for the chain. Jost pulled himself onto the links and waited for Steiner to hook the automatic pistol and explosives on his belt, then he began to climb with Julius and the others following close behind.

They vaulted soundlessly onto the deck and ducked into shelter among the crates and boxes, already piled there, ready to be unloaded. Their luck held. The large hold cover was open with the crane positioned overhead for the morning. In the hold dim emergency lights glowed outlining the cargo.

Steiner stabbed a finger toward the steel ladder that led into the hold.

Jost glanced at his wristwatch. "We have fifteen minutes to rig the crates and another fifteen to reach the shore."

"Let's move!" Steiner whispered.

One by one the commando descended and turned on their shaded torches. Steiner and Jost quickly inspected the cargo. The inscriptions were in Chinese and Russian, but thanks to the widespread illiteracy in Mao's empire the crates were also meticulously illustrated with stickers, depicting grenades, shells, dynamite, mortar bombs, and land mines.

"Perhaps they represent the local equivalent of the warning: Explosives, handle with care," Jost murmured.

Moving like shadows, the men placed their mines and incendiaries, chosing places where the charges could neither be spotted nor easily removed. With half of the job done, Steiner looked for access to the bow. From several steel doors he chose the outermost one, which opened into a corridor and passed by the machine and boiler rooms down below. The commando came face-to-face with a pair of bewildered sailors, hauling a tray of tools. Jost and three troopers overwhelmed them before they could utter a sound. A quick stab in the heart. The men concealed the corpses under a pile of oilcloths and moved on.

The rear hold contained trucks, semi-track vehicles, and artillery pieces. One trooper found twenty crates of small arms and ammunitions, which were quickly mined. On the way back to the prow, Steiner dropped a pair of incendiaries between some oil drums, then signaled scramble.

Halfway to the beach they rested and looked back. Reassuring silence prevailed on the deck of the *Huang-Po*. The first part of the perilous mission had been accomplished.

At midnight, Paul Kretz and Ernest Landauer from Gruppe Drei fired four explosive slugs into the transformer box. With a brilliant flash of light the transformer burst into flames. The lights in the camp went out.

We darted toward the perimeter, drew the wires apart, and rolled across the gap. We waited for an instant to orient ourselves, then darted toward our assigned objectives. I heard distant shouts and a brief altercation. Battery torches flashed around the distant barracks, the guardhouse, and the railway cars, but no beam turned in our direction. The enemy was still preoccupied with the burning transformer.

It took only a couple of minutes to mine the fuel drums at fifteen places, while Riedl's group rigged the trucks. Then, with a dull thudding sound, the generator started up. The perimeter lights began to wink, then lit up, although much dimmer than before. We kept in the shadows, away from the watchtowers, a pair of which turned on their searchlights and swept the ground along the fence. Groups of soldiers were running around the guardhouse and the barracks. Shouts and orders filtered down to where we squatted. I wondered how Krebitz and Stolz were faring.

At 12:15 P.M. troopers Metzger and Schindler fired a pair of bazooka shells into the generator shack. For the second time the perimeter lights went out, and we rushed for the fence. The explosion triggered a cacophony of shouts and high-pitched commands. Soldiers scrambled from their barracks. Hundreds of battery torches now swept the eastern part of the compound and a hand-driven siren began to howl.

RECALL TO INFERNO

Alarm!

Then the sky above the sea lit up with a dazzling flash and a gigantic detonation ripped apart the the Chinese freighter, which disintegrated in a towering funnel of fire and smoke. The shockwaves wrecked the pier and stirred up dust inside the dump. Running toward our point of assembly, I wondered what would happen when the fuel and ammunition behind us exploded.

To my relief, Steiner and Jost were already back, tired but content. Krebitz and Stolz showed up five minutes later.

"Let's get the hell out of here!" Rudolf gasped. "In fifteen minutes we'll have a new Hiroshima here. . . . I managed to break into one of the cellars full of dynamite from floor to ceiling, and we mined the lot."

Relieved of our heavy load of explosives, we hurried westward, no longer caring to conceal ourselves but following a dirt road. Behind us the doomed supply dump was now illuminated with car headlights, many of which were moving toward the gate.

"It's too late to evacuate the place," Riedl commented, but the vehicles were only moved into positions to illuminate the enclosure.

"Soon they'll have more light," Krebitz remarked, then looked at his watch and shouted. "Take shelter!"

We dived into the grass.

The earth beneath us heaved and rocked. The land toward Bo Trach vanished behind a rising wall of smoke, inside which more and more explosions cast flaming lightning in every direction. Moments later the shockwaves reached us, flattening trees, tearing brush and grass, knocking the wind out of our lungs. Earth and dust covered everything, as if we were in a sandstorm in the Sahara. When the dust finally settled, I saw thousands of glowing metal shards and burning bits of wood raining down on the forest and the fields. Shells and mortar bombs streaked through the air. The secondary explosions blew fuel over the railway line and highway. Telephone poles crashed down. The high tension line along the road collapsed. Dong Hoi was hidden in pitch darkness.

Kretz and Schindler were Stalingrad veterans and Alois

Fuchs had been through hell at Monte Cassino, but none could remember having seen a similar devastation.

When the smoke momentarily lifted we observed the site through our field glasses but all we saw was a burning desert. The buildings, watchtowers, fences, and railway cars had disappeared, pulverized, and their debris was blown into the sea and the nearby fields, where hundreds of small fires burned.

The commando marched through the night. Toward dusk, Krebitz spotted three pairs of headlights behind us. We crossed a stream with a plank bridge, which Steiner and Stolz demolished with grenades. Positioning ourselves on the far bank, we waited with the bazookas and the remaining six shells.

We no longer felt like playing hide-and-seek with the enemy.

The trucks with a platoon of troops emerged from the wooded bend and halted in front of the broken bridge, bumper to bumper. Someone shouted, "Disembark!" then Kretz's bazooka slammed a projectile into the foremost vehicle. Schindler and Landauer hit the second and third truck in less time than it takes to wink, while we opened up on the scattering soldiers.

Ignoring the random shouts of the survivors, we withdrew and marched away. If we were lucky, hours might pass before the district commander would know about the incident. Even if one of the trucks had carried a wireless set, it probably had been destroyed or damaged.

We were already five hundred yards away when the North Vietnamese began blazing away at the empty brush along the stream, and no one seemed eager to follow us.

The rising sun found us near the Bai Dinh–Tuyen Hou road and a guardhouse with overhead phone wires. Our sharpshooters shot away the line, then we overran the station, manned by eights guards, of whom only three survived our Blitz. Krebitz tried to gather some information about military dispositions along the road to Bai Dinh, which the prisoners refused to furnish. There was no time to waste on the third degree. Krebitz and Steiner finished them off.

The men ransacked the guardhouse and collected all the transportable food, mostly rice and dried fish but also some canned beans, bamboo shoots, and meat, all which were promptly distributed. Unaware of what might lay ahead, I decided to abandon the road and disappear, once more, in the unbroken wilderness of gradually rising hills that eventually grew into towering mountains.

Safety before speed! We were no longer incognito but hunted.

In order to confuse eventual pursuers, Krebitz and his men marched half a mile down the road discarding evidence of alien presence to suggest that we'd taken a southerly route. He then retraced his steps and we entered into the jungle.

Toward the west, in Laotian territory, loomed the Chiai Truong mountain range with its peaks of six to seven thousand feet. At the rate we were advancing it appeared as world's end, hopelessly beyond reach.

Out came the machetes, and we embarked on another tortuous ascent, hacking and slashing at creepers and brushes. Our flimsy native garb offered no protection against the thorny weeds, sharp splinters, and rough bark. After two hours of excruciating advance and at the end of our strength, we were perhaps two miles inside the wilderness. Around eleven o'clock, sore in every muscle and worn, I ordered halt near a brook to bed down for the day. The men were so spent that no one bothered to wash off two days' filth or to eat; they just slumped to the ground where they happened to be standing and dozed off.

I followed their example.

Krebitz posted sentries to be relieved at half-hour intervals. Otherwise they would have fallen asleep. As a matter of fact, both Jost and Kretz did fall asleep, and for the first time in many years, if only briefly, our survival had been left to chance.

When I woke up at 4:30 P.M. Rudolf and Helmut were standing in the brook, in their underwear, washing. I joined them in the chilly water and felt a great deal better afterward.

The men were still snoring under their mosquito nets, now serving against flies. Krebitz boiled some coffee and we ate our last biscuits and sardines.

"From now on it's going to be the native diet," Rudolf remarked, hefting a lump of dried fish, wrinkling his nose and grimacing.

I turned toward Helmut. "You'd better raise the men. They'll have to wash themselves and eat something, then we should push on. I want to get closer to the border before dusk."

"If Father Ho's apes find us and give us chase, the border won't stop them, Hans," Krebitz reminded me.

"I know, but we'll be closer to home."

"That's true. Laos lies closer to Germany," Rudolf cracked.

"Germany?" Riedl's chin lifted. "I've even forgotten what she looks like."

Krebitz chuckled. "Well, she doesn't look the way you remember her, that's for sure."

"We should visit home," Helmut said nostalgically.

"All right," Rudolf replied with a nod. "Show the way."

It took some time and effort to get the men back on their feet amid quiet laments and soft curses. A few of them had to be marched into the brook virtually at "gunpoint."

The commando moved on shortly before 6 P.M. and marched until it was too dark to negotiate the ravines and rock-strewn acclivities. We bivouacked at the chilly altitude of about five thousand feet, and to render our trip more miserable, a drizzly rain began to fall. We were traveling light, without anything unnecessary, including burlaps. There was nothing else to do but "go native"—cut down saplings, gather boughs and leafy branches, and build ourselves four makeshift shelters. Ours weren't as perfect as their native counterparts, but where the roof leaked we stuffed it with grass. In the end we were able to light two small fires to warm ourselves and dry our clothes.

Krebitz tried to calculate our location and came to the "happy" conclusion that we had some 120 miles to go before we could turn eastward, below the armistice line, and reenter into South Vietnam.

"The closest Laotian village, Bhan Nha Phao, should be twelve miles away," he told me over a cup of warm soup. "We should avoid it because of the Laotian garrison stationed there."

"Once inside Laos we should come across some easy paths," Stolz said. "The former Vietminh trails, now abandoned on account of the shorter routes."

"If we find one, we'll take it," Krebitz replied. "Or else we won't get home until Christmas."

"We might bump into a random Viet party," Jost said.

"Or the Pathet Lao," Riedl added.

"In which case we'll get more food," I cut in.

"Food . . ." Stolz repeated, looking as if he were about to vomit. "Do the vile bastards eat anything else but rice and fish?"

"Why won't you teach them to prepare *Wiener Schnitzels*?" Krebitz suggested.

"Well, the next time you catch Vietcong, don't go bumping them off, but let us teach them to make some decent meals," Stolz answered.

Riedl exclaimed, "Will you please stop talking about *Schnitzels*? You can kill a guy with your blabberings."

Two days later, in Laos and marching south along a comfortable path, my walkie-talkie beeped. Krebitz reported a small party of Vietcong with some fifty coolies resting near the stream, boiling rice. I told him to stay put until we arrived. Confident in our guerrilla outfit, we moved on boldly, singing aloud the revolutionary song "*Ho kéo Phao*."

> The valleys are profound,
> But our hatred is deeper,
> Roll your gun forward and
> Turn the battlefield into
> A graveyard of the enemy.

We came into view. The guerrillas scrambled and gathered on the trail in loose groups without making any hostile gesture. They watched us descend along the shrubby slope, gesticulating, chattering, waving hands, and hollering greetings.

Our ruse worked. We waved back, then opened fire. With cheers and smiles turning into terrified expressions of horror and disbelief, the enemy fell like ripe corn under the scythe. Leaving their loaded bicycles, fires, and pots, the unarmed coolies bolted for the woods. We hunted them down in groups or in pairs, in the bushes, hollow tree trunks, crevasses, the rushing stream.

Then we helped ourselves to the already prepared warm lunch. There was enough rice, already cooked, to last for several days. Every man carefully wrapped his share in fresh latania leaves. We also found eggs and salt, the latter carried in hollow segments of bamboo.

The corpses were frisked for money, cigarettes, matches, grenades, and watches, but on this occasion our "booty" was meager.

They weren't even decent guerrillas, only armed vagrants," Krebitz grumbled.

What delighted us the most were twelve sturdy Thai horses, which the men discovered in the forest. "Hooray!" Riedl exulted when he saw Jost and Steiner leading the horses. "Here we go a-riding home!"

The horses could not accommodate all of us, but we could take turns and they also carried our knapsacks. Marching was easier without a load on the shoulder.

We heaped the guerrilla equipment and supplies in four large piles: food, weapons, ammo, and the rest; wrecked the bicycles, most of them French Peugeots, others Chinese-made; and set fire to the lot.

Bypassing the village of Phao, we traversed a pair of streams in rugged gorges, where our advance guard bumped into an overzealous Laotian lieutenant with a patrol of six troops, who "trapped" Krebitz and Jost Waldman at the southern extremity of a plank suspension bridge. Rudolf beeped us the appropriate signal. Soon we captured the lieutenant and his soldiers and "liberated" our companions from their twelve-minute captivity.

Trying to appear extremely official and composed, the lieutenant, who spoke fluent French, frostily reminded me that members of the French armed forces in Vietnam were illegal trespassers in neutral Laos.

In a similar tone, I calmly asked him where the North Vietnamese were getting their entry visas from. He stiffened and replied that there were no North Vietnamese soldiers in Laos, only Vietnamese refugees. He delivered this twenty-four-carat shit with immense dignity and without batting an eye.

In turn, I casually informed him that we had nothing to do with the French forces, a statement that baffled him.

"Then who are you?" he asked, and I told him that we were a group of buccaneers, returning home after a raid in North Vietnam. From his puzzled expression I deduced that he didn't know a buccaneer from Adam.

"We are a group of pirates, Lieutenant," I enlightened him amiably.

"Savage pirates!" Riedl added for good measure. He unfurled

our fancy Jolly Roger and began to wave it. His playful antics drew an unexpected reaction. In a wink the lieutenant's authority crumbled. His composure faded, transformed into a look of sheer misery. He stepped back and stared at us with wide eyes.

"But you—you must be—what Hanoi calls the Commando of Death!" he muttered haltingly, and now it was our turn to stare in disbelief.

"Holy shit and three thunders!" Riedl exclaimed. "I didn't know we were that famous!"

"It seems we are," Krebitz commented with a grin. "And I like this kind of popularity too."

The lieutenant began fumbling with his belt, wanting to unbuckle it. His soldiers dropped their rifles.

"Heavens—no!" I stopped him. "No one has told you to lay down your arms, sir," I protested. The lieutenant seemed more dumbfounded than before, so I added for good measure, "We have no trouble with Vientiane. You are free to leave."

"Back toward Nha Phao," Krebitz added, indicating the way north with his thumb. "Not toward Kavak, which happens to be our direction."

The bewildered Laotians were only too eager to decamp.

"By the way," I said casually, "you might come across some Vietcong, likewise traveling without visas.... We met them five miles uptrail."

The lieutenant, who had recovered some of his former demeanor, said determinedly, "If they are still there, I shall arrest them."

"I guess they'll be there," Riedl reassured him. "But you won't be able to arrest them."

"Are they—many?" he asked warily.

"About twenty. All dead.... *Bon voyage.*"

We saluted him. Somewhat hesitantly, he returned our gesture. We marched across the bridge, the cables of which Krebitz cut to forestall any unwanted tailing.

I waved a friendly hand toward the still-gazing group, then stabbed a finger southward. *"Los! Weiterfahren!* Move on!"

In five days of relatively uneventful trekking, our commando traversed the headwaters of the Sé Kong and Sé Noi rivers, plus a dozen streams and brooks that flowed into them. We spent one night in the hut of a peasant family, the head of which, an elderly man and his son, had treated us very kindly. In his youth, the farmer had served in the French Colonial Army and retired with the rank of corporal. He had been decorated for bravery and proudly displayed us the weather-beaten leather box in which he preserved his medallion.

"We must live with the Vietcong," he explained in halting French. "They are close. The French are far. But even if they would be closer, they could not protect us from the bandits. . . . And there's also the Pathet Lao. Sometimes worse than the Vietcong."

He slaughtered a dozen hens to provide us with a good meal, and his wife prepared sixty boiled eggs for the road. In exchange I presented him with our horses, which gesture that struck the man speechless. It also made him rich.

Riedl said afterward, "You made me feel like a Boy Scout who has done his good deed for the day, Hans."

Steiner slapped him on the shoulder and said with a chuckle, "It won't unlock the gate of paradise for you."

"But you shouldn't worry." Krebitz joined in the farce. "Lucifer won't let us enter into hell either. He needs no competitors."

Jost Waldman threw his arms wide. "I know! We'll be roaming in the damned jungles and swamps of Vietnam until the end of time—like some landlocked Flying Dutchman."

"Sure," Riedl retorted. "I think if I popped off right here, my ghost would be marching after you all the same."

Eleven days after the destruction of the North Vietnamese supply dump and the Chinese freighter, we reentered the Republic of Vietnam, without having sustained a single casualty.

We'd given Hanoi a powerful demonstration that the Ho Chi Minh trail was wide enough for two-way traffic.

Having read a copy of my report to General Houssong, Major Roy Cooke commented, "You know, Captain Wagemueller, apart from the material success of your expedition, you revealed a very important sideline: that, although very powerful in the south, the Communists are rather weak inside their own territory. . . . It's a very useful fact to know."

14.

Deadly Dew

For quite some time I was wondering what might the reason be for Schulze's ardent cultivation of Captain Spata's friendship. The two were spending many evenings together in the cabarets of Cartinet Street, or at Erich's place, where Mike became a frequent guest, sometimes alone, sometimes in the company of Sergeant Starr. Every now and then Krebitz and Riedl would also participate, and I had the queer sensation that Erich and company were brewing a top hush-hush affair, from which I was tacitly excluded.

But whenever I even hinted at their mysterious plot, centered in the annex of our transport repair shop, which was kept under locks and seven seals by Schulze, Erich would casually brush aside my query. "We're working on a small invention, Hans. If and when it is ready, you'll be the first to know," he'd say, or something similar.

One quiet Sunday morning I called Erich over the phone and told him that I wanted to discuss something urgent. He bade me to come over.

I found him in the living room, sprawled on a couch, a pair of fans stirring a small hurricane around him. Before I could say as much as a hello, he rose to one elbow and, striking the newspaper with the back of his hand, he boomed, "Look at this one here! The French Communist party decided to adhere to the new Kremlin directive . . . like a good dog."

"Is that news?" I asked sarcastically, and went to fetch myself a beer from the fridge. "Whose directives should the Communists adhere to?" I continued, dropping into an armchair. "Dwight Eisenhower's?"

"But how could the government tolerate Thorez and his crowd of traitors openly siding with the enemy?" he complained.

"The Russians are no enemy for Thorez and company," I

reminded him, wondering how I could change the subject. I knew that unless I managed to sidetrack our conversation, I would be in for a long political merry-go-round.

"This is why France is losing everywhere," Schulze fumed. "There are spies and saboteurs sitting in responsible positions, advising Moscow on every important move the government or the army plans."

Trying to take a pleasanter tack, I said casually, "At least there's no Communist party in our new *Deutschland*." Germany had just received full independence from the Western Allies.

"Let's hope it'll stay that way," Erich commented, groping for his slacks. "Otherwise we might as well pack up Task Force-G and go home, guns and all."

"Where's Suoi?"

"She's gone out shopping with Noi. . . . You'll stay for lunch, of course."

"If I'm invited," I said with particular emphasis that hinted at my previous exclusion from Erich's dinners. He failed to take notice.

"Consider yourself invited." He picked a beer for himself and sidled down opposite me. "You wanted to talk about what?"

"Well, now that we're alone—it's my old sob story."

"Schiess los!"

"The annex."

"Ah." He grinned. "Our special undertaking. . . ."

"In your very special workshop. All very private and confidential."

He chuckled. "You couldn't get in, eh?" He drew a key from his pocket and tossed it into my lap. "There's the key, if you want to quench your curiosity, but all we have there are a couple of mortar shells."

"That's bullshit and you know it."

"The shells are special," he admitted with a grimace.

"Okay, Erich—what did you concoct this time?"

"A new kind of shell for the 81-mm mortars."

"With Spata and Starr?"

"Heavens, no! Mike is an expert in chemistry, and I needed his theoretical help to make something."

"Something—what?"

"A new pesticide," he replied. "To fill the shells with. "Co-Cl-two."

"What the hell is that stuff?"

"Phosgene!" he stated matter-of-factly. His reply almost knocked me from my chair. I knew that Schulze and Krebitz were a pair of resourceful devils, but to team up to make a poison gas . . .

"What for?" I blurted without thinking. I could have answered that question myself.

"What do you mean, what for?" Erich exclaimed. "To shell the soldiers of Father Ho, naturally."

"Naturally," I repeated with a hint of irony. Then I lighted a cigarette and drew a deep breath.

"Let me have one too," he said, and I passed him my cigarette case and lighter.

"Are you producing that stuff in our motor pool annex?" I asked warily.

Erich shook his head. "We have a couple of local experts with a properly equipped lab to do the manufacturing. We're only placing the ready containers into the mortar shells."

"Without even wearing a protective mask?"

Schulze's eyes kindled and he replied candidly, "Why did I ask Uncle Sam to send us some scuba gear, Hans?"

"I thought you wanted to mine some Vietcong sampans on the Mekong," I taunted.

"Of course. That'll come too. . . . The scuba gear is also perfect for handling gas."

I leaned back in my chair and sipped some beer. Erich cracked a broad, confident smile and beamed exuberantly. *"Jawohl, Herr Kommandant,* we are brewing the greatest Mickey Finn the Vietcong ever swallowed."

"So it seems."

He observed me searchingly. "What do you say?"

"May I ask if you have already brewed some gas?"

"Twenty shells," Erich conceded. "We should have at least one hundred to clinch the job."

"What job?"

"Wiping out a large Vietcong base south of the Mekong, near the Cambodian border. . . . Without any fighting, mind you."

He clambered to his feet and beckoned me to a wall map. After picking up a bamboo pointer, he showed me the site.

"Here it is. Five miles south of Nha-bang. . . . All rice paddies and swamps with a forested hill toward the border."

Toying with the pointer, he dropped his words like coins on the table. "Creepers. Elephant grass. One peak of two thousand feet. No roads. Only canals. All navigable by sampans. No villages around."

"When did you find it?"

"We weren't sitting idle while you were up north, you know. . . ."

"If you were already so close, why didn't you attack that camp?"

Schulze rolled his eyes and uttered a sound of bitter amusement. "Attack it? Mensch! With Krebitz, Riedl, and you absent? That base is a fortress, Hans. Ringed with heavy MGs and 37-mm guns. There are at least eight hundred Viets in the camp . . . perhaps a thousand. They gunned down a pair of copters and a low-flying B-26. Two months ago Saigon dispatched a battalion to clean up the site. Only two hundred of them returned."

"It should be a difficult target."

"Difficult?" Erich exclaimed. "It's impossible. . . . Open fields, paddies, and swamps on three sides. The last five hundred yards without any cover."

"Therefore you want to try your fancy shells."

"Lobbed from a distance of eighteen hundred yards. Out of range for the machine guns."

"But not for the 37-mm guns," I reminded him.

"I've thought of that too. There are dikes. The mortars could fire from the far side. . . . With the phosgene you don't even have to aim, just lay down a creeping barrage. Before long you may move in to count the corpses and wreck the base at leisure."

"Wearing the scuba gear, I presume."

"Richtig," Erich confirmed. "All we need is a fine, sunny day."

"To speed up the catalysis between the carbon monoxide and the chlorine?"

Schulze stared. "How do you know that?"

"Before forty-nine, the S.S. were still instructed in the technicalities of gas warfare."

"Congratulations. Your memory is excellent." He lifted his bottle of beer. "Cheers."

He drank, parked the bottle on the table, and added with a chuckle, "Imagine wiping out a thousand Vietcong in ten minutes, Hans. They can't even flee. You cannot run far with lungs blistered to bleeding shreds."

"And you just imagine what'll happen if the news of your crap should reach the newsmen," I replied wryly.

Erich waved a hand. "Why should it ever reach the newsmen?" he asked. "After the coup we'll pile the corpses around the ammo depots and blow everything to smithereens. . . . The whole damned forest will burn down to the paddies."

There was a pause. I looked at him levelly. "Is Captain Spata somehow involved in all this?"

"Of course not. But he's a chemical engineer, and I screwed the manufacturing formula out of him."

I rose and tapped him on the shoulder. "Let's get Krebitz and Riedl. I'd like to have a look at your gas company premises."

"Now?"

"That's right."

Twenty minutes later we gathered in the mysterious annex and stood in front of a pair of ammo boxes containing twenty 81-mm mortar shells, neatly marked with three yellow crosses.

"Will it work?" I asked Krebitz.

"We tried it on mice."

"I mean the releasing mechanism. Is it reliable?"

"There's no mechanism to malfunction, Hans," he explained. "We have only removed eighty percent of the explosive to make place for the container. Like the ones here." He opened the lid of another box with padded compartments and straps to hold the fragile-looking containers in place.

"They look like the inner tubes of Thermos flasks," I remarked.

"They are Thermos flasks," Erich said. "When the shell explodes, the flask breaks and out comes the phosgene."

I turned my attention back to Krebitz. "Do you agree on testing your cocktail on the Vietcong?"

Rudolf grinned. "I'd hate the idea of experimenting on Rhesus monkeys," he said in a casual voice.

"And monkeys cost money," Riedl cracked. "The terrorists are participating free of charge."

Schulze said searchingly, "I hope you're with us, Hans."

"You know that as the commander of Task Force-G, I cannot consent to using a weapon that's been outlawed by the whole civilized world," I said, not very convincingly.

"Also, dann es ist alles in Ordnung," Riedl quipped. "Everything's okay. Onetime S.S. killers don't belong to the civilized world."

"Stop playing, will you? This isn't something to monkey about," I said reprovingly.

"Even General Houssong said that we may use any method or weapon," he argued.

"I remember what Houssong said. But he didn't mean either the H-bomb or poison gas, Helmut."

Erich cut in. "Mensch! Don't make us chuck our fine shells into the Mekong."

"It might have been better for me not to know anything."

"It was you who insisted."

"Now I resent it," I stated flatly. "And I know nothing."

"Abgemacht!" Krebitz boomed. "Excesses perpetrated by your subordinates without your knowledge."

"Sure, Rudolf. Those who voiced similar excuses during the Nuremberg trials were hanged good and proper. . . . Who else is in on this?"

"Stolz, Jost, Steiner, and Altreiter," Erich replied.

"And the Vietnamese in the laboratory," Krebitz added.

"What's the name of the laboratory?"

"Star Chemicals. Produces rat poison, insecticides, and the like. Four chemists and two technicians."

"Our official request was for pesticide," said Schulze. "Stahnke scrutinized the background of the locals. They were badly wronged by the Communists, Hans: brothers executed, wives, children, and parents killed in terrorist bomb explosions. . . . They also know that being talkative could be as dangerous as the phosgene they're producing for us."

"When do you intend to attack that base?"

"When we have at least one hundred shells ready. It'll take some weeks. Everything must be made by hand."

"We already have a code name for the operation," Riedl told me exuberantly. "Deadly Dew."

"Fitting," I commented dryly. "Let me know when you're ready. The details must be worked out carefully, for there can be no mistake. I hope you realize that."

"Naturally," Schulze said reassuringly, visibly satisfied.

"And not a word to the French, I recommend."

Krebitz said, "Captain Dessault knows."

I frowned. "How come?"

"From Stahnke."

"That's shit!"

"Dessault hates the Commies so much that he would turn the plague on them if he could. He lost his brother at Dien Bien Phu."

"I know. . . . What does he think of your idea?"

"Dessault? He said we should wait until we had five hundred shells, then make a trip to Hanoi instead," Riedl retorted.

But there were other considerations as well, mostly technical ones. We had only ten scuba outfits, although Krebitz was sure that more might be borrowed from the Saigon navy, or perhaps we could even purchase them. In the end he managed to procure fifty gas masks from the local fire department, each equipped with a small container of air, enough for half an hour. The masks would ensure that the mortar crews would also be protected in case of an unexpected change of wind.

A commando of about seventy men should suffice to carry twenty mortars and their shells, including some regular ones.

During many nights, while lying sleepless in my bed, I pondered over Erich's scheme.

I was trying to reassure myself with self-presented arguments. Until now the Communists had not protested against the explosive slugs we were using against the Vietcong. Perhaps they didn't notice it yet. (Naturally the United Nations would never discuss the guerrilla methods of using poisoned arrows and punji stakes, or bullets and shells that had been stored in animal carcasses, so that even light wounds might cause death through blood poisoning.)

The guerrillas were not yet equipped with flamethrowers, but they began to use phosphorus shells with napalmlike effect, made in China. In the never-ending war both sides constantly tried to improve the methods of mass destruction. The Vietcong dropped cholera- or typhoid-infected excrement into wells. We returned the courtesy by poisoning their water sources with arsenic and strychnine. We often permitted them to capture much-wanted medicines—poisoned or substituted. Chemical warfare was not something new in Vietnam.

What difference should the phosgene make? Solid, liquid, or gaseous, poison remains poison.

As long as we kept the affair top secret, there would be no difference at all.

The day of action dawned.

The weather forecast seemed reassuring. Three days of sunny, warm weather with only sparse local precipitation over the central highlands.

At 4:15 A.M. we boarded the four GMC trucks of the South Vietnamese Army, which were to take us near Chau-dôc, a village on the southern branch of the Mekong, situated only two miles from the border. Chau-dôc was a well-know guerrilla sanctuary.

The only passable road was a circuitous one, running from Saigon to My-tho and from there to Vien-lang by ferry across the river, passing Cân-tho, then toward Cambodia along the Mekong, across hundreds of canals. A trip of 350 miles through government-held townships and guerrilla-controlled villages, over roads whose ownership seemed conveniently divided. The Saigon forces controlled them during the day, the Vietcong during the night, when no decent soldier would set foot outside his fortified camp. This merry state of "divide and rule" had existed for quite some time.

When I asked our native driver how long it would take to arrive at Chau-dôc, he replied, grinning, "With or without Vietcong attacks, sir?"

The length of the trip would also depend on other factors, he said; mostly on how many bridges over canals had been wrecked by the guerrillas during the night.

The first part of the trip was uneventful. We passed innumerable South Vietnamese checkpoints where the troops, having nothing else to do, pestered bus passengers and peasants on their way to the city markets, checking identity papers, baggage, and merchandise. As if the Vietcong should need to smuggle a couple of pistols or grenades into Saigon, concealed in the bottom of wicker baskets laden with fruits and vegetables. The guerrillas had the roads all to themselves during the night and could haul hundreds of tons of supplies into Saigon by trucks!

We traversed the Mekong under the "protective cover" of two howitzers and a pair of armored cars. They looked very martial, and a casual visitor would have been impressed by the orderly tranquillity they commanded. However, we knew that as soon as the sun dipped behind the hills of Cambodia, those war machines would return into their fortified base and roll up the pavement for the night. The ferry service was continued by the Vietcong.

A large number of sampans were moving toward the delta and along the innumerable canals, laden with passengers and merchandise. Along the road we passed peasants carrying baskets suspended on both ends of short poles; young women in closely fitting, ankle-length dresses, the married ones wearing their hair in a cylindrical chignon, while the girls let their long hair flow freely.

We were accustomed to such picturesque spectacles, and I wondered how many guerrillas with their deadly load would reach the capital or the delta before the day was out. Erich must have entertained similar ideas, for suddenly he exclaimed, "I bet that Hanoi could send half its army to Saigon without anyone noticing a thing."

There were no bridges blown, only tires. The trucks had not been sniped at but broke down from natural causes—a choked carburetor here, a leaking fuel pump there, all of which our men fixed. At Lang-xuyen our driver took the wrong turn, and it was only after some miles that we were able to turn around on the twelve-foot-wide road.

"Can't you read the road signs?" I browbeat the driver, whose distraction had lost us almost two hours.

He shook his thumb toward the corporal sitting next to him and replied with genuine indignation, "I am only driving, sir. Corporal Truong is checking road signs."

"Well, isn't that fabulous!" Schulze commented sarcastically.

"He only drives! And should his corporal fail to notice a ten-foot warning, *Achtung Minen,* he would drive straight onto the minefield!" He shook his head. "He only drives!"

After another breakdown due to a fused ball bearing, we were obliged to crowd into the remaining three vehicles.

Krebitz said wryly, "I'm sure the trucks have gone through half the war without the wheels being greased once."

"Why should the Viets bother?" Stolz commented with a shrug. "When something breaks down, Uncle Sam will send a replacement."

The corporal told me reassuringly that if we couldn't make it to Chau-dôc before dusk he would pull up for the night in the nearest fortified camp, because not even sweet Jesus (he was a Christian) would make him drive along the Mekong in darkness. And so it happened that the motorized part of our voyage terminated fifteen miles past Lang-xuyen, near a canal that ran a southwesterly course. We were about thirty miles away from Tri-ton, west of which lay the swamps that surrounded the Vietcong base. We decided to continue on foot. The South Vietnamese wondered why we should accept so great a risk.

"Marching along the road at night?" the garrison commander, a young lieutenant, asked us, puzzled. "In two hours the full moon will shine and the guerrillas will ambush you."

"Don't worry." Krebitz waved a hand. "We've been through guerrilla country before, and the only ones who suffered were the Vietcong."

He treated us to a good dinner of roast buffalo steaks and the inevitable rice, after which we marched off toward Chau-dôc, seemingly adhering to our original plan. Three miles down the road Task Force-G turned onto a footpath along a canal and melted into the darkness. We moved in single file, keeping a distance of ten yards between the men. Krebitz and the trailblazers were three hundred yards ahead of Schulze and myself. We communicated through the WTs.

Shortly before 10 P.M. the full moon rose. Marching became easier but also more dangerous on account of our sharply outlined shapes.

Thanks to the American night scopes, Rudolf spotted a group of guerrillas sailing along the canal in eight laden sampans. He passed the word and we prepared a trap. Taking twenty men, Schulze crossed over to the far side and we lined both banks of the canal with submachine guns.

The unsuspecting enemy drifted into our fiery reception. Some fifty submachine guns, blazing away from a distance of fifteen yards, at people massed in boats. It was all over in a few seconds. Sixty corpses lay sprawled along the slippery banks, in the slowly drifting boats, in the brush, partly submerged in the water. Krebitz had the sampans lashed together, then mined the lot with fuses set for ten minutes, and we hurried on.

The explosion shot a hundred-foot flame and tore a fifteen-foot gap in the embankment. The canal's water gushed into the outlying fields and paddies.

Fifteen minutes later Krebitz reported sighting a group of civilians. "Men, women, and kids," he told me. "Apparently without weapons."

"Probably locals coming to inspect the site of the detonation," Erich remarked.

"There should be no village around here."

Schulze shrugged. "That we know of. . . ."

"Let them pass," I told Krebitz.

We clambered down on the grassy declivity of the embankment and lay low in the grass until the group of some twenty chattering natives passed by, then we resumed our march. (Until this very day I have no idea where those people had come from. We saw no hamlet on either side of the canal for miles.)

It was sunrise when we camped down on a wooded hillock that emerged from the paddies like a small island. It was covered with huts, inhabited by some fifty families, perhaps two hundred people altogether. They were terrified to wake up and find the area occupied by the *Thays*—foreigners. Erich and Krebitz reassured them that if they were neither Vietcong nor custodians of terrorist caches, they had nothing to fear. They also said that for the time being no one should try to leave the hamlet.

Riedl and Altreiter posted sentries with orders to stop anyone from leaving and capture those trying to enter. Krebitz, Stolz, and Steiner inspected the huts, but except for ten vintage shotguns and one French revolver, no arms were found. The revolver belonged to the elderly headman, who showed me a yellowed license, dated 1936. I returned his gun and also restored the shotguns to their owners, a gesture that reduced their concern. The inhabitants of the hamlet were apparently trying to keep out of trouble and offered no sanctuary to the guerrillas. Krebitz reasoned that it was probably the guerrillas who left the people alone, perhaps because the place was so isolated and wide open to aerial or artillery bombardment.

The headman seemed worried because of the restrictions we imposed, and after a brief consultation with my companions, I agreed that the women and youngsters should attend to their daily work in the paddies. Otherwise some neighbors might become curious. "Tell your people not to try to escape, for they'll be shot without warning," I warned him sternly. "In the evening we shall leave for Rach-gia, on the seashore, and after we depart you may do as you please."

I gave the false direction intentionally.

With endless bowing and bobbing amid broad smiles, the headman reassured me that my orders would be obeyed, although it didn't end our problems. Around two o'clock in the afternoon four women and two men happened along the path. Carrying baskets, they entered into the village and were stopped and searched by Jost Waldman. Finding them clean, they were released within the confines of the hamlet to barter their goods.

We slept in turns. The inhabitants were docile—neither overly friendly nor hostile, and they even offered us some boiled rice, which I politely declined. The natives gathered around us in small groups, especially the youngsters, whom Krebitz and Schulze treated to biscuits and bars of candy. Elderly women with round, creased faces huddled together on the nearby steps and terraces of their huts of wood and straw, conversing in low voices. Most huts had cooking pots hanging from tripods in the open, with fires going underneath. Pigs and hens strolled between the dwellings in peaceful coexistence with cats and dogs. Water buffalo idled in the shady bog.

The dwellings were well made of wood, bamboo, and straw with wickerwork partitions and entrances covered with colorful linen cloth. They were clean. In fact, the entire village appeared astonishingly clean, and when I mentioned this to the headman, the plump little man in his late fifties proudly showed me a first-aid box with a selection of French-made drugs, among them antimalaria pills and antibiotics.

"In my youth I attended the French missionary school in Cholon," he told me in a slow but correct French. "I am trying to keep diseases away from our village. . . . Also the war."

Speaking earnestly, he admitted that the inhabitants were paying a toll to the Vietcong: 100 pounds of rice, 200 eggs, 20 hens, and 150 pounds of fish every three months.

"In exchange, they let us live in peace," he explained. "We may carry our goods to the city market without being robbed or killed."

Trustfully, he showed me his *Laissez Passez,* given by the Vietcong and signed by a certain Commissar Kwang Lien-hu.

"He is not Vietnamese but Chinese," the headman explained.

The name rang a familiar bell.

"Have you ever seen this Commissar Kwang?" Schulze asked.

The response was affirmative. "He has come here two or three times in the past to ascertain how much we can offer to the cause of the liberation."

"Is he a short man, close to sixty and with a scar across his left cheek?"

"Oui, c'est lui," the headman replied without hesitation. "It's him."

"Herrgott, Hans!" Erich exclaimed. "He's the same fellow we encountered when we conducted our ideological debate in front of those Meo villagers up north."

"Together with Commissar Kly," Rudolf added. "Sure. . . . Kwang must be the same troublemaker we permitted to leave."

"And live!" Riedl cracked. "You see, we shouldn't have done it."

"He has certainly come a long way from the Chinese border," Krebitz said. "It'd be fun to meet him again."

"Not for Kwang, though. . . ."

I turned toward the headman. "Do you happen to know where the commissar and his Vietcong are?"

"In a camp somewhere near the border. Perhaps inside Cambodia."

I did not wish to mention the base west of Tri-ton, so I dropped the subject.

The commando departed at dusk, and the night's march landed us north of the Vietcong base. Once again Krebitz followed a canal. According to the sketch that Schulze had drawn of the region, the canal should have flowed into a stream coming from Cambodia and discharging into the Gulf of Siam. Erich's point of reference lay six miles northeast of our target, which, as we later discovered, was also a training camp for guerrillas. From that hypothetical point our way continued across weedy swamplands that terminated in an open patch of paddies five hundred yards wide. Beyond the paddies rose the forested elevation and the enemy base.

Somewhere between the paddies and the swamps we planned to set up our mortars at twenty-yard intervals and shell the woods from a distance of about one mile. The sky was spangled with stars and the gentle breeze from the northwest suited our plan.

Led by Krebitz, Gruppe Drei entered the morass. We followed them at a distance in ankle-deep, weed-infested water. Sometimes we sank knee-deep in the mire but, sweating and cursing, the men plodded on.

Unexpectedly the sharp staccato of a machine gun ripped into the frogs' steady chorus.

Halt!

The troops squatted or kneeled down and waited tensely.

Krebitz called. "There's a lookout platform," he said quietly. "Right in the water, erected on piles. . . . Three bastards with a Chinese MG. I recognized it by its tune."

"And you're properly illuminated too," I said, referring to the moon.

"One cannot be careful enough." Rudolf grunted with dismay. "Anyway, they only stirred the swamp and stilled the frogs."

Naturally Krebitz held his fire, permitting the enemy gunner to wonder whether he had been shooting at an illusion. Twilight can play strange tricks on taut nerves and strained eyes. And hearing no exchange of fire, the guerrillas in the camp might think that the brief salvo was accidental.

"Can you knock them out?" I asked Krebitz.

"We're about to do it, Hans."

I was familiar with his routine. Three Vietcong on the platform; three silencer-equipped precision rifles, now with the

American night scopes; three slugs fired at the same time; three holes in the head.

Krebitz was back on the WT. "It's done, Hans. You can move on."

A few minutes later we arrived at the lookout platform camouflaged with water weed. Krebitz and his men were dismantling a Russian wireless set and the machine gun, throwing the parts into the water.

The enemy had a radio transmitter.

"There goes our surprise attack," Riedl announced dryly.

Naturally when the camp called the platform and received no response the enemy commander realized that something happened to his lookouts.

"There's now a fine red alert in the woods," Helmut added.

Schulze spat. "So what? The apes will be alert and ready when the phosgene hits them, then—good night, Fritz."

We came to a transverse canal approximately at the right distance from the base, and the northern side of the embankment was suitable for the mortars. Using trenching spades, Gruppe Drei excavated the flat platforms, while others assembled the mortars and set them up along an artillery front five hundred yards long.

The enemy was indeed aware of impending trouble. Soon a platoon of thirty guerrillas emerged from the woods and began to cross the paddies, coming roughly in our direction, drawing wide apart as they approached. We permitted them to close in to about 150 yards inside the coverless morass, then Gruppe Drei opened up on them, first with the precision rifles, then with the submachine guns. After losing half its men, the platoon turned and fled back toward the forest line, pursued all the way by the seldom-missing slugs of our sharpshooters. The fugitives tumbled and fell one after another. Only a handful managed to reach the safety of the woods.

This aborted attempt prompted brisk movement in the enemy camp. Through field glasses we saw a dozen field guns being rolled into position. Minutes later the Vietcong opened up with 75- and 37-mm guns, raising geysers of water and mud, but gradually the shells began to register closer and we received water and mud in our faces too. Lying prone on the safe, northern slope of the embankment, I told Erich to start with the ranging shots—ordinary explosive shells to register distance and elevation. After the third salvo, Krebitz landed a few shells right between the enemy howitzers and turned his muddy face toward me.

"We are ready, Hans."

"Go ahead," I said. "Starting with those gun emplacements, then lower the trajectory and move the barrage inland."

"Zu Befehl!" He saluted jokingly.

We had 170 shells marked with yellow crosses—eight salvos from twenty mortars and ten more projectiles for good measure. From the forest line the guerrillas fired again. A pair of their three-inch shells blasted a huge chunk from the embankment and tossed earth and gravel over me. Erich turned. I nodded.

"Los!" he shouted.

We observed the muffled explosions along the forest line. The second salvo landed fifty yards farther inland. For a short time there was no visible effect. The guns kept firing. The enemy must have been wondering about the feeble detonations of our shells, for they made hardly any sound. Our third salvo went home, after which the howitzers began to phase out. Watching the enemy through his binoculars, Krebitz said tersely, "It is taking effect, Hans."

It was indeed, and the effect was terrible—a spectacle from Dante's *Inferno*. Large groups of guerrillas darted from their guns, staggered, tore at their clothes, and crashed to the ground. The next series of shells struck deeper in the woods. The fifth salvo landed. In the base entire platoons disintegrated before our eyes. Terrified groups of screaming men burst from the underbrush and dashed into the paddies—and fell, tried to rise, then dropped, never to move again. When, for an instant, I dropped my field glasses to wipe my perspiring face, I caught a glimpse of Jost Waldman; his face tense and running with rivulets of sweat as he stared at the abominable spectacle with his lower jaw hanging. Schulze's face was rigid like marble, and Stolz was shaking his head as if he couldn't believe his own eyes.

Our last ten mortar bombs landed a mile from the howitzers, targeted on the center of the base.

"Continue with HE and incendiaries!" Krebitz ordered the gunners.

Sixty more shells streaked toward the hostile woods, now a gigantic graveyard, and crashed into the base with resounding detonations, setting fires, felling trees, and overturning guns.

Erich turned toward me. "Do you want to move in?"

"Wearing the scuba gear?"

"Not the wetsuit." He shook his head. "You couldn't walk a hundred yards in it without going up in steam."

Krebitz spoke. "The wind's still holding direction."

"All right," I said. "Let's move to the forest line."

"Do you want to return here?"

"It'd be the shortest route to My-tho, and we already know it."

"Then we might as well leave the mortars here," Rudolf suggested.

"*Sicher*, Rudy. We'll pick them up on the way home."

Leaving our heavy equipment on the embankment in the care of Altreiter and forty troops, we advanced across the paddies, strung out in a wide arch, ready to drop into the mire at the slightest sign of hostility, but the woods ahead remained silent.

The high ground loomed closer and closer. Krebitz drew a flask and let some transparent liquid soak into wads of cotton. He tucked one in the breast pocket buttonhole of my jungle fatigues and distributed the others.

"If your wad turns orange put on your face masks," he warned us. Needless to say, we kept the cotton in sight all the time.

We halted again about one hundred yards from dry ground and observed the gun and machine-gun emplacements carefully. Piles of corpses were strewn far and wide in the distorted positions of agonized death that arrived amid crippling convulsions. Karl Stolz called our attention to a pair of finches prancing on the ground.

"The gas has already drifted from here," he said. "We can move on."

The sight that awaited us was even more abominable. Our incredulous eyes beheld hundreds of Vietcong lying where they had fallen—a handful here, fifteen there—entire platoons in random heaps. Corpses with bulging eyes and with noses and lips covered with blood. Some bodies were seminude, as the suffocating victims had ripped away their shirts and pajamas, gasping for oxygen. Others lay facedown in their own vomit. I saw faces distorted in the ultimate agony; jaws hung open, frozen in the last desperate shriek or gasp; rigid hands clawed into gun carriages, into the flesh of other corpses, into earth. Eyes seemed blown from their sockets. Tongues bitten through, and hair torn. Images from the *Inferno* of the Italian painter Orcagna.

The men advanced carefully, keeping an eye on their wads of cotton. When someone coughed or merely cleared his throat, the others would grab their face masks.

More dead guerrillas; dead birds, hens, and pigs.

Dead flies and wasps.

Krebitz signaled halt. "Put on your masks. There's still gas around."

My wad of cotton already had acquired a pinkish hue.

With our expressions now hidden beneath a pair of large, round glass eyes, we advanced like the silent knights of the apocalypse, devil's guards, or the angels of death. I knew that my troops were deeply moved by the immense power of destruction that had been unleashed against their enemies. The thought occurred to me that after today's attack they could rightly ask: "Why should we storm guerrilla strongholds and camps, or engage them in bloody hand-to-hand brawls? Why should we risk our lives and suffer wounds? There's no need to fight the Vietcong. Just turn on the gas."

The center of the base must have been hit by a slow-drifting layer of phosgene. There were bodies everywhere. In the doorways, on the low terraces and stairs, fallen over bushes. Carcasses of horses and pigs, hens and ducks.

Krebitz beckoned us into the headquarters barracks, which resembled a well-equipped German World War II command post: wireless sets, phone switchboard, microphone to external loudspeakers, wall maps of the Mekong delta. . . . A record player with stacks of records.

On the floor the dead operators still wore their earphones. Dead officers, judging by their holsters and automatic pistols. The commander of the base lay halfway out the window of his hut. In the bed a woman, perhaps his wife—her mouth and chin covered with blood. In an adjoining longhouse fifteen women and, to my sorrow, also children.

Corpses everywhere, human and animal.

Stolz, Steiner, and Altreiter counted 785 dead.

Gruppe Drei rolled drums of fuel between the huts and rigged them with explosive charges. The howitzers and machine guns were wrecked where they stood. Schulze collected the North Vietnamese flag from a pole next to the commander's office, together with a smaller one, featuring the silver-embroidered numbers: 307/57 and TRA DINH. It belonged to the 57th company of the so-called Iron Division. Tra Dinh was Dien Bien Phu in the local dialect.

We did not find the body of Commissar Kwang, whom we had captured, then let go, sometime in 1950. His luck still held. He had already escaped death by shooting. Now he escaped the phosgene too.

I took a small memento from the record rack: a Communist revolutionary song. Rudolf blew open the commander's safe. It yielded fifteen files of confidential documents and about $30,000 in francs and local currency. The documents went to Karl Stahnke, the cash into the coffers of Task Force-G.

With the explosive charges placed and the timers ticking away, we evacuated the base and were already two thousand yards away when the charges exploded, blasting an estimated two hundred tons of ammunition and fuel sky-high. The deflagration uprooted the forest and devastated the site in a twelve-hundred-foot circle. Smashed tree trunks, stripped of their branches and bark, were hurled three hundred yards into the paddies. The base became engulfed in a roaring conflagration that raged for three days. The following night, from a distance of twenty miles, we could still see the fire-tinted skyline.

Schulze remarked during the march to Lang-xuyen, "There should be nothing left to show that the base wasn't destroyed by conventional means."

"Let's hope you're right."

"I came. I saw. I conquered," Erich quoted Caesar's famous report to the Roman Senate after the battle of Zama. "We didn't suffer casualties—not even a scratch. . . . After all, it was a sensible idea."

"I'm already wondering what your next sensible idea might be," I replied with mild sarcasm.

Erich grinned. "Perhaps we should also try the formula CH_4-H_8-Cl_2-5."

"Commonly known as?"

"Mustard gas," he enlightened me casually. "Easy to make and store. What do you say?"

"Geh zum Teufel!" I replied. "Go to the devil!"

When we arrived in Saigon, we found Captain Spata and Joe Starr back from their home leave and eager to learn what Task Force-G had been doing during their absence. I told them briefly about the wholesale destruction of the large Vietcong base and training camp, naturally by conventional means.

"Imagine the luck we had," Krebitz narrated with charming insincerity. "One of our shells landed right on top of two hundred tons of explosives. Almost a thousand Vietcong perished in the blast."

To change the subject, I interposed cheerfully, "I'm sure that you've had a much better time. . . . What's the news at home?"

Starr, who had gone to San Francisco, shrugged his shoulders and answered casually, "I guess the biggest news in Frisco is Rocky Marciano's KO win against Cockell."

15.

Silent Hawks

After an intensive five-week training period at the military airfield, conducted by two American instructors, Stefan Escher, Hubert Mohr, and Hansjuerg Woss were ready to take charge of the Silent Hawks. Our pilots had completed a night flight of two hundred miles and returned with infrared films of conspicuous concentrations of sampans and men at odd places. During the four-hour flight the gliders' engines had been turned on only briefly during the return flight to Saigon.

The threesome landed flushed with enthusiasm. The enemy never scatter or scramble at their approach. They seemed ignorant of the silent overflights.

"These are the airplanes to win the war with," Escher exulted. "The enemy has no warning."

"They should be altered to carry at least some small bombs," Mohr suggested. "We could raise hell along the Ho Chi Minh trail."

"Why don't you work it out?" Schulze asked. "How to fit the bombs?"

"We'll come up with something," Woss said assuredly. "Four to six bombs per plane should suffice. . . . You won't believe it, but we swooped down in a valley with a Vietcong convoy on the move: laden bicycles and buffalo carts—fifty of them, and the apes only stared."

The photos disclosed groups of men and barges in marshes and canals around the Mekong; a guerrilla camp and a convoy in the ravine. No scattering people. No panic. No weapons aimed skyward. Only staring faces.

Our Commando of Death was ready to embark on a combined land-aerial operation, guided by the gliders to the right place at the right time. And it didn't take long before our airmen (and naturally Schulze and Krebitz) began to ponder over diverse technical problems, looking for loopholes where useful innovations might be inserted. They spent days scrutinizing the service manual, using the slide rule to make improvements with regard to the glide-payload ratio, which hovered around the 1:50 mark. This meant that our Silent Hawks could glide five thousand feet for every one-hundred-foot loss of altitude, in windstill and in the absence of upcurrents, which Woss called an American engineering record for gliders of that size.

In the end, our amateur engineering team concluded that the Hawks could be fitted with racks to carry six small bombs of twenty to twenty-five pounds each, next to the wing studs. But there were no such bombs in the air force arsenal, so Krebitz settled for regular 105-mm mortar shells.

Another problem, however, remained. The additional load reduced the glide ratio to 1:28. To avoid this drop in efficiency, the navigator-observer would have to weigh less than 120 pounds, and such individuals were not to be found in our ranks.

And as I wasn't sure what nasty methods we might use against the Vietcong, I discarded the idea of borrowing navigators from the Vietnamese Air Force.

We were discussing the problem over dinner at Erich's place, when Suoi unexpectedly came up with a proposal.

"Why shouldn't Noi and I give a hand? Neither of us weighs over one hundred and ten pounds."

At first neither Erich nor Helmut would even consider the idea, but our young ladies remained adamant and spiritedly began to recite their various overland excursions with our one-time Battalion of the Damned. "With bullets flying all around," Noi emphasized.

"I don't consider flying any more dangerous than trekking in the North Vietnamese mountains." Suoi hammered on the theme, and Noi promptly added, "Just remember when the Vietminh and the Chinese militia attacked us on the hill, and you were hard-pressed in a hand-to-hand brawl with a superior enemy."

"We know, we know." Riedl, who must have heard that particular story quite a few times, waved a dismissing hand. "Together with Schenk, Thi, and Chi you saved the day when you opened up on the enemy reinforcements with your submachine guns."

"Well, then—" Suoi shrugged, perhaps considering the dispute closed. "What else is there to discuss?"

"What else?" Erich exclaimed, both frightened and irritated. "Very well, you've been with us in the jungle, participated in actions, proved your bravery more than once, but that wouldn't turn you into either navigators or photographers. . . . You've never flown in your life."

"And what prevents us from learning?" Noi asked flatly.

"Oh, Allerheilige Gottesmutter." Schulze rolled his eyes and blew a sigh of exasperation. "What's the use of it?" he cried. "Airmen can be shot down, too, you know."

"One can get shot while trekking in the jungle," Suoi retorted.

This lively four-way altercation continued for some time with Krebitz, Stolz, Altreiter, and me playing the role of the innocent noncombatants. None of us interfered, for we never doubted the eventual outcome of the discourse: the victory of the weaker sex.

The following week Suoi and Noi began their training at the Vietnamese Air Force base and progressed amazingly fast. In the third week the girls were already performing parachute jumps and practice glides, to the bemused delight of their husbands. Six weeks later they were navigating blind flights between the Gia Dinh airfield and Cân-tho and guided Woss and Mohr back to the airstrip—at night. After the successful conclusion of their training, Suoi and Noi reported to my office, still clad in flight overalls, and I received a pair of smart salutes.

"Mais, mon cher commandant," Suoi addressed me in her charmingly original martial style, "what do you say now?"

I seated them with a laugh. "What do your husbands say?" I countered, chuckling.

Noi opened her hands and replied innocently, "Oh, sir—our dear husbands are resigned to *le grand fromage.* Are we accepted?"

"Avec plaisir," I responded with admiration. "I've just finished reading the report on your accomplishments. You're a formidable duet, *mesdames."*

"We know that," Suoi stated matter-of-factly, in a self-congratulatory tone. "We are very agile. . . . When do we start?"

"Now—wait a moment!" I raised a restraining hand. "Erich and Helmut have set some rules."

"What rules?"

"That you'll be flying only over South Vietnamese territory."

Noi stared. "Why? Are you planning to fly elsewhere?"

"Over Cambodia and Laos."

Suoi said in a firm voice, "I can't see what difference it should make. The enemy is the same anywhere and so are their bullets."

"That's true," I conceded, amused. "But if you have to land in an emergency, you come down on friendly ground, my dear girl. . . . That's a big difference."

"Friendly ground?" Noi snapped ironically. "Will you please show me on the map that bit of Vietnam?" In a sense she was right. There were Vietcong everywhere. She added, "Anyway, we won't be operating far from Task Force-G on the ground."

"Certainly not. We'll always stay within WT range."

"Then where's the problem?" Noi concluded. "We should be going wherever we are needed."

"That's right." Suoi placed her dot after the discussion.

In the evening, looking utterly dejected, Erich lamented, *"Je suis à la mort, mon ami.* . . . What if they fly into a barrage of 37-mm slugs, Hans?"

I tried to lessen his concern. "The girls will be flying mostly at night at an altitude of six thousand feet, Erich," I said persuasively.

"Sure!" he cut in. "That's why we fitted the racks. To bomb the Vietcong from six thousand feet, at night! The girls might as well chuck those bombs into the Mekong."

"When the gliders descend to bomb they might be flying one hundred and eighty miles per hour, coming in without making any sound. . . . Now, be realistic. By the time the guerrillas notice that they're being attacked, the gliders will have dropped their bombs and sped out of range. Cheer up, man!"

"Come on, Hans—I don't want to see her killed."

"Suoi could say the same when you are away on a mission, sometimes for weeks."

"It's not the same."

"It's the same to her, Erich. Remember that wherever the

gliders might be, you won't be far away either. Perhaps you'll be closer to your wife than ever before."

He blew exasperatedly. "Oh, *merde alors*, Hans. You've always been good at presenting the shit as if it were gold."

In any case, I had already decided that Suoi and Noi should wear a simple native dress beneath their flight overalls and carry the regular identity papers whenever on a mission. I advised them accordingly.

"If, for some reason, you land in hostile territory, get rid of your overalls and leave the site immediately to become a commonplace native—out to pick berries."

"Or assume the role of a brave revolutionary," Noi suggested. "Which would also justify our being armed."

I stared stupefied at her resourcefulness.

Suoi added, "We could even help our pilots to reach a nearby fort, or the task force."

"How?" I blurted, still baffled.

"By assuming the role of a guerrilla escorting a prisoner."

"You don't lack ideas, do you?"

Suoi uttered a soft, tingling laugh. "It might be a good idea if we carried only Russian or Chinese guns, Commander."

"Well, you do have a point there," I admitted, shaking my head.

Krebitz threw back his head and laughed. "I told you not to worry about them, Hans."

I myself had participated in a test flight with Woss piloting *Silent Hawk One*. I wanted to get a good grasp of the glider's capabilities. Therefore we requested no towing, but took off from the runway under the glider's own power.

To my pleasant surprise the slender plane rose after a short run of only three hundred yards, although the climbing was a slow process: it took half an hour to reach an altitude of 3,000 feet, where Woss found an upcurrent and corkscrewed the glider to 6,800 feet. I asked him to fly to the Vietcong base near Tri-ton, which we had destroyed with phosgene.

His expert handling of the glider, making use of every updraft and the gentle northeasterly wind, permitted us to cover the hundred miles in seventy minutes, without reverting to power.

I scanned the derelict base through my field glasses, looking for signs of life or reconstruction, but saw only desolation. Two square miles of uprooted, burned forest with a three-hundred-foot crater in its center where the ammunition depots had been, now filled with ground water. Of the 150 huts and wooden barracks, not even traces remained.

With the engine idling at a low RPM, Woss descended to three hundred feet to give me a better view. Still there wasn't a living soul around, not even birds or monkeys.

Strangely I didn't feel elated or even satisfied, for I never considered the event a victory over the Vietcong. There had been no fighting at all, only wholesale slaughter. The enemy had no chance to defend itself.

Nevertheless, I knew that, if necessary, I would do it again and again, subjugating every other consideration to my will to prevail against our insidious antagonists, to provide a solitary precedent in a tiny part of this remote earth to show that the Red Monolith cannot always win. The Vietcong were the "Golden Horde" of the Nuclear Age, led by modern Ghengis Khans in Moscow and Peking, and I was resolved to treat them accordingly. As Krebitz had said, "If you want to kill a rat, use a trap. If you want to kill ten rats, use poisoned bait. But when the whole place is infested with rats—resort to gas."

We were certain that the North Vietnamese Communists wouldn't stop at the much-publicized reunification of the two Vietnams, naturally under Hanoi's rule. They would want much more. The moment the country was pacified, they'd export their aggression into the neighboring countries. Ho Chi Minh and company were only discardable pawns on the grand Moscow chessboard, and the lords of the Kremlin wanted to gain control over much of Southeast Asia. And since Peking's aims were very much the same, the two Communist giants would collide sooner or later.

We were also certain that the Reds weren't planning a new global conflagration that would surely burn them too. Instead, Moscow and Peking would foster hundreds of small local wars worldwide; rebellions here, overturned governments there, wrecked law and order somewhere else. It'd be easy for them to kindle new Vietnams elsewhere. Anyplace where large masses of impoverished people were looking desperately for a way out of their misery—the wretched ones, whom the apostles of Marx and Lenin could easily incite with the revolutionary slogan: "You have nothing to lose but your chains—fight!"

After the disaster of Dien Bien Phu, France had hurriedly restored Moroccan independence. Now there was a civil war in Morocco with the various tribes killing each other and the French settlers. Algeria, too, was on the verge of going up in flames. Such were the kind of wars the Communists preferred. Every small war caused a small fissure in the foundation of the great democracies, and the tiny shocks would eventually grow into a giant quake. There was still time to stop them, but to do it, the free world needed leaders with cast-iron will and dauntless unity among the free nations.

But capitalist nations seldom united their forces before the final hour. There were too many conflicting commercial interests.

Woss steered northwest and prodded our *Silent Hawk One* to five thousand feet. We crossed the silver band of the Mekong and headed home. He cut the engine and once again the only sound I heard was the rushing of air around the cockpit.

It was not Saigon intelligence but Karl Stahnke who provided the information about Vietcong Convoy 327 on its way south along the Sé Kong valley, in Laos. If Stahnke's source was reliable, the convoy was composed of 1,200 armed Vietcong, 150 horses and mules, 50 buffalo carts, and some 600 coolies, pushing laden bicycles. The convoy's destination was a major North Vietnamese logistics base situated in the Mondulkiri district of Cambodia, near the headwaters of the river Srépok. Stahnke had its approximate location marked on our operational maps. The base lay only twenty-five miles away from the South Vietnamese village of Tu-soay.

A convoy of such magnitude could easily transport anything up to a hundred tons of supplies. Consequently it would advance slowly, covering perhaps twelve miles a day over difficult terrain with countless acclivities and declivities. According to Karl, the column was presently moving toward the Cambodian border along the Sé Kamane and could reach the base in about fifteen days.

It was enough time to prepare an assault on both convoy and camp.

Stahnke procured some old aerial photos of the Mondulkiri segment of the guerrilla route: fifty miles long and winding, as it followed the capricious course of the upper Srépok in narrow valleys and ravines.

Following General Houssong's proposal, Task Force-G was transferred to the village of Buôn-mé-thuôt, 175 miles northeast of Saigon and only 50 miles from from the Vietcong route, as the crow flies. It featured a fortified airfield, which we needed for our gliders. Captain Spata and Sergeant Starr requested my permission to participate in the expedition, and I consented on the condition that they would not be carrying anything American on them, would follow my instructions to the letter, and would speak only French in front of any natives we might encounter—including members of the Saigon army.

Just when we were about to leave, our CIA count, Jeff Robertson, appeared, clad in jungle suit and paratrooper boots, ready to join up. When I asked him for the reason behind his hurried decision, he casually told me that he wanted to see the gliders in action and perhaps learn something useful for the future.

But later, when we were sitting around the fire, sipping tea, he confessed to having a more profound reason for coming along.

"Say, Hans," he began, "do you happen to know what the abbreviation OSS stands for?"

"Shouldn't I know?" I responded with a chuckle. "It's given us enough trouble during the war: the intelligence service of Uncle Sam."

Robertson nodded. "Something along that line," he confirmed. "Office of Strategic Services. . . . A bunch of tough guys, many of them with Burma experience—like the One Hundred First detachment. . . . Well, two years ago they formed the Tenth Special Forces Airborne Group, under the command of a certain Colonel Aaron Bank, based in Fort Bragg, North Carolina."

"Now they're called Green Berets," I said quietly.

The CIA count stared. "You know?"

His startled expression made me chuckle. "The French also

have an intelligence service," I replied with a grin. "A wild bunch of top-quality experts, like the guys of Task Force-G. Their selection is very tough. Out of one hundred applicants, seventy-five won't make it through the exams. . . . Well, if Uncle Sam wants to help Saigon, he should send them over. We should be able to work together very well."

"Sure. They do the clean part of the job, Task Force-G does the rest," Erich quipped.

"It might happen, guys," Robertson said thoughtfully. "If the Commies are pushing us too far, it might happen."

"The Commies will never stop pushing and provoking," I said.

Robertson sipped some tea, then glanced up. "I believe that you were trained at Bad Toelz, weren't you?"

"Correct. At the S.S. academy."

He looked at me candidly. "Well, do you know that some units of Green Berets are training at Bad Toelz right now?" he asked. Now it was my turn to pull a baffled expression. "Are you surprised?" Robertson prompted me.

"I'm surprised to hear that our installations are still standing."

"They've been enlarged to faciliate tests and training."

"Any idea what our number-one test used to be, Jeff?"

"Nope."

"Well, when a guy applied for admission into the *Waffen S.S.* —before the war, mind you, because later, when the house was already afire, they'd accept any trash—our drillmaster, *Shaarfuehrer* Heinz Kunert, would make the applicant stand at attention with a primed hand grenade on top of his helmet. . . . Naturally it was a training grenade without splinters, but the detonation was the same, and if the fellow didn't shit his pants full, his application would be considered. Otherwise Kunert would send him back to mama."

Our CIA count uttered a snort of mirth. "Hell, Hans—our Green Berets often train with live ammo and if someone gets hurt, it's just too bad," he countered. "That's no joke either."

"Then your Green Berets are on the way to becoming invincible," I commented flatly. "And Uncle Sam cannot afford to be weak. . . . But what has it all to do with your being here?"

"Well, I'm trying to give the Special Forces some help. Enemy strategy and tactics, weapons and methods the Vietcong are using in the woods, in the hills and swamps—that sort of information."

I said firmly, "You'll get all the help you need, Jeff. We have no secrets."

"Save for one or two," he remarked candidly.

I had no idea what he meant, but answered with a smile, "We all have some little secrets."

"Sure. . . ."

Colonel Phu Ninh Xen, the commander of the battalion that guarded the fort and airfield at Buõn-mé-thuōt, had been advised by Saigon to provide us with every possible assistance—without being inquisitive. He didn't question Task Force-G's mission or the pair of strange aircraft that drew the attention of the local airmen like a magnet attracts iron. But even more sensational was the presence of Suoi and Noi, whom the South Vietnamese pilots tried to engage in spirited conversations without much success. Nevertheless when they saw our girls clad in flight suits, climbing into the cockpits, they broke into enthusiastic cheers. Suoi and Noi were probably the first local women ever to see the inside of an airplane cockpit.

The local air force featured a colorful assortment of planes: two World War II Dakotas, three Mosquitoes, five Bearcats, six B-26 bombers, a couple of Mustang trainers, and two Alouette copters.

I sent *Silent Hawk One,* with Hubert Mohr and Noi, on a reconnaissance flight to take more pictures of the Srépok valley and, if possible, to locate the exact site of the North Vietnamese logistics base. In order to maintain secrecy, our pilots were told to leak the word on reconnaissance flights over Bon-ho in the north. Mohr was to cast off the tow line at 8,000 feet, then fly for some minutes away from the Cambodian border, turning west only inside the clouds and after the tow plane had left the area. To faciliate their return, estimated at some time after midnight, a vertical beam of a searchlight would serve as beacon, and when Mohr fired a green flare, the airstrip landing lights would be turned on.

Silent Hawk One took off around 8:15 P.M. and returned at 1:17 A.M. with a reel of infrared film shot of the areas we were

RECALL TO INFERNO 229

interested in. One of the Mosquitoes flew it to Saigon for developing and returned the next afternoon with the results.

The North Vietnamese base and the trail leading to it were clearly defined by the heat emissions registered on the film. Small fires within the base, hidden under the unbroken foliage, depicted sites where the guerrillas were cooking their meals. Temperature differences indicated people and animals along the trail. Some isolated smudges of heat pinpointed gun emplacements that flanked the trail for about one mile.

We were no longer striking at the enemy blindly. We could see them under the trees, in the underbrush—even in pitch darkness.

Then days later, in the dead of night, the full complement of Task Force-G marched toward Don, a hamlet near the Vietnamese part of the Srépok River. There were 280 troops in four combat groups, or *Kampfgruppen*, under the command of Schulze, Riedl, Altreiter, and me. The thirty specialists of Gruppe Drei were led by Krebitz.

Although numerically small, when judged by combat experience and firepower, Task Force-G's actual strength equaled that of a South Vietnamese regiment. Each group transported six flamethrowers with three reserve tanks for each, a pair of 12.7-mm and eight 9-mm machine guns, and six 60-mm mortars with twenty-four rounds each. Submachine gun, six hand grenades, and a bayonet constituted the trooper's standard equipment, apart from the obligatory change of underclothes, trenching spade, canteen, spirit cubes, and food. Counting everything, each group transported a ton of arms and ammunition and nearly as much in other equipment and victuals. Each trooper carried around fifty-five pounds, so it was no wonder that the men were always eager to engage the enemy. Combat would reduce our burden.

The Vietcong fared better. Marching along their well-maintained trails, they could utilize bicycles, carts, and pack animals. Our strength lay in our mobility over untrodden ground, in the trailless wilderness, where neither machines nor animals could move.

Captain Spata, Sergeant Starr, and our CIA count (who somehow managed to look spotless even in the jungle) insisted on taking their fair share of our load; and since we observed no difference between officers and ranks, I divided with Mike the load of a dismantled mortar and its shells. Joe Starr shouldered a heavy MG, while Robertson hauled a spare flamethrower tank.

As we approached a wooden bridge across a ravine, Krebitz signaled halt. Almost instantly a couple of shots rang and a machine gun spluttered a brief salvo. We dropped behind the roadside boulders and bushes. Rudolf informed me of the presence of guerrilla lookouts on the far side of the bridge.

"And you let yourself be caught with your pants down," I commented tauntingly. "Rudy, you're getting old."

"Kuhscheiss!" Krebitz grunted over the walkie-talkie. "They're in a damned good position, Hans. Fifty feet high on the rocky slope and command trail and bridge."

I heard several single shots, then once more the sharp staccato of the Chinese machine gun.

"Stay under cover," I told Krebitz. "I'm coming over."

I elbowed myself forward with Erich on my side. "The village is not far." He gasped. "It must be a real viper's nest."

"And the folks surely hear the shooting," I replied.

"We'd better do something before the monkeys on the cliff get reinforcements."

Near the bridge we found Gruppe Drei blocked.

"They're over there!" Krebitz explained, pointing. The moment he raised his hand the enemy machine gun opened up and the slugs chipped the boulder behind which we sheltered. "You see?" he asked. "A difficult target even by daylight."

The Vietcong position was beyond flamethrower range, and I didn't feel like wasting precious mortar shells against a couple of individuals. As if he could read my mind, Erich called Riedl over the WT.

"Say, Helmut—couldn't you cross the ravine where you are?"

"I'm going to have a look."

"Do that. . . ."

He surveyed the cliffs and swore quietly. *"Merde, quel dommage. . . .* Unless we pass here on the double, the apes across the border will be alerted."

Riedl called, "We can cross but it'll take some time."

"Do it all the same," I replied urgently. "Send only a few men with grenades."

"I'm going over myself."

"Okay, but look out, eh?"

I turned to Schulze. "Erich, take your group across the hills and get beyond the village to block the trail toward Cambodia. Don is only a mile away."

He conned the rugged, looming acclivity he was to climb. "It's going to be a rotten mile, Hans, but"—he tapped me on the shoulder—"so is life. See you later."

"Keep in touch over the WT."

He crawled back to where his men were sheltering. The guerrillas fired another random salvo and received a pair of explosive slugs in exchange, which, however, did not stop the MG.

And to our bemusement, the Vietcong gunner seemed to be changing position all the time. "That's all we need now." Stolz cursed quietly, as the moon popped into view between the slow-drifting clouds, illuminating the bridge and our side of the ravine, while the guerrilla snipers remained in comfortable obscurity.

"Keep your heads down," Rudolf advised us as a new short salvo ripped across the trail, throwing up grass and earth. Bullets ricocheted off the boulders.

"*Verdammt nochmal!*" Jost Waldman swore. "There must be not one but two machine guns, each firing briefly to avoid spotting." He let go of a salvo of frustration.

"Hold your temper, lad," Krebitz calmed him. "You're only chipping the rock. . . . There's only a single MG, Jost, but a couple of apes are setting off firecrackers to draw our response to the wrong place. It's an old Chinese guerrilla trick."

My WT crackled.

"I'm across the ravine with six men," Riedl reported in German. "Hold your fire. We're moving toward the bridge."

"Stay well above the snipers."

"Where are they?"

"Directly opposite the bridge, fifty feet above the trail."

"Excellent. . . . try to keep them distracted, Hans."

We began to fire single random shots toward the snipers, to draw their response. The guerrillas were apparently content with having pinned us to the boulders and preventing our crossing.

"We're looking down on the village," Erich mused over the WT. "There's a bunch of apes gamboling toward the bridge. I could buzz them from here but it'd give us away."

"You just think of getting beyond the village," I replied briskly. "Leave the apes to us. How many are they?"

"Not more than twenty."

Our conversation was momentarily interrupted by movement on the acclivity. Battery torches knifed into the darkness, illuminating the boulders, drawing shouts of surprise and fear. Mitras clattered. Grenades detonated, setting off a cascade of earth and stone. Erich asked tersely, "What's going on?"

"I think Helmut has just opened the way for us."

Riedl cut in. "The way's free, Hans."

"How many were there?"

"Five. All dead."

"You've done a great job, Helmut. Join us at the bridge."

We clambered to our feet. "Forward!"

Gruppe Drei crossed over and we followed, taking position just in time to receive the Vietcong reinforcement. Gruppe Drei's submachine guns caught them at twenty yards. Stolz and Steiner bayoneted the wounded and brought back five prisoners. Wasting no time with preliminaries, Krebitz grabbed the closest ex-soldier of Father Ho by the front of his probably stolen French army shirt and drew him closer.

"How many of you are left in the village?" he asked angrily.

The guerrilla said nothing, he only stared sullenly without a flicker of interest in his dark eyes. Krebitz drew his automatic and shot him through the left foot. Crying out in pain, the fellow dropped to one knee. Krebitz repeated his question, but the only response he got was a spiteful "Long live Uncle Ho." A second slug through his right foot knocked the guerrilla flat on the ground.

"Into the ravine!" Krebitz told Steiner. The bayonet glinted and struck home. Stolz kicked the corpse into the stream. Krebitz turned his attention to the second prisoner, a shallow-faced, hollow-eyed character of perhaps twenty years.

"All right." Rudolf addressed him. "Where do you want to go, home or to hell?"

He repeated his question. Silence.

The automatic roared, putting a slug through the prisoner's cheeks. His nose and teeth exploded in a fountain of blood.

He, too, was put to the bayonet.

The third one in the row screamed. "Xuyen and Trengh are heroes!"

"They *were* heroes," Krebitz said emphatically.

"They're only corpses now. Will you talk or do you prefer to have the same treatment?"

"I have nothing to tell you, accursed French fascists!" The prisoner sneered.

"We are German fascists," Krebitz corrected him coolly.

"Kill me too! Iron Gnoc will revenge us." The Vietcong sneered spitefully, calling General Giap, by his nom de guerre.

Krebitz shot him between the eyes and snapped his fingers toward Stolz. "The next one!"

Like a dentist calling in his next patient.

I caught a glimpse of the Americans, staring at the abominable spectacle indignantly.

"All right, Rudy." I stopped Krebitz. "They're a hard lot and we have no time. You'll have your answer when we enter into the village."

Krebitz shrugged. "Wipe them out, Karl," he told Stolz.

Captain Spata spoke. "They're brave men, Hans. Can't you spare them for a change?"

"I'm sorry, Mike—the answer is no."

"Why not?"

"It's a matter of policy. Hanoi has nicknamed us Commando of Death. We're trying to live up to the distinction."

"You never really interrogate your prisoners?" Jeff Robertson asked.

"This kind here? Never! Sometimes when we capture a top cadre, we send him to Saigon."

The rest of the prisoners were shot and pushed into the ravine.

"They weren't chicken for sure," Starr remarked.

"I admire their steadfastness myself, Joe—but in the game we're playing there's no room for humane sentiments," I told him evenly.

Erich called over the radiotelephone. "Did you get them?"

"Selbstverständlich," I answered. "Naturally. We're moving into Don."

"They seem to be panicky . . . the folks in the village. Dashing left and right like freshly shorn sheep."

"Where are you?"

"About five hundred yards past Don."

"Can you cross the ravine?"

"We're already across," he replied with a chuckle. "Kretz found a footbridge."

"All right, Erich. Don't let anyone escape toward the border."

"They could only fly, Hans. I have the trail under control. . . . I think you'll have a good haul. The village must be full of Hanoi goodies."

Behind me Krebitz was grumbling at Riedl over the WT.

"Where the hell are you?" he queried gruffly. "You should have been down here long ago."

"Perhaps you'll kindly tell me how I'm supposed to get down," Helmut responded amiably. "Fly like birds, or crawl like spiders?"

"Come down the way you went up."

"I wish I could remember the way," Riedl lamented. "Whichever way I turn—sheer drops."

"All right, Boy Scout, I'll light up your way."

He sent a dozen troopers to illuminate the declivity and, after a while, we saw the torchlights descending between the jagged boulders. Riedl and his companions sprang onto the trail. Worn and torn, they looked like a bunch of KZ inmates.

Zeisl dressed their cuts and bruises, then we moved on.

Plodding next to me, Jeff Robertson asked quietly, "Must you torture your prisoners before finishing them off?"

"Torture?" I asked with pretended dismay. "We call it reeducation."

"With a bullet through the foot?"

"Sometimes it makes the ape talk."

"But you would gun him down anyway."

"Not always, Jeff. When I promise a prisoner his freedom, he goes free."

"But all the others die."

"What else could I do with prisoners?"

"You could escort them to the nearest fort, for instance, and hand them over to the South Vietnamese."

I shook my head and asked quietly, "Have you ever been in the army, Jeff?"

Robertson seemed surprised. "Of course. For three years during the war."

"Fighting against the Japs, or against us, Teutons?"

"Against you damned Teutons," he replied with a grin. "In North Africa, in France, in Germany, and I beat the hell out of your *Panzers* too. Twelve of them in a single day."

"Did those *Panzers* run out of gas and ammo?" Erich taunted him.

"Would your meticulous S.S. *Verfuegungsabteilung* permit your tanks to run dry? Anyway, I always escorted the prisoners to a camp."

I asked nonchalantly, "How many men did you have?"

"I was a regimental commander."

Erich whistled softly. "Then we should answer you with 'yes, sir'—loud and clear, Colonel."

"I was a major."

"Yes, sir," said Schulze. "And you commanded three thousand troops. We have only three *hundred*. We capture Vietcong every day. If we kept sending them back, by the time we reached our objective, there'd only be Hans and myself to do the job."

"To escort five prisoners in the jungle, ten guards are necessary. The Vietcong are fanatic bastards who wouldn't hesitate to bite through your jugular if given a chance. Besides, there are guerrillas all over the country. The prisoners might not march five miles before being freed by their buddies, and where would that leave the escort?" I continued. "The American pioneers used to say that the only good Indian is a dead one. We say the same of the Communists."

"I don't share your view, but I can understand it," Jeff commented.

Distant gunfire interrupted our discourse, but it was short-lived. Erich reported that a group of sixty people, guerrillas and villagers, had tried to escape toward the border. He stopped them.

"Wipe out the Vietcong and bring the rest back to Don." I told him, "Maintain the roadblock."

The prolonged bursts of several submachine guns told us that Father Ho had lost some more soldiers of the revolution. When we entered into the village, the inhabitants were already gathered between four pyres of burning cane, which illuminated their terrified faces and also kept the mosquitoes at bay. Erich had the headman placed under guard—a nervous, lean individual with a dyspeptic countenance. Willingly and without any persuasion, he revealed all the sites where the Vietcong had deposited arms and ammunition. He even called Krebitz's attention to a cleverly concealed pit, two hundred yards from the village, which otherwise would not have been found. About thirty locals who had been helping the Vietcong by providing them with shelter, food, and concealments for army matériel were separated from the rest. Noticing the consternation on Captain Spata's face, I hurriedly reassured him that we had no intention of shooting the civilians and would only punish them. "I must teach the people that helping the enemy can be costly," I told the Americans. "Without local assistance the guerrillas would be lost, but if the natives keep helping them, this damned war will never end."

"What do you intend to do?" Spata asked warily.

"Gruppe Drei will destroy whatever they possess," I replied flatly. "Their dwellings, stores, livestock—everything."

"How can they survive then?" Starr cut in.

"At the expense of their kin, I guess. They won't have anything left for the Vietcong."

Jeff Robertson shook his head. "You are a hard-hitting bunch, Hans," he said, neither approvingly nor disapprovingly.

"So are your marines," I answered equably. "And so will be —I hope—your Green Berets. Battles aren't won by weaklings."

We rested in the village for the night. Before Task Force-G marched off at dawn, Krebitz dispatched Kretz, Fuchs, and Schindler to position themselves upon the cliffs and observe the trail through the telescopic sights. We left the village, but once we entered the forest, we bivouacked in the roadside thicket. Once again Rudolf's caution brought a dividend. Fifteen minutes after our departure, six locals hurriedly left Don in the direction of the border. They carefully avoided the trail and took a path over the hills. Our sharpshooters spotted them and killed them as they climbed the acclivity. Naturally they had wanted to alert the guerrillas across the frontier. Among the corpses we discovered the younger son of the headman, who probably wanted to reduce the gravity of his treason by giving us away to the Vietcong, as he had given away the Vietcong caches to us. Perhaps he only wanted to maintain good relations with both sides.

It didn't prevent Gruppe Drei from returning to the village to wreck his property too.

Task Force-G maintained the blockade throughout the day. It netted us another group of eighty guerrillas, who marched into Krebitz's trap. Perhaps this was the unit the messengers wanted to alert.

Finding themselves enveloped by a superior force, the Vietcong scattered in the riverside underbrush and put up a tenacious resistance. Unwilling to expose my men to unnecessary peril, I turned the flamethrowers on the enemy. In the tall elephant grass and shrubbery the fire spread quickly, and the heat eventually compelled the guerrillas to surface; but the moment a head popped into view it was riddled with bullets. Groups of hollering guerrillas with their clothes on fire dived into the stream and were either shot or swept away and crushed against the boulders by the rapids. The few who dropped their guns and raised their hands were knocked back into the spitfire by machine-gun salvos. The slaughter continued for twenty minutes and ended with a handful of guerrillas making a desperate dash toward Don. They ran into Altreiter's reception party and perished in a shower of slugs.

"This trail must be a principal infiltration route," CIA Count Robertson remarked, while our troops frisked the corpses for valuables and documents.

"Do you always do that?" Spata asked me, somewhat astonished.

"Collect booty?" I chuckled. "Why shouldn't we? The villagers would take everything anyway."

"It's still a kind of—indecent, or don't you think so?" he responded. "For soldiers, I mean, to loot soldiers . . ."

"The Vietcong aren't soldiers but bandits, and we aren't

soldiers either, only mercenaries who sustain a rotten regime, Mike. We take whatever we come across."

"Well, why do you support a rotten regime?"

"You could ask the same question in Washington." I chuckled. "And get the same response. . . . Because the only alternative would be communism and that stinks even more."

Schulze came back beaming. He tossed a knapsack at our feet. "Twenty thousand dollars worth of Laotian kips, Cambodian riels, and French francs," he announced. Slapping Starr on the shoulder, he added, "At least Father Ho is paying for our *fatigue,* Joe. Did you learn something useful?"

"Sure." The sergeant grunted. "We should keep warplanes, armor, and artillery at home and send Diem a few thousand Sioux and Comanches with plenty of flamethrowers and submachine guns."

"When the British ran into trouble with the Communist guerrillas in Malaya, they brought in Dayak headhunters and Papuan cannibals to clean them out. They cleaned them out, all right."

"And probably ate them too," Spata quipped. "Well, the British have more experience in colonial affairs."

I told Mike, "You've already earned two hundred dollars each for a day's hardship, Mike."

"What do you mean?"

"Your share of the booty."

"There'll be more by the time we return to Saigon," Schulze continued. "The Communists are no longer proletarians, Mike. They're rich capitalists."

"We can't accept any such money."

"Come on, Captain—don't play that old record again. You promised to follow our game rules; alas, taking your share of the booty is one of them."

"Besides, you did accept the cash after the Bin Xuyen cleanup in Saigon," I added.

"That was a reward given by the government," he repeated the lie I'd told him. "This is something different. . . . Don't make us turn back, Hans."

Erich laughed softly. "Turn back where? Christ! Three brave Americans trodding along a Vietcong trail. . . . You wouldn't last two miles." He turned toward Jeff. "Say, CIA Count, suppose your agents happen to gun down a couple of Russian spies with a suitcaseful of dollars on them. What would you do with the cash?"

"It would be turned over to the Treasury."

"All of it?"

"We might receive an official reward."

"Merde."

"Why *merde*?"

"It sounds stupid to me."

"But that's the way they're doing things at home." Jeff laughed. "Otherwise everybody would want to work for the police or the CIA. We can't keep our booty."

I interposed mildly, "You should continue your discussion in Saigon, folks. Now put on your Vietcong garb and let's hit the trail."

We donned our guerrilla pajamas and bamboo helmets and marched toward the frontier, which we crossed without encountering a soul. It was not even marked.

At midnight Task Force-G had an appointment with *Silent Hawk One*, flown by Woss and Suoi, on a reconnaissance flight along the Srépok valley.

We came to an eastern branch of the river, which the men crossed with the help of rope hand- and footholds, fitted with grapnels, and shot over to the far bank, then continued westward across the moonlit hills. At 11:30 P.M. we camped down on a wooded crest and turned on the WTs. Working the shortwave wireless, Krebitz contacted Escher and Mohr. Speaking in German, Escher told us that Woss and Suoi had taken off on schedule and we should be in contact with the glider soon.

The men began to prepare their dinners. I sat with Erich next to the WT, waiting for the call, the first one under actual combat conditions.

Woss's signal came at 12:17 A.M. *Silent Hawk One* was on its way back to base with an exposed reel of film.

"One of the Dakotas will fly it to Saigon," Woss told me. "You should call Berger for the result at fourteen hundred hours, but I think we spotted elephant two miles south of point six-three-three, circa B-miles-eight from your actual position."

In our code, elephant meant convoy; six-three-three defined

the Cambodian village Lomohat, and B-miles-eight equaled twenty-eight miles.

Krebitz said thoughtfully, "The convoy should be at the ambush site sometime in the afternoon the day after tomorrow."

Erich wanted to talk to Suoi. She sounded very enthusiastic about her experience, but following my earlier advice, she did not mention the words *flying* or *glider*.

"We'll return tomorrow night, the same time," she told Erich. "Don't worry."

"Okay, sign off now." I gestured him to conclude. I wanted to keep transmissions as brief as possible, in order to avoid even the remotest chance of enemy radio triangulation. The North Vietnamese were still unaware of our silent overflights, and I preferred it that way. The gliders were a formidable weapon against the guerrillas.

After a good night's rest, morning wash-up, and foot care, we continued toward Point A (for ambush), which we'd chosen before we left Saigon. It was thirty-four miles north of the logistics base where, for two miles, the trail ran between perpendicular rock faces and traversed an eighty-foot ravine over a truss bridge, constructed by the French. We planned to lock the convoy into a coverless section of the ravine. Occupying the nearby heights, Task Force-G would destroy them at leisure.

At 2 P.M. we contacted Lieutenant Berger. In a coded message we were informed of the results of Suoi's photography. Woss had indeed spotted Convoy 327 as it was advancing along the Srépok; two lines of men, pack mules, bicycles, and carts, extending for two miles. And, to our delighted surprise, there was a smaller convoy too, tailing 327 at a distance of eight miles —Suoi's discovery. The existence of this latter convoy had not been previously known.

During the afternoon *Silent Hawk Two*, with Mohr and Noi in the cockpit, glided low over the crest and dropped a container with photographs of the North Vietnamese logistics base. Carefully evaluated by Captain Dessault and Stahnke, the pictures depicted the base in detail. It comprised sixty-four stone and wooden buildings, arranged in neat rows, twenty semi-buried ammunition cellars, and stacks of one-hundred-gallon fuel drums, everything expertly camouflaged beneath the natural canopy of trees.

Exposed fuel drums! The dream target of every bomber crew, commando, and saboteur operating in hostile territory.

There were also four rows of pillboxes within the base and six more along the trail, to cover the approaches. A dozen MG emplacements defended the base. At the first glance it was evident to any veteran soldier that no hostile ground forces could ever use either the trail or the flimsy wooden bridges, which would surely crumble under the weight of a tank; and without armor the base could never be approached. The valley was impregnable even to paratroops.

After having studied the pictures and the intelligence evaluation, Krebitz advised me to abandon the idea of assaulting the base. Our American friends agreed with him.

Erich told me under his breath, "Instead of HE for the gliders, we should have filled the bombs with phosgene and lewisite."

"Don't say that you have also lewisite now?"

"Some," he replied in a subdued voice. "Only to see one day how that stuff works."

Suoi had also taken pictures of the valley and the bridge where we planned to ambush the Hanoi convoy, and they gave us a nasty surprise. The bridge was guarded by a Cambodian platoon, which manned a guardhouse and sandbagged machine-gun emplacements on either side of the river.

"I guess your plan needs some revision," Jeff said as he reviewed the pictures. "You don't want to kill Cambodians, do you?"

"Naturally not."

I had no intention of causing Cambodian casualties, and especially not among the troops of King Norodom Shihanouk, whose shaky throne was already rocked by internal strife among Communist, Conservative, and Neutralist factions.

"You should take those guys into custody for the duration of the assault," Robertson suggested. It was the only sensible solution, and I accepted it on the spot.

When we came within two miles of the valley and the bridge, I split our forces into three groups. Horst Altreiter and fifty troops were to move a few miles north, descend into the valley, and traverse the river at the first suitable place. Their task was to march toward the bridge, masquerading as a guerrilla party coming from Laos.

"When do you intend to capture the bridge?" Captain Spata asked.

"Tomorrow at dawn," I replied.

Spata turned toward Horst. "I think your best chance to reach the bridge without trouble would be by twilight, when it is already bright enough for you to see the guards but still sufficiently obscure so that you won't be recognized as Europeans even through binoculars."

Krebitz took over. "Time your action to coincide with the movements of Stolz and Jost. They'll descend into the ravine by ropes. Keep in touch through the WT and seize both MG positions simultaneously. The slightest error could jeopardize the entire mission."

"And no shooting between us and the Cambodians," I advised.

"*Verstanden*. Understood," Horst agreed. "But what if they start shooting?"

"You're an expert. Don't give them the chance."

Pointing out the details on his sketch, Schulze explained his battle plan. "Once you've neutralized the Cambodians, you should escort them over here. . . . The rings mean caves. About three hundred yards from the bridge. The guards should be safe there. Afterward we'll occupy the western bank, with me on your flank, and we'll have half a mile of coverless trail under our guns at eighty yards."

He glanced at the listening Americans. "What do you think of it?"

"A bonanza," Starr replied flatly. Captain Spata seemed to be considering his response, and the CIA count grimaced.

"There's a catch," he said finally, scratching his head. "The Viets will notice the absence of the guards and might become suspicious."

"I was thinking the same," Spata remarked.

Erich said dispassionately, "I can always dress up a couple of my men to man the bridge, Jeff."

Robertson pursed his lips. "It might work if the convoy travels without an advance guard, Erich," he responded soberly.

"Before we look ahead too far, we should see the site," Spata ventured.

"We'll come up with something," Riedl said positively. "We always do."

"Good luck!"

Schulze and Altreiter marched away northward. We continued toward Point A, cutting our way through the all-entangling creepers and up on the last, rock-strewn acclivity, covered with thorny shrubs.

Ten minutes of climbing.

Ten minutes of rest.

Forward!

Perspiring and cursing, halting again and again to catch our breath, we moved on. The last three hundred yards were excruciating. The men had to remove their packs and ascend the cliffs with the help of ropes, hauling up the equipment afterward. Still, by five o'clock in the afternoon we occupied the cliff five hundred feet above the road and the bridge. Half an hour later Krebitz and Riedl embarked on a brief reconnaissance trip to search for a site where descent would be practicable—behind the guardhouse and out of sight of the Cambodians in the ravine.

I was keeping in touch with Erich and Horst, talking in coded German, using Bavarian, Schwabian, and even Swiss dialects. Altreiter's group was already descending to the river, two miles north of the bridge, with Schulze following them. When I asked my friend how he was feeling, Erich replied bluntly, "Like a mountain goat."

16.

Holocaust in the Srépok Valley

After having hacked a six-hundred-yard path to a cluster of striated cliffs behind the guardhouse, where descent seemed practicable, Rudolf and Helmut returned for a last consultation with Schulze and me, then assembled their groups and moved to the site. Using ropes, the men descended into the valley, carrying only their guns and grenades. The rest of their equipment was lowered after them. I followed Gruppe Drei's progress from an overhang until both groups were safely down, three hundred yards behind the guardhouse and the machine-gun emplacement, and had melted into the lush undergrowth.

What followed was a long night's vigil in absolute silence without movement and no smoking. Making themselves as comfortable as possible, the men tried to catch some sleep.

At long last the horizon began to lighten and gradually the trail emerged from the gloom. Altreiter reported that he was moving toward the bridge, and soon his pajama-clad "guerrillas" came into view. I advised Krebitz and Riedl to get ready.

Rudolf took Gruppe Drei to within fifty yards of the guardhouse, while on the far bank the Cambodians stirred and strolled onto the road, watching Altreiter's approach. I could hear dull shouts, which sounded more like greetings than calls of alarm. Lying next to me on the slab of stone that overhung the valley, Robertson observed the scene through his field glasses and said quietly, "The ruse is working."

The Cambodians had taken our commando for just another Vietcong unit marching south, a familiar sight.

The final tense moments. The last twenty yards.

A harsh challenge in Khmer. A solitary shot. Horst's troops lunged forward and engulfed the Cambodians in a brief melee. I shifted my binoculars to the momentary confusion around the guardhouse where Gruppe Drei was already in possession of the

MG emplacement, while Rield's men were rounding up the guards together with their sergeant and corporal.

"The guardhouse is taken," Krebitz reported. "You may descend."

We joined them at the bridge. The Cambodians were terrified, but their sergeant spoke French and my firm-voiced reassurances lessened his consternation. "We came to destroy a Vietcong convoy without harming the local people," I told the sergeant, whose name was Tuc Daun. To our genuine astonishment, his response was most unexpected. "At least someone does something about the canaille," he said spitefully. His corporal nodded in accord.

A reassuring sign. They didn't sound like Vietcong sympathizers.

More friendly words and freely distributed cigarettes dispersed the last vestiges of concern. The soldiers became amiable and talkative. The sergeant told us that the wireless set, which Krebitz had discovered in the guardhouse, belonged to the local cell of the Khmer Rouge, the Cambodian Vietcong. Some twenty-five Communists had gone north the day before to check the trail and remove possible obstacles, such as boulders and trees, that might have fallen down the precipice.

"Whenever a Vietcong transport arrives here, they notify another station twelve miles to the south," the sergeant told us. "The news is relayed to a large rest camp near the border."

The good sergeant believed that the huge North Vietnamese logistics base was a simple rest camp for weary guerrillas and their coolies. He had never been there because the Vietcong had declared the entire region off-limits to natives. It was a fair picture of how things were in Cambodia—the Vietnamese Communists defined where the inhabitants could or could not go in their own country.

"It isn't unusual," Krebitz told the sergeant, his voice carrying an ironic tinge. "They're doing the same in the Communist holy land. When Ivan in Moscow wants to visit his uncle in Kiev, he needs twenty different permits."

Sergeant Tuc Daun and his soldiers were certainly not hostile, so, with genuine pleasure, I permitted them to come and go freely, though under the polite supervision of Gruppe Drei.

Jeff Robertson questioned the sergeant about the situation in

Cambodia. "The accursed Vietnamese are coming and going in our country like it was their own," the sergeant complained bitterly. "A Vietcong *hai-shi*—corporal—could order a Cambodian colonel to shut up."

"Why don't you try to resist them?" Jeff asked.

Sergeant Tuc uttered a short nervous chuckle. "What can we do? We have only thirty thousand troops. They are half a million. We may only live with them or die."

I noticed that our CIA count was most interested in Sergeant Tuc, so I let him run the interrogation. Jeff asked, "What does your commanding officer think of the Communists?"

"I have three commanding officers, sir," the sergeant replied spitefully. "One from Phnom Penh, one of the Khmer Rouge, and a third one in Hanoi."

Erich uttered a wry laugh. "I think he's actually looking forward to the convoy's destruction," he said in German.

"I have the same impression," said Robertson, who then turned back to the sergeant and asked if he would give a hand by manning the bridge, as if nothing happened. It was something I have never done and probably would not have done, but it worked. Tuc Daun, his corporal, and the soldiers promptly, almost eagerly, agreed to help us set the trap, and their participation was a welcome addition to our design. It made everything easier.

"There's a chink, though," Starr said. "If the Cambodians remain around the bridge, they'll be right in your line of fire when you open up on the convoy."

It was an argument to consider, and I discussed it with the sergeant, who talked to his soldiers. In the end, Spata suggested, "When half of the convoy has passed the bridge, Sergeant Tuc and his men should quietly evacuate their stations and withdraw toward Schulze and Riedl on either side of the river."

His proposal was accepted. I told Krebitz to give the Cambodians back their rifles and machine guns, and they then resumed their routine. We prepared our positions with open fields of fire from sheltered sites. Erich sent a pair of lookouts a mile uptrail to report the arrival of the convoy. By noon our theater of action was ready, but from then on time seemed to slow down to mere crawl, as we waited tensely for the enemy.

At 3:20 P.M., *Silent Hawk One*, with Escher and Suoi and four bombs under each wing stud, swooped down and glided over the bridge with its engine idling.

"Elephant sighted at 8-miles," Escher reported. "*Hawk Two* will join at sixteen hundred hours."

"TFG to *Hawk One*," Erich responded. "Stand by to mail parcel at red flare to point yellow."

"*Verstanden*, TFG."

The glider rose slowly between the cliffs as Escher revved up the engine. It cleared the crest and disappeared from view. The Cambodians stared after it, dumbfounded.

"What kind of an airplane was that?" the sergeant wanted to know. "It flies like a ghost."

"It was made to," I answered evenly.

I assembled my own group and moved some eight hundred yards south, where we positioned ourselves among the boulders, thirty feet above the trail, set up the machine guns and mortars, then settled down to the long wait.

With their grudging consent, I sent the three Americans to a safer place, fifty feet higher up, where a cluster of crevasses offered protection against slugs and splinters.

A mile-long section of the exposed trail was covered with machine and submachine guns, mortars and flamethrowers. It seemed impossible that anyone would be able to flee or fight back effectively. Convoy 327 was doomed.

At 5:15 P.M. our lookouts reported sighting the convoy, then returned to Schulze. From that instant everything ran like a Swiss clock. Our taut nerves relaxed. Our inner tension eased or vanished altogether. The enemy became tangible. The situation was familiar. We were about to play a game we had been playing for years.

"*Hawk Two* to TFG. . . . Elephant at sauna thirty," Woss called.

"Roger, *Hawk Two*. . . . Mail parcel at red to green. Over."

"*Richtig*, TFG. Over and out."

"TFG to *Hawk One*!"

Escher came on. "Here's *Hawk One*."

"*Bereitschaft*-B!"

"*Verstanden. Kriegspiel nach Rotlicht.* Over."

"Wargame at red flare. Correct, *Hawk One*."

The ambush site was seemingly deserted. The Cambodian sentries were walking their beat. The unsuspecting convoy marched into its doom, with a handful of local Khmer Rouge troublemakers forming the advance guard. The Cambodians around the bridge raised hands and shouted greetings. The Khmer Rouge began to cross the bridge. My men's eyes were riveted to the trail.

Through the gunsights.

Eight hundred yards . . . 750 yards . . . 700 yards . . .

The Cambodians began to vacate their positions, strolling away on both sides of the ravine.

Six hundred yards . . . 550 yards . . .

Around me tense faces, running with rivulets of perspiration.

"Hawk Two to TFG. Ready!"

"TFG to *Hawk One*—go!"

I fired the red flare. It drew a yellow one from Altreiter's position to mark the site where Noi should release her bombs. The glider swooped into the ravine, leveled out, and dropped six bombs into the foremost company of the convoy, blowing apart men, animals, and carriages, blocking the trail with debris. Woss and Suoi devastated the rear of the column, causing instant panic.

"Los!" I ordered fire, and the valley erupted with the violent clatter of automatic weapons and the sharp detonations of grenades. Cries of pain, fright, and anger mingled with the deep, drawn-out whistling notes of the mortar shells. A series of explosions ripped along the convoy; men were flung into the stream like broken dolls; disemboweled mules thrashed in agony; broken bits of wood, chips of stone, shards of earthenware, mangled human limbs, flour, and rice rained over the trail. Abandoning ranks and loads, the guerrillas and their coolies scattered and dashed for cover between the boulders and in crevasses and chinks, falling by the scores to the laces of slugs and whizzing splinters. Men and beasts stampeded across the bridge and down the precipitous banks, looking desperately for shelter, but there was none. Those who found protection against Krebitz and Riedl's guns were mowed down by those of Altreiter and Schulze. Within minutes the trail and bridge was hidden in acrid cordite smoke but the mortars, well aligned, kept firing. The air carried a thick layer right in our direction,

RECALL TO INFERNO

and I told the men to stop wasting ammunition, for we couldn't see a thing beyond a dozen yards.

Making good use of the God-sent cover, the enemy dashed into the canopy of smoke to break out toward the south through my position. We could hear them coming but saw nothing before they were almost on top of us.

"Di! Di!" someone shouted in Vietnamese directly in front of me. "Advance! Advance!"

"Watch out!" Julius Steiner cried, gesturing toward a dozen obscure shapes dashing from the smoke with guns blazing. We found ourselves facing a forest of bayonets.

"Achtung!" Kretz yelled as he swung around his machine gun and opened fire against the oncoming mob at twelve yards, with devastating effect. But there were too many Vietcong.

"Look out—grenades!" someone shouted. An instant later a pair of grenades detonated nearby. The blast stunned me and stabbed into my ears like sharp needles. Kretz and his gun disappeared in fire and smoke. Splinters whizzed past my head; submachine salvos threw up dirt and chipped stones, ricocheting in every direction. A third grenade emerged from obscurity and landed with a dull *clank* between the boulders barely twelve feet from where I squatted. Some reflex forced me to hurl myself aside. The rocks deflected the blast somewhat but I got its pressure and a mouthful of grit. Lying with my back against the rock, I fired like a madman toward the Vietcong. Darting from boulder to boulder, jumping over bushes, corpses, firing their guns and stabbing our wounded with their bayonets as they went, the guerrillas fled southward. I spotted Rolf Schneider the moment he was hit. He rose, staggered, vomited blood, and crashed to the ground. A pair of guerrillas sprang from a boulder and landed directly in front of me. I fired half a mag into their tottering bodies. A third one darted straight for me. I shot him. He reeled, steadied himself, and charged on, screaming *"Xung-Phong!"* My second slug caught him in the throat, and that stopped his screaming, but his bayonet ripped along my left upper arm before he dropped his gun, twirled, and went over backward. Five yards from me, Alois Fuchs discarded his empty submachine gun and drew his automatic to pump slugs into a group of shouting guerrillas. His automatic housed eight bullets. The enemy were twelve strong. Fuchs hit five of them. Others came on, firing from the hip. Our dauntless *Kamerad* now drew his bayonet, but was hit by a submachine-gun salvo.

With effort I changed mags. My left arm felt numb. Fighting for equilibrium, I managed to rise, then dive for cover as four more guerrillas darted past my refuge.

Fire erupted from overhead and for an instant I feared another Vietcong unit, but then I saw our Americans on the ledge of the overhang, blazing away. Their timely intervention relieved the pressure, and my men could gather themselves.

Steiner crawled over and bandaged my arm, raw, red, and swollen around the four-inch gash the bayonet had torn across the muscles. The Americans clambered down the slope. "Are you okay?" Jeff asked.

"I could be better," I replied with a wry smile. "Thanks for your intervention. It came just in time."

"About a hundred of the Viets escaped," Captain Spata told me glumly. "Now the logistics base will be alerted."

"I guess I can't do anything about it," I said, wincing as Julius applied the disinfectant.

Farther along the trail and around the bridge the fighting continued. I called Erich over the WT. "How are you doing?"

"Splendidly," he answered. "Can't you see it?"

"There's too much smoke."

"Some of the bastards must have gotten through your line, Hans," he said.

"I couldn't stop them. Got a bayonet slash in my arm."

"Serious?" he asked anxiously.

"Only painful."

"Any casualties?"

"Kretz and Schneider for sure. They're dead. There might be others. . . . What about you?"

"A couple of wounded. None serious. . . . I'm going to send Zeisl over."

"Zeisl can wait. Who's working the roasters?"

"Krebitz and Riedl. . . . Frying the survivors in the crevasses. Take care of yourself, Hans."

The shooting gradually phased out, with the salvos giving way to single reports. The smoke cleared, unfolding a scene of carnage, with corpses lying singly or in random clusters all the way to the bridge and on the jagged banks: men and animals lying in coagulated pools of blood in distorted positions; blown-up carts spilled their cargo and at places our men were walking ankle-deep in rice, flour, and dried fish.

On our side of the ravine the battle ended and the sharpshooters were picking up the handful of fugitives who had managed to crawl up on the precipice to hide in crevasses, fleeing from one death to another. They were all hit and came tumbling and cartwheeling back to the trail.

On the western bank some two hundred diehard Vietcong still resisted, but their situation was hopeless. Gruppe Drei crossed the bridge and was advancing on them under the cover of four flamethrowers, or roasters, as the men had nicknamed them.

Julius Steiner assembled our group, and the men gathered our seventeen dead and gave first aid to twenty-six wounded. Apparently my group had borne the brunt of the fighting, as we lay directly in the way of the enemy breakout, which I had failed to anticipate. It was a grave tactical error that cost us dearly. I should have deployed more troops in our section of the valley to frustrate any such attempt.

Riding a small Thai horse, Kurt Zeisl came over to treat my wound, but I sent him off to help our more seriously wounded comrades. Among them were men with abdominal shots. All Kurt could do for them was to ease their suffering with morphine. Three of them died within two hours; a fourth lingered on until dusk. In the end our casualties increased to twenty dead and thirty-eight wounded, the heaviest loss we ever suffered.

Because of my lack of foresight. My companions and even the Americans tried to convince me that it was only a freak chance that the smoke drifted toward my sector and provided cover for the Vietcong, but it was small comfort to me. Such freak chances decided the issue of many great battles of history.

In the northern section of the trail the battle ended with the remaining Vietcong and coolies pushed into the stream, while a platoon ended up caught in a gully and was annihilated with flamethrowers. The Cambodian soldiers returned to the bridge and stared dumbfounded at the mass destruction.

Speaking to Sergeant Tuc Daun, Erich boasted, "You see,

Sergeant—we are only three hundred strong, yet we defeated a thousand enemy. . . . Even the much-dreaded Vietcong terrorists can be beaten."

"If you know how to do it," Starr added with good humor.

Jeff cut in, with a grin, "Well, Hans and company certainly know." Tapping Erich on the shoulder, he added jestingly, "You S.S. son of a guns sure know how to raise hell."

"*Sicher,*" Schulze agreed. "Imagine what an S.S. *Kampfgruppe* would do to the little gnomes of Father Ho."

Krebitz chuckled. "With the *Kampfgruppe* Sepp Dietrich, we would be dining in Hanoi the day after tomorrow," he stated confidently.

Captain Spata laughed softly. "Why not tomorrow, Rudolf?" he asked tauntingly.

Krebitz threw out his hands. "That'd be quite impossible, Captain. The roads up north are rubbish. You couldn't drive faster than thirty miles an hour."

Spata chuckled. "To tell you the truth, I'd gladly buy a ticket to such a show."

"So would Diem in Saigon."

In the valley the last of the guerrillas died. The guns fell silent. We gathered at the guardhouse. The troops began to destroy the enormous quantity of equipment and supplies scattered along the trail. Gruppe Drei searched the corpses and Robertson joined them to scrutinize every document the men discarded, tearing up some, pocketing others.

"They might come in handy one day, Hans," he told me over his shoulder.

"Even Hanoi restaurant bills?" I asked him, laughing, noticing what he had put aside.

"Even Hanoi hotel bills," he conceded. "Everything here can be of value. Even private letters."

"Suit yourself, Count." I was unconcerned. "You might find some important Party papers."

"Are you not interested at all?"

I shrugged. "What for? High strategy and politics are for the top brass. We're engaged in local tactics."

"But the papers might contain important political revelations, Hans," he insisted, somewhat astonished.

"Ah, the essence of Communist policies never change, Jeff. They're the same since Lenin."

Mike Spata and Joe Starr joined Jeff to give a hand at sorting the papers, which they placed into different knapsacks. The stunned Cambodians recovered their former cheerful mood when I permitted them to join Gruppe Drei in frisking the corpses and to keep whatever they found. Here, too, to our delight, the Vietcong were carrying a fair amount of cash.

Krebitz and Stolz counted nearly seven hundred Vietcong and four hundred Dang Cong corpses. Some eighty horses, mules, and buffalo, thirty carts, and fifty bicycles had survived the holocaust. We selected twenty strong mules to transport our wounded; the rest of the livestock I offered to the Cambodians. Sergeant Tuc politely declined my gift, saying that he could not possibly hide the animals from the Vietcong; but there was a very poor village nearby whose people would surely welcome the beasts. I told him to summon them on the double, for I was already concerned with the second convoy, which should arrive within six hours, unless, by some chance of bad luck, they stopped elsewhere for the night. In that case they would come only in the morning.

If . . .

They could also be alerted by wireless. Some of the Vietcong evaders could reach the guardhouse fifteen miles to the south by the morning. Sergeant Tuc thought they would reach there by midnight.

A pair of soldiers trotted off on horseback. We buried our fallen comrades in three crevasses and Krebitz blasted hundreds of tons of earth and rock over the entrances. With the help of the Cambodians, we cleared the northern section of the road of corpses and rubble and the troops set up new positions behind a row of flamethrowers poised at twenty-five yards, to where the enemy would pass.

Led by the Cambodians on horseback, a group of villagers gamboled down the trail, heading for the guardhouse, chattering. A grinning Tuc Daun conducted them to the grassy lay-by where his soldiers had already collected carts, bicycles, and animals. It took some time before the shy, introverted natives became convinced that everything was theirs for the keeping, and we received a tremendous ovation, a torrent of garbled words of gratitude, gentle back-slappings, bowing handshakes, and even smacking kisses—from toothless old matrons, to our bemused pleasure. The carts were laden with food and utensils—rice, flour, salt, fish, pots and pans—also matches, cigarettes, Chinese and Russian canned food, shoes, underwear, and the like. Through the sergeant's labored interpreting we were told that the food would be enough to feed the entire hamlet for several months. The youngsters were already riding away on the bicycles—luxury items the regular purchase of which would have swallowed up a local farmer's income for five months. The same might be said of horses, mules, and buffalo.

The gratitude seemed unending. I urged the people to leave and warned them not to brag about their good fortune before strangers, for then the Vietcong might retaliate. At long last they departed, leaving the site ready for action.

The Americans considered it a good idea to use the Vietcong supplies to benefit the wretched villagers, like a message of goodwill. I thought it was only a message: "Those who are not against us are with us." (Those who were against us we exterminated with merciless ferocity.)

It was our second night with hardly any sleep. I was feeling spent and my arm in the sling throbbed incessantly. Zeisl's tetanus shot gave me a slight fever and a headache. My companions insisted that I lie down in the guardhouse and get some sleep.

"I can take care of the smaller convoy," Erich argued. "Go and have a rest."

"You should have a rest yourself," I countered mildly. "You've done the same mileage, Erich."

"But I didn't get a bayonet through my arm," he persisted, but I remained adamant. I wanted to follow the action from the piled terrace of the guardhouse.

Tuc Daun's soldiers prepared a strong tea for us, which we appreciated.

"Small, hard-hitting teams of experts—that's what are needed in Vietnam," Captain Spata murmured, sipping tea. "Neither warplanes nor tanks, only well-equipped counterguerrilla specialists."

I asked Robertson, "Did you find any interesting papers, Jeff?"

"I don't read the local lingo, but several documents seem to come from high places. I'm going to send the lot to headquarters. We have some bright guys back home."

"Who understand the local *beach-la-mar*?"

The CIA count chuckled. "Understand? I guess some of them could write poetry in the local dialects, Hans."

The second convoy, comprising three hundred armed guerrillas and as many coolies, arrived shortly after 11 P.M. and marched into a devilish snare of Rudolf's making. It was laid out in the form of a minefield three hundred yards long and twenty yards wide, set with the Chinese antipersonnel mines Riedl had discovered in some carts of Convoy 327. Gruppe Drei created a deadly barrier between the road and ourselves and between the road and the river. The mines had been arranged so that they would permit the enemy to advance along its entire length before the foremost ranks would trigger the first detonations.

The idea came from the CIA count and was based on experience in the Philippines during the Japanese occupation.

"When the head of the column bumps into the mines, those behind would instinctively scatter and run into the mines planted on both flanks," he explained.

This is exactly what happened. When the mines started to explode, the bewildered guerrillas and coolies dashed off the trail to seek shelter and succumbed to a series of subsequent detonations. The same instant a hundred powerful battery torches illuminated the milling multitude. The submachine guns and flamethrowers had done the rest. The terrified, blinded, and deafened enemy ran amuck between laces of tracers, exploding mines, and hand grenades, knocking down each other, pitching left and right riddled by bullets, shards of metal, and stone, blowing themselves to mangled chunks of flesh or shriveling up in the vicious jets of the flamethrowers. Here, too, the Vietcong learned the hard way that discarding weapons and raising hands would not help. Our Commando of Death were living up to its Hanoi-given name and shouldered arms only when there was no enemy left to shoot at.

Riedl swung his submachine gun over his back and strolled to the fountain behind the guardhouse, humming one of his latest fancy rhymes to the tune of an old German song:

> Oh, du lieber Augustin,
> Cong ist hin, Dang ist hin,
> Futter, Waffen, Geld ist hin,
> Alles ist hin. . . .

Roughly translated, it ran something like this:

> Oh, you dearest Augustin,
> Cong is gone, Dang is gone,
> Weapons, food, money are gone,
> Everything's gone. . . .

Schulze and Krebitz joined us. Rudolf warned Sergeant Tuc Daun against tampering with the corpses or the discarded enemy luggage along the far bank, which lay in the middle of the minefield. Thinking of the Cambodian civilians, he had already removed the remaining mines from the road, but those along the flanks remained.

"Let the Vietcong tackle the problem," he told the sergeant. "But put up warning signs, so that your folks won't be strolling off left and right and get hurt."

There were many things to do and coming actions to discuss but first of all we needed some sleep. The men were so tired that they wouldn't even open tin cans to eat something. After posting sentries on the bridge and twelve more along the road, Task Force-G camped down behind the guardhouse and dozed off. Fortunately our much-deserved rest was not disturbed either by other guerrilla convoys or enemy counterattack. It was midnight and some of the platoons that had broken out of our trap might have reached the other guardhouse and informed Hanoi by wireless. Some Communist counteraction could be expected soon.

We rose at six in the morning virtually reborn and in good spirits. Zeisl changed my bandages and noted with satisfaction that my wound was clean, although his stitches still hurt like hell.

Over breakfast we discussed the situation with the Americans. However much we loathed the idea of abandoning the second phase of our expedition, the attack upon the logistics base, we were in no condition to continue as planned. Our wounded companions needed proper medical care, surgery, and hospitalization. Zeisl had also discovered several cases of painful foot and leg sores that our suffering *Kameraden* were trying to conceal. Our plan had to be drastically modified.

We debated over various alternatives and eventually Spata suggested that Schulze, Krebitz, and I should stay in Cambodia with fifty of our ablest men and the best of Gruppe Drei, and continue southward. Riedl and Altreiter, both lightly wounded by splinters, should take our wounded companions back to base by the same way we had come, now familiar and free from obstacles. The proposal was accepted. Following the existing trails and paths, even at the cost of long detours, would have been impractical, because of the constant guerrilla movements.

But retracing our steps called for negotiating the rock face upward. There was no alternative.

Using the ropes by which we had descended into the valley, and which had been left in place, Krebitz and Gruppe Drei ascended to the crest—a genuine Alpine feat—in seventy minutes. After a short rest to gather themselves, the men began to construct a pair of crude winches to move primitive hoists, while the Cambodians gave us a hand at roping together sturdy bamboo platforms for our stretchers and the mules. Joe Starr, who had had some experience in carpentry, insisted on going up to help Rudolf. He was hauled onto the overhang. Others followed his example, and while the hoists were being completed, half of our complement ascended. The work on the winches speeded up.

Trees were felled, cleaned of bark, and cut into suitable logs; then joined and fastened properly by the troops of Gruppe Drei, the only ones among us who carried axes. It was a work that the Legionnaires of Julius Caesar might have done two thousand years earlier, when they constructed their siege machines. But in the end, Krebitz contrived a crude mechanism for lifting and lowering the platforms by means of long-handled capstans, turned by sixteen men. The transport of the wounded could commence.

Bound and hooded, the mules followed, then the rest of the troops and their equipment ascended. The newcomers relieved those at the winches. The operation took the better part of the day, but was concluded without incident. Around four in the afternoon Schulze and I took our leave of Sergeant Tuc Daun and his soldiers, giving a parting counsel.

"They'll surely question you, Sergeant, and you should stick to your story. You were overwhelmed, disarmed, and immobilized moments after the attack began. This is important because the escaped Vietcong were first to cross the bridge and they'd seen you manning your positions. Those who came after them are all dead."

The sergeant understood the significance of my warning and promised to follow it to the letter. We shook hands and parted like good friends. I sincerely hoped that neither Tuc Daun nor his men would suffer retribution for having assisted us.

We took our primitive but functional elevators to the crest. Gruppe Drei gathered the ropes but left the winches intact for (only God could tell) use in the future.

Robertson told me meditatively, "I wonder if you shouldn't have enrolled Sergeant Tuc as a quiet collaborator of Task Force-G, Hans. . . . He's a genuine anti-Communist who hates the North Vietnamese and has a wireless set at his disposal. He could have furnished you with top-quality intelligence about guerrilla movements along the Srépok. . . . Don't you think so?"

"The calling code of the guardhouse wireless is OLX—ANX —Three. Frequency sixteen-point-six kilocycles," Krebitz stated matter-of-factly. "I'll call him up next week to ask what's going on in the valley."

The troops gathered their equipment.

Forward!

We followed the path that Krebitz and Riedl had cut two days ago toward the clearing that held our former camp, from where our trail ran toward the border. The mules were docile and easy to handle; they carried our heavy equipment and the wounded who were capable of riding. When the going was rough, the troops decided to carry the stretchers themselves.

I decided to camp down for the night. Schulze spoke to Escher through the wireless and informed him of the change of plan. He exchanged a few words with Suoi, then handed the mike to Riedl, who spoke to Noi. I told Woss to stand by for further communication at the same time tomorrow and the day after.

"If we should manage to wreck the logistics base, the lion's share of the job will be yours," I told him, to which Krebitz added with his traditional professionalism, "You'll have to use delayed action fuses, Stefan," he counseled Escher. "Fifteen seconds should suffice to get clear of the blast."

"All right, Rudy."

"Good luck!"

Shortly after sunrise, Zeisl prepared our wounded companions for the long trip home. The stretchers were fastened onto the mules with a pair of troopers in attendance on either side. I decided to send Zeisl along too. In our group I was the only one who might need medical attention. Helmut and Horst Altreiter had thirty wounded to care for.

Handshakes. One last embrace. Gentle back-slapping and good-luck wishes. Then the major part of Task Force-G departed eastward and soon disappeared in the all-encompassing green tangle.

Our commando of fifty troops, including the three Americans, continued along the untrodden crest, strewn with sprawling cairns of boulders, following the course of the valley and once again cutting our path across the virgin wilderness, crossing fissures and gorges, climbing rock faces, frequently with the help of our ropes. Not shirking hard labor, Spata, Starr, and Robertson joined Krebitz up in front and shared the work of the trailblazers.

Climbing boulders was not exactly the sport my sore left arm needed, but after a while I got the idea of wrapping a bit of bark over the bandage, which protected the wound when I bumped or scraped it accidentally. In the wilderness we were absolutely safe from hostile interference, but we also advanced very slowly. From morning until one o'clock in the afternoon we covered only about three miles. After lunch and a short rest, the march continued until dusk with the gain of five more miles. We covered places where it took an hour to advance five hundred yards. Every now and then Krebitz would dispatch a reconnaissance party to the precipice to get visual orientation. We were still following the Vietcong trail down in the ravine. At the rate we were moving, we'd reach the southern guardhouse in two days. Only fifteen wretched miles in three days was worse than tortoise crawl, but the jungles of Vietnam, Cambodia, and Laos were no parade ground. Our advance guard stirred to life an amazing range of wildlife, mostly noisy, crested birds, but also a pair of indignant eagles, which sprang from their nest, surprised by our intrusion, and kept circling above us, crying angrily We passed a large python, basking on a sunlit slab of stone, wholly unconcerned about us. Sergeant Starr believed he'd seen a leopard.

We also got caught in a thunderstorm and had barely managed to rig up our burlaps before the downpour hit us, fortunately without the customary gale to go with it. But even so we spent five miserable hours, constantly shifting places to escape the rivulets of water that seemed to be following us stubbornly wherever we sat or lay down for short periods of slumber.

The sky cleared after sunrise. Krebitz found a brook with a spacious natural basin and we bathed, then changed into clean underwear, shirt, and socks. It was a necessity I never permitted the troops to forgo. Our physical fitness depended on proper body care—an important precondition to survival in tropical jungles.

We also received the confirmation that the news of the double disaster in the Srépok valley had reached Hanoi. It came in the shape of a MIG 15 fighter, which streaked along the valley, probably surveying the trail between the bridge and the logistics base, looking for us. The jet bore Chinese markings. Although Ho Chi Minh did not yet have his own air force, his Chinese and Russian friends often gave a hand when it came to flying special missions that did not call for dogfights over foreign soil.

Krebitz tuned in on the MIG's frequency and we overheard the singsong exchange between the pilot and an airfield somewhere in North Vietnam. As Jeff pointed out, the MIG carried no spare tanks, so it could not have come from China. The conversation sounded bona-fide Chinese to us. We didn't understand a thing, but the pilot was probably reporting the absence of hostile troops along the trail. He never bothered to inspect the crests. He probably considered the inaccessible heights a place for monkeys and birds but certainly not for men. Even so, the unexpected appearance of a warplane was unwelcome due to the scheduled flights of our gliders. The MIG could return tomorrow or the day after and also when the Silent Hawks were flying missions. The mere thought was enough to rekindle Erich's smoldering concern.

"No more daylight overflights for the gliders!" he stated after the MIG departed. "The girls will have to bomb at night."

I agreed with him, but my support wouldn't cancel the fact that Suoi and Noi had not one chance in a thousand of hitting the fuel dump at night. It would be a difficult target for experienced bomber crews by daylight.

Unless we could place markers, or enclose the target in a quadrangle of tracers, as we had done in North Vietnam in 1952, during Operation Firefly. Some nagging doubts, however, lingered. Even if we could reach the cliffs above the base and target the base for the girls, they'd need additional training for the delicate job of releasing the bombs in the right moment, purely by feeling. The gliders carried no targeting devices. Altitude, flying speed, wind direction, and bomb release had to be timed by instinct and experience.

We discussed the problem. Krebitz insisted that there was still enough time for our pilots to fly Suoi and Noi on dry practice runs under simulated night conditions against a mock target, pinpointed by tracer salvos. Captain Spata suggested we transmit our problem to General Houssong. Erich jotted down the message, which Krebitz transposed into digital code and transmitted to Lieutenant Berger. The same night we received the general's response. Berger would fly to Buōn-mé-thuōt the next morning to take charge of the matter personally.

"Now I'm sure she'll make it." Erich beamed. "I know my wife. She'll do it again and again until it works."

"I know Suoi myself," I reminded him, "but there's also the element of time, and it's pressing."

Captain Spata said, "At least the preliminaries are in good hands. I consider Berger a very capable officer."

"So do I," Krebitz commented.

My previous foreboding about the Chinese fighter reawoke when the MIG returned the following morning; or rather another MIG, for the markings were different, at least according to Robertson.

"Don't tell me that you can also read Chinese?" Schulze boomed.

Jeff shook his head. "Read? No, but I can recognize a pattern of designs after I see it once."

"You should sign up with Task Force-G, Jeff," Schulze cracked.

"Nope!"

"Why not?"

"Because then I should command it. A matter of seniority of rank. I was a major."

The men chuckled. Krebitz said meditatively, "So, they've got two fighters north of the seventeenth parallel. I wonder what happened to yesterday's?"

"Some mechanical problem," Riedl quipped. "Built in. . . . They seem to make them one-way planes, like the Zeros of the Kamikaze."

The fighter flew past the crest where we sheltered at a distance of only three hundred yards, and a couple of well-placed salvos could have downed it. Gruppe Drei's men were full of enthusiasm for trying it and so was Starr.

"You could easily bust that skyjerk," he said pugnaciously. "Why won't you do it?"

"Because we shouldn't look for complications," I answered in a firm voice. "If the MIG crashed in the valley the wreckage would be examined and our bulletholes would be found and likewise our presence in the hills, so close to the logistics base, would no longer be secret."

We let the Chinese pilot disport himself and return to base undisturbed.

Jost said, "We'll have a real shit of a situation when Hanoi has its own warplanes."

"Aber was." Krebitz dismissed the idea with a flick of his hand. "By then we won't be in this godforsaken country but somewhere in Haiti."

"Or in hell," Karl Stolz added flatly.

Krebitz rolled his eyes. "I've already told you that Lucifer would never admit us into hell, *mensch.*"

"He'd be scared of losing his job," Jost retorted, then, glancing at the Americans, he added teasingly, "Anyway, Father Ho's air force will be a problem for Uncle Sam to tackle."

"It'll take some time before the airmen of Father Ho can

stand up against the Amis," Schulze commented, meaning every word of it.

Robertson chuckled. "And by the time they gain the experience they'll have no planes left to fly. Remember what happened to the MIGs in Korea."

We also received good news. Riedl and Altreiter had arrived safely and our wounded companions had been flown to Saigon. Assisted by the men of Task Force-G, Lieutenant Berger was working with Suoi and Noi, and they were making progress. I began to recover my wobbly confidence in the eventual outcome of the raid. Helmut and Horst knew very well how our tracer quadrangles worked in practice. They could be of great help.

During the rest of the excruciating trip, the MIGs remained comfortingly absent. We passed the Cambodian guardhouse with a tall aerial, down in the valley. Nearby spread a vast complex of straw-roofed bamboo huts, a Vietcong transit station, now vacant, but able to accommodate several hundred men and animals. Lying on an overhang, we conned the place through our field glasses, using shades over the lenses to prevent them from glinting.

The camp featured barracks, huts, kitchens, mess halls, and a bathhouse. A separate smaller compound was probably for women. Despite all their crudeness, sexual behavior in the Vietcong ranks was governed by strict moral principles. (One positive point I readily conceded to the Communists.) Man and wife could sleep together. Others were segregated. When a young lad and a girl were sitting on the moonlit riverside they'd probably pass the time by singing revolutionary songs or discussing the wisdom of Lenin, Mao, and Father Ho.

There were also extensive bamboo enclosures with mangers for animals.

On the way back to our encampment, Robertson remarked, "I presume that neither Sergeant Tuc nor his soldiers revealed how we left the valley. Otherwise this plateau would have been guarded."

It was a welcome change to know that among the simple natives of onetime French Indochina, there were still trustworthy men whose minds had not been twisted into following blindly the crooked path of the Marxist troublemongers.

Forward!

The commando trudged on for ten to twelve hours every day. On the sixth day we finally arrived on the plateau that overlooked the tangle of green on the far bank, which concealed the North Vietnamese logistics base, surrounded by an enormous line of ruddy cliffs.

There was nothing to reveal the site, save for a short branch of the trail leading into the forest, but even this was cleverly camouflaged with overhead netting, studded with green bits of canvas.

We spotted a cluster of guerrillas lounging along the stream, holding fishing rods. A line of coolies was hauling water into the camp in carts laden with large water jars.

Had we ever entertained the idea of blowing up the enemy fuel with phosphorus MG slugs, we would have abandoned it on the spot. The masses of trees were protecting the drums like a wall of concrete.

We carried no mortars. It would have been impossible to negotiate the trail we had taken with the extra load.

We established ourselves on the wooded flat. Krebitz, Stolz, and Joe Starr went to reconnoiter the rock face and select the sites for the machine guns that were to mark the base for Escher and Woss. The attack was planned for the following midnight, when only a thin crescent of moon would show above the horizon.

The day was spent in the feral tangle, except for the time I spent on the overhang with Schulze and Krebitz to align the MGs. The perimeter of the base could not be determined visually. The infrared photos had to be compared with the actual landscape, a task in which Jeff Robertson excelled. It was amazing how many different things our CIA count was capable of doing expertly. Jeff had certainly helped Erich to establish the essential points of reference for lining up the twelve machine guns at fifty-yard intervals. The job was much like marking the exact site of a sunken ship merely by coastal references.

Once aligned, the guns were locked in position.

At 8:30 P.M. Krebitz called Woss. The gliders were ready to take off at 11 P.M. I talked briefly to Lieutenant Berger, who reassured me that our girls were now sufficiently prepared for their job.

"They've been practicing for twelve hours a day with excellent results," Berger informed me. "Twenty to thirty drops daily, using duds of the same size and weight."

"Their score?" I asked tersely, since it wasn't the drops but the hits that counted.

"Eighty-six percent for Suoi. Ninety-one percent for Noi," he replied.

"Fair enough," I conceded. "What was the altitude?"

"One thousand feet."

"Let Suoi bomb first," I told him. "I want to reserve Noi for the second run if necessary."

"Merde!" Erich exclaimed, taking my proposal as a personal affront. "A difference of five percent is nothing."

"A difference of five percent could also decide between hit or miss, Erich."

I turned my attention back to Berger. "Thank you for all you've done," I concluded, ignoring my friend's grumbling.

"Rien de tout," Berger responded. "Call me after the raid. I'll be at the wireless and probably the general too. *Bon chance.*"

Dusk brought us a welcome premium: the tattoo of an electric generator. Points of lights flickered through the foliage, and we also spotted fires. Krebitz, Stolz, and Steiner occupied their respective positions. Jost Waldman sat down behind the solitary MG, which would pinpoint the center of the camp. The Americans and I remained near the wireless close to the precipice, while the rest of the commando spread out to watch the coming spectacle.

At 11:05 P.M. the long-expected wireless signal came. The gliders had taken off and should be with us in thirty to forty minutes. The MG crews were alerted. The gunners and their helpers made a last-minute inspection and prepared the spare mags.

Heavy, uneasy silence blanketed the crest. The faces around me glistened with pent-up tension. Jeff Robertson's eyes were glued to his binoculars. Spata studied the map by the light of his hooded battery torch. Starr had gone to assist Jost Waldman. From the North Vietnamese base the faint notes of merry music, singing voices, and laughter filtered up on the precipice.

Time stood still in eternity.

At 11:30 the WT began to transmit.

"Here we go!" Jeff exclaimed, scanning the sky.

"*Silent Hawk One* calling TFG. . . . Confirm target."

"TFG to *Hawk One*—affirmative. *Lichtspiele* in ninety seconds. Over."

I called Schulze. "Tracers in ninety seconds, Erich!"

"Roger, TFG. Over."

"Watch flare!"

Robertson called out, pointing, "There she comes!"

I fired the red flare. The machine guns opened up. Four steady lines of white tracers traversed the valley, converged, and crossed at treetop level above the enemy base, forming a sparkling, elongated quadrangle that boxed in the target. Jost Waldman's steady salvo marked its center.

Down below the merriment abruptly terminated. The fires vanished. The generator conked out.

"TFG to *Hawk One*. Target marked. Over."

"*Hawk One* to TFG. Start of bomb run."

"TFG to *Hawk Two*. Stand by!"

"Here's *Hawk Two*. Distance two miles. Attending."

We followed the glide of *Silent Hawk One* as she streaked toward our flashing quadrangle along a level flight path. The clatter of the machine guns echoed and reechoed between the cliffs, which increased the roar tenfold.

I was counting the seconds.

Five hundred yards . . . four hundred yards . . . The glider was silhouetted against the lighter sky like a giant prehistoric bird of prey.

Two hundred yards . . .

"Drop it now!" I exclaimed. The same instant we saw the six dark dots drop away from the fuselage at split-second intervals and plunge into the blazing quadrangle. *Hawk One's* engine thundered into life. She banked and lifted, clearing our crest at two hundred feet.

"Eight . . . nine . . . ten . . ." Captain Spata counted the seconds.

"TFG to *Hawk Two*. Stand off."

"Affirmative!"

"Fourteen . . . fifteen . . ." Mike droned on.

Across the ravine, the valley erupted with four violent detonations, followed instantly by a fifth, gigantic explosion that shot a five-hundred-foot rolling ball of fire and smoke skyward with incredible speed.

"They've done it!" Robertson cried. "By God! The girl hit the fuckin' dump square in the center!"

Our machine guns phased out. Down below a series of detonations flattened the trees and engulfed the valley in flames.

Burning fuel drums shot high in the air; some exploded, raining cascades of fiery streams, others arched back like blazing bolides.

"*Hawk One* to TFG," Suoi called. "Are you there, Hans?"

"In person, *ma cherie*."

"Do you see what I see?"

"You've done a greater job than all of us here together."

"Don't exaggerate."

Erich cut in, speaking openly. It was no longer necessary to talk in code, or use riddles. The enemy had no time to eavesdrop and the guardhouse upstream was beyond WT range.

The gun crews reported in.

Detonation after detonation rocked the valley.

"We'd better get the hell out of here!" Starr shouted over the pandemonium. "When the ammo blows up, this overhang might crash into the ravine."

It was a sensible proposal. Grabbing our gear, we retired to a distance of about three hundred yards, from where the cliffs looked like blazing volcanoes. The brightness was so intense that we could see bugs crawling on the boulders.

"*Hawk Two* calling TFG." Escher came on. He sounded disappointed. "We'll unload the bombs and return to base."

The gliders couldn't land with primed bombs.

"Affirmative, *Hawk Two*. Drop on target. Altitude two thousand feet minimum."

Escher glided in, heading toward the inferno. Noi dropped her bombs, three of which landed in a tight circle and raised towering fountains of fire.

Noi spoke. "I am taking some pictures for your report. Just to do something useful."

"You shouldn't say that," I answered in a gently reproving tone. "We're working as a team, you know."

"I know. . . . I'm sor—"

The rest of her sentence was obliterated by the primeval explosion that rocked the cliffs and heaved the plateau where we sheltered.

"The ammo dumps are going up!" Krebitz shouted. *"Jetzt wird es wirklich heiss.* . . . Now it's going to be really hot."

Stripped, mangled tree trunks and stumps, large boulders, and glowing shards of metal cascaded into the valley, into the stream, and upon the cliffs. A fiery shower landed on the overhang where we had been lying minutes before. The pressure of the detonation stripped the rock face bare of shrubs. Fearing that *Hawk Two* might have been caught by the blast, I called Woss over and over. Finally, to our relief, he responded. The glider was already six miles away heading for home.

"You see," I taunted Noi, "your bombs went to the right place. You hit one of the ammo cellars."

"It's like a volcano even from a distance of six miles."

"You'll probably see the fire from thirty miles. . . . Land safely. Greetings to Helmut. We'll be seeing you in two days' time."

"Good luck, Hans."

I turned off the walkie-talkie and called Krebitz. "Assemble the folks, Rudy. We're moving out."

"Now?" Schulze cut in.

"Now!"

"We might receive visitors, Erich." Krebitz backed me. He understood why I wanted to move. Now Schulze got it too.

"Ah, you mean the MIGs of Father Ho?"

"Precisely," I answered. "We'll camp down for the rest of the night at some safer place."

We were two miles away when a squadron of six MIG 15s streaked over the vacated crest, bombing and strafing the boulders, trees, and underbrush for twelve minutes.

17.

Unconventional Warfare

Our successful operations against the guerrillas were rooted in four important factors: speed of movement, constant surprise, misleading masquerade, and innovations regarding weapons and tactics. I never permitted the enemy to fit Task Force-G into a frame of set patterns. Our modus operandi and the weapons used changed as necessity warranted, to suit the different tasks.

The motor-pool annex of our base became not only a warehouse of unconventional weapons and ammunition, but also a well-equipped workshop, where Schulze, Krebitz, Riedl, Stolz, and many other experts were constantly experimenting with new sophisticated or crude methods of destroying Vietcong.

Erich's latest and already functional invention was his socalled *Partisanschreck*—"guerrilla terror," a smooth-bore machine gun, fashioned from the barrel of a 37-mm cannon, altered to accommodate the barrel of a 12-gauge shotgun, firing twenty-four 4-mm pellets at the rate of 140 shells per minute to an effective range of sixty yards. Schulze chose the name because the gun's effect against exposed guerrillas at close quarters was truly devastating. Firing 3,360 pellets per minute was no joke. While testing the gun under operational conditions against dummies positioned in the shrubbery, Erich's guerrilla terror had virtually cut shrubs and dummies to shreds. With its bipod support and full mag the gun weighed fifty-five pounds, not exactly the ideal commando weapon. However, when it came to presenting the Vietcong with some nasty surprises, we never shrank before any difficulty.

Schulze and Krebitz "owned" a large locker with machinegun bullets, grenades, and mortar shells treated with curare, the South American arrow poison used by the Amazon Indians. A row of massive, double-locked metal chests in the basement contained eighty phosgene shells, and during my latest visit in

Erich's top-secret domains, I also discovered two boxes of mortar shells marked LWTE and MSTG: lewisite and mustard gas, produced by Schulze's local associates.

I never consented to the use of either gas. This was not on account of any humane or moral considerations, for, when it came to killing terrorists, I had none, but rather because both substances were persistent and would leave definite traces. They would also cause horrible blisters that promptly incapacitated the victim, but death could be delayed for days. Some of the less severely affected victims might get away to die elsewhere and provide the enemy with convenient *bodies*.

Our CIA count, Jeff Robertson, impeccable as usual, came to see me a few weeks after our raid in the Srépok valley. He sat down. I offered him a drink. He asked casually, "Say, Hans—how many of those special mortar shells have you got left?"

His snide query almost knocked me from my chair, but I managed to gather myself enough to pull a puzzled look and respond nonchalantly, "You mean the ones treated with curare?"

Robertson would not be sidetracked. With a smirk hovering on the corners of his mouth, he observed me candidly. "Come, now—Captain. You can sell me something better than curare."

"What, for instance?" I temporized.

"Phosgene!" he stated blandly.

"How the hell did you—"

"Find it out?" he cut in. "I've just returned from a trip to your private little Hiroshima near Tri-ton—still full of traces."

"Phosgene leaves no traces," I replied, wondering how he found out about the gas, for surely none of my companions had talked. Robertson himself confirmed that fact.

"No traces in the area devastated by the fire," he conceded. "But I happened to do a bit of survey farther south, toward the sea. A mile or so from the camp, where the trees weren't even singed, I found my clues."

"I'm listening," I said. "I'm also curious."

"So am I, Hans." He chuckled. "Damned curious."

"Okay. What did you find?"

"Lots of little carcasses and skeletons. Birds, foxes, otters, jackals, egrets, and the like, and they didn't pop off of the chicken plague either. I guess there was a light wind, carrying your stuff to the sea to bump off everyone in its way. Also, a couple of fishermen were hit by a mysterious malady that choked them to death, Hans. . . . The rest was easy to deduce."

"I'm glad you're not working for the other side, Jeff," I commented. "I'm also sorry about those people."

"Well, sometimes the bombers miss the target too," Robertson replied consolingly. "Where did you get the phosgene?"

"We had it manufactured by a small lab that produces pesticides."

"You don't say!"

"I do say, and I hope you'll keep your mouth shut, Jeff."

He uttered a soft laugh. "Oh, I've had good training in keeping secrets. Besides, I don't want your supplies cut off by the Pentagon."

"Why should the generals be sorry for a few hundred dead terrorists?"

"They don't care a damn about the terrorists, Hans, but they sure as hell care about the political repercussions, should a leak reach the newsguys. We have our leftists too."

"Starting with the newsguys," I agreed. "Most of them are pink."

"We live in a big, free country, Hans, where everyone may say or write whatever he feels like telling."

"Too much freedom can be poison too."

We drank. I brought in some crackers. After a while Schulze and Erich came with Riedl in tow.

"Did you find something useful among the papers you collected at the Srépok?" Erich asked Jeff cheerfully.

"Sure. And I'm still wondering why should you ignore important enemy papers?"

"We're mainly interested in papers that say 'This bill is legal tender,' Count," Erich replied spiritedly.

Krebitz said, "Sometimes we do collect documents for Karl Stahnke."

"The Gestapo guy?" Robertson blurted, then added, "Well—formerly."

"The *formerly* no longer counts, Jeff," I remarked.

He reverted to our former subject. "Now, about that phosgene, Hans. . . ."

My companions assumed the mildly curious aspect of innocent bystanders. "What phosgene?" Krebitz asked with the expression of a newly born babe.

I waved a hand. "You may drop your antics, Rudy—Jeff knows."

"Ah—"

Robertson asked, "How many shells do you have left?"

"Eighty!" Erich stated. "Why?"

There was a brief pause. "Because I might need some against a specific target."

Now it was our turn to stare. "Precisely?" I asked.

"I can tell you in a couple of days," he replied. "The target is probably heavily guarded, and no explosives should be used because of the material I'd like to recover intact."

"I see," Erich said. "The guards should be bumped off without damaging the installations."

"Exactly," said Robertson. "You've already tried the phosgene. It worked, and it might be the best solution for what I have in mind."

I shrugged. "Suit yourself, Jeff. Just let me know when you're ready. We'll handle the rest anywhere in Vietnam."

He looked grave and said soberly, "I'm afraid that the target won't be in Vietnam, Hans."

"Then it might be too risky. I don't feel like leaving evidence for Hanoi to holler about."

"That might be prevented."

I blew a sigh. "Work out how, then we'll discuss the matter in detail."

Robertson parked his glass, observed us levelly, then said with a grin, "You're the greatest bunch of SOBs I ever worked with."

Erich laughed. "Is that an insult or a compliment, Jeff?"

"You guess."

"About those papers you collected," Krebitz said. "What were they?"

"Communist party directives."

Riedl pulled a grimace. "Political stuff—all shit."

"In a Communist state such party directives regulate life, Helmut," Robertson continued seriously. "Internal, external, and military matters, as you should know."

"I know," Schulze said. "I've been in Russia—although we gunned down the guerrillas without reading their party directives first."

"Wrong policy," said Jeff. "I found documents that forecast Vietcong offensives, define objectives, prescribe tactics."

"We're familiar with the Vietcong tactics," Krebitz said self-assuredly. "We also have a fair idea about the guerrilla objectives, and the moment they assemble enough men and hardware to start an offensive, we know about it too."

Robertson shook his head. "And what about the Vietcong attack against Camp Dizier last year?" he asked with a skeptical smile. "The North Vietnamese were able to assemble men, artillery, and armor within a few miles of the camp without the garrison noticing a thing."

Rudolf grinned. *"Also, gut—hast Recht."* He struck his banner before Jeff's irrefutable argument. "You're right. I'm no God either."

Our CIA count's mysterious target turned out to be a field headquarters of the 151st Vietcong (or rather North Vietnamese) Regiment of Engineers of Dien Bien Phu fame. This was the regiment that constructed the jungle roads for motorized transports and the formidable gun emplacements, from where Giap's artillery demolished Fort Béatrice on the vital Hill 506, and Fort Gabrielle, two miles to the northeast.

The field headquarters was located in "independent" Laos, snug in a sharp bend of the Sé Kamane river that surrounded it on three sides. Only twenty miles away from the border, as the crow flies, but there was a 6,500-foot peak of the Truong Son range between, and translated into practical infantry terms, the distance was closer to forty-five miles. The closest place to reach by air transport was Công-tum, from where a drivable road ran through Dac-bo to Hue, along the Sé San river.

Over Vietcong-controlled territory.

"A pleasantly murderous march of eighty-odd miles," Erich commented. "Right across the mountains. . . . What's so damned important about this base, Jeff?"

Robertson considered his answer, then spoke. "We have reason to believe that the North Vietnamese are turning the Laotian section of the Ho Chi Minh trail into a real highway, suitable for wheeled transport."

"Tanks, trucks, artillery," Riedl said.

"Right," Jeff confirmed. "Some papers I collected talk about earth-moving machines, special tools, and bridging materials stored in the engineers' base." He consulted his notes. "There should be detailed plans, maps, and directives stored in the camp. Once we have those, we'll know everything about the Vietcong supply routes and depots, down to the smallest detail."

I understood the significance of Jeff's argument. The presence of the famous engineering team in Laos suggested that Hanoi was already preparing for the eventual invasion of South Vietnam.

In two years—five years—ten years—we were sure that it would come. The Communists are long-range planners. They steadfastly pursue far-reaching policies in which the immediate future plays little role and only the distant consequence counts. This is contrary to our capitalist society, where the prospect of immediate profit is decisive, while the distant, negative consequences are conveniently ignored.

With French assistance (and U.S. finances), the Saigon government had constructed a heavily armed defensive line along the seventeenth parallel.

Hanoi was already constructing the roads to bypass it altogether, like the German *Wehrmacht* had bypassed the formidable Maginot Line in 1940.

Perhaps already thinking of the future, the Americans began to gather intelligence on the North Vietnamese lines of communication. (The definition of "Vietcong" became irrelevant, because since the partition of Indochina, they could not be distinguished from the North Vietnamese regulars.)

During our discourse, our formidable CIA count politely requested us that none of his fellow Americans in Saigon be informed about our planned use of phosgene against the North Vietnamese in Laos. The request sounded superfluous because we were perfectly aware that the fewer "outsiders" were privy to our secret, the better it would be for us. Captain Mike Spata presented no problem, for he was on leave and had gone to Japan, but I truly disliked the idea of leaving Joe Starr out of it.

He was an enthusiastic and reliable companion who shirked from no peril and who would always share our burden and fatigue. In the end, Robertson agreed to talk to Starr, after which he told me that the sergeant was okay, he'd keep the affair to himself.

Stefan Escher and Hansjuerg Woss had transferred to the Công-tum airstrip with *Silent Hawk One*. From there the two men flew several photographic missions along the Sé Kamane river, taking infrared pictures of the target and its environs. They had not been detected. There was no alarm. The base remained dimly illuminated.

From the sixty photos, we gathered that the enemy had learned something from the past debacles. At the distance of about one mile, the base of the 151st Regiment of Engineers was virtually encircled by a defensive perimeter, composed of blockhouses, trenches, foxholes, barbed-wire entanglements, and perhaps also mines.

Not an easy nut to crack. If we tried to break through the perimeter by conventional means, the shooting would alert those in the camp. Robertson was right. The only way to neutralize a section of the perimeter defenses in silence was to use the phosgene.

The barracks and tents in the camp could accommodate about three thousand engineers and workers, very likely every one of them a trained guerrilla, ready to pick up a gun and join the army detachment if necessary.

Schulze, Krebitz, and Stolz got down to manufacturing gas canisters. Riedl procured twenty oxygen tanks, the kind used in surgical theaters, to fill with phosgene under pressure. Krebitz and Gruppe Drei made screw-together aluminium tubes to fit the tanks. Extendable to fifty feet, the special bangalores would serve to convey phosgene across the obstacles direct to the enemy positions.

In silence.

Task Force-G transferred to Công-tum, together with Jeff Robertson and Joe Starr. Schulze brought along his cherished *Partisanschreck*, which he wanted to test under actual combat conditions. He did not lack the occasion.

Our commando of eighty troops left its camp of tents in the evening. The rest of Task Force-G remained at Công-tum to engage in daily field exercises and to conduct short-range excursions "to search for Vietcong" in the nearby villages. I left Riedl whose sore leg hadn't yet healed in command. Stolz stayed in camp, too, with a bad cough.

I wanted our camp to preserve its regular appearance for the benefit of the local Hanoi spies. As we learned, we couldn't quite fool them.

We followed the road only until we crossed the Sé San river. Around 1 A.M. our rear guard stopped a pair of natives on muleback, riding in the same direction. It was most unusual for peasants to be on the road at night. Jost Waldman and Julius Steiner questioned them briefly. Ostensibly the men were on their way to Plei-kiu's market with vegetables and birds. They carried neither weapons nor anything suspicious, but the presence of four large pigeons in bamboo cages stirred some childhood memories in Steiner's mind. He decided to escort the locals to Krebitz.

Rudolf scrutinized the pigeons. The owner insisted that they, too, were for the market. Rudolf thought they were too old for the grill, then offered to buy them on the spot, saying benevolently, "So you won't have to carry them all the way to Plei-kiu."

The fellow procrastinated, hemmed and hawed, and did not seem happy at all about Krebitz's generous offer. Shifting uncomfortably, he said at length, "The pigeons, sir. I cannot give you. They are paid for—already—by a very good client."

Unperturbed, Krebitz doubled the amount, saying amiably, "All right. Now you may repay your client and still have the full price."

"But—but what can I say to my client?"

"Tell him that your pigeons escaped, or popped off," Erich interposed casually.

Jeff Robertson, who had been listening, remarked quietly, "He isn't going to sell those birds, not even if you paid in gold. They're carrier pigeons."

"Naturally," Krebitz agreed. "That's why I offered to buy them."

Ignoring the owner's feeble protest, he took one of the birds and tossed it in the air. It promptly made a beeline for the Cambodian border. "It'll settle on the nearest tree until dawn,"

Rudolf said. Then, to the peasant, he continued. "How strange.
. . . You're supposed to live in Công-tum but your birds seem
to be at home somewhere else."

A more careful search then brought to light eight small cane
segments with fine leather straps. The segments were hollow
and contained bits of blank paper.

"Here it is!" Krebitz commented triumphantly.

The "birdman" was stripped nude and spread-eagled on the
ground with his balls between a pair of trenching spades, which
Steiner squeezed a bit for better understanding. It wasn't long
before the fellow confessed to being one of the local "eyes and
ears" of the Vietcong. As soon as he was certain which way we
took, one of his birds would have carried a message to a Vietcong operational center near Attopen, in Laos.

The two spies were bayoneted. Krebitz discarded their luggage, freed the hens, and loaded some of our heavy gear onto
one of the mules. At his bidding I jotted down a couple of bogus
reports in French and a request to the commander of the local
Saigon garrison to translate them into Vietnamese. Riding the
second mule, Steiner went back to Công-tum, raised Major
Xeng, and returned two hours later with the text I wanted.
Erich copied the first report, placed it into the cane segments,
tied it around the neck of the second pigeon, and wished the
bird good homecoming.

The report briefly stated that our eighty-strong commando
was marching southward in the river valley in the direction of
Ratanakiri—far from our real target.

A mile past the bridge we left the road to follow a footpath
across the undulating, forested ground toward the Laotian border. The path took us to a branch of the Sé San, which we
forded, then advanced by the compass, cutting our trail, negotiating acclivities and gorges, making a "good" twelve to fourteen
hundred yards per hour. Two days and eight miles later,
Schulze released the last bird to confirm our presence twenty-five miles to the south. If all worked out well, the Vietcong
might mobilize its resources along the Sé San to ensnare us in a
valley—while we would be on our way in the woods of the
Truong Son range.

Twelve days of laborous trekking brought us to within two
miles of the enemy perimeter, where we bivouacked and set up

a sort of operational base. Three subsequent flights of our glider confirmed the tranquillity of the North Vietnamese installation, and no changes were evident inside the security zone. We settled down to the final preparations, moving only under the cover of darkness.

Elbowing their way through the underbrush, Gruppe Drei cut the distance between us and the wire entanglement to three hundred yards. To my relief the Vietcong hadn't cut down the trees and the thorny shrubs in front of their perimeter to widen the field of view and fire—probably because the barren patch of land would have betrayed their presence along the crests. True to tradition, the guerrillas preserved the natural camouflage the overhead foliage provided, but it also permitted us to crawl up to their obstacles with relative safety.

Jost Waldman came crawling to where I sheltered with Schulze and the Americans, perhaps twenty-five yards from the wire entanglements. With his Mitra slung onto his back, he elbowed himself slowly, warily, studying the ground before he placed his arms and knees, careful not to crack a bough or stir the greenery. His gas mask hung from his neck.

"There's a stretch of punji stakes on the far side of the wires," he reported in a crusty whisper. "Krebitz is already working on them."

"Is he across the wires?" I asked, surprised.

Jost nodded. "Some wires and mines won't stop Rudolf."

"What about the blockhouse, Jost?"

"Two machine guns and a dozen apes inside."

"What else?"

"MG emplacement about a hundred yards to the left with lookout stand above it on a tree. We can neutralize the MG crew with the gas canisters but the lookouts should be taken care of by the sharpshooters, using silencers."

"What's Steiner doing?"

"He's preparing the tubes to send the phosgene into the blockhouse through a gap in the logs," Jost replied. "He needs three more tubes."

He gathered the sack with the aluminium tubes, wrapped in cloth in order not to clank together, and crawled back toward the obstacles.

RECALL TO INFERNO

"The wind is still with us," Erich said quietly.

"Well, just keep your masks ready," I advised him. "It might shift."

We waited tensely. From the blockhouse dull voices filtered into the open. Laughters. Music. My WT beeped twice, paused, and beeped again—the signal that Gruppe Drei was ready for action and we could move ahead. I passed the word.

"Gas masks in ninety seconds!"

More laughter. The blockhouse loomed closer and closer as we crawled forward. A North Vietnamese regular in uniform walked into the open and began to urinate barely five yards from Julius Steiner. "I could have blasted off his prick," he told me later.

Three beeps. Pause. Three beeps.

We put on the breathing apparatus and checked our watches. The filters should be changed in twenty minutes. My crawling troops were converging at the ten-foot gap Gruppe Drei had opened in the entanglements and the six rows of punji stakes. Ahead of us the phosgene began to flow, an invisible cloud of death, filling the blockhouse, the MG emplacement, the foxholes. The canisters crashed and cracked open. The pair of sentries on the elevated platform gasped and, choking, tumbled to the ground. Prodded by the gentle breeze, the gas spread over the ground, engulfed the obstacles farther south, crept insidiously into trenches and foxholes.

Warning no one. Sparing no one.

Unconventional warfare to make up for what we lacked in manpower.

The seconds ticked by. I heard the sounds of commotion. High-pitched exchange of words, choked shouts, long, painful fits of coughing—a gurgling death cry. A sentry clutched at his throat and toppled from the stool he was sitting on. Bewildered, the crew of a machine-gun emplacement bolted from their sandbagged hole, ran a few yards, gasped for air, and stumbled. The door of the blockhouse flung wide and a pair of living corpses staggered into the open, pitched off the stilt-supported balcony, and fell.

No loud cries. No panic. No shooting. Only choked gurgles and gasps, convulsions, and, ultimately, death.

We clambered to our feet and moved into the zone of death.

Jost cut the overhead phone wires. Steiner occupied the MG emplacement. I halted briefly at the blockhouse door. Erich flashed his battery torch inside.

Six corpses on the floor. Six more in and around the bunks along the wall. Two in the doorway. Both North Vietnamese officers. Robertson frisked them and took their papers. Starr picked up a pair of leather map cases stuffed with more papers. I jabbed a finger toward the expensive field glasses that lay on the table. Joe nodded and picked them up too.

Schulze tapped Altreiter on the shoulder and made a fast whirl with his index finger. Horst nodded, turned, and signaled his men to deploy. Forty troops spread out along the conquered section of defenses to secure and hold it until our withdrawal. Erich waved the rest of the troops forward, and we moved downhill along the comfortable enemy trail. Halfway to the engineers' base I held up a hand and the men began to assemble the mortars.

With Krebitz, Robertson, and Starr, I advanced almost to the bamboo fence of the base, which was hemmed in between the river and towering rock faces. It was an ideal target, for the phosgene couldn't disperse quickly.

12:20 A.M.

Except for a handful of sentries and a pair of lookouts in the center watchtower, the camp seemed sound asleep. I sent the signal to Erich, and the first mortar salvos began to register, then crash into the compound with systematic precision, covering the ground at some twenty-yard intervals. Some shells crashed into the barracks and the complex of tents. The rustling of the woods obliterated the dull reports of the mortars, and there were no explosions where the shells landed. Using silencers, our sharpshooters killed the watchtower lookouts, whose elevated platform was out of reach of the heavy gas. Even so someone had managed to sound the alarm before dying. Scantily clad regulars, guerrillas, and workers darted into the open—and into the layer of phosgene that blanketed the ground.

From nearby, the spectacle was even more horrible than our first attempt near Tri-ton. As the alarm spread, so did the panic. Seminude engineers and technicians, regulars, and Vietcong were dashing left and right amid terrified screams. They bumped into each other, tottered drunkenly, tore at their shirts and pajamas, clutched at themselves, and keeled over to die in convulsions.

Behind us on the crest a red flare arched across the sky, and the silence was shattered by the reverberating clatter of machine guns and detonating grenades. The enemy troops farther south, unaffected by the gas, had discovered that something had gone wrong with one of the blockhouses and that the camp was under attack. A patrol dispatched to investigate had run into Altreiter's guns.

And the phosgene! The shooting soon petered out, then stopped altogether.

The mortars fell silent. We dashed into the base—now a vast morgue. There could be no orders given, only signs made. But every man knew his task. One detachment of Gruppe Drei rolled fuel drums next to the buildings and holed them. Krebitz and twelve men began to demolish the more distant barracks and the tent complex, using flamethrowers. With astonishing self-assuredness, Jeff Robertson darted straight for the construction headquarters with Sergeant Starr. I followed them.

There was neither a safe nor lockers to break open. Construction plans and documents were stored in large drawers or lay stacked on tables and chairs. Robertson and Starr stuffed everything into large jute sacks, which a pair of troopers carried outside. The nearby office of the base commander, a North Vietnamese colonel, yielded another bagful of political and military documents. We found his corpse outside his bungalow.

At 12:50 A.M. we changed filters and by 1:15 A.M. our groups were back on the acclivity, high enough to be safe from the gas. Krebitz tested the air, then removed his mask. We followed his example and blew deep sighs of relief.

Krebitz said boisterously, *"Also, Herr Obersturmfuehrer, wir haben es geschafft. . . .* We made it."

"Herr Hauptsturmfuehrer," our CIA count corrected him. "Hans is a captain now."

"Jawohl," Krebitz acknowledged, then added with a grin, "After this coup, Diem might promote him to major."

"Colonel!" Erich cut in. "Don't you know that in the Saigon army they're jumping grades, Rudy? The size of the jump depends on the social status of your dad and how much dough he has."

The CIA count said tauntingly, "I think Hans has just promoted himself to a top-class war criminal. Unconventional warfare, prohibited weapons, crimes against humanity." He chuckled. "Eventually you'll all hang, busters."

"Sure!" Erich said. "Between you and Joe and it should be funny too. I wonder where the judges will come from?"

"Hanoi and Moscow!" I cracked, cutting into their merriment. "All right, people, we have no intention of visiting either Hanoi or Moscow—let's finish our job and move on."

The gunners began to fire phosphorus shells into the drums; the mortars fired two salvos of incendiary bombs. Within a few minutes the base turned into a sea of flames.

My WT crackled to life. Altreiter reported that his position was already free of phosgene and that he was eliminating the rest of the enemy perimeter south of the blockhouse.

We returned to the blockhouse. The men fired into the corpses to disguise the fact that they'd died without visible wounds, then blew up the buildings. Following Altreiter's men, we moved south along the defense perimeter, demolishing obstacles, blockhouses, and MG emplacements that the bewildered enemy had evacuated. Erich attacked some positions that hadn't received the phosgene with his 12-gauge *Partisanschreck*, the nerve-shattering salvos of which stripped the underbrush and peppered entire enemy platoons into screaming, trashing invalids.

In the camp the fire raged, consuming everything, wrecking even the heavy earth-moving machines and dump trucks. The blockhouses and foxholes that still resisted were shot full of phosgene canisters. Unable to comprehend the nature of the disaster, the rest of the enemy platoons fled toward the valley and the road.

With the first light of dawn the men continued to erase the evidence of our unconventional warfare.

At 7:15 A.M. five truckloads of Vietcong and regulars arrived and halted near the entrance of the burning camp. Gruppe Drei eliminated them with bazookas, submachine guns, and flamethrowers, loaded the corpses back onto the trucks, engaged the gears, and let the vehicles roll into the blazing inferno.

Two weeks later we learned that 60 percent of the complement of the 151st Regiment of Engineers had perished in the raid, including 1,200 construction workers and technicians and 900 North Vietnamese regulars and Vietcong guerrillas.

When Sergeant Starr asked me jokingly, "How do you feel, Hans?" I answered wearily, "Like the Angel of Death."

18.

War Without End

News from Vietnam had all but vanished from the pages of the free press. To the world at large the Indochina question terminated with the division of the country. Firmly entrenched in the north, the People's Democratic Republic of Ho Chi Minh was making its preparations for the reunification of the country by the force of arms.

For the time being, Hanoi refrained from embarking on a large-scale, open aggression against the Republic of Vietnam similar to that of their North Korean comrades, perhaps to avoid triggering a similar U.N. counteraction. Ho Chi Minh preferred a slow but safe war of attrition—many small shocks instead of one great quake. Communism was an infectious disease; Task Force-G was a blocking agent but not a cure. We knew perfectly well that despite any losses we inflicted on the Vietcong, the course of events wouldn't radically change. Human lives counted little to Father Ho and Nguyen Giap, and the material losses would be made good by Moscow and Peking. The Communists had long since learned that if they persevered, the free world would eventually bow to aggression and let them have their way. Especially if the contested area lay in some remote, godforsaken part of Mother Earth and not in the immediate neighborhood of the wealthy European democracies. And however wealthy and powerful it was, the United States could not repel worldwide aggression without the active participation of its allies, who, except for England, were very reluctant ones, ready to receive benefits, wary to discharge obligations. They'd move only when the flames were leaping over onto their own roofs.

The French and the South Vietnamese were expecting a massive American intervention, and more and more signs indicated that it would eventually come. Those happy signs, however, also made the local government and armed forces sluggish, reluctant—overconfident in the idea that if the bad turned worse, Uncle Sam would land a million troops, ten thousand tanks, five thousand warplanes, or drop the A-bomb on Hanoi and end the problem in a month. The intelligentsia were talking about an American invasion of North Vietnam on the scale of the D-Day landing in Normandy; about bombing raids with one thousand bombers, like those of World War II against the German cities. Whenever they spoke of American troops and machines, the local elite always tacked on four zeros.

Knowing how martial matters were run these days in the free world and especially in America, I had my reservations. The days of the glorious warlords were over. Now the generals were commanded by disinterested and most often indifferent civilian "supervisors," many of whom could probably not distinguish between a Cadillac limousine and a half-track assault gun.

To defeat the Communist aggressors, the Moscow-inspired popular image of "a poor, small country fighting against a mighty military power" must be erased. When viewed statistically, the per capita armaments of the "poor, small country" would outnumber that of the mighty military power's by five to one. Massive offensives, five hundred bomber raids like those against Nazi Germany, the relentless destruction of enemy industries, communications, military installations, the enemy's capability to wage wars at all, was the only way to convince the Communists that it might be better to live in peace. Truces, armistices, and similar temporary solutions would only postpone aggression but never prevent it. The Communists don't care a fig for treaties and to them, cheating on the capitalists is only a part of the overall Marxist-Leninist strategy.

The silent, insidious war in Vietnam continued.

Task Force-G killed guerrillas. We collected our wage of blood in money and in booty, and tried to survive. Krebitz and Riedl were daydreaming about settling in Haiti or Bermuda in happy retirement. Erich and I considered a visit to Germany. We were wealthy enough to live in comfort until the end of our days, without having to do anything but write our memoirs. We'd spent very little of our regular wages, and what we'd taken from the enemy surpassed it tenfold.

* * *

After their tremendous success in the Srépok valley, our Silent Hawks began to fly regular missions within and outside Vietnamese territory, carrying out reconnaissance flights for the benefit of the Commando of Death and surprise bombing raids with excellent results. Moving along their remote trails, the guerrilla convoys were deprived of the timely warning engines of approaching warplanes conveniently provided. Gliding out of the blue, our pilots would swoop down, straddle the convoys with six splinter bombs, then bank into a gap between the cliffs and disappear.

Suoi and Noi were no longer "amateurs" but commissioned officers of Task Force-G, drawing a regular salary like we all did. The girls were fond of flying and attended a regular training program at the South Vietnamese training center at Ghia-Dinh, to learn piloting and navigating powered planes.

Their overflights were so successful that our Silent Hawks began to spearhead regular air force strikes against Vietcong convoys and camps. Once the gliders spotted the enemy and marked the site where it lay concealed beneath the foliage, B-26s and Bearcats could saturate the limited area with 250- and 500-pound bombs. They decimated the guerrilla ranks, even when the guerrillas themselves were not actually visible.

Our CIA count Robertson was extremely interested in the achievements of the gliders and eventually became convinced that, once fitted with a more powerful engine, proper bomb racks, and a 37-mm gun, a new model could become the principal warplane against the Vietcong.

The season of the winter monsoon was approaching when, one morning, Escher and Noi returned from a reconnaissance flight over the Mekong with a reel of film. It revealed a handful of large sampans in an arbored inlet of Tan-chau island, near the Cambodian border. Since the sixteen-mile island was subject to irregular inundations, it wasn't permanently inhabited, and the few makeshift fisherman's huts did not justify the presence of such a large number of barges, so cleverly camouflaged that a subsequent conventional reconnaissance check with planes flying low above the river could not spot them.

Escher and Noi had come across a major Vietcong shipment that lay concealed during the day and traveled during the night, eventually to disperse in the innumerable branches and canals of the delta.

Dark wavelets lapped against the shore, rocking the tangle of water weed back and forth. The air was alive with sounds, the buzzing of insects, the chirping of crickets, and the steady chorus of frogs.

Lying in the soggy grass in the riverside undergrowth, Erich scanned the shimmering surface. "There they come!" he said quietly.

The surface stirred. A pair of wet suit–clad heads and shoulders popped into view. Jost and Steiner glided into the shallows and pushed up their goggles. We helped them onto the bank.

Steiner wiped his face and gasped. "The sampans are loaded to the rim and the island is crawling with apes. . . . Give me something to drink."

Riedl handed him his canteen of tea. Steiner gulped some, then handed the flask to Waldman.

"They're still loading crates, jute sacks, and oilcloth bags," Julius continued. "Think they'll be leaving soon."

"So it seems," Jost added. "We'd better get down to the job right away."

On this particular occasion there were only five of us: Schulze, Riedl, Steiner, Waldman, and myself. There had been no time to organize a proper raid. We just gathered our gear and hopped onto the first available copter to take off with the approaching dusk. The South Vietnamese pilot flew us within two miles of the Mekong, dropped our already-inflated rubber dinghy into a canal, and landed us on the back. After wishing me good luck, he left for the base at Cân-tho. He would pick us up at the same place around 2:30 A.M. It wouldn't have been safe to park the copter on the canal bank for several hours. We were in Vietcong country.

"I wonder if he'll find us," Schulze commented sardonically. "I'd hate to walk back to Saigon."

We rowed to the river and hid the dinghy in the shrubs. Jost and Julius had swum over to the sampans to have a closer look at our target.

Jost suggested that we should embark two hundred yards upstream to compensate for the current. Leaving our guns in the dinghy, we walked along the bank until Steiner found a suitable place to embark in silence. After donning our wet suits and tanks, we clamped the mines onto our belts, tested the regulators and the mouthpieces, and entered the river. We swam halfway on the surface, then submerged, trying to stay together. Despite our efforts, we soon drifted apart and landed at different muddy spots, unable to communicate. We'd foreseen such an eventuality, however, and each of us headed toward his assigned targets.

Swimming downstream, I encountered Riedl and later also Steiner. From the reconnaissance pictures taken by the *Silent Hawks* we knew the location of a machine gun and a 37-mm AA gun, which guarded the islet against attack of gunboats or warplanes. We passed them submerged and surfaced near the sampans, which were anchored in five rows of four barges each. My targets were the innermost ones. We split and each of us swam toward his own "pigs." The sampans were still connected with planks. I saw brisk comings and goings with coolies arranging loads, armed Vietcong standing guard, and boatmen working on the rigs, chattering in low voices.

Our charges were the magnetic type, unsuitable for wooden hulls, but Gruppe Drei's experts had converted them into self-adhesive ones. Drifting along the low-slung hulls, I attached my mines in the midsection, except for the foremost sampan, which I decorated with a second mine in its prow.

My job was done in six minutes. I ran for the place where we left our dinghy and landed fifteen yards downstream. Schulze and Jost returned next. A few minutes later Riedl showed up, then Steiner waded ashore. We dried ourselves, dressed, and sat down to drink tea and wait.

The timers had been set for thirty minutes.

Across the river the sampans were preparing to leave. We could hear the rasping sound of the planks being drawn. Dull commands filtered down to us. The engines began to chug-chug. Erich was gazing at his watch, then said tensely, "Now!"

At the isle a dozen fountains of fire and water erupted with shattering thunder, followed by a series of detonations in quick succession.

"*Erledigt!*" Riedl exulted. "It's done!"

One by one the sampans disintegrated in a fiery display of

skyrocketing material, much of which landed far and wide on the isle and in the Mekong. Some shot across the water and splashed into the river close to where we sat. Of the sampans, there were only traces left. Whatever remained above the surface burned fiercely. Observing the site through my field glasses, I saw no scattering people. The guerrillas on and around the boats must have perished in the explosions.

"I wonder how much Russian and Chinese hardware has gone to devil," Jost remarked.

"Plenty!" Erich replied flatly.

Riedl said meditatively, "I've no idea how much matériel we destroyed or how many Vietcong have been killed, but one thing is sure, we've probably saved thousands of lives tonight."

Helmut was damned right.

"Come to think of it," Erich said, "for every hundred Viets we gun down, we save the lives of one thousand Viets." He chuckled. "After all, we aren't that bad, are we?"

Contrary to Erich's expectation, the South Vietnamese copter pilot knew his country and his job well enough to land right where he had dropped us off. By five in the morning we were back at the base and happily in bed. For the benefit of our curious *Kameraden* (who would surely come to query us with the first sunlight), Helmut hung a hastily scribbled note on the door of my quarters with his brief report in rhymes.

> Oh, du lieber Vater Ho,
> Sampan weg, Cong sind weg,
> Arme Giap liegt im Dreck,
> Alles ist weg. . . ."

The English version ran something like this:

> Oh, you dear Father Ho,
> Sampan's gone, Congs are gone,
> Poor Giap lies in the shit,
> Everything's gone. . . .

It wasn't exactly Schiller, but Helmuth's silly rhymes helped to keep up our spirits, and to the men of Task Force-G, good spirits were just as important as good shooting.

* * *

The Vietnamese New Year was approaching with the first full moon in January—the Tet, with its continuing drizzle and cold winds. I was lying on the couch, reading General Chassin's book *La conguête de la Chine par Mao Tse Tung*, when the sergeant of the guard called me over the phone, announcing a lady visitor. It couldn't have been either Suoi or Noi, for they both had passes to enter the base.

"Escort her up," I told him, then had a quick shave before a soldier knocked on my door.

"Enter!"

He saluted. Next to him stood a pretty, auburn-haired young woman whose heart-shaped face looked vaguely familiar. I dismissed the soldier and invited her inside.

"I am Hans Wagemueller," I introduced myself in French, ushering her into the living room.

She smiled, extended her hand, and replied in German, "I know you, Hans, from many letters and pictures," she said airily. I stared at her, puzzled for an instant, then an incredible thought began to dawn in my mind.

"But you are . . . you must be . . ."

"Erika," she said. "Karl Pfirstenhammer's sister."

"Oh, du lieber Gott!" I exclaimed. "Erika!" I was so carried away with joy that I grabbed her, crushed her against my chest, and kissed her on both cheeks. She seemed a little surprised by my greeting but I meant every bit of it, and she returned it in the same spirit.

I seated her in a club chair and stared some more. "Erika Pfirstenhammer," I repeated warmly. "Karl's little sister."

"The little sister has grown," she corrected me with a self-conscious smile. "She is now Dr. Pfirstenhammer."

"Of course, Doctor," I replied. "You were studying medicine when—" I quickly swallowed the "when Karl died" and substituted an awkward "did you land?"

"This morning," she replied. "I took a cab and came straight here . . . to avoid getting lost in Saigon."

"Well done, Erika!" I exulted. "Did you have your breakfast?"

"Not yet."

I rose. "I'm going to boil some coffee. . . . Fried eggs with bacon okay?"

She joined me at the kitchen door. "Let me do the eggs."

She was tall and graceful like her brother had been, with a sweet face and large, dark eyes.

"There's the fridge," I said, pointing. "Eggs, bacon, cheese. . . . All's there. Please feel at home, Erika. Karl was like a brother to me." And I told her briefly how I met Karl at the Danube in 1945, two fugitives in their own country.

"Thank you, Hans," she said warmly in her soft contralto voice, "for having told me this. Also for your hospitality."

"Where's your luggage?"

"I've only two small suitcases. . . . left them at the airport."

"Why?"

"It's easier to look for a hotel without luggage."

I shook my head and said resolutely, "You'll do nothing of the sort." I took her by the hand. "Come along."

I led her into the guest room and waved a hand about. "What do you say?"

"It's a nice room, Hans."

"Well, it's all yours. I'm sure a few feminine touches will make it look even nicer," I added persuasively. "Stay as long as you wish."

She looked at me searchingly. "I—I don't want to be—"

"You won't be." I cut her short. "I'll be happy if you stay and so will everyone else. . . . Anyway we spend much of our time in the wilderness. Here you'll be comfortable and safe. The guards will help you shop."

She uttered a soft, tingling laugh. "Karl told me that you have a persuasive personality."

We had breakfast. She asked how Schulze, Riedl, and Krebitz were doing. Then she embarked on the painful tack I wanted to avoid as long as possible.

"Tell me about Karl," she said soberly.

I told her about our happy days with her brother; about our battles, how Karl had shelled the daylights out of the Vietminh with the howitzers he had taken from them; about our two raids into Communist China, riding in captured Chinese army trucks. And I told her about her brother's sudden death in the well with the secret entrance into the Vietminh tunnels.

"Karl would never send his troops into unknown peril, Erika," I told her. "When there was a particularly dangerous job he would do it himself. That's why he died."

Erika's face clouded over and her eyes glistened but she listened to my sad narrative bravely and remained composed.

"Did he die—quickly?" she asked finally.

"Instantly, Erika," I lied. "He didn't suffer." And the recollections of my friend with the shaft of a four-foot spear in his chest made me shudder inwardly.

"I'd like to visit the place where you buried him, Hans," she said quietly. "Can you take me there?"

I said gravely, "You can't go there, Erika. Karl's grave is in North Vietnam."

I told her how we buried Karl with rifle salvos and by the old tunes of the *Wehrmacht* farewell to fallen soldiers, *"Heil Dir Im Siegeskranz."*

"No one will ever disturb his tomb," I said in a reassuring voice. "Krebitz blasted half of a mountain upon his grave."

She said sadly, "I can't even place a bouquet of flowers on it . . ."

"Perhaps your bouquet can be dropped—from a plane," I replied impulsively, thinking of our *Silent Hawk*s and forgetting how far north Karl's grave was.

"I would gladly do that."

"I wouldn't let you fly along but one of our pilots might drop your flowers and bring back some pictures of the site."

There was a brief, uneasy silence. I went to fetch Karl's old *Wehrmacht* belt and curved pipe, which I had safeguarded ever since, and offered them to Erika. "I kept them for such an occasion, Erika, here—or in Germany. . . . Karl carried his belt and pipe in Russia, Indochina . . ."

She picked up the belt and held it almost in awe. *"Gott Mit Uns,"* she read the engraving on the buckle. "Thank you, Hans. . . . Thank you from my heart."

I wanted to leave her alone for a while and asked for the key to the airport locker, so that I might send someone to fetch her suitcases. She took a shower but didn't feel like sleeping. "I slept most of the flight," she told me. Instead she wanted to see Schulze, Krebitz, Riedl, and Kurt Zeisl. I called them up and they hurried to my place with Suoi and Noi. Erich thought it was the greatest event of the year. Riedl was speechless, and Krebitz found it necessary to dab his eyes. There was no formality, no awkward silence while the proper words were being considered; the encounter was spontaneous and sincere, as if Erika had been a lifelong friend returning home after a long absence.

"Of course you're going to stay!" Erich boomed, as if giving an order. "You're one of the family . . . a large one, to be sure. Karl wouldn't let you go."

"My return ticket is valid for twenty-one days," she began hesitantly.

Riedl cut her short. "Only three weeks? Out of the question."

"Otherwise I'll lose my ticket."

"How much did it cost?"

"Almost nine hundred dollars."

Riedl struck the table with his clenched fist. "Nine hundred once . . . nine hundred twice . . . nine hundred third . . . It's sold!"

Erika laughed. "To whom?"

"To Task Force-G, naturally—that's us. And we're big capitalists, you know."

"I've never heard of rich soldiers."

Erich chuckled. "Rich soldiers, no, soldiers of fortune, yes. We're pirates, Erika." He patted her hand. "Karl talked a lot about you. He wanted to bring you here after you finished your studies."

"And I wanted to come so much."

"You see? Your place is with us."

Zeisl interrupted. "We could also use a good physician," he proposed with quiet emphasis.

Erika smiled. "It would be a long time before I acquire a tenth of your experience, Kurt," she said modestly, then added, "But if you are willing to experiment with me . . ." She left her sentence unfinished, a polite consent.

"Hooray!" Helmut exclaimed, as Zeisl embraced Erika and kissed her on both cheeks.

My friends were content that now I was no longer alone. Erika's presence ended my dreary years of virtual solitude. With the passing of time we became inseparable friends. She was a superb companion and, like her brother had been, steady in friendship, steely in will, and serious in profession. She brought some sunshine into my dreary routine, perhaps the only sunshine I'd ever known. Our relationship blossomed, and finally we agreed to get married after my service in Vietnam was over.

The winter monsoon turned the unpaved roads into paddies and the paddies became treacherous swamps. Along the Mekong and in the valleys of the other principal rivers, on the plains the rivers traversed, nothing was permanent and enduring. Where yesterday was dry ground a river flowed the following morning; an island at dawn would turn into a sea of morass by dusk.

Only the grass-overgrown jungle trails remained more or less negotiable. The footbridges across gullies and ravines were now safe from sabotage. The Vietcong needed them as much as their antagonists. It was high season for the guerrillas. The Foreign Legion had already left, save for a token expeditionary force. The South Vietnamese Army had taken charge of the fortified villages and camps but they were still amateurs. Grown-up kids playing war. Content with holing up in their concrete bunkers, behind the walls of forts, wire entanglements, and hastily laid minefields, to spend the days and weeks of rain in merry idleness that resembled lethargy. At places, the Vietcong High Command in Hanoi considered unimportant, a convenient "live and let live" system existed between the Vietcong and the local garrison. The guerrillas refrained from attacking the fortifications and the soldiers of Saigon let them pass undisturbed toward their distant objectives. Incredible as it may sound, but in some fortified hamlets the minefields had been laid only to furnish the Vietcong with HE free of charge. For when the Hanoi engineers came to remove the mines in broad daylight, the South Vietnamese troops in a bunker with machine guns and a 75-mm cannon would only look on indifferently. The mines were not French but American. What if the Vietcong hauled off a few hundred? Uncle Sam would send more.

But the monsoon season was also the high season for the Commando of Death. Drizzle or rain, we would be on the field, especially around the period of Tet, which would always bring about an upswing of guerrilla activity.

The well-maintained trails across southern Laos and Cambodia were abuzz with Vietcong supply convoys, and the Mekong teamed with hostile shipping.

The French Air Force had long departed to easier hunting grounds in North and Central Africa. Most local airmen could take off and land only in daylight with visual reference to the airstrip. Instrumental and all-weather flying remained the privilege of the handful of French-trained elite, whom Diem would never risk on account of some raggedy guerrillas, who, daring the storms and rains, trudged east along godforsaken jungle trails.

Task Force-G was expected to play the role of attacker, defender, air force, navy, and intelligence.

With 307 men!

Then came the sad day when Lieutenant General Simon Houssong, his adjutant, Lieutenant Bernard Berger, and Captain Dessault were leaving for home too. Karl Stahnke's section stayed to work for the Saigon government.

General Houssong's job was taken over by a friendly, perpetually smiling Vietnamese colonel who could organize splendid garden parties and plan sweeping fancy raids. Sometimes we pleased him; sometimes, when the realization of a "plan" would call for the resources of an armored division, we politely sent him to hell. But Saigon was paying us well and we also enjoyed lots of "fringe benefits," so we kept our part of the bargain by making the guerrillas' life as miserable as possible.

It was a dreary day with gray overcast portending rain. We were in the Binh-Thuan mountains, tailing a Vietcong outfit that had raided the airfield of Phan-thiét the night before and wrecked half a dozen parked aircraft together with their ground installations, recently constructed with American aid. Though there had been only fifty Vietcong in the commando, it had raised enough hell for five hundred.

Their commander must have been a seasoned veteran. He didn't follow any of the existing trails but cut across the hills as the crow flies, obliging us to dog them where going was hellish and visibility almost zero. Not knowing when and where we might run into a clever ambush, we advanced with redoubled caution. The fact that good old Krebitz was trudging ahead of us with his trailblazers was no consolation, for I didn't feel like losing him either.

Still, I was calm and resolved but I cannot say that I was also unconcerned. I had my moments of weakness like everyone else, especially in the beginning of an action when everything still appeared uncertain and often unsafe. As on this special occasion when (a rare occurrence) I recognized my adversary as an expert.

The jungle takes no side. The green hell is neutral. It gives no warning, no hint where our formidable antagonists might be lurking in the undergrowth, in the four-foot grass, or between the boulders. Death could be waiting behind every tree, rock, mound.

I was afraid and so were Erich, Riedl, Krebitz, and the rest of us on many occasions. Our apparent calm and cheerful wisecracking was only a sort of self-defense, a façade of dauntless heroism.

Still, there's a difference between the fear of the seasoned jungle fighter and that of a newcomer. The veteran might experience fear while he's stalking an invisible foe; he might dive for cover or pale when a surprised deer bolts from its cover in front of him. But in the moments of real peril, when his adversary had revealed himself, the veteran becomes cool, self-controlled, efficient, and just as dangerous as his antagonist. When the green recruit might freeze with terror, the expert would react with his nerves and muscles under perfect control. He would never panic.

We came across an abandoned camp of crude bamboo-and-straw huts. Krebitz found ample evidence that the occupants had decamped in great hurry. Sleeping mats, utensils, fried fish, and boiled rice were lying around the vacant shelters. Hungry as they were, our troops wouldn't touch anything the enemy left behind ready and inviting.

Apparently they had spotted Krebitz and his party and had been astute enough not to attack him and reveal themselves, but pushed on. Perhaps the Vietcong commander wanted to leave the issue undecided and us floundering in suspense. Perhaps he knew that Task Force-G preferred action to suspense, the roaring of guns to ominous silence, and decided not to play along.

We hit a forested hillock that sloped to the bank of the

Langa. After a brief search, Krebitz discovered the place where our foes had crossed the swollen stream by wading and swimming across the cold, turbulent water. Once again the rain came pouring down. The gusts of wind whipped spindrifts and obliterated every other sound. Our antagonists could have opened fire on us from twenty yards without us hearing anything. Why would the crafty Vietcong commander miss such a chance?

I wouldn't send my men across the stream to get soaked to the skin without any possibility of building fires to dry themselves. We were in no hurry. We seldom lagged more than a mile or two behind the Viets, who kept leaving behind ample evidence of their trespassing in untrodden forests. They weren't cutting a path, which would facilitate our pursuit, but rather pushed through the undergrowth as best they could and suffered the consequences in the form of cuts and bruises. Krebitz and his men found shreds of cloth and hair on the thorny twigs, broken boughs, trampled grass, and imprints of guerrilla sandals fashioned from tires in the soggy soil.

Gruppe Drei blasted six young trees that were long enough to reach the far bank and the commando passed the stream on the improvised bridge, erected in twenty minutes.

Forward!

We moved on until Rudolf discovered that the enemy was leading us by the nose in circles. Why? he wondered. I myself was mystified.

The rain was still beating down fiercely. Under the hastily rigged burlaps we discussed the situation, while the troops prepared themselves a cold meal. Erich suggested that the Vietcong commander didn't consider his forces adequate to attack us.

"We're over one hundred strong. He has only some fifty men, perhaps some of them wounded and unable to fight."

"But he could have had the advantage of opening up first," Riedl argued. "This merry-go-round play doesn't make sense."

"Or else the group has used up most of its ammo and grenades in the attack against the airfield and hasn't got the means to attack," I said thoughtfully.

Krebitz's chin snapped up. "That's it!" he exclaimed. "Their guns must be dry."

Riedl stared. "But why lead us in circles?"

"Because of their lack of ammo, Helmut."

"I still can't see the tie-in, Rudy," Erich said.

"I can't either," Riedl added.

"It's very simple," I said. "If the Viets are dry, they need supplies, but in order to get ammo they should return to base, and they can't return to base with us tailing them."

"You mean their base could be that close?" Jost Waldman asked.

"It must be somewhere in these woods."

"A razor-sharp deduction" Krebitz commented. "We're going to end this *Karussell.*"

"To begin with we'll split into three *Kampfgruppen,*" I said, "Like in the grand old times. Rudy with forty men is going to follow the Viets—they're already used to seeing him. Erich and I will advance on the flanks with fifty troops each and envelop the crafty lot between the gradually closing arms of the pincer." I illustrated my idea on the map. "Our pincer will prevent the enemy from continuing their merry-go-round antics. If their commander wants to get away from us, he'll be obliged to cross this gully here." I pointed out the spot. "And that's where the pincer will snap shut."

We divided our forces. Krebitz and Gruppe Drei continued tailing the fugitives, while Schulze and I advanced along the flanks in a sweeping arch. Two hours later our antagonists tried the *Karussell* trick for the third time and ran into Riedl's submachine-gun salvos, which sent them back on a beeline to the gully. The fact that they still refrained from firing confirmed our former supposition. The group had indeed run out of ammo.

Now, dropping all precaution, we began to advance rapidly and caught the small unit of Vietcong in the ravine, exactly as we had envisioned. There were forty-three men of the 312th Vietcong Regiment of Infantry—all expert sappers and scouts.

They surrendered on the first challenge, for they had only a total of thirty cartridges left. Their commander, a handsome young Hanoi engineer, was so upset that, seeing me advancing, he threw his bamboo helmet on the ground and trampled it flat in a fit of impotent rage. Then he cursed nonstop for two minutes, calling us all kinds of canaille, *tête de merde,* sons of bitches, and whoresons in perfect French, and made our troops bray with guffaws.

It also saved his life.

We weren't mad. On the contrary, I felt pleasantly dissipated. It was such a funny sight seeing him squashing his helmet, and his companions discarding their useless guns with expressions of sheer disgust, that we couldn't stop laughing.

Instead of bullets and bayonets we gave our adversaries cigarettes and biscuits. There was no need to question the unhappy Vietcong leader because in his map case, Krebitz found a sketch of the region with the site of the guerrilla camp marked. It was only about three miles from the ravine. He'd had no time to destroy his papers.

Slapping him gently on the shoulder, Erich said patronizingly, "Congratulations, colleague. We're going to pay a visit to your boss in camp two hundred six."

At this the guerrilla chief sank into the depths of gloom and sighed as if life were becoming a burden to him.

"They'll shoot me for this," he stated glumly.

"That's why we'll let you live."

They hadn't killed any of us and, as Erich had put it, they were good sports.

I had them bound and left them under guard, while we marched against the nearby base. It wasn't large, having only twelve huts and four community tents, but everything was expertly camouflaged on the crest of an arbored hillock. We overran and eliminated it without any trouble. Its arsenal contained submachine guns, rifles, mines, plastic explosives, mortars, shells, and ammunition sufficient to sustain about two hundred guerrillas for a month or so. As far as I know, we left no survivors.

We returned to the ravine and released our prisoners. I sent them on their way, advising them to return home and use their skills in some peaceful activity. Almost all of them were North Vietnamese.

Nine miles to the northwest, near the village of Bao-tôc and the road to Da-lat, Krebitz bumped into a cart laden with MG ammo and escorted by twelve Vietcong who were blown to kingdom come when the solitary bazooka shell Jost fired hit the ammo crates square in the center.

Schulze remembered having seen a large cave in the region during a previous expedition. Gruppe Drei found it the same afternoon. The cave happened to be occupied by eighteen guerrillas, cooking rice and drying clothes around a bonfire with their rifles neatly stacked. After our sharpshooters eliminated a pair of sentries, Gruppe Drei stormed inside with submachine guns blazing. The corpses were rolled down on the precipitous slope and we took possession of the comfortable rest house with a fire already going and rice cooked. We helped ourselves to a good meal of curried rice and Chinese meatballs at Hanoi's expense. The cave featured a creek. We all bathed. Worn socks and underclothes were washed and dried. We enjoyed a roof overhead for the first time in twelve days, most of them rainy.

Over the wireless, Krebitz contacted Stahnke, who was the only person in Saigon we were keeping in touch with. Only he knew our whereabouts, destination, and itinerary. We trusted no one else. Not even our new commander, Colonel Xan Ghuyen Bo. We would send him regular reports on our accomplishments but never a word on battle plans.

Horst Altreiter with the rest of Task Force-G was to leave for the Da-dung valley, to meet us in three days ten miles west of Kin-du, on a hill marked 1640 on our operational maps. From there we planned a large-scale assault on a Vietcong base located in a sharp bend of the river. According to Stahnke, the base was supplying arms and ammo to sixteen guerrilla groups operating in War Zone 6/B—6,400 square miles of highlands, dotted with strategically placed forts, stubbornly contested by the Vietcong. The base, marked 6-116, was supposed to cater to over a thousand Vietcong, of whom four to six hundred were permanently present in the camp.

The long rest made us feel strong, and by the time we were ready to leave the cave the rain, too, had stopped. Task Force-G marched north, ready for action, although since General Houssong's departure we lost much of our earlier zeal. In the old days of our Battalion of the Damned, we fought the Communists by conviction; now we killed the guerrillas for a good wage and for booty.

The knowledge that no matter what we had done or could do, the enemy would eventually prevail was very depressing.

"It's like trying to squash an anthill with your heels," Erich said in a moment of exasperation. "It doesn't matter how many of them you squash, there'll be others, more than before."

He was right, although a "final solution" was still available— a drastic solution but the only one, which the French did not, the Saigon government could not, and the Americans would not pursue: the total war of extermination in the south and the north, using every available weapon including poison gas and nuclear shells to eliminate the Communist power north of the seventeenth parallel forever.

But I believed that the mere threat of using such weapons would have been enough to bring Hanoi to reason. The only argument the Communists would accept as valid and convincing is that of the gun. The A-bomb dropped over Hiroshima had extinguished 150,000 lives. It also saved the lives of a million U.S. servicemen who might have fallen during an invasion against the Japanese home islands.

A single bomb dropped in Korea, or in Vietnam, perhaps around Dien Bien Phu, would have altered the course of history and probably stopped Communist aggression everywhere in the world. It would have rendered aggression too costly.

One may taunt a cat at large but never a tiger. The leaders of the free world were scared even to threaten.

When we arrived at Hill 1640, Horst Altreiter was already there, camped on the crest. His group had brought along our heavy equipment and reserve tanks for the flamethrowers.

To my combined astonishment, delight, and concern, Erika, Suoi, and Noi were also there with Kurt Zeisl, all three of them properly clad and equipped for the rainy season and radiating joy. So were our American friends Starr, Spata, and the CIA count, who greeted me with a resounding "Hi, chief—you see, it's not so easy to sneak away from us."

Altreiter handed me a sealed envelope, bearing the seal of Ngo Dinh Nhu, President Diem's brother. It contained not an order but a request that Task Force-G proceed to Lomphat along the river Srépok, then follow the Ho Chi Minh trail to Siem Pang and Attopen in Laos to destroy Hanoi convoys and troops, reportedly on their way south in large numbers.

Our ever-smiling colonel in Saigon had simply endorsed and forwarded it, naturally without a word on the logistics problems such an expedition would present in terms of boots, let alone food and ammunition. Our "employers"—rather than superiors—seem to have become used to the fact that Task Force-G would manage somehow, it always did, because the Germans were a resourceful bunch of bastards.

"Do they think we can shit mortar shells and MG ammo?" Krebitz grumbled openly. "Why? From here to Attopen is a good four hundred miles, one way. What are we going to shoot with by the time we get there, slingshots and bows?"

"One of the Dakotas will drop more supplies at Ghia-nghia," Altreiter stated, opening his hands as if to say "I'm innocent."

"At Ghia-nghia?" Schulze exclaimed. "It's near To-soay and the whole *Verdammte Scheissland* is crawling with Vietcong!"

"*Sicher,*" Krebitz agreed. "Half an hour after the drop the whole Cambodian guerrilla network would be on red alert."

"Yes, the proposal sounds a bit crazy," Captain Spata agreed. "You can't start a secret mission with an airdrop over hostile territory."

Stolz advised, "You'd better start taking notes regarding Saigon idiocy, Captain. They might come handy one day, when you'll have to cooperate with them."

"Don't worry," the CIA count replied reassuringly. "I already have a notebook full."

The route of penetration into Cambodia and Laos that Saigon suggested was a familiar one. It traversed the Mondulkiri and Ratanakiri districts, where we had already demolished Vietcong bases and convoys and also encountered Sergeant Tuc Daun. Near Lomphat lay the North Vietnamese base from where the attack against Camp Dizier had been launched and which we later destroyed with Major Lapautre and his paras.

But we disliked following routes suggested by a third party.

Through Karl Stahnke's office I politely turned down the proposed airdrop near Ghi-nghia and requested delivery right where we were, on Hill 1640.

"It's going to be a damned long trip," Erich remarked as he scanned the map. "Two months, or more."

"That's why we wanted to come along," Erika said. "Two months is a long time to spend in suspense."

"But you have no jungle experience at all." I voiced my concern. "The jungles of Asia are not the *Thueringer Wald.*"

"Suoi and Noi will tell me what to do."

"And what not to do," Krebitz added emphatically. "Can you shoot?"

She shook her head. "I've never done it."

"Well, you'll have to learn how to handle a gun."

"I promise to be an attentive pupil," she retorted, smiling. "But I want to save lives, not destroy them."

I turned back to Horst. "Any other news?"

"The Communists are stirring up trouble in Burma."

Erich uttered a soft, ironical snort. "I expected it. Why shouldn't they? No one is going to stop them. Just wait. Hanoi'll gobble up Cambodia, Laos, Thailand, and Burma. The French and British colonial empires will be replaced by a Communist one."

"And it'll end up like the Third Reich," Riedl cut in, "occupying scores of nations, then fighting insurgents everywhere and bleeding to death in the process like the *Wehrmacht.*"

I shook my head. "You're wrong, Helmut," I said gravely. "There's a fundamental difference. Then and there in Europe the irregulars were fighting against a foreign invader—the Nazi *Wehrmacht*. The Communists are working from within, using regiments that are already inside the country they wish to conquer, and they can do it by proxy, by creating puppet governments that would conveniently invite them to invade, to provide brotherly support against the reactionary enemy. Are there any partisan wars in the East European countries occupied by the Red Army?"

"That's true too," Helmut conceded. "Asia might sink in a sea of Communist shit."

The following afternoon the Dakota came. Schulze signaled the site with smoke candles. Circling the crest, the plane dropped a dozen large bales and chuted down large metal containers.

To be honest, Saigon was most generous. We received more weapons, ammunition, medicines, canned food, cigarettes, spare boots, clothes, fifteen small Canadian tents, surgical instruments and plasma, et cetera. When Rudolf finished his inventory, he told me casually, "We'd better start looking for mules, Hans, for once I divide the load between the men, each of us would carry a ninety-pound backpack."

"Very well, we'll buy some mules."

Jeff Robertson told me on the march, "If Sergeant Tuc Daun is still at the guardhouse, I'd like to have a chat with him. He might be willing to give us a hand in the future."

I looked at him candidly. "A hand to TFG or to the CIA?"

"Both," Robertson replied nonchalantly. "We're working hand in hand, Hans—aren't we?"

"Sure, Jeff. . . . What is ours is yours, what is yours TFG has nothing to do with. The CIA seems to have a one-track mind, you know?"

"I know," he replied flatly.

"Suit yourself all the same."

He added, "Perhaps we could halt briefly at the North Vietnamese logistics base the gliders destroyed."

"We won't be going that way, Jeff."

He looked at me, surprised. "But the itinerary I got from your colonel—"

"—is a piece of paper, a copy of which might be under scrutiny in Hanoi in this very instant."

"You don't say!" He still looked astonished. "You don't even trust Diem's brother, Hans?"

"It's a matter of principle," I answered casually. "While the French were in charge, we were dealing with General Houssong and his immediate staff and with no one else. To tell you the truth, if the Saigon government consisted of Jesus Christ and his twelve Apostles, I would still keep my security measures."

"They might not like that, Hans."

"They can take it or leave it. I'll tell Saigon where we've been but never where we shall be."

He threw an inquisitive glance at me and asked tauntingly, "Say, Hans—do you trust me?"

I slapped him on the back. "Well, it was you who got us the night scopes and the *Silent Hawk*s," I replied with a grin.

Krebitz cut in. "We'll hit the Ho Chi Minh trail at Tuc Daun's guardhouse. Perhaps we can still use the trails and the winches we left in place."

"Okay." Jeff shouldered his gun. "Carry the torch."

The Vietcong camp marked 116 of Operational Zone 6 was hiding snugly in the northernmost bend of the Da-dung river.

Unaware of how near they had been to death, some five hundred guerrillas of Father Ho had been given a new lease of life.

Heading for Mondulkiri in Cambodia, the Commando of Death bypassed them by only three miles.

The endless war continued.

GEORGE ROBERT ELFORD

DEVIL'S GUARD: THE BATTALION OF THE DAMNED

The brutal and shocking testament of a Nazi mercenary.

This is a first hand record of an unregenerate Nazi who escaped the war crimes trials in Europe after World War II and joined the French Foreign Legion.

Sent to Indochina to fight the Viet Minh, the German battalion shot, bombed, tortured and bayonetted the enemy.

Devil's Guard is one man's personal document of reprisals and counter-reprisals, of criminal violence on both sides, of outrages against humanity, of war at its rawest, cruellest and most gruesome.

Post·A·Book

A Royal Mail service in association with the Book Marketing Council & The Booksellers Association.

Post-A-Book is a Post Office trademark.

GEORGE ROBERT ELFORD

THE SONNEBERG RUN

The Hell Pit, men had called it in the war. Forced labour gangs from the concentration camps, driven on by the lash and the jackboot, had sweated and died in its many-levelled depths, hacking out the coal to fuel the Nazi war machine.

Now, long disused, its tunnels dynamited and half-flooded, it stretched for miles beneath a new landscape of horror: the minefields, watchtowers and barbed wire of the Iron Curtain.

But to a group of desperate, hunted men – and one woman – it was more than just a place of bitter memories. *The Sonneberg mine was about to become the deepest escape route in the world.*

HODDER AND STOUGHTON PAPERBACKS

MORE THRILLERS AVAILABLE FROM HODDER AND STOUGHTON PAPERBACKS

GEORGE ROBERT ELFORD

☐	01336 7	Devil's Guard: The Battalion of the Damned	£3.50
☐	05908 1	The Sonneberg Run	£1.95

J. C. POLLOCK

☐	41382 9	Crossfire	£3.50

THOMAS BLOCK

☐	05839 5	Airship Nine	£2.50
☐	05726 7	Forced Landing	£1.95
☐	05160 9	Mayday	£3.50
☐	05556 6	Orbit	£2.99
☐	41555 4	Skyfall	£3.50

All these books are available at your local bookshop or newsagent, or can be ordered direct from the publisher. Just tick the titles you want and fill in the form below.

Prices and availability subject to change without notice.

Hodder & Stoughton Paperbacks, P.O. Box 11, Falmouth, Cornwall.

Please send cheque or postal order, and allow the following for postage and packing:

U.K. – 55p for one book, plus 22p for the second book, and 14p for each additional book ordered up to a £1.75 maximum.

B.F.P.O. and EIRE – 55p for the first book, plus 22p for the second book, and 14p per copy for the next 7 books, 8p per book thereafter.

OTHER OVERSEAS CUSTOMERS – £1.00 for the first book, plus 25p per copy for each additional book.

Name ....

Address ....

....